A Russian Tale

– STEPHEN B. MORRISEY –

An environmentally friendly book printed and bound in England by
www.printondemand-worldwide.com

This book is made entirely of chain-of-custody materials

www.fast-print.net/store.php

A Russian Tale
Copyright © Stephen B. Morrisey 2012

All rights reserved

No part of this book may be reproduced in any form by photocopying or any electronic or mechanical means, including information storage or retrieval systems, without permission in writing from both the copyright owner and the publisher of the book.

All characters are fictional.
Any similarity to any actual person is purely coincidental.

ISBN 978-178035-495-8

First published 2012 by
FASTPRINT PUBLISHING
Peterborough, England.

For Elizabeth

Prologue

St Petersburg, Russia

TUFTS of dirty hair stick out from underneath the hood. The bruised cheeks are tear-stained. The huddled figure of a child, defiant now to the icy cold, is shuffling its way to the gate. No-one watches, no-one cares. In its hands is a necklace. It is plastic and soiled but it is the only item in the world that gave the child a reason for being. They should never have taken it from him, ripped it out of his hands and thrown it out of the window into the frozen mud. They never dreamt that he would go outside into the biting cold for it; that would be to risk the severest of punishments. All he had done in the first place was to run the beads through his fingers and make little lassoes as he swung it round in front of his face. It was dark inside and the necklace hardly made a sound as it threw off tiny dull circles of an amber light. But it had been too much for the prematurely middle-aged woman cuddling her bottle of vodka. She had snatched it from him and slapped him across the face with such force that he had fallen out of his damp bed. Now the ice cold had numbed his face and frozen his tears.

He reached the gate and pushed it. It was locked. The moon was bright and lit up the snow. All round there was a peacefulness in the air. Snow fell quietly. He was breathing calmly. The tiny gasps of air from his mouth condensed into small droplets down the front of his coat and froze into glittering miniature icicles. He had had no time to find a hat or gloves from the big basket in the corner where the woman had fallen asleep and dropped her empty vodka bottle. As he pushed the lock of the gate his fingers stuck to the metal. He pulled them away quickly and sniveled as a warm burning pain shot through his fingertips making him drop the necklace. He bent down and picked it out of the snow. He caressed it, wrapped it into a ball and put it into the pocket of his coat. His coat, or rather the coat he was shoved into when he and the other children were thrown out into the garden for the afternoon regardless of the temperature – this coat was too big for him and it slowed him down. But now he did not care, he was never going back. He moved along the fence and found the gap used by the dogs who sneaked in at meal times to whine and howl outside the kitchen. All the children watched them wishing they could give them their own food, but if any of the children showed a reluctance to eat, the blows were swift, hard and deliberate.

He lay down on the snow and crawled into the gap. He was too big. He took a deep breath, closed his eyes and squeezed his head under the fence. The ice scratched his head and he pushed again. He turned his head to one side and as he pushed again his ears filled with sharp pieces of ice. He forced himself forward again and again using his hands and every muscle of his small body. He pushed hard again and slipped through up to his waist. He lay half way through. The pain all over was now too much and he let out a string of small sobs. Lifting one leg he used his knee for a final attempt and was through. The cold had flooded through his coat and he could feel sticky liquid across his chest. He slowly struggled up and on to his feet. He took out the necklace and held it up to the moonlight. He twirled it around and around wondering at the way flashes of the now bright amber light broke out and shone through the soiled surface of the beads. He tried but he could not smile now. The muscles of his scratched face were frozen. All feeling was now knocked out of him, almost.

He carefully wrapped the necklace up again and put it in his pocket. He turned towards the road desperate now to run but he could barely force one foot in front of the other because of the numbing cold. He closed his eyes. As he stumbled forward two large lights dazzled him. He dared not open his eyes and yet somehow he could see. A car was heading straight for him. And then a roar – the wild roar of an animal in danger. With the roar the lightly falling snow was whipped up in front of him, the snow thickening instantly and then whirling around and around in a frenzy of flashing white. The car swerved violently off the road to avoid the whirling snow, the eyes of the car's driver wide with terror as the child listened to the sound of screeching tyres and shattering glass being muffled by the thick white bank of snow at the side of the road. The child stayed still and then opened his eyes to see the wizened face of the old man with the piercing dark blue eyes. The old man was smiling at him with such warmth through the whirling snow.

One

CRASH! He woke and could not move. The explosive sound of glasses simultaneously smashing into peels of hysterical laughter had stopped as abruptly as it had started. Strange! The house was now at its quietest. He could not hear any other sounds. The temperature outside had dropped to minus twenty degrees centigrade and had frozen the two-storey country house in its own bubble protecting it from the numbing harshness of a Russian January in St Petersburg. The young boy, Alex, turned his head slightly and watched as the numbers on his clock flipped to 04.00. He had to go back to sleep. The sound must have been a dream coming to an end. Whatever else that there had been in his dream was over now, buried back in his subconscious. He snuggled his face into the corner of his thick duvet and rummaged around with a hand to grab hold of his well-worn cuddly teddy bear. He had time yet. He would not have to leave the cosy warmth of his bed until seven o'clock at the earliest. That was when he would have to start to get ready for school.

He closed his eyes and then opened then again in a flash this time sitting bolt upright. This time it was not a loud noise but a sharp tingling in his fingers, a tightening in his chest. Silently he got out of his bed and took the few short steps across his bedroom to his desk. He pulled out a plastic toy tub from underneath his desk. He knelt down and fished out a cloth bag from the bottom of the tub. As always the cloth bag felt slightly warm and the tingling in his fingers increased. He put one hand in the bag and withdrew a piece of light rock. The rock was the shape, size and thickness of one of his school exercise books. He held the piece up and the dim light from his night light by his bed hit the piece and a warm glow of whirling amber lit up his face. He smiled at the piece and gently put it away. It was his greatest find – a piece of real treasure found buried in the woods near their new house in this new country – it was the reason why his new life in Russia was starting so well. Now he would sleep and sleep soundly. He snuggled down in his bed again. As he began to fall back to sleep he saw himself smiling as he sat in the front seat of his mum's chauffer driven car on the way to school.

Alex was last up that morning. He was nine years old and of average build for his age. His hair was fair coloured and his eyes were light blue. Compared to the rest of the boys in his class he had a slightly more mature look. To his mum, of course, he looked angelic no matter what state he was in! His mum and dad were already dressed and eating breakfast as Alex came down the wooden steps from upstairs and shuffled over to the table in the kitchen. The house had wooden floors. It also had wood-covered walls and wood-covered ceilings. It was a truly odd construction. It was based on a traditional Russian dacha - a type of summer house - but built out of brick on the outside rather than out of wood. Wooden panels and strips of wood, however, had then been added throughout the inside of the house to give it the 'dacha' feel. A sauna almost. It had been partially adapted to Western design so that an ex-pat family could live in the Russian countryside all year round and not just in the summer as Russians do. This meant bathrooms inside and room had to be found in the kitchen for a washing machine. There were four such houses in the compound. They had all been built with whatever materials the Russian construction company had been able to find during the turbulent times of the breakdown of the former Soviet Union's command economy and the start of 'perestroika' or the 'redevelopment' of the economy. The resourcefulness of the construction company had impressed the Western firms which had rented the four houses for their senior executives and their families. Coca-Cola,

Unilever, Citibank and Miller Lombard were at the vanguard of the 'new' Russia – they were dedicating experienced staff and they were the first major foreign multinational companies to open their own offices and operations in St Petersburg now that Russia was opening up. After over seventy years of Communist rule the age of the new and wild Russia had dawned.

It was January 1995 and St Petersburg was seen as the new window into Russia – a neat one-hundred-and-eighty degree flip on St Petersburg's original purpose – built almost three hundred years ago by Peter the Great as quite the opposite – built on marshland as Russia's 'Window into Europe'; the 'Window' through which Peter would haul a backward Russia into the modern European era. St Petersburg was designed on Amsterdam and Venice with traces of London. Now once again Russia had been rocked to its core. This time by the fall of Communism. Communism had finally fallen in 1991 when Boris Yeltsin stood on a tank defying the die-hard Communist leaders who had attempted to restore Communism after the changes had started. These changes known as 'perestroika' had been started by Gorbachov and had led to Communism losing its control over the vast Soviet Empire and much of the Eastern Bloc of European countries. The fall in 1991 was an event almost as spectacular as Communism's revolutionary rise of 1917 but this time with considerably less violence - so far at least. What it was bringing, though, was as wrenching an effect on the structure of the country and on daily life as the Revolution of 1917 had brought. Now all business was up for grabs with the imminent sale of most of the country's companies through the process called 'privatisation' – the sale of companies by the State into private hands. The problem though was that privatisations could be made in lots of different ways. Both Russians and foreigners were now frantically engaged in trying to work out how the rules of privatisation would work – or rather how to make and influence the rules in the first place - and then how to make them work to their own advantage. So far with the brave but increasingly erratic Yeltsin in the Kremlin uncertainty was the only certainty of each day.

Into this maelstrom of political and business intrigue and deal-making, the Western, largely American, firms had enthusiastically parachuted in executives and their families. It was as if they were on their way to a land 'full of milk and honey' which was ripe for the taking. Along a gold-bricked road. The four families in the town of Pushkin, fifteen miles to the south of St Petersburg, were cocooned in a compound akin to a Little America; they were chauffeur-driven everywhere in foreign vehicles, all well cushioned from the harsh reality of the bitter and dark St Petersburg winter. Deep snow had been on the ground now for over two months and the view out of the Hampton's kitchen window was thrilling. A large green crested woodpecker sat on the compound fence behind which rose row after row of silver birch trees twenty meters high. Dull beams of weak sunlight twinkled through the trees and the snow-covered branches glistened. The compound had a story tale feel to it - just like the dawn of Christmas Day on a Christmas card.

"Alex," said his mum, Ellen, in a hushed voice. "Come quick. The woodpecker is on the fence." Alex joined his mum at the kitchen window and shuddered so strongly despite his dressing gown and thick slippers that his mum wrapped her arm around his shoulders. "Are you cold, Alex?" she asked.

The house was really well heated by thick hot water pipes throughout which were fed by a huge gas boiler in the basement.

"I'm fine, mom," replied Alex, "I just thought I saw one of them again." He paused and looked up at his mum. "You know a man in the village told the Millers next door that they will come right up to the fence now that they have woken up."

"Alex," said his father putting down the papers he was reading with his breakfast, "we should not listen to all the gossip in the village, you know. Some people here are not used to anyone except Russians. They would prefer us to leave. That's why they make up all kinds of stories to scare us."

Alex's father, John Hampton, was a forty-five year old lawyer and head of the Russian operations of the leading London law firm called Miller Lombard. He was tall and well built. His black hair showed its first flecks of grey which suited him. He had had a short but distinguished career in the US military prior to retraining as a lawyer. What he now lacked in legal expertise found in lawyers of his age and position he more than made up for in his life experiences and military background. In contrast to the gung-ho approach of the large US consumer product companies and banks, the major US law firms were still not ready to make their push into Russia. The Russian legal system was as complex, contradictory and unclear as the most devious legal minds could have made it and no American law firm would currently venture any legal opinion on any legal matter in Russia. The British law firms, though, were somewhat more pragmatic and Hampton had been delighted to have been headhunted by Miller Lombard to lead the firm's expansion in St Petersburg. The law firm already had an office in Moscow and was building up a separate team of ex-pat and Russian lawyers in St Petersburg with the bold aim of winning Russian and foreign clients before any other law firm. It wanted to be the leading foreign legal adviser on Russian privatisation. Russian privatisations were being seen as a potential gold mine by foreign lawyers and accountants who were keen to apply the highest fees to what they were only too happy to classify as complex and 'ground breaking' work.

"Maybe, dad," replied Alex sitting down to start his breakfast, "but I am sure I saw one of them. In the trees behind the fence."

"Was it in a dream?" asked Ellen slowly and with a pointed look at her husband who once again put down his papers. Ellen was two years younger than her husband. She kept her hair short and was attractive without the use of make-up which in any case she had little time for. They had been in St Petersburg for six months and Alex had fitted in well at the Anglo-American School in St Petersburg. The school was run by the American and British embassies and catered for children from diplomatic and business families.

Ellen had managed to secure a job in the school as a classroom assistant. She had put her journalistic career on hold in the short term to help the family settle into Russia. The family had lived in Chicago until their move – their first move – and Alex had been as excited as both his parents, if not more so, by the prospect of living in another country for a year, maybe two. The upheaval, though, could not be underestimated and Ellen was convinced that it was having an effect on Alex. He took in everything he saw and heard with great eagerness and he had started to dream a lot more. Ellen was a trained journalist not a psychologist but she was sure Alex's mind was being stretched more than normal for a boy his age. He was developing an uncanny sense of reading his mum's mind. This had unsettled her on several occasions recently. She had not mentioned anything yet to her husband as she knew that he faced tremendous pressures at work and she was able to stay close to Alex virtually twenty-four hours a day. Perhaps it was just that - the constant closeness which was making Alex think like his mum. Maybe she would look to break their routine more as soon as the winter weather let up a little.

"No, I'm sure it wasn't a dream," replied Alex eating into his bowl of cereal.

"Maybe it was the dull light," suggested his dad. "Shapes might be difficult to make out. Or a tree might come to life." He smiled at Alex who seemed to think for a moment and then smiled back. "And we don't want to be frightening your mom with the idea!" Alex smiled even wider and gave his mum a furtive glance. "Anyway the dark days will soon be behind us and I'm sure any such creatures have far better places to hang out than round here. Right, I'll get my stuff and be off."

"It is a real bear, mom. You know I saw it," said Alex looking intently as his mum.

"I'm sure you did," replied his mum. "I heard the same stories from Mrs Miller next door. Apparently hibernation has finished early this winter and there are a couple of bears out in the woods looking for food. But not near the compound."

"Ok," said Alex leaving the table, happy that his mum did not disbelieve him but also happy not to push the point any further.

Hampton had gone to the small room near the front door which he used as a makeshift study. He put his briefcase on his small desk and then turned to a large metal unmarked cupboard at the side of the door. When they had moved from Chicago this cupboard had been flown in specially and separately from their household items. He used a key and turned two dials to open the door. He looked at the rack of rifles and ammunition and mentally made a full inventory and check. Save for the hunting rifle under their bed everything else was locked in here. His wife knew of the cupboard but had never been shown inside. Alex did not know it existed but he had been told that his father had brought his hunting rifle from the States to try some hunting in Russia one day. He left the room picking up his case.

"Ellen, is it ok if I go ahead?" asked Hampton putting on his rubber-soled shoes and taking his fur coat from the coat-stand near the front door.

"Of course, John," replied his wife coming across to the front door. "How do you think your new English recruit will be feeling this morning?" she asked.

"Raw, I should think. I'm sure they continued his welcome party till the early hours. But I think he will work out fine. He was well trained in London and has spent nearly two years in Moscow. He seemed to get on well with our Russian staff. I've already given him a complicated legal case to look at, so fingers crossed." He kissed her on the cheek. "Have a safe drive."

"You too."

Hampton opened the front door and stepped out quickly. He walked over towards two parked cars which both had their engines running and a driver standing by the door. Both cars were dark coloured Volvos with yellow number plates, the tell-tale sign of foreigners in Russia on a business visa. Russians have white number plates and diplomats the much sort after red ones. The yellow plates are a magnet to the Russian traffic police who always pull over such cars whether a traffic offence has been committed or not. Hampton exchanged a brief good morning with both drivers in his basic Russian. He sniffed the air and the air froze the insides of his nostrils. 'At least minus fifteen centigrade,' he thought as he quickly got in the car.

Alex and his mum took another thirty minutes to get ready to go to school. Alex was really excited about a school trip later that day to the Hermitage Museum, the former Imperial Palace of the Tsars. His class had been studying Russian history all school year and this was their reward for their studies. A private tour of the Hermitage. The class had been a buzz with tales of treasures hidden away in the Hermitage and in the other Imperial Palaces around St Petersburg and today would be a real chance to learn more first hand. Alex was specifically interested in finding out what had happened to the treasures in the palaces near where their house was. Their house was in the town of Pushkin which was where the two great Summer Palaces of the Tsars were built – the Catherine Palace and the Alexander Palace. Their compound was in walking distance from the Catherine Palace down a secluded country path or a short drive along a couple of roads. Like the Winter Palace in the centre of the city, which had been converted into the Hermitage Museum, these palaces contained many works of art. Many of these works and treasures had been hidden away when St Petersburg was besieged by the Germans during the Second World War and there were many rumours that some had yet to be found again. Unbeknown to everyone Alex already had found his first treasure, the piece of amber. The piece he had found buried a couple of feet underground in the woods within days of the family moving into the house at the end of the previous summer. He had been walking in the woods and thought he saw something shining under a pile of leaves. There was nothing under the leaves and without any thought he started to dig through the soft earth with his hands and then with a small stick. He found the piece of light rock wrapped in a thick velvet cloth. It was a secret find. Something at the back of his mind told him to keep it secret.

Alex put on his boots, thick coat, hat and gloves and picked up his bag. He pushed open the heavy metal front door and ran over to the car. His mum followed straining as she pulled the door shut. The builders had insisted on this large metal door which was padded on both sides with a waterproof material. A door to an apartment or a house was its weakest point, the builders had explained, and all Russian apartments, be they on the ground floor or the fifteenth floor of a building, had such a door. It was a definite given for houses whose lower floor windows normally also would have metal bars on them. It had taken Ellen almost a week after moving in to realise that the house did not have a back door. Instead at the back of the house there was a flight of wooden steps leading to a small veranda. The veranda was reached through the landing on the first floor but the door could only be opened from the inside. At first she had put it down to the oddity of the house but soon realised that this too was very much a safety feature. The house's doors and windows together with the high fence around the four buildings and a twenty-four hour Russian guard on the gate completed the security of the compound and Ellen had to admit on occasions that it gave her great comfort moving as they had from a quiet small town outside of Chicago. She turned the large key in the front door three times and walked over to the car.

As she walked over to the car something did not look right. She stopped as the driver opened his door on the left of the car and got out, hastily brushing crumbs off his old overcoat. Alex! She thought. He should be in the back seat of the car but the back seat was empty.

"Good morning, Madame," said the driver in heavily accented English. "We go now?"

"Good morning, Slava," replied Ellen sighing to herself quickly as she saw her son's head in the front passenger seat. "Yes, please," she said with a smile as Slava moved quickly to open the passenger door for her. Ellen followed and then knocked on the window of the front seat.

"Alex," she said, "why are you sitting there? You know you should sit in the back. It is much safer. And the roads are very icy."

"Please, mom. Just for today. Please!!"

"Your father would not let you," replied his mum just stopping herself from opening the front door. She looked at Alex. His eyes were shining bright and he had such a large smile on his face.

"I won't tell dad. I just had this weird dream last night and in it I went to school in the front seat of the car."

A fleeting furrow ran across Ellen's brow and a tiny shiver went up her spine. "Very well," she said keeping her composure, "just this once. And I mean once."

The guard lifted up the barrier and the car turned out of the compound. Its tyres crunched on the snow-covered short country road that took them into the town of Pushkin. They then took several roads until they turned on to the M10 and the twenty minute drive into St Petersburg. The roads were relatively good being a long established route between the city and its famous Tsarist Summer Palaces and city dwellers' wooden dachas. It was still free from any real traffic. The roads had been very difficult in November when the first winter snow had blanketed the whole area. Meters of snow had fallen over a couple of days, but once the roads had been cleared and the surfaces treated with the Russian version of salt – a chemical composition which as well as keeping the surface of the roads clear can make holes in the soles of rubber boats within minutes of contact – then the roads were easy to drive. The fun remained in the side roads and country roads which had no such treatment. To negotiate these roads after a snow fall required a plethora of equipment from spades to planks of wood and pieces of cardboard and an ability to bounce a car up and down to get traction under its wheels. This was when the Russians came into their own and one of the reasons why until now the Hamptons had not driven their own cars. This and the constant attention of the traffic police who expected every car they stopped to make a financial contribution. It was not for nothing that the traffic policeman's baton is known at the 'Please' stick.

"Mom, I can't wait to go to the Hermitage, today," said Alex excitedly and turning his head to look at his mum. "Are you coming on the trip?"

"Sadly, no, Alex. It is only your class going and I'm helping out in first grade today. But I am sure you will tell us all about it."

"I will," smiled Alex. "Even dad has not been on a private tour."

"He hasn't. Hopefully we will all be able to visit more when the new museum committee he's helping with gets going. Your dad is quite an expert on paintings and other works of art, you know."

"I know, mom. You are always telling me."

Ellen smiled at her son's matter-of-fact way of thinking. Her husband's main interest both academically and hobby-wise was art and he was well connected in art circles in Chicago, New York and London. Coming to Russia was fuelling her husband's drives in both his new profession and the main interest in his life. Ellen had her Alex and since the day he arrived she had put everything in to caring for him. Now as Alex had turned nine years' old, events outside their tight family life from time to time had started to pique her journalistic instincts. Throwing all these ingredients into the fascinating world which the new Russia promised would give all three of them a life-defining opportunity which would make any questions from the past melt into insignificance. She closed her eyes for a moment as the car drove towards the city.

Even though there was little traffic there was always a short hold up on the M10. Police check-point. A vestige of the former Soviet times which had now turned into a money-making enterprise and one of the first to prosper in the dislocated phase the Russian economy was bobbing around in. The police officer knew the car and its occupants. He stopped the car every day. Ellen had thought from day one that this traffic police officer was related to their driver but she and her husband literally turned a blind eye to the couple of one dollar bills silently handed over to the officer with the car's documents and the driver's papers. 'Office expenses' covered a multitude of sins but without which nothing in their daily life would move forward. No wonder the American law firms were still running scared of setting up offices in Russia where nearly every daily act broke one Russian law or another. She waved and smiled brightly at the officer who returned her gesture with a slight nod of the head. They left the check point.

As the driver accelerated away the car did a sudden jump and the driver braked and then accelerated again going up through his gears with a heavy deliberate motion. It seemed as though he may have hit a pot hole or a brick on the road. The car seemed to be driving fine, but as was the habit of both their drivers, as soon as he could, he pulled over to the side of the road and switched off the car's engine. Without commenting he jumped out of the car and quickly did a tour around the car bent over checking wheels. He came back to his door having gone all round. He then stood up and looked at the car windows. He frowned and jogged round to the right passenger car door. Ellen followed him with her eyes and gasped as the driver stopped and was examining a small hole in the window. The driver pulled the door open and stuck his head into the seat next to Ellen. He said something in a harsh tone under his breath and with a fast and powerful action used one of his keys to dislodge and pull a small object out of the top of the seat. He did not look at it but put it straight into his pocket and avoided eye contact with Ellen. Ellen though had seen the object. It was a bullet and she had immediately realized that the car had taken a gun shot through the window without shattering the glass. Had Alex been sitting in his normal seat in the back of the car then the bullet would have hit him square in the chest.

Two

CRASH! He woke up and jumped out of his bed. He looked around the room feverishly and shivered. None of the other boys stirred. Strange! He shook his head and then quickly got back into bed. It would take him a few minutes hugging his two worn blankets as close as he could before his body would warm up enough for him to sleep again. It was the dead of night and the only time that this old building fell silent. It was 'Children Home No. 8.' in St Petersburg and yet there was nothing in the slightest child-friendly or homely about it. It was a block-shaped building of four floors built to the same design as the majority of Soviet government buildings. A large rectangular building in grey concrete. Each floor had a corridor running the length of the building with an equal number of sterile rooms off each side. The rooms could be offices, meeting rooms, kitchens and every other possible use. In this building the rooms on the first, second and third floors were dormitories crammed with six to eight beds in each. The first floor was for boys, the second for girls and the third for 'special cases.' The ground floor had all the communal rooms and offices of the Home.

A deep clanging noise almost made him jump up again but the noise repeated itself and he realised that it was the large old clock in the corridor outside the dormitory. It chimed three more times and the boy, who was called Sasha, was struck by how soothing it was compared to the racket in his dream of glasses smashing to fits of laughter.

He knew he would be woken in little over an hour by the other young boys in the dormitory and then the long day would start. He hoped it was not his day to fetch the wood from outside. This time of year in the early morning it was pitch black outside and anything could lay waiting in the wood store. Anything, animal or human. He had tried to ask why the building no longer had hot water pumping through the thick metal pipes high up on the walls which ran through every room but he was ignored. All that the children knew was that the rooms on the ground floor now depended on wood or oil burning stoves for heating, cooking and washing. One of the staff was constantly complaining that the building was worse than during the 'Great Siege' and that the quicker the Communists returned to power, the quicker they would have their hot water running again. The children were used to the never ending moaning of the adults in the building and were perceptible enough to work out that none of the adults wanted to be in the building any more than they did. It created an unspoken bond of solidarity and was the closest that any of the children came to a feeling of support or care. As his body warmed he managed to fall back asleep. This time his dream was peaceful with no glasses smashing nor fits of laughter; this time he was sitting in the back of a large foreign car driving further and further away from Children Home No. 8.

He stayed curled up in his bed as long as he could. No-one knew his age for sure as one night he had literally been dropped off at the entrance to the Home. He had blondish hair and clear blue eyes and a discernible presence or confidence about him despite being abandoned at a time in his young life when he easily understood what was going on around him and the predicament that he was in.

The other boys in the room had gone down to the ground floor as soon as they had woken up. Sasha could picture them all huddled around the stove in the kitchen waiting without a sound for the temperature in the room to rise above zero and waiting for a bowl of warm porridge. Despite whatever happened in the day, the bowl of warm porridge was the only sure highlight. The Home's cook rarely had enough food for all the children to eat both a lunch and a dinner but she always made sure that every child had porridge and porridge made with milk, fresh or powdered, and she would not let any of the staff who had been on night duty or herself touch a drop until she had fed every single child. 'If we cannot give them hope in life we can give them porridge,' was her saying. Said every day like a prayer.

Sasha finally left the comfort of his blankets to brave the icy cold. He took a pair of training shoes from the side of his pillow and untied the laces which were tied onto the metal frame of the bed. Since being dropped off at the door of the Home a year ago he had mastered life in the Home with a level of composure really seen in the Home. He had been living in a small village outside the city with his grandmother who had brought him up. They had had very, very little money and his grandmother survived on the money she earned looking after a small chapel and sewing lace shawls. From an early age Sasha had spent many days in the chapel being looked after by his grandmother. It was in the chapel that Sasha had learnt the one true joy that nothing – and nothing during his darkest days in the Home could take from him. The true joy of singing. He had been dropped off at the Home by one of the old men in the village and it had taken him several months and an appearance in a meeting full of adults for him to find out that his grandmother had been found dead one afternoon in the chapel, or, rather that the old lady who looked after him had been found dead. She had died from a heart attack and her identity was in some doubt. For Sasha her death was sad but whenever he had felt he was going to cry her face would appear in his mind and he would hear her teaching him to sing and then he would start to sing inside and not finish singing until the sadness stopped.

With his training shoes on he stood on the metal edge of his bed and stretched up the wall to the large pipe running around the top of the wall. The one advantage of the pipe no longer being used to heat the building was that he had been able to unscrew the section above his bed. He had seen a couple of the Home's workers do this one evening on the first floor. They had unscrewed a small section to take out two bottles of clear liquid. He just took a quick look inside to check and the quickly screwed the pipe back in. His bag was there safe and untampered with. He could now risk going downstairs and queuing for his porridge.

"Sasha, my favourite Sasha, is here at last," said the cook handing Sasha his bowl of porridge. "I hope we will be hearing you sing this morning. Do you have a lesson today with Yelena Matrovna?"

Sasha looked at the cook and thought hard. It was always difficult to remember which day of the week it was as life in the Home never varied day from day. "What day is it today?" he asked with a smile.

"Friday, Sasha," replied the cook with a small smile back.

"Then, yes," said Sasha sniffing his porridge as his stomach started to rumble. "Friday! And I might even have a visitor. She comes most Fridays."

"You are a lucky boy, Sasha," continued the cook, "I don't think you will be in here as long as the rest of the boys and girls."

Sasha looked at her briefly as a whole list of questions rose in his mind pushing his hunger to one side. "Now eat your porridge," said the cook quickly sensing that she had said a little too much to him, "before it gets cold. Eat it up." Sasha did as he was told. He sat at one of the long tables and quickly ate most of his porridge. He then paused and looked back over to where the cook had been. She had left and had taken her large cooking pot with her. He looked over to a window and for a moment again he saw himself sitting in the front seat of a large black car. He shook his head and slowly ate the last few spoonfuls.

At the main entrance of the Home two visitors were standing outside. The first, a shortish man in a long fur coat, had pressed the intercom on the main door and spoken quietly. An old lady shuffled to the main door and took her time in opening the locks. The second visitor was a young woman also in a long fur coat. She waited until the man had gone inside and then pressed the intercom again. The old lady shuffled again to the door and opened it. Inside the young woman took off her boots and put on a pair of shoes from the bag she was carrying.

"You'd better keep your coat on, Miss," said the old lady. The young woman smiled and took the old lady's hand. The old lady was visibly shocked as she pulled her hand away to reveal a couple of red bank notes. "Bless you!" she whispered. "Bless you!" The old lady crossed herself several times with her head bowed as the young woman passed her.

This was the young woman's tenth visit to the Home. She was on her way to the office of the law firm where she worked and she was able to work this thirty minute slot into her routine and to visit the boy, Sasha, before the singing lesson he took most mornings. She was single and two years into her job after studying law at Moscow University and graduating with top honours. Her family was originally from St Petersburg but her father had worked his way up in one of the top Ministries and had had to move his wife and daughter to several postings in Russia and the wider Soviet Union and Eastern Bloc, as they were then known, in order to advance his career. Her father was now retired and had stayed in Moscow with her mother who was much younger than her husband. Anna had jumped at the opportunity to return to St Petersburg to start her own career. Her early childhood in St Petersburg in the 1970s had been magical and she felt no ties to Moscow which had been all-consuming study, study and more study.

On returning to St Petersburg to live with an aunt she had not reckoned with Sasha. Sasha it had been discovered was not related to the 'grandmother' who had brought him up and his origins were being investigated. So far the authorities were of the belief that Sasha had a possible connection to Anna's family. The only identification document found on his 'grandmother' was old and worn. Sasha's family name appeared to be 'Tyublonski' or 'Tvublonski'. Anna's family name was Tyublonski and the authorities had contacted twenty or so families in St Petersburg with the same and similar names. This was because these family names were relatively uncommon. All but Anna's family had dropped any interest when the reason for the contact from the authorities was revealed to be an orphaned boy. Anna's family, on the other hand, had decided to find out whether there was a connection but so far the trail was proving elusive. On the request of her mother Anna had taken the step of visiting Sasha and the visits had now been going on for almost three months. As a lawyer Anna was well placed to become involved in the search process but so far she had limited herself to getting to know the boy. The American training shoes had been a real success.

"Anna. I had forgotten that it was a Friday!" said Sasha running in to the room on the ground floor reserved for visitors. Save for four chairs, a table and a broken samovar the room was as bare and sterile as the rest of the building. Sasha threw his arms around Anna and hugged her.

"How are you, Sasha?" asked Anna putting her hands on his shoulders and looking with warmth into his eyes. There was a wonderful look in his eyes which always struck her. Despite the awful conditions he was living in, his spirit seemed to shine through his eyes; there was no resentment or vacancy which she saw in most of the other children in the Home. More and more she hoped they would find a relationship link between Sasha and her family. As a single young woman she would have next to no chance of adopting him if he was not related and there was no one else in her family who would realistically be able to. And in any case any adoptable children, especially the young children, were now reserved for adoption by foreign families who everyone knew were prepared to pay large sums of money. Sums which in turn had to be shared by lots of the people involved in the adoption process and paperwork.

"Tell me about your work, Anna?" asked Sasha excitedly. "What is it like working with people who aren't Russian? There are lots in your office aren't there?" Sasha always asked similar questions and Anna readily sat him down and talked. She produced a pencil with the words 'Miller Lombard' embossed on the side and Sasha gratefully took it and stared at it in awe immediately making a note of where to hide it. He held it with the reverence that his grandmother used to hold the small wooden icons in the chapel which she dusted once a week. Anna also produced a thick pair of socks which she made him put on over the ones he already had on. She gave him eight small bars of chocolate and he knew he had strict instructions to give one to each boy in his dormitory. In her bag she also had a bottle of vodka, two large bags of dried pasta and a large bar of chocolate. These were destined for the Director of the Home on the condition that the boys' chocolates were not taken off them and that one bag of pasta would go to the children's meals and one would go to the staff's meals. Such was the balance needed to preempt jealousy and theft in the Home.

There was a knock at the door and a middle-aged woman walked in. She was tall and thin with a long black dress and a purple lace shawl over her shoulders. Her hair was thick and tied in a bun with an ornate heavy clip. A gold chain round her waist held a small pair of reading glasses. She held a folder of papers with musical scores sticking out. Her face showed signs of wrinkles but her skin was clear albeit pale. "Anna Petrovna," said the woman with purpose, "it is so good to see you visiting Sasha. It always makes him happy before his lesson."

Anna smiled as the woman stroked Anna's arm. "Yelena Matrovna, good morning. I hear he is a good singer," said Anna brightly. "I think he must have learnt a great deal from his grandmother."

"Yes, he is excellent and especially good at the complicated Church hymns and chants. It obviously comes from deep within his heart."

"Well I think I should leave you to your lesson." The three of them chatted for a few more moments before Anna hugged Sasha and wished him a good singing lesson. She left to see the Director of the Home.

The other visitor to the Home that morning was sat in the office of the Director of the Home. He was a short man and in contrast to the drably dressed staff in the Home he was dressed in Western jeans, an expensive shirt and a sports jacket. He too had changed his boots and wore a pair of designer Italian leather shoes. He had a pepper-coloured and neatly trimmed beard which gave him an air of being much older than he was. A pile of bank notes was set out of the desk in front of the Director of the Home and the man was reading through a list of two pages.

"Valentina Alexandrovna, I am sure that I can arrange these items as usual," said the man quietly.

"Roman Felixovich, you are a great help to our Home," replied the Director swallowing hard. She found it difficult to adjust to the new world. Two years ago the Home received all its heating and food for the children without question. The food was very basic but available. Now the wonderful new world of the free economy meant that she had to beg for food and for fuel. The city gave her some funds but that only went far enough to pay her staff a basic wage. Food parcels came intermittently from a local church; wood and the occasional can of oil came from sources she did not even know; and clothing came from a foreign charity. Without the foreign-clothed man, whom she knew to be in his mid-twenties despite his older look, sitting in front of her, the Home would be in a catastrophic situation. And yet the sight of the young man filled her with a deep sense of betrayal and, whether it went against her own very good even saintly nature or not, a touch of disgust. He was the most visible sign of the corruption of her whole world. Two years ago young men like Roman Felixovich operated underground in the bowels of the black economy which every Russian knew existed but very few openly admitted. A black economy which ran alongside the mighty Soviet command economy plugging gaps, oiling wheels and providing the Western goods that the once all powerful Soviet Union did not produce. The Soviets could produce massive intercontinental ballistic missiles but not an espresso coffee machine! Now the black marketeers were the new masters and the accumulators of cash in piles of dollars, dollars and more dollars. Even Valentina Alexandrovna took dollars instead of roubles now whenever she could and with every deal there were conditions. Cash ruled but the centuries old Russian tradition of favours still flourished. In her case, the basement of the Home was being used by Roman Felixovich to store some of the goods he traded in and which he wanted to keep completely confidential. This was the price she was paying for the weekly supply of food and oil.

"I have arranged for the boy to sing for his Holiness The Metropolitan. The boy will not see his Holiness. The boy will be told it is a choir practice only." Roman Felixovich looked at Valentina Alexandrovna. This time it was his turn to feel uncomfortable. He was at his happiest doing deals, making faceless calls on his selection of state of the art mobile phones, counting his cash and privately enjoying the fruits of his growing wealth. His wealth was still tiny in comparison to the riches which he saw his counterparts in the West enjoyed but he was already putting an increasing gap between himself and the vast majority of the people of St Petersburg. He was driven to be one of the small handful of new businessmen who would dominate St Petersburg in the years to come and possibly the whole of Russia itself. Being involved with an orphan boy at the request of the Director of the Home was something he found incredibly uncomfortable but it was part and parcel of the deal he had with her and he at least admired the fact that she of all people was showing an ability to deal to get something she wanted!

"That is excellent, Roman Felixovich," replied Valentina Alexandrovna with the first trace of warmth in her voice. Roman Felixovich looked to the floor. "I'll have my driver fetch him now and take him to the cathedral," he said quickly and quietly.

"Will Yelena Matrovna accompany him?"

"If you wish."

Sasha had only just sung two songs for Yelena Matrovna when the door to the room opened and a man in a long leather coat wearing sunglasses stepped in and signaled for Sasha to come out. Yelena Matrovna whispered to Sasha to go get a coat and then come down to the main door. She spoke abruptly and purposefully to the man who peered at Yelena Matrovna over the top of his sunglasses and did not reply.

Yelena Matrovna met Roman Felixovich near the main door.

"You'll need your coat, also," he said to Yelena Matrovna with authority in his voice. "I've arranged for him to have his singing practice in the Cathedral you wanted."

"Really!" replied Yelena Matrovna with complete surprise and an immediate feeling of excitement. "The acoustics there are marvelous. There is nowhere like it. Why are you..?"

"No questions. Just take him there."

"Of course," nodded Yelena Matrovna with an increasing smile on her face. "This is a great honour for the boy and for you to be helping like this."

Roman Felixovich looked at her. His expression hardened and Yelena Matrovna looked away from. "No questions," she said quietly before adding, "helping him is a brave act, Roman Felixovich. Especially for someone from your family." She turned theatrically on her heels before he could reply.

Five minutes later Anna had put on her coat and was hurrying out of the main door. As she made her way along the pavement she looked up as a sleek black Mercedes swept past her. The car's windows were blacked out but one of the windows had been wound half down and Anna could have sworn that she saw Sasha sitting on the back seat of the large foreign car with a huge smile across his face.

Three

INSPECTOR Bushkin closed the door of his unmarked police car and looked at the old fashioned building in front of him. He lit a cigarette as much to keep his ungloved fingers warm as for the inhalation. He wore a long dark coat with an unpressed suit underneath. His hair was thick and dark and his face worn. He was on the Moika Embankment in one of the oldest parts of St Petersburg. The building in front of him still had an air of wealth and substance about it despite the ravages of time and the weather. The building was Number 94 and was the former home of Russia's richest noble family, the Yusupovs. It had been built at the height of their wealth to house the largest private collection of art in Russia. Its walls were a yellow colour and Inspector Bushkin could not quite remember what the building was now used for. He had come on his own to see if an 'incident' required an investigation. He threw the half-finished cigarette into the road and took out a crumpled up piece of paper from his pocket. He read the badly typed message:

'Report by anonymous caller. Ground floor windows blown out, two rooms with considerable damage and four bodies piled up in a corner. Address – Moika Embankment 94. Complaint of lots of noise – voices and breaking glass at four am at same address also received this morning. Please investigate and determine course of action.'

The message was from the city's Chief of Police and addressed to Inspector Bushkin 'only'. It was now nearly ten o'clock. He furrowed his eyebrows at the mention of bodies. He was one of the city's top murder detectives with a growing list of unsolved murders and the prospect of adding another four did not appeal. The majority of the cases he had were the result of battles between the main criminal gangs in the city – the recently termed Russian 'mafia' gangs who aped the American gangs in the Hollywood movies. These murders were instantly recognisable and would never be solved. This case did not make any sense to him. For once maybe there would be something even his bumbling and now largely unpaid team might take an interest in, assuming that is, that they could tear themselves away from their multiple moonlighting activities. Remaining a policeman in the new Russia required just as much extra-curricular income earning as civic dedication. He himself was looked after by a number of the rising new businessmen in the city for the advice and information he could provide. He had not become too greedy or too indebted to any one person or group and he would keep it that way.

He went up to the main door of the building and stopped. He looked at the windows to the left and went over to them. The widows had been blown out as his message had said but without any damage to the walls around the windows. He would have expected plenty of visible damage had a bomb or similar device caused the windows to smash. It seemed as though the glass in the windows had been pushed out. He took out his radio and contacted his station asking two of his team to come to the building. He lit another cigarette and waited. As he heard the distant siren of one of the police cars he decided to make a start. He stepped up to the front door and rang the bell on the right side. As he did so he pressed on the large ornate door which swung open. As there was no sound of anyone coming he stepped inside.

The corridor inside was imposing and lead to a wide sweeping marble staircase. The rooms with the blown out windows were on the left and he took the first door on the left. He entered a room and blinked at the lavishness of the blue colors of the walls and of the furnishings. He was stepping straight back in to the Tsarist times with their overblown imitation Italian extravagance. The walls had more garishly coloured material on them than any bed would have. Perhaps the Revolution had been good for some things after all! He returned to his task and inspected the room. There were no marks on any of the walls, floor or ceiling and he examined the blown out windows from the inside. He thought long and hard but he just could not work out how the glass had been blown out. It was if someone had taken a small hammer and gently cracked the panes of glass and then pushed the glass out. Shards of glass lay outside under the windows. Again, had there been an explosion, the glass would have been blown into much smaller pieces and out onto the pavement. He would ask his team to photograph the windows.

He looked round the room and saw a door leading off to the left. He walked over and opened it. There was a spiral staircase descending down. He paused. He thought hard for a moment and then realised what was bothering him. The silence. The lack of people. What was this building now used for? He thought he had been here before but nothing was jogging his memory sufficiently. He assumed that it was one of the few well-kept buildings formerly used by Communist Party officials since the Revolution and now probably used by the same people but under a different organisation. He was sure it had not been rented to a foreign company yet, although that would probably be its fate once whoever lay claim to it won control of it. There were a growing number of attempts now by people to claim previous family ownership of buildings confiscated by the Communists, although property laws were a minefield and the process of restitution was only just being considered.

He started to go down the stairs and then tumbled backwards as a force rushed by him.

"My God!" he shouted his voice bouncing off the walls.

"Inspector! Where are you? Are you alright?" shouted a voice from the room above.

"Fine," shouted back Inspector Bushkin as he re-emerged into the room, a little disheveled and straightening his overcoat. "Did you catch him?"

"Fraid so," laughed a second voice. Two large policemen in shabby police coats and hats were in the middle of the room. One had a large ball of fur in his arms. "Quite a large cat, this one, Inspector. You must have given him quite a shock." Without allowing the Inspector time to reply the policemen left the room quickly and a large cat scream echoed in the doorway.

Inspector Bushkin turned to the other policeman. "Let us see what is really down there shall we? After you." The tight held smile on the policeman's face evaporated as Inspector Bushkin stood back to let him pass to the door and descend the stairs.

"Sorry, Inspector," came a voice from behind them. "Got rid of the cat. Do you know that.." before he could finish a loud bang rang out from the room below and the other policeman yelled a lengthy obscenity which made Inspector Bushkin and the other policeman smile to each other. Their colleague had fallen heavily over some form of obstacle. A broken chair by the sound of the obscenity.

"I know," Inspector Buskhin said briskly to the other policeman, "and I bet that the four bodies will be fine once we pick them up."

"You've been here before then, Inspector?"

"A long time ago and it took me a while to remember."

They both went down into the room below and helped their colleague get up. His pride had taken the brunt of the fall.

"What shall we do with the bodies?"

Four full size waxed models had been thrown on top of each other in the corner of the room. It looked as though they had been deliberately shoved together with their arms and legs twisted to comic effect.

"Leave them. I seem to remember that this museum is shut for most of the winter except for private tours. Can you have someone contact whoever runs it these days and tell them they need to fix or board up the windows and come and check their exhibits." Inspector Bushkin made his way to the next room and looked in. The main exhibit was sitting calmly and unmolested at his table. Poisoned cakes were laid out before him and yet he had a serene look on his face. Inspector Bushkin smiled at the wax figure. "It seems his noble assassins are about as effective now as they were in 1917!"

The two policemen peered into the room and then quickly looked back out. One of them crossed himself. "We should not look him in the eyes," he said with a genuine tremble, "or he will see into our souls and he might decide to put a curse on us."

"Nonsense," replied Inspector Bushkin with a contemptuous snort. "What have we to be afraid of? This is the building where Rasputin finally got what had been coming to him for a long time. And he lost all his so-called powers when he drowned in the river after being poisoned, stabbed and shot here! Killed three times over! His curses only ever work in fairy tales. Let's go."

Four

HE felt a sharp light hit his head and he moved his hand to cover his face. His heart thumped. He swallowed a horrible stale gulp and opened his eyes. The sunlight dazzled him. He propped himself up on his elbow. He was lying on a sofa. He stretched out his hand and an image flashed across his mind - smoke bellowing across a disco floor, girls dancing. He could taste the smoke - fingers were undoing his tie, bodies moving in front of him. He snapped his eyes shut and the vision got louder. He snapped them open and stared at the window. The light was streaming in. Time! What time was it? His watch! He lifted his left arm up and fell back on the sofa. Ten thirty! Wallet! He saw his jacket slung over the back of a chair opposite. He got gingerly to his feet and made his way to the chair. His wallet was there. He sat back down on the sofa and breathed deeply. All the stories he had been told about foreign men in Russia having their drinks drugged by girls in bars, then being coaxed and led away with promises of a good time only to be robbed or worse...

Where on earth was he? It could not be ten thirty. He looked out of the window and saw the giant clock on a church opposite. Ten twenty something! Can't be right. He stared at the finger hand as it jerked sharply clockwise. This was not his hotel! The church was not the Kazan Cathedral he normally saw through the window of his hotel room. Again the previous night flashed through his mind. The girl was smiling all over, her blonde hair was cut and styled to frame her young face and flow down onto her shoulders, her lips were full and her eyes sparkled; she was barely in her twenties and had the look of a model. He was at the bar buying drinks. He closed his eyes and saw himself dancing. 'Idiot! Adam, you are a real idiot!' he said to himself. He opened his eyes again.

His head throbbed as he focussed on the room. His heart jumped as he saw an open door. Again he got gingerly to his feet. He approached the door and peered in. There was bedding all over the floor and he almost collapsed as his eyes landed on the sight of a body lying face down and at a strange angle on the bed. Blonde hair hung over the side of the bed. He stood back, grabbed at the door handle and closed the door as quickly as he could. The body had not shown any sign of life.

Adam opened the front door of the room and then slammed the door shut behind him. From the view from the window in the room he guessed that he was on the third or fourth floor of an apartment block. During his two years in Russia he had been in enough of the soulless and identical Soviet built apartment blocks to be able to guess the way out without any difficulty regardless of the state he was in. Not the lift. He stumbled down the stairs banging against the walls for support. His legs were numb. His head was pounding.

"Watch where you're going," growled an old man carrying a plastic carrier bag in each hand. He mumbled a light expletive and darted out into the sun. His throat ached. Ten thirty! He should have been in the office of the law firm he worked for at least an hour ago.

An old black Mercedes heavily dented on the driver's side was parked twenty meters away opposite the apartment block. The driver had obviously not wanted to look at him but their eyes locked for the slightest of moments. The driver had a visible scar above his left eye. Adam's heart was in his throat. The vision flashed back. The man behind the wheel was remonstrating with the girl in a corner of the bar. The car moved off and he sank down and sat on the edge of the pavement. Hell!

He held his head in his hands for several seconds and composed himself. Where was he? He looked up. He started to shiver as he realised he had no coat on and that he was sitting in dirty snow. He stood up and wiped a mixture of ice and dirt from the back of his trousers. He had to get a move on. He decided to find a river or a canal to work out his bearings. After several futile attempts which took him further into the seemingly never ending sprawl of dour ten floor apartment blocks, he walked out on to a canal. Following the canal for five minutes he whistled under his breath as he could see a wider expanse of water and the River Neva which flows through St Petersburg, the main waterway which transverses the city. A few brisk paces and the skyline opened up and beyond a row of old three story merchant houses he spied the Winter Palace, once the palace of the Russian Tsars and now the Hermitage Museum, one of the world's greatest art galleries. He had often been struck by the contrast of the impressively built and attractive colonial merchant houses and the grey monotony of the crumbling Soviet apartment blocks. Now he was just glad that he was back in civilisation. He jogged up to a bridge and the first sighting of traffic.

The cold was now beginning to bite and his head was thumping harder. He threw out his hand at the first car he saw which braked and slid to a halt perilously close to mounting the pavement. Where else in the world can you stop any private car and negotiate a ride? Normally he would not dream of doing it without a Russian friend or colleague but after the night he had had! He closed his eyes as he sat next to the driver and this time the other girl jumped into view, smiling at him, her hair was black and in a ponytail half way down her back, her nose was slightly large and her eyes partly glazed. 'Olga', her friend with the blonde hair had called her, 'Olga!' He opened his eyes and shook his head.

The car crossed the River Neva at the Troitsky Bridge and sped up Nevsky Prospect, the main street in the centre of St Petersburg. The car jumped across lanes paying no attention to the cars around it. As it flew past the turning to the Grand Hotel on the other side of the road Adam caught a glimpse of flashing lights and lots of cars parked in a fan like arrangement. He strained back to look but the car drove on another couple of hundred yards before doing a sharp right and a U turn back down Nevsky Prospect. He was about to try to ask the driver about the commotion and the flashing lights when he was drowned out by the wailing siren of a police car coming up alongside. The diver started to pull over as the police car shot in front. Adam swore as the driver banged on his brakes. The police car in front did not stop but lurched off around the corner into the turning to the Grand hotel. The driver started up again and motioned to Adam that he would stop again the further side of the turning. Adam felt a cold sweat spread down his shoulders to the small of his back. How would he explain where he had ended up? He could hardly remember. How would it look? A foreign lawyer from a major English law firm waking up in a completely unknown apartment and with a body in the bedroom which was lying dead still. He could hear his heart thumping.

"Twenty," the voice was patient and gruff, "twenty, you said twenty."

"Twenty!" Adam shouted as he stared at the man only to realise it was the driver.

"Twenty roubles. Pay dollars if you want."

"Twenty, yes, twenty." Adam took out a fifty rouble note, stuffed it in the driver's hand and climbed out of the car breathing heavily.

The road to the Grand Hotel had been cordoned off and he could see the police car which had overtaken them had joined the other cars. Lights were flashing but the sirens had subsided. He could also see a fire engine and fireman pouring water from a leaking hose into the second floor of the building opposite the Grand Hotel. The fire engine reminded Adam of a model he had had as a child with its large cylinder of water and little driver's cab in front. He jogged along the road desperate to get to the hotel and tried not to look at the police.

A group of large elderly tourists were making their way through the doors and metal detectors out of the hotel. They were fussing and talking in loud voices. Americans.

"Well, have they caught him yet? They say they saw a man running away and that he was wearing a suit. Western looking," a large woman bellowed over her shoulder to the man behind her.

"Gee, Margaret, haven't you been looking round you. This city is full of men in suits. It looks like Chicago was in the thirties."

As if on cue their gaze honed in on Adam as he dipped his head and excused himself to pass them.

"And just look at all those cars. It's just like stepping into a gangster movie," the man continued as he stopped to train his video camera on a row of black windowed BMWs parked in a line across the street to the left of the fire engine.

"But won't you just look at the state of that fire engine, now that's the real Russia," bellowed the woman again as the group in unison charged off across the street hurriedly getting out their cameras. "The real Russia!"

Adam took out the crumpled paper with the plastic room pass in it from his wallet. Room 515. Thankfully he was there and in the room in seconds. The room had a strange orderliness about it. He looked around. Why? The cleaner had been. Of course! He opened the bathroom door. Everything cleaned up. He took out his wallet and shuddered. Credit cards? Wait. He jumped down and opened the main wardrobe and pulled out a pile of towels. He unwrapped them and sighed as he found his black briefcase. He unzipped it and searched through the pockets. Amex, Visa all there. Also a green plastic folder full of yellowing pages. He started to relax. Anything else? He stood up and looked round the room. Passport? He picked up the phone and dialled reception. They confirmed that they still had his passport from his registration.

He took a quick shower and shaved. His clothes did not look too bad. A stain on his suit jacket came off pretty much with a little water. His career as a lawyer at Miller Lombard was coming back into view. Staying out late was understandable in the circumstances, he said to himself, and Russia was such a difficult place for all professionals to work in. In any case he had been putting in the hours to match any of his contemporaries in London and beginning to make a name for himself in Russia. Last night had been 'Welcome Drinks' for him after his first week in St Petersburg. His boss had planted the company credit card behind the bar with instructions to all the staff there to enjoy themselves and for Adam to practice his Russian. Lessons, yes Russian lessons, he vowed he would concentrate on those seriously this time. The vision flashed back and he was making a pathetic attempt with the girls to speak Russian trying to pronounce 'another' in Russian. How stupid. The vision was less intense but clearer. He was sobering up and with it his head was beginning to ache even more. And then a terrifying thought hit him – he was a lawyer, the law was his career and would be his life and yet he had just abandoned the scene of a crime - no matter what had happened in the that room, what would happen when they found out that he, a lawyer, had been there and had left the scene?

The receptionist handed over his passport with a brief smile.

"What are the police doing?" he asked in a firm voice.

"Investigating a bombing, Mister Carter."

"Oh?" he replied.

The receptionist looked at him sternly and then at his suit. Adam followed her eyes down to the stain which looked worse than before. He put his hand over it. "Really?" he continued, "was anyone hurt?"

"They never tell us anything," she said as she walked off sharply.

Feeling a surge of energy and more comfortable now in his warm coat he strolled out of the hotel and turned to walk to the offices of Miller Lombard, a brisk five minute walk away. He surveyed the scene across the road. Things were winding down. The firemen were rolling up their hoses. The wall around one of the windows in the building was coated in a jet black soot and the smell of burnt wood and rubber hung in the air. Only one police car remained.

He smiled to himself and looked to the left at the rank of cars working as taxis for the hotel. The men turned lazily to look at him and his eyes shot in horror from one driver to another. The vision flooded back in full colour. The driver of the Mercedes was back again and this time he had taken hold of one of the girls in a corner of the bar. Adam had jumped forward towards them but the strong grip of the blonde haired girl, 'Lena', she had shouted her name to him above the music, 'Lena', had pulled him back almost begging him not to go over. "Dance, let's dance". Her sparkling eyes implored him with a mixture of strength and playful submission. "Please, please. Stay with me. Don't you like me? Let's dance, please, let's dance". And that's when everything must have really started. And over? No, it was not over.

Five

ROMAN Felixovich was in his private office. His office was on the top floor of yet another standard issue Soviet building. This building was the Leningrad Oil & Gas Research Institute. In Soviet times it was a hive of activity full of geologists and researchers covering all aspects of oil exploration. Experts came here from all parts of the former Soviet Union. The senior figures of the Institute, all Communist Party members, enjoyed the privileges of the Soviet elite – good housing, cars and access to the special shops. Now the Institute was manned by a handful of Soviet stalwarts all of whom were of pensionable age but continued in the Institute to hang on to the few privileges that they could hope to keep – their apartments and use of the Institute's several large dacha complexes outside of the city. The Institute's real assets, especially its maps and information on oil fields, had vanished the moment Yeltsin came down triumphantly from the tank outside the White House in Moscow. Several shootings had been penciled into the 'Theft from the Len O&G Institute – murder case(s)' file at police headquarters.

The only activity at the Institute of any note now was the renting out of its rooms to new private businesses. The ground floor had several cafes, a printing company and a travel agency whilst the top floor was rented to private businesses. Roman Felixovich had rented half of the top floor for a monthly rent equal to the price of a couple of pairs of Western jeans. His contract was at this price for ten years and he had ambitious plans for his part of the building. The area he had now was largely empty save for a few desks, a room of sample products, his work office and his private office. His work office was kept exactly as the office was in Soviet times. Several faded maps and posters on the walls, a cabinet with several pieces of rocks and the 'T' shaped desk arrangement – the abiding feature of the offices of the head of a department or an enterprise anywhere in the Soviet Union. The head sat behind one desk placed horizontally; the other chairs were placed two on each side of the second desk set perpendicularly to the first desk to make the 'T' shape. Whilst the head spoke to the others who were side on to him; the others faced each other and had to turn to talk to the head. The arrangement reinforced seniority. As did the telephone system. Whilst the head had a telephone with buttons on it to dial out, the rest of the key workers in an enterprise had phones with no buttons on – they could be called by the boss, but could not call anyone else. The Soviets took the 'don't call us, we'll call you' management philosophy to its ultimate extreme.

Roman Felixovich's private office was a complete contrast. It was secured behind two metal doors, had steel shutters on its windows and was invisible from the outside. Inside the furnishings were lavish and more akin to those in a Venetian palace rather than even the most lavish Russian apartment. This was Roman Felixovich's most private room and a room he only shared with his most trusted Russian business partners.

He was reading a copy of the English language St Petersburg Times newspaper, the second English language newspaper to be launched in Russia after the Moscow Times. He normally enjoyed the few pages of local news and then would go through the pages of advertisements in minute detail. The vast majority of the ads aimed at ex-pats for cars, household appliances, computer and office equipment, drivers and security services were from one or other of his operations. He had cornered these markets and guarded them fiercely. They were highly lucrative as he charged premium prices, often up to three times the price in the West, whilst using very low cost labour, and mostly recycled stolen goods, especially cars. He also held the import licences and distributorships for several Western computers and household goods brands. Today, though, his attention was spoilt by the article on the front page. The headline of the article read:

'Is this the work of Grigory Yefimovich?'

The article explained the bizarre happenings in the Rasputin Museum housed in the basement of the former Moika Palace now known as simply 94 Moika Embankment which had had windows blown out and the full-sized wax exhibits tampered with. It further reported on noises of a late night party in the neighbourhood which no-one had been able to locate. Smashing glasses and hysterical laughter had been reported in the early hours of the morning which was surprising because this time of year - it was in January, after Russian Orthodox Christmas (which is two weeks after Western Christmas) - was normally the quietest as well as the coldest time of the year. Roman Felixovich continued to read the article and swore under his breath. "Rasputin was killed once and for all," he muttered with contempt under his breath as he read the reporter's conclusion:

'We should not be surprised at the timing of the mysterious event,' ran the final lines of the article, 'because it happened in the early hours of the 22nd of January - the date of birth of Grigory Yefimovich Rasputin. The last time something very similar happened was on this day in 1942 as the Siege of the city entered in most terrible phase. Many people believe that is was the day when Rasputin came back to help the starving citizens of the city and now today St Petersburg is once again facing one of its most uncertain moments in its history – the start of privatisation and the massive effects this will have on the citizens of the city. Has he returned to help again?"

Roman Felixovich folded the paper in half. He felt like throwing it in the bin but stopped. He would go and see the newspaper's editor. He was the biggest advertiser in the paper. He would instruct the editor to drop this story. It had not appeared in any of the Russian newspapers who were concentrating most of their articles on the upcoming privatisations. He would make sure that the St Petersburg Times took the correct view of the great benefits the privatisations of the city's factories and assets would bring and at the same time bury all this superstitious nonsense where it belonged - deep underground with this long dead rogue of a peasant. A peasant who had risen to have such a malevolent hold over the Tsarina and the Tsar until the noble families had sorted him out. Privatisation was going to lead to the vast redistribution of wealth to the few who were smart enough to take the opportunities that were coming. Once again St Petersburg would have a wealthy elite – the clock was going back almost eighty years. The Revolution was finally being undone. Roman Felixovich's long lost family wealth would be regained.

Six

THE shrill ring of his second mobile phone came two seconds after his fist mobile had rung. Leonid Marlenovich ordered, "not now," into the first one, and then politely answered, "yes, yes, I will look into it and I'll call you back as soon as possible," into the second one. Leonid Marlenovich was seated on a long leather sofa. He was late middle-aged with leathery skin, small piercing eyes and well groomed hair. He was dressed in a suit which was somewhat old fashioned. Some light filtered in through windows at the top of the walls. The room was in a basement and there was no need for curtains on the windows as they were caked in mud on the outside. A sweet smoky smell hung in the air. The room had a state of the art music centre and next to it facing the sofa was a large flat screen television which was now showing the news. Leonid Marlenovich stood up and pointed a remote control towards the ceiling and started the low hum of an air conditioner.

"Who was that?" asked a voice in an adjoining room.

"No-one for you, Olga," replied Leonid Marlenovich with a yawn.

A few minutes later Olga came into the main room and put on a long fur coat. Her hair was black and long and had been put up in a bun. Her eyes were brown and looked tired. She opened the door from the room into a dark corridor. The stale sweet smell from the main room was replaced by a pungent mixture of tobacco and fruit. The door to a room across the corridor was open slightly and there were signs of recent activity which had left a stack of discarded packets next to several crates of exotic looking fruits.

"Should someone not tidy up the mess that's been left in there?" asked Olga.

"I'll get someone to do it later," lazily answered Leonid Marlenovich, "it is more important that the goods are now on their way in good time. They are more important than everything else we do."

"But surely leaving such a mess like that means someone might raise some questions," said Olga raising her voice slightly.

"Now, now, Olga, I don't think there is any need for starting to argue like this. No need for any more arguments. No more family tiffs," yawned Leonid Marlenovich again.

"You are not our family," replied Olga with a glare.

"Think of me as your 'godfather'," said Leonid Marlenovich slowly and with a deliberate and large smile.

"That's pathetic. You have been watching two much television from America."

Olga walked along the corridor. She then climbed some steps and opened and closed an unmarked door behind her. She was now in the street and she walked along a wall made of old brick. Writing on the wall in very faded paint proclaimed, 'All glory to the workers!' and honoured the heroism of the workers in their historic victory over the fascist invaders in the Great Patriotic War. The drawing of a man holding up a large sword had been sprayed over to enlarge the parts of his lower anatomy with the quotation below amended to say how lucky the workers were to be treated that way ever since. She reached the corner of the wall and crossed over to another building which was built out of grey concrete. She entered the building which housed a large and modern designed showroom with glass cabinets and shelves full of wooden and plastic models. The staff in the showroom were also brightly dressed. Two old ladies in white aprons and hats who were sweeping the floor with brooms made of brushwood were the only indications that the showroom was still in Russia.

Back in the basement room Leonid Marlenovich took out a third mobile phone which was much smaller than the others and pulled out its thick antenna. He pressed a series of numbers.

"Victor Nikolayevich, are you alone?" he asked curtly.

"Yes," came back the reply.

"Victor Nikolayevich, are you alone?" he repeated with an edge in his voice.

As he asked the question for the second time he pressed the remote control on the television and flicked through a series of grey and grained pictures showing different parts of the inside of a large factory and work yards. He stopped as he reached an office. At the bottom of the picture the caption read 'General Director'. In the office a large grey haired man was sitting behind a desk. He looked old and tired. The top button of his shirt was stopped from fitting by a thick neck which also revealed a worn and grubby collar. His hands were on the desk and his fingers were thick and stubby.

"Now, now," tut-tutted Leonid Marlenovich, "Victor Nikolayevich, for the third time, are you alone?"

The General Director turned to the side and watched as a white coated lady, previously out of camera shot, moved quickly to the door.

"It was only Larissa Arkadovna," Victor Nikolayevich said softly.

"I don't care. These days, you know, that we can trust no-one," came back the reply.

"But Larissa Arkadovna is our head book-keeper and my..." his voice trailed off.

"I don't care. Do you want to put everything at risk?" said Leonid Marlenovich sternly.

"Of course not."

"Then do as we have agreed. Why did you call?"

"We have a problem. Did you not see?" His voice was like a frightened child.

"I have been rather busy," he said coldly. "What is it?"

"The government is going to," he looked at a piece of paper in front of him, his hands shaking. He put on a pair of heavy glasses, "privatise us." He stopped and then looked up. "Privatise us. What does that mean, Leonid Marlenovich? I mean you understand all these new changes. Just tell me is it good or bad."

"Neither," answered Leonid Marlenovich bluntly.

"Leonid Marlenovich, please explain this to me. All the people in the company are talking about it and I must tell them something. They expect me to know." He was close to tears.

"Tell them we have been waiting for this." Leonid Marlenovich was thinking fast as the implications began to sink in. "Tell them that no-one knows how to privatise better than us." He was searching for an easy formula to give to the General Director, who was formally his boss, but whose only real use was to keep the mass of dim-witted workers from getting any ideas above their station. "That we are planning to increase the production of our most famous boats to meet the demands of the new market economy and the best way to do this is if we are privatised."

"That sounds perfect," sighed the General Director rapidly scribbling the words down with his thick pencil. "Perfect. We will build more boats when we are privatised. Privatisation will be good for everyone. Perfect."

Leonid Marlenovich could tell that Victor Nikolayevich did not understand what he was writing down let alone believe it. This was the news he had been warned about. The process of privatisation of their company had started and he would have only one objective from now on – to protect what he had and to make sure that the privatisation of the company did not change anything. They would continue to build boats as always and more importantly to run their new activities which were starting to flourish in the now effectively uncontrolled economy which no-one now had any command over.

Seven

ADAM wanted to run to his office but his legs again felt numb and he stumbled along the slippery pavement. The contrasting windows of the shopfronts on Nevsky Prospect failed to excite his normal curiosity. A display of expensive furs and underwear in a chic Parisian style boutique was followed by the dull cardboard boxes of a chemist. Next came a gun shop with stand after stand of tightly packed weapons, a dimly lit Russian tea shop, and a largely blacked out computer shop. This block was completed by a bakery with bare shelves, a glitzy twenty-four hour bar and a Finnish supermarket. Post-war austerity intertwined with London's Knightsbridge or New York's Fifth Avenue. Today he kept his head down. After another three blocks he turned left into a side street. The small gold coloured metal plaque on the wall humbly stated 'Miller Lombard.' Nothing else and no instructions about how to find the entrance to the St Petersburg office of one of London's leading law firms. It was on the left side of a heavy wooden door. On the other side was a key pad with eight buttons but with blank labels. Adam pressed a code and entered through the heavy door. Inside it was actually darker than the entrance of the apartment block he had so recently exited. He steeled himself against the visions and laboured up two flights of stairs. His legs were aching again.

He rang the doorbell and went in to be met by pristine white walls and strong light; except for the lingering smell of a pizza he would have thought he was entering a private clinic of some sort, not an office. His jokes about being in a hospital were still not understood by the Russian staff who made up the majority of the twenty professional and support staff in the office. He hung up his coat on the coat-stand and tried the door to the toilets. It was locked and he heard feet scurrying around. He walked past and into the small kitchen where he saw the remnants of lunch. It was pizza which no doubt meant clients had come for a working meeting. Strange that John Hampton, the managing partner of the St Petersburg office, had not mentioned it to him. Had he had a meeting he certainly would not have carried on so late with the Welcome Drinks the night before. All Hampton had wanted him to do was for him to pick up some files and start going through the papers in them. He flicked a piece of cold pizza over and heard a sharp burst of giggles. As he turned round he just caught sight of Vera, his boss' secretary, emerging from the toilets. As he walked back over to the reception Janna, the receptionist, looked at him with a frown.

"Are you ok?" she asked concerned.

"I was coming out of the hotel and everywhere was blocked," he said sheepishly expecting her to understand.

"Mr Hampton asked me to call you this morning but there was no answer from your mobile or from your hotel room," Janna continued not quite understanding what he had said.

"Late breakfast reading through my notes. It was very claustrophobic in my room." Adam knew he was not making sense. The vision was streaming back with great intensity. His cheeks burned. The young woman, Lena, was smiling; she looked remarkably similar to Vera, his boss' secretary.

"Really are you ok?" Janna was sounding more and more concerned.

Vera had returned and was standing behind her. He stared at her and no, no, Vera was much taller and the girl's nose had seemed much cuter. Vera was coming over to him.

"Can I get you a diet coke or a glass of water, Adam?" asked Vera.

"I can manage," he spluttered and turned to the kitchen. "I think that I might be going down with a bug or something."

At that moment the door to the main meeting room behind the reception area swung open and with it a burst of raucous noise and laughter signalling a break in the meeting. John Hampton bounded out with his sleeves rolled up.

"Ah, Adam," he boomed, "there you are. We thought for one horrible moment that you'd been caught up in that terrible mess opposite the hotel this morning."

"You could almost say that," replied Adam looking at the floor. "I mean it meant that I couldn't get here before now." He was mumbling.

"Come in. I want to introduce you to Dominic Corley from the British Redevelopment Fund. He has worked with our colleagues in London quite a few times and he is absolutely delighted to find that we have an office in St Petersburg."

"Yes, I know the Fund," replied Adam grateful to be back on safe ground.

"Before we go in, Adam, were you able to finish that review of the papers on the buildings on Anglisky Prospect?"

"I got the papers late last night," replied Adam patting his case to indicate where they were. "It'll be finished today." As he patted his case again his mind flashed back to receiving the papers as instructed from the Russian lawyer he had been told to meet. The lawyer had come to his hotel. After taking the papers Adam had gone for a quick drink with the lawyer in the hotel bar and noticed the young women in hotel reception as the lawyer left. They had smiled at him. He had then gone back to his room, put the papers in his case which he then had hidden and then gone straight back down. He had then had a rush of courage and invited them to the bar where his Welcome Drinks were going to be. Idiot. Luckily he had not told them that he was a lawyer. He had described himself rather as a management consultant. But they had not been that interested in what he did, had they? He was just a foreigner with dollars. Could not have been anything more.

"Let me introduce you," said Hampton sensing Adam's discomfort at being late in finishing his work. He also seemed a little shook up by something, he thought, but he knew that Adam had been solid during his two years in Russia and had made a good impact in St Petersburg so far. Hampton was sure that Adam could be trusted with the firm's more delicate work and he knew from his Moscow colleagues that Adam almost invariably met work deadlines. He was only in his late twenties but he was fast tracking through the law firm with apparent ease. "Donald, this is Adam Carter. Adam, this is Donald Corley from the British Redevelopment Fund or rather the 'British Redevelopment Fund for companies in the Former Soviet Union' to give the fund its proper title."

They shook hands and Adam proceeded to discuss the work Miller Lombard had done for the Fund in London and the people they both knew. Adam was finally sounding and feeling like himself. The excitement of being a legal pioneer in Russia started to come through in his observations and anecdotes about his time so far in the new Russia.

After a few minutes the door to the meeting room opened and Anna walked in and smiled around the room her round wide eyes shining brightly. She had changed on arriving at the office. Her dark hair was now clipped up and her elegant light grey dress and bright scarf made Adam glance down at his unironed shirt and crumpled suit trousers. Adam guessed she was in her mid-twenties and she seemed to Adam to have an air of sophistication; the air which seemed to elude the other young Russian women in the Miller Lombard office despite the designer clothes they wore. Adam had spoken briefly to Anna in the office and at the Welcome Drinks but had not gotten to know her yet.

Anna for her part did no yet know what to make of her new colleague. At times he seemed to speak as he was now doing with great confidence whilst at other times he seemed all at sea with day to day tasks. He was already a source of great gossip with the secretaries in the office but her interest in him and their boss was much more professional. She had joined a foreign law firm excited at the prospect of working on complex transactions with foreigners many of whom were strange, larger than life characters. People who went charging around trying to make things happen and giving a seriousness to their work which was something hard to find in most of her own Russian relatives and most family friends; their lives tended to consist of getting by or in some cases avoiding life as much as possible. She was curious to know whether work was really that important to foreigners and why it appeared such a motivator for people.

Wages in foreign law firms and banks were certainly a great attraction, but was there much of a real point to it? So far she could not decide. She enjoyed the new situations and was intrigued by the foreign people and companies she met. She felt most at home, though, dealing with Russian companies struggling to adapt to the demands now of a 'market' driven economy. An economy where the laws of supply and demand for goods had replaced the old Soviet system of dictating the production of goods irrespective of whether the goods were wanted or not, or more often than not, whether the goods were of much actual use or value compared to Western-made goods – the great 'command' economy of the Soviet Union. Although it may have been ineffective and slowed down technological development, everyone knew where they stood and what they were commanded to do – now they had to face the world economy and daily uncertainty. Nearly all the Russian companies and their management were also facing interaction with foreign companies for the first time. Anna could put herself firmly in their shoes as that was her world so far – they were her relatives, she understood them, their vacillating bouts of fear and then pride, their unbound ambitions followed by unstoppable pessimism. Now she was excited more and more by the prospect of learning as much as she could from the foreigners.

Anna sat down next to Dominic Corley. He was an impeccably dressed middle-aged man in a pinstriped suit and Hermes tie. His English diction was wonderfully precise and Anna enjoyed listening to the sound of him talking as much as to what he was saying.

"So if I understand this correctly, John," Corley resumed his conversation with Hampton again, "these vouchers are being exchanged for actual shares in companies?"

"Correct," replied Hampton, "the programme of so-called 'mass privatisation' is now moving in to it next phase. Under mass privatisation vouchers were given to the management and workers of companies and to members of the public. These vouchers can now be exchanged for actual shares in companies."

"And foreigners can then buy these shares?"

"Yes, with one or two exceptions. Military mostly, as you would expect. In fact, however, the majority of companies now being privatised are not part of the military industries or other sectors that the Government wants to keep. The companies of the so called military-industrial complexes which accounted for great swathes of Russia production often running whole towns and cities. Many of these are in terminal decline and would not be attractive to anyone to own or to invest in."

"Everything seems to be happening a quite a pace," commented Corley.

"That seems to be the Russian way," added Adam. "They could have taken a gradual route but by the end of this year some five thousand large companies will have been privatised."

"It is quite remarkable, you know, how simply they are doing it and yet, as I understand it, so many companies do not have any basic financial records as we have in the West," replied Corley.

"Yes, and so it is being done on a very simple and straightforward basis," said Hampton, "and that is the beauty of it. Each region, each city and each town across Russia has the same basic infrastructure built during Soviet times – power station, telephone exchange, food manufacturers, shops and they can simply be privatised for each region, city and town by creating new companies with the relevant assets and operations simply put into them in each geographical area." He stopped for a moment to see if everyone was following and then continued. "Also larger companies such as the oil companies can be privatised based on the oil reserves and the production which they have. And quite often a city produced all the items of a particular sort for the whole of the Soviet Union – light bulbs in Estonia, washing machines in Perm, for example, and these can also easily be privatised. The only complex cases which we can see are those companies which already existed before Communism. These are companies such as trading companies, shipping lines and old style manufacturing companies such as ship builders. We have some of these companies here in St Petersburg. They have existed for many years and were taken over by the State during Communist rule. We believe that there might be some legal cases around these companies concerning who the rightful owners are."

"Plenty of good challenging work for you lawyers then," quipped Corley, "and not to mention the fees."

"And plenty of great investment opportunities for funds such as yours," shot back Hampton.

"One should not say this too loud," continued Corley dropping his voice, "but one has to take every advantage of the chance to buy cheap." For once Anna was disappointed by what Corley was saying. He had seemed such the epitome of an English gentleman and of a professional but now it seemed as always to come back to one thing - money. But what else did she expect? This was capitalism. "From the research we have done I have my eye," continued Corley, "on several companies in St Petersburg and we have lots of funds to invest. Please let me know if you come across any investment opportunities in these privatisations. I am particularly interested with companies which have properties in good locations. Some of the properties in this city will be worth a fortune in the future."

"We will, of course," replied Hampton with a big smile. "Adam will you make a note of that? Now before you go, can

I explain to you about the work we are starting with the Hermitage."

"Now that would be the ultimate privatisation not to mention property investment!" quipped Corley again.

"Well I don't think even Russia would go that far," responded Hampton. "Our work is going to be to assist in locating and exhibiting many of the works of art which have been stashed away and have not seen the light of day for many years."

Adam and Anna excused themselves to go back to their desks. Adam was now sounding like his normal self. Anna though was slightly saddened by the light-hearted attitude of the senior men in the meeting. Perhaps she would have to try and understand their humour more, if that was what it really was. Privatisation sounded a very seductive proposition and a once in a lifetime chance but only probably for a very small minority of people. In the companies involved and in the general population it had created a sense of danger, a foreboding that big changes were again just around the corner. She vowed to make sure she would understand everything that mattered and find her own part to play in the changes. She left as soon as she could at the end of the afternoon and went to the Home.

Valentina Alexandrovna unlocked the large steel filing cabinet in her office in the Home and took out a yellow file. Anna was sitting on a chair on the other side of the Director of the Home's desk. The office was small and looked lived in. It had a tidiness about it and yet it was crammed full of papers, photographs, small objects and mementos. It had a samovar and cups and saucers in one corner and a tall lamp in another. It had no windows and its walls were covered in certificates and photographs.

"Sasha's file is full of papers but few of them are of any use," sighed Valentina Alexandrovna putting the file on her desk and sitting down. "Here are the papers found in the old lady's possession and here are copies of letters and letters of enquiry sent to try and find out where Sasha and the old lady came from."

Anna took the papers and had a quick look at them. The papers from the old lady were in a plastic folder. They looked very old and they were barely legible.

"You can see how difficult it is for us even to be sure of Sasha's family name. His date of birth is completely illegible as well."

"I can," replied Anna, "not even a magnifying glass would help. Parts of the words look like they have been scratched out."

"Perhaps, or just worn away. Probably not well looked after. We have had very few replies to the enquiry letters. And those we have had have all been negative. This is a rare case, Anna. We have lots of abandoned children in the Home but we know where nearly all of them have come from or we can easily trace where they have come from."

Anna looked at Valentina Alexandrovna. She did not know her age. She looked old but as she studied Valentina Alexandrovna's face, Anna could see the deep lines under her eyes on what was not an old person's face. Having the desperate plight of some hundred plus abandoned or orphaned children in her care was a tremendous weight. Anna found it very hard to think of the conditions in the Home and with each visit the state of the Home started to weigh more and more on her. For one quick moment she felt a nervous laugh inside at the thought of proposing to her boss and to the rich Western investors that they privatise the Home, though she doubted they would understand her Russian humour. Valentina Alexandrovna had perhaps sensed the laugh and she looked quizzically at Anna.

"Can you tell me more about how you find out information, Valentina Alexandrovna? Maybe there are ways I or the law firm I work in can help."

Valentina Alexandrovna smiled and gave Anna a fifteen minute talk through the process of identifying children from the registration of their births onwards. The Soviet Union had been run on paperwork. People literally could not move without the correct papers – by correct normally meant a flurry of stamps and the signature of a bureaucrat. Sasha and his 'grandmother' did not have the correct papers and had stayed under the bureaucratic nets by living in the country and being aided by the Russian Church. The papers with the disputed family name were those of an internal Soviet passport and Valentina Alexandrovna had to admit to Anna that the papers might not have been genuine. Immediately, however, to stop Anna worrying she explained that the few words that Sasha could write were those of his name. The document may have been false but they had no reason to doubt the name. The likelihood was that the woman had needed some papers to travel to St Petersburg and had had them made on the black market and would have had no reason to make up new names. Anna visibly relaxed at this explanation and her pulse returned to normal. The thought that there may not be a family connection to Sasha after all was something that she did not wish to contemplate. More and more she wanted the connection to be proven so that Sasha's life could be improved – she wanted to improve his life at least. Maybe all the changes that she wanted to play her part in during the privatisation work might lead to a chance to help some of the other children too. It would not take much to improve their lives – if funds were made available they could go a long, long way to improve so many things in the Home.

"There is one thing I wanted to ask you, Valentina Alexandrovna, if I may?" Anna's voice had become serious.

"Of course, Anna," replied Valentina Alexandrovna slowly.

"Sasha has not really been to school has he?"

Valentina Alexandrovna nodded. "He can read music and some books but his writing is poor. He has lacked formal instruction."

"Since he has a singing teacher, would it be possible for him to have some writing lessons as well?"

Valentina Alexandrovna looked at Anna with a deep smile. She knew how much Anna wanted to help but there were two problems with her question. "I will answer you but I may disappoint you," she said as she gathered the papers on her desk back into Sasha's file. "There are two problems. The first is the cost. The singing lessons from Yelena Matrovna are paid for."

Anna lifted her head up in surprise. This was the first time she had heard this. "Really?" she said. "Can you tell me who pays for them?"

"I wish I could, Anna," replied Valentina Alexandrovna with another smile, "but the donor wishes to remain anonymous. And," she lowered her voice, "I myself do not know. Only Yelena Matrovna knows. It is an unusual arrangement. Yelena Matrovna brings me money each week and I pay her for her lessons out of it. I can see what you may be thinking but Yelena Matrovna will not reveal who it is."

Anna remained silent. She did not quite know how to react to this. She would have to think it through. Someone else must have an interest in Sasha. "And the second problem," continued Valentina Alexandrovna, "are the other children. Everyone accepts Sasha's gift for singing but if we also give him writing lessons many would think he was being favoured. I am sorry, Anna."

"Is there any other way?" asked Anna. She was blushing slightly out of embarrassment. She must have sounded very selfish.

"Let me have a think. Life is changing here every day and we don't know what may happen tomorrow. Let me have a think."

They chatted for a few more minutes and then exchanged goodbyes. For once Anna felt like crying and she did not really know why.

Eight

THE young school children all wrapped up in brightly coloured ski jackets, hats and gloves descended from the yellow school bus in a loud buzz of excitement. The bus was a standard issue American school bus and its bright yellow colour bounced off the hard packed snow across Palace Square. The bus shrank in size, however, as the children saw the imposing building of the Hermitage Museum from close up in front of them. To the children its magnificent green facades, white columns and lavish golden window surrounds were awesome. Nearly six hundred metres wide and twenty three metres high its sheer size stunned them. The incongruity of a single decker yellow American school bus parked on the edge of the deserted Palace Square in front of one of the most palatial sites in the world was striking. No-one could imagine a single decker bus rolling up and parking at the side of a deserted Buckingham Palace or the White House in Washington D.C. Yet here in St Petersburg the Tsars had long left their Winter Palace, originally started by Peter the Great's daughter Elizabeth and then finished by Catherine the Great to house the vast amount of art she collected from all over Europe. Its saving grace had been the Communist revolutionaries' decision to convert it into a museum and art gallery. On a crisp winter's morning the soft light shimmered off the snow and illuminated the green facades giving the whole building and square a magical aura.

The children raced to the entrance. The large door had just been opened and the class from the Anglo-American School were the day's first visitors. Their private tour meant that they would have an hour to visit the rooms and halls before the museum opened to the public. As they entered the children were shepherded by several elderly ladies to a large cloakroom where they all quickly took off their coats, hats and gloves. The high pitched voices of the children with an overwhelmingly American accent echoed loudly in the foyer and visibly unsettled the elderly Russian ladies who struggled to hang up the piles and piles of children's clothing in the cloakroom. One of the two women with the schoolchildren quietly clapped her hands.

"Fourth Grade," she said calmly, "Fourth Grade, please pay attention." The children all quietened down. "Remember, you are in a famous museum and as the signs say," she paused and pointed to several large signs in Russian and English at the side of the wide marble staircase that led from the foyer through to the halls, "'Rule 1 - Do not touch any exhibits. Rule 2 - Please proceed quietly.' We must obey the rules." The children had fallen silent but most looked puzzled. "We all know that Russians do most things a little differently to us but we must respect their rules." At that moment a middle-aged woman walked over to her and smiled. "You are from the Anglo-American school, are you not?" she said.

"We are. And I am Miss Marshall, their teacher," she replied.

"I am very pleased to meet you, Miss Marshall. I am Olga Valentinovna. I am your guide for your visit."

"Great," replied Miss Marshall.

"Our rules are a little, how do you say – 'old fashioned?'" Miss Marshall smiled with a small nod in reply. "But I am sure that if the children do not make too much noise," continued Olga Valentinovna, "then no-one will mind."

"That's a relief," replied Miss Marshall. "The children are so excited and keen to see the great treasures and paintings you have here."

Olga Valentinovna smiled. She had worked in the Hermitage all her life and she had seen great changes in the types of visitors over the last thirty years. Despite the world-class nature of many of the exhibits and especially the paintings, more than anything else it was the faces of children she liked to watch - Russian children, and now for the first time foreign children, - as they moved from exhibit to exhibit putting the life back into the Palace – a Palace which deserved to be full of life and laughter.

"Which of the children is Alexander Hampton?" she asked.

Miss Marshall looked at her puzzled. "Alex," she said, "where are you?"

"Here, Miss," said Alex brightly pushing his way past the children in front of him.

"Very pleased to meet you, Alexander," said Olga Valentinovna. "We are so grateful for the work your father is doing for the museum. Please tell him how grateful we are."

"I will," said Alex bowing his head.

"Well let's start. Let's go," said Olga Valentinovna with a wave of her hands and her voice visibly rising in volume in clear contravention to Rule 2. "Follow me!"

The children started to run up the wide staircase but the stern look on Miss Marshall's face slowed them down and they settled into an orderly, if noisy, procession. The halls genuinely interested the children. Olga Valentinovna explained many of the exhibits in a concise and academic sounding manner. The actual worth of many of the Old Masters from Leonardo Da Vinci to Rembrandt was largely lost on the children, the Impressionists puzzled them and the nudes made them giggle, but they generally understood the overall stature of the exhibits. It is, after all, as they had been told, the world's best art museum. The children had been instructed to make a note of their favourite exhibits – the bronze 'Peacock' clock which looks like its dial is on top of a huge mushroom was number one on the list closely followed by the double-headed eagles painted in the Peter the Great Hall. What price a multi-million dollar Monet masterpiece to school children!

Since it was a private tour Olga Valentinovna was able to let the children look behind the scenes briefly and she took them to one of the main working rooms were works of art were being restored. The children were amazed by the amounts of paints, brushes and other materials. There were several canvases stretched on big frames with clear plastic sheets covering them. It was an art room to die for. Sensing several wandering hands and over inquisitive gestures Olga Valentinovna moved the children on quickly. Next they passed through a large room full of crates. They could see hundreds of wrapped up objects and what were most probably paintings. Most were wrapped in lawyers of paper which had yellowed with age and were tied up with thick string. Many had large and elaborate wax seals and were covered in ink marks.

"As you can see," said Olga Valentinovna, "we still have many, many exhibits which we have not yet put on display."

"There must be some real treasure in here," said Alex quietly under his breath to one of his classmates. "My dad says there still are hundreds of hidden treasures in here that no-one knows about. Stuff the Soviets took back from the Germans and other things they found at the end of World War Two. Lots of them don't have proper records." Alex had stopped and was looking at a crate which was largely hidden by several others in front of it. The crate had one object in it which was probably a heavily wrapped painting. Miss Marshall was watching Alex with rising curiosity. Alex squeezed himself between two crates and very gently started to raise a hand to touch the object. At that moment Miss Marshall caught Olga Valentinovna's eye. Sensing that Alex was on the point of breaking Rule 1 of the museum, Miss Marshall quickly moved over to Alex to block Olga Valentinovna's view of what Alex was doing. She quickly put her hand on Alex's arm and drew it back. Alex blushed deeply. As Miss Marshall turned round, Olga Valentinovna had moved over to her.

"Alexander," she said in a high pitched voice. "Alexander," she said her voice now under control. She hesitated as Miss Marshall stepped behind Alex and put her hands on his shoulders. Alex was staring at the floor.

"What do you think you have found?" asked Olga Valentinovna a large smile slowly spreading across her face. She had made a quick decision to take a positive step with the young boy. His father was a leading expert in art and more importantly she and her superiors in the museum had great hopes of his father raising funds for the museum and other art collections in St Petersburg.

"I'm sorry," replied Alex looking up and his cheeks cooling, "but I can kind of feel something from this object. I was not going to.."

"You have no need to be sorry, Alexander," said Olga Valentinovna sweetly. "You should be proud of your knowledge."

Alex turned his head and looked at Miss Marshall who shrugged her shoulders slightly.

"My knowledge?" replied Alex.

"Yes," continued Olga Valentinovna. "That object is probably the most valuable work in this room. It is a stained glass panel from the Saint Sophia Cathedral in Kiev. And can you tell me why it is so valuable?"

Alex had recovered his normal enthusiasm. He had felt an attraction to the crate. He had been drawn to it over the other hundreds in the room. And he had had a slight tingling in his fingers. "Easy. Must have jewels in it?" he replied excitedly.

"Correct! Gold and precious stones. I'll ask one of our curators to see if we can put it on display or at least show it to you and your father when he comes here. It is spectacular. Would you like that?"

"You bet!" replied Alex. "Just wait till my dad hears about this."

The children's visit finished just as the doors opened to the public. It was very difficult for Miss Marshall to round them all up and it took nearly thirty minutes to get them all dressed in the coats, hat and gloves and out across Palace Square and onto their school bus. Olga Valentinovna had been genuinely nonplussed by the young American boy's attraction to the Saint Sophia window and she decided to write to the Head Curator to inform him. If the young boy had such an obvious affinity to priceless objects like that, and then, if it ran in the family, what level of art knowledge and interest might his father have?

At the end of the school day Ellen and Alex met Miss Marshall in the school corridor. Miss Marshall had also been intrigued by Alex's attraction to the wrapped up stained glass window.

"Alex has your husband's feeling for great works of art," she said with enthusiasm. "So much knowledge! It was a great trip, wasn't it, Alex?"

"Super," replied Alex. "And mom, I found one of the hidden treasures?"

"Really?" said Ellen raising her eyebrows and looking at Miss Marshall. For some reason the image of the bullet in the back seat of her car flashed through her mind.

"Well kind of," replied Alex again grinning. Ellen looked again at Miss Marshall.

"He found a crate," said Miss Marshall.

"In a room full of hundreds of crates," jumped in Alex.

"He found a crate," repeated Miss Marshall, "which had a very valuable window in it full of jewels. From a famous cathedral."

"What did it look like?"

"We never saw it," said Alex. "It was wrapped up but I could tell what was inside."

"True," said Miss Marshall. "All through the visit Alex seemed to know all the treasures and most of the paintings. This window with jewels was the icing on the cake or else it was a very lucky, lucky guess!"

"No," said Alex, "I just knew and then the lady said what was inside. She did say they will put it on display when dad goes."

"True, again," said Miss Marshall. "Alex was our star of the trip. Will you excuse me?" she asked with a smile, "I need to catch the Principal."

Ellen smiled at Miss Marshall as she walked past them. She then looked at Alex. His excitement was clear and it was so good that he was sharing his dad's greatest passion. At that moment she decided not to tell her husband about the bullet and would leave it with their driver to deal with.

'I agree,' she heard Alex say, 'he has lots of work and worries at the moment.' But she was not sure if Alex had actually spoken to her or if he had just read her mind.

Nine

SASHA and Yelena Matrovna crossed themselves as they entered the Cathedral of the Resurrection or the 'Cathedral of Our Saviour-on-the-Spilt-Blood' to give it its true title. The cathedral was built on the spot where Tsar Alexander II was assassinated by a terrorist bomb in March 1881 and hence its odd sounding name of 'blood being spilt'. The Tsar's assassination had notoriously been foretold by a fortune teller and mystical forces had been said to have gripped the city in the years after the bombing. In many respects this act of terror was the forerunner of the bloodshed which would be unleashed in the Revolutions of 1905 and 1917. There is nothing in the slightest bit odd about the cathedral, however. Its exterior is as sumptuous as it is classical. It has eight onion-shaped cupolas around a middle drum with a tent-shaped pointed structure supporting the top cupola. Four of the cupolas are covered with gilded and enamelled cooper sheets and the other four in a wonderful mixture of blue, green, gold and white patterns. The cupolas are completed by golden crucifixes on top of each of them. Set in niches around the base of the cathedral are twenty granite plaques with carved depictions of the key events in the reign of the assassinated tsar. It is without doubt one of the most impressive cathedrals in Russia.

The interior of the cathedral matches its exterior. Its walls are adorned with multicoloured Italian marbles and Russian semi-precious stones. Its inner canopy, crowned with a rock-crystal cross is mounted over the exact spot where the Tsar was assassinated. Its vault is decorated inside with stars made from topazes and other gemstones and rests on four columns of jasper. The vault and walls all look as if they are covered in a mosaic carpet.

More importantly for its visitors who were coming through its door, the layout and size of the cathedral was perfect for acoustics – it magnified the intimacy found in village chapels - village chapels which stretch across the breadth of Russia by its vast geography and which sing out of the deepest depths of the Russian soul echoing the turbulent years of the country's religious past.

Yelena Matrovna, who had put on a head scarf on entering the cathedral, went forward to the altar and without hesitation prostrated herself on the ground. Sasha stood in the middle of the cathedral and drank in the beauty of the walls. The magnificence was overwhelming and yet there was also a feeling of simplicity and of warmth – the feeling he had had every time he went to the chapel which his grandmother had looked after. All of a sudden out of the corner of his eye he caught sight of a figure moving. There had been no-one in the cathedral when they had arrived. It was a quick movement and then he saw a face. The face was the image of his grandmother. He closed and opened his eyes and the face was gone. It was replaced by a figure dressed in very old clothing. The figure was in an alcove near the door. Sasha watched as the figure raised a hand and beckoned to him to come over. The figure was that of a large man. Sasha took several steps and then looked over his shoulder. Yelena Matrovna was still on the ground deep in prayer. He ran to the alcove and stopped his foot making a banging sound on the stone floor. Gone. The figure had gone. Sasha turned and this time walked over to Yelena Matrovna who was now standing up.

Vladimir Melnikov, the Metropolitan of St Petersburg and Ladoga, the Metropolitan being the Russian Orthodox Church's equivalent of an Archbishop, normally led services in the city's largest cathedral, the Kazan Cathedral, attired in his white robe, mitre and golden crosses. Today however he had come to this cathedral on a private visit and was dressed as such in a simple ankle length black cassock. He was accompanied by another man dressed the same. The second man walked over to Yelena Matrovna and Sasha and greeted them warmly. Yelena Matrovna reverently kissed his right hand and Sasha followed. The Metropolitan melted in to the alcove near the door. The second man spoke to Yelena Matrovna quietly and then with a smile at Sasha he left them and walked over to the door. Sasha shuddered slightly as he heard the loud turn of a key in a lock. Yelena Matrovna put her hands on Sasha's shoulders and spoke quietly.

"We have been given thirty minutes in here by ourselves to practice and to hear your voice, Sasha. Are you ready?"

"Yes," replied Sasha in a whisper. His throat was dry and his hands were shaking,

"Very good. We will start with 'The Invincible Lord of Hosts'."

Sasha took a deep breath and looked at Yelena Matrovna. There was a worried look on his face. He opened his mouth and then paused. He took another deep breath and this time opened his mouth fully but silence. Sasha seemed to look around himself. He breathed and tried again. Silence again. Yelena Matrovna took hold of the glasses on her chain, lifted them up and peered at Sasha. She did not speak. She looked down at the open music book in front of her. Sasha half turned round and looked to be listening. He breathed again and then with a smile started to sing. Yelena Matrovna was convinced that Sasha was following someone else's lead but she could not hear another voice. Sasha's voice rose and rose – its melodic tones making small echoes high up in the cathedral's roof. His voice sounded like many voices singing. As he ended, Yelena Matrovna gave a small clap as was her way of signalling her approval. Sasha took a deep breath and with the faintest of smiles launched himself into one of his favourite folk songs – 'Down the River Volga'. At the end of this song, a few beads of sweat had appeared on Sasha's forehead. "Take a moment, Sasha," said Yelena Matrovna quietly. "Those songs were beautiful. Bravo."

Sasha looked around. The walls and roof of the cathedral now seemed brighter than when they had arrived. He felt the walls themselves were warming. He closed his eyes and could imagine the peasant dancers in his folk songs starting to twirl round. Yelena Matrovna tapped him on the arm and he opened his eyes. "Sasha, your voice is warm. Let us now try the chants. I will start and then you continue." It was Yelena Matrovna who this time closed her eyes. She licked her lips and then started to sing very, very quietly and very, very slowly. Sasha closed his eyes and joined her singing. After several moments their voices melted together and they started to sing more quickly and then more loudly and then Yelena Matrovna's voice began to drop in volume and gradually it stopped. By now Sasha's voice had reached a minor crescendo and once over that his voice picked up its pace again, the rhythms varied like waves, the pitch of his voice undulating with immense vocal dexterity. Although his eyes were shut, Sasha's face was beaming as if he could see through his eyelids. The inside of the cathedral was chanting with him. The regularity of the sounds hardened as if Sasha was spinning and to anyone watching they would have thought Sasha was in a trance. The effort was showing through the beads of sweat down the side of his face. The singing was physical as much as it was spiritual.

Yelena Matrovna had also her eyes closed. And then a loud sound interrupted the singing as if a glass had shattered on a floor in the middle of the night. Sasha stopped abruptly. As the final notes of his voice resounded around the cathedral in a dying flourish and he and Yelena Matrovna stood eyes open, both bodies rooted to the ground, a coarse laugh seemed to bellow through the cathedral and a gust of wind flew across the floor making Yelena Matrovna's music papers flutter as if in a violent panic. Yelena Matrovna crossed herself and rushed Sasha and herself towards the cathedral door. To their surprise the door had been unlocked and opened. They stepped quickly out into the snow without looking behind. The sharp light off the snow on the ground blinded them momentarily as the laughter, much mellower now, slowly faded away into the sounds of the songs that Sasha had just been singing.

Ten

JOHN Hampton and Adam were in Hampton's Volvo. They were on the way to the Peter the Great Shipyard and were being driven the short distance from their office just off Nevsky Prospect. They were driving towards the Neva River and then along its embankment. The Neva's embankment was lined by impressive large three and four storey buildings from the Tsarist era. Many of Europe's colonial cities would be more than proud of these well-built and imposing buildings. The impact of the Soviet Union though was also clearly felt on the embankment. Every few hundred metres or so much less impressive and drab buildings, factories and shipyards had been squeezed in between the buildings from the Tsarist era. This was particularly the case in the area to which the Volvo was headed. The Volvo left the road along the embankment and crossed over onto Dekabristov Street. A few minutes later it turned right onto Anglisky Prospect.

The Peter the Great Shipyard occupies a large site which is bounded in an oblong shape by the Anglisky Prospect, the end of Dekabristov Street, a small canal in parallel and opposite to the Anglisky Prospect and finally at the bottom end by the River Neva itself as befits one of the city's longest established shipyards. The site itself inside is divided internally into three large oblong areas which run in parallel with the Anglisky Prospect and the canal. The first area facing the Anglisky Prospect contains an office building and a showroom of typical Soviet construction and then a much older brick-built building at the end which borders the Neva. The second area houses a covered ship yard, a workshop, a foundry and a dry dock and the third area bordering the canal and the Neva has a large open dock and slipway.

"Have you been here before, John?" Adam asked Hampton.

"No, first time," replied Hampton, "but I have met one of the company's Directors before. This is one of the companies we expect is going to be privatised soon. Anna has been checking all the official announcements printed by the City Council and by the St Petersburg Property Fund which is the department in the City Council responsible for the privatisations."

"I haven't seen anything in the St Petersburg Times about any companies being lined up for sale," said Adam.

"And you won't. Not until the deals are done. And very little in the Russian press. And even the official announcements of privatisations, which are stuck up on a couple of public notice boards, nearly always go missing as soon as they are put up."

"Really?" Adam had not heard this before.

"Adam, information is the most valuable commodity here now." Hampton had lowered his voice. "Some companies want to stop their own privatisations or more likely want to keep them to themselves. So they make sure the process is kept from as many people as possible. Anna has two of the Russian legal assistants checking the main public notice boards every day and doing whatever they have to in order to make sure we know what is being announced."

"How do they do that?"

"'Office expenses', Adam," laughed Hampton. "There are some Russian ways of doing things which we are better off leaving to the Russians. I think we are here."

They arrived at the entrance and could see the three buildings which bordered the Anglisky Prospect. Two were soulless two-storey grey concrete blocks whilst the third which led down to the river bank was old and brick-built. It seemed to be a classic clash of Tsarist versus Soviet construction styles. There was also a large structure which appeared to stride over the entrance which was between the two concrete blocks. Adam stood back to try to make out what it was. As he looked closer he was sure that the bases of the structure were two large black old-fashioned boots. A number of workers in overalls were standing around the base. One was smoking and depositing ash into what looked like an eye hole of a boot's laces.

"Someone you must recognise," said Hampton

Adam was puzzled. He stared up from the boots and could make out calf muscles and up further to where the legs joined.

"Well it is some huge statue of somebody," observed Adam.

"Well, we are at the Peter the Great Shipyard, Adam," smiled Hampton.

Adam took several steps back but could still see no further than a huge belt buckle which had become the perching zone for a flock of what looked like large magpies.

"Cross back over the road and you'll see properly. Watch out for those Siberian crows."

Adam turned, stumbled into a foot-wide pothole, managed to retain his balance and crossed over the road. He looked up above the belt and followed the line of a tunic until a huge bearded jaw and imperious eyes glared down at him blocking out the sun. He moved his head to the left and raised his hand as the sun shot past the head and dazzled him. He refocused and followed the raised left arm to its end where a large sword was held aloft in a mixture of rallying cry and triumph. There was no doubt now. This was a very striking image of a great of a man, of Peter the Great himself. Adam shivered slightly. A sharp breeze from the River Neva had risen and caught him between the shoulders. The sheer size and solidity of the statue was a powerful reminder of an ambitious and powerful past.

"Now you can see that there is something to this country," Hampton said calmly, "when they get it right. Anyway now let's prepare ourselves for what lies inside."

Adam's sense of awe evaporated as they entered the foyer to the first grey building. It was drab and shoddy. There were several exhibiting glass cases which contained large but very old looking models of boats. The foyer was busy with people milling around the entrance who paid no intention to the exhibits. Instead they were carefully studying and feeling a selection of items on a stall on the other side. It was assortments of children's clothes and household cleaning items. On the wall Adam saw a number of notices. From his very basic written Russian he could work out one or two of them. One was about the company's dental clinic which would now open on Tuesdays and Thursdays. Another seemed to announce that those wishing to join the annual summer boat trip and weekend at the company dacha should ensure that they send the names and passport details of all those wishing to come to the General Director's office by 4th April. Adam knew that the dacha would be the company's recreational complex in the country but he could not see why passports would be needed. He put it down to his poor Russian but made a mental note to ask Anna.

"Gentlemen, how very good to see you," said a man politely in English. "John, how are you this morning?"

"Very good, Leonid Marlenovich. And you?" replied Hampton shaking Leonid Marlenovich's hand.

"Good as always, John," replied Leonid Marlenovich who then whispered in the ear of a large scowling woman sitting at the side of a rusting turnstile. Any official visitor to the company's offices had to pass through the turnstile. Her scowl blushed and without a word she motioned to Hampton and Adam to go through the turnstile.

"And how is Victor Nikolayevich this morning?" inquired Hampton as they went through.

"As fretful as ever."

"I see. And how is his health?" replied Hampton touching the side of his throat with his fingers.

"Oh, don't worry, John, it is much too early for that. It's not yet eleven and Victor Nikolayevich is completely sober. 'As sober as a judge,' I think they say in England, don't they?"

This was, of course, a complete misrepresentation of events. As soon as the guard at the front barrier had telephoned up to Leonid Marlenovich in Victor Nikolayevich's office to say that the Volvo had arrived, Victor Nikolayevich's hands had started to shake and Leonid Marlenovich had calmed him down with two large vodkas.

Leonid Marlenovich and his visitors made their way up a flight of stairs and along a corridor where all the doors had simple numbers on them and were shut. At the end of the corridor they went through a door and into a corridor with glass walls on each side. They went out of the glass corridor and into another large entrance area. It was as if they were stepping back into time. The ceilings were high and the walls all wooden-panelled two-thirds of the way up with glass on top up to the ceiling. A large iron clock hung down from the centre of the ceiling. Offices led off from the centre like small booths. It was quiet and orderly. They walked across to two large doors. To the left of the door was a large brass sign in both Russian and English. Adam stopped to read it. 'The Peter the Great Shipyard established in 1703, rebuilt after the Great Patriotic War. A Hero Factory in Russia's Second Hero City.'

"Hero City?" Adam whispered to Hampton.

"It was made a Hero City because it survived the German siege in the Second World War," replied Hampton.

Leonid Marlenovich had walked straight in and the others followed. In front were two desks. Behind one sat a young woman of no more than twenty dressed exquisitely in blue as if she had walked of the front cover of Vogue. Behind the other sat a middle-aged lady dressed in a shapeless floral dress. Doors led off at either side of the room with name plaques for the General Director and Deputy General Director. To the left was a large glass display cabinet housing more large and old looking models of boats. Leonid Marlenovich turned to the younger woman.

"Shall we go in?" he said more as a command than a request.

"Let me just check." The girl jumped up and scurried off into the office.

"I'm sure that would not be necessary," moaned the middle-aged lady not hiding her distaste for the enthusiasm of her much younger colleague. "They're always like that at the beginning," she said resignedly to Leonid Marlenovich. "Why do we have to have such young girls nowadays?"

"Come, come. We all know who is really in charge here." His tone was mockingly soothing.

"But why do I have to put up with all these young girls?"

"Now, now we'll talk about this later. We have to move with the times. Let me have a quick word with the Deputy General Director."

He walked straight into the other office and almost straight out. "Good, good see that they are all ready and packed on time," he said quietly as he came back out closing the door behind him.

Adam tried to catch a glance of the Deputy General Director whom he assumed would be a typical fifty-year old production manager responsible for the supervision of production at the shipyard. He could not quite see behind the door but as he craned his head forward to look he could just make out the Deputy General Director's shoes. They were high heeled. A woman? Before he could look any further the door to the other office flew open and the young woman beckoned them over announcing in heavily accented English, "Victor Nikolayevich is very happy to see you. And I will translate for him."

They went in. Victor Nikolayevich greeted them warmly one by one. His top button was open and his red cheeks gave the impression that his tie was slowly strangling him.

He shook his guests' hands using both of his own and the strength of his grip took Adam by surprise. The office was in wood like the foyer. It was if a company from the time of Peter the Great himself had been rebuilt inside the grey Soviet shell of a building. Opposite the door was a large desk in front of which was a long table with chairs arranged in two lines facing each other.

On the wall behind the desk there were two maps. One was a large map of St Petersburg and the surrounding region. Groups of different coloured pins were stuck in the map giving it a faintly military air. Perhaps still in use from the Second World War, Adam wondered, briefly studying various heavy lines drawn on it around the centre which could well have been marking battle lines. The second map was a map of the world. This time pins were stuck in several Russian cities, in cities around the Baltic and Northern Europe and one as far away as Cuba. A large window filled the wall to the left of the entrance and looked out over the other buildings and yards on the site. It also had wide views of the Neva and the Fortress of St Peter and St Paul in the distance. The opposite wall was lined with wooden and glass cabinets filled again with small trophies and plaques and a large ceremonial sword about two feet long with a blue banner attached to its handle. To Adam it all had a quaint air somehow unreal but somehow solid. On a table at the side stood a large bowl overflowing with chocolates in multicoloured wrappers and an ornamental silver tray with six small glasses.

The young woman waited dutifully for the greetings to finish and then asked, "tea, coffee please?"

"Tea, my dear, I think," smiled Victor Nikolayevich, checking to look at Hampton who nodded. The young woman stepped out briefly and then returned to translate for Victor Nikolayevich and the others as necessary.

"Victor Nikolayevich, these are the lawyers I explained to you about. They are from one of the best law firms in London." Victor Nikolayevich nodded at Hampton and Adam in turn. "And they work here in St Petersburg." Victor Nikolayevich nodded again.

"Leonid Marlenovich, should we invite some of our other colleagues to join us in our discussions?" asked Victor Nikolayevich.

"I think we can keep this just with us. Do you agree Mr Hampton?" said Leonid Marlenovich.

"Of course, I think that the important and strategic matters in a company should only be discussed with those who are in charge."

Victor Nikolayevich beamed at the compliment.

"And I understand that the company is very fortunate in having someone who has been in charge as long as Victor Nikolayevich has been," continued Hampton.

"Yes we are," interrupted Leonid Marlenovich, "having a strong leader through all the changes is clearly in the best interests of the company."

"And in the best interests of all its workers," Victor Nikolayevich said, though he stopped for a second and looked nervously at Leonid Marlenovich, "if I am allowed to say such things these days, now that all these privatisations are about to happen."

"Of course, Victor Nikolayevich, you are well-known for looking after all your employees."

At which point the older woman entered with a tray and started to pour out the tea.

"And do you know, Mr Hampton, just how important we are to the city of St Petersburg?" said Victor Nikolayevich.

"You are one of the biggest employers in the city and, of course, your ships and boats are famous across all Russia."

"More than that," he said lowering his voice and head slightly excited at the thought of knowing something more than the others did. He shot a mischievous grin at Leonid Marlenovich. A frown began to break across Leonid Marlenovich's face and he raised his hand about to say something.

"We are the second biggest tax payer to the city," Victor Nikolayevich proclaimed banging his hand down with delight.

Leonid Marlenovich emitted a sigh of relief.

"Do you know who is the largest?" then asked Victor Nikolayevich continuing the subject. Before anyone had time to react he blurted out, "the October Vodka plant. Vodka and boats!" he roared laughing, "after all the years of building up military factories, heavy engineering, steel plants - the only businesses to any make profits are vodka and boats. Vodka and boats!!" He was laughing so much that it brought tears to his eyes which he wiped away with his hands. "Yes, all we do is pay money to our Government with nothing in return," he continued. "Do you know how much we pay in taxes?"

Hampton shot a glance at Leonid Marlenovich and then at Adam who looked at the papers he had put on the table. These were the briefing papers on the company prepared by their office. Adam swallowed and then said with a slightly trembling voice. "I think the information we have indicates you reported paying taxes of two million dollars."

Victor Nikolayevich beamed at Adam. "Two million some say, but it was much more than that!" he exclaimed.

"Not according to Western ways of accounting, Victor Nikolayevich," said Leonid Marlenovich.

Victor Nikolayevich visibly made some mental calculations. "We paid more. We paid nearly twice that."

"But that includes many different types of taxes and payments." Leonid Marlenovich was speaking slowly and clearly trying to gently steer Victor Nikolayevich from the subject.

"Yes, there are those which go to the Mayor's office and the others to the police funds. Also to cities where we have repair yards. When we were at the dacha deciding..." Victor Nikolayevich was starting to sound confused.

"Victor Nikolayevich, I'm sure that such a famous law firm as Miller Lombard does not need to know about our internal planning and tax matters here in St Petersburg. Management of the company is for us. Is that not so, Mr Hampton?" His tone had acquired a slight edge of authority.

"Of course," replied Hampton.

"Let me just order some more drinks," said Victor Nikolayevich going to his desk and pressing the buttons on one of the three phones on his desk. Adam was struck by the fact that one of them was without key pads. He was also amazed at the sight of the General Director, the head of such a famous and large company. The research he had been given detailed a famous history and a long list of iconic boats and vessels which the company had built and yet the man in front of him seemed a total wreck. He looked a mess and even with the help of the translator Adam was having great difficulty understanding most of what he was saying. He could not see any positive reasons why a foreign investor would want to invest in a company with a head like Victor Nikolayevich. Adam had been in Russia for over two years now and knew that there was only one thing to do in situations like this – suspend his judgement. Things were often very different from how they appeared on the surface and the best approach, especially in the hope of winning a lot of legal work, was to be patient and to wait and see. The meeting had started well and there obviously was some form of previous contact between his boss and Leonid Marlenovich. And it was Leonid Marlenovich who definitely seemed to be the one pulling the strings.

Eleven

ROMAN Felixovich was seated in a corner table of the 'Old Customs House' restaurant on Universitetskaya Embankment. The restaurant had been converted from a Nineteenth Century customs house which was made up of large cellar like rooms. In the past these cellar rooms stored vast ranges of valuable goods, such as alcohol and tobacco, before the customs duties were paid on them and the goods were then released and could be sold in the city and further afield. The large cellar rooms with low ceilings and brick built arches had plush interiors and were ideal for privacy during meals. A large area in the centre had been remodeled as a more normal restaurant with an arrangement of tables. The cellar rooms were by far and away the most used. It was just after midday and the restaurant was largely empty. Roman Felixovich ate alone. One of his assistants, a man of similar age and dressed in plain jeans and a shirt, sat on a chair back from Roman Felixovich's table and held a pile of papers in his hands and had several briefcases at his feet. Roman Felixovich finished his soup and beckoned his assistant over. The assistant brought one of the briefcases with him.

"Have you checked everything, Misha?" asked Roman Felixovich in a very friendly voice.

"I have. All the money is there," replied the young man.

"Good. That needs to go in the safe and next week you need to fly to Cyprus to put it in the bank. Book your flight."

"Straight away."

"Soon I hope we will have our own bank set up here. I have more meetings this week and am looking for the best partners."

The young man did not reply. Roman Felixovich did not expect him to. The young man was a relative of one of Roman Felixovich's oldest friends and he was proving himself to be very loyal and dependable. He worked for his friend and increasingly for Roman Felixovich. Roman Felixovich had never risked depositing a single rouble, let alone a dollar, in the old state banks or the newly formed Russian banks. He could not imagine a greater risk. Taking cash out to Cyprus was the preferred route for money made in Russia of which more than ninety-five per cent was in dollars with small amounts of Deutschmarks, French Francs and Sterling. Roubles had to stay in Russia for now. If he was able to set up his own bank then life would become more easier and transfers abroad would be at the touch of a button.

One of Roman Felixovich's mobile phones rang and he answered. He had a brief conversation which finished with a string of curt 'da's or 'yes's. He beckoned his assistant over again.

"Misha, take out five hundred dollars and have a driver deliver them to this woman at this address this evening." His assistant nodded as Roman Felixovich wrote down a name and address. Roman Felixovich smiled to himself. He had just added one of the now largely defunct Leningrad Oil & Gas Research Institute's oldest professors to his pay role. His office occupied most of the top floor of the Institute which had pretty much stopped functioning now that virtually all of its previous funding had dried up. The knowledge it held in its hay day though was priceless and Roman Felixovich continued to track down all of its key staff who had left and the files which had all been taken in the days after Communism fell. With the help of the father of one of his other school friends he had calculated that Russia's greatest wealth lay underground in the vast oil and gas fields and he had drawn up a 'hit list', in the nicest sense of the word, of those who had worked in the Institute who would know where the best oil and gas lay or better still where the Institute's research showed it was and never yet explored properly by the now defunct Soviet Oil Ministry. He had acquired a storeroom full of maps which he believed were originals and unlikely to have been copied given the paranoia of secrecy that was the lifeblood of Communism. How grateful he hoped he would be for that paranoia. He was ticking off the experts, as he called them, one by one as they joined his pay role as consultants or over whom he had contrived to gain some form of hold.

His main course of filet mignon and French fries was brought to the table along with a bottle of Evian water. He picked up a copy of the St Petersburg Times as he ate his food. His assistant sat quietly on his chair back from the table. He was glad to see that the newspaper had no information on privatisation. On reflection he had decided against any approach to the paper as its biggest advertiser to suggest it stopped the stories on Rasputin – in fact he was thinking of encouraging them. Much better to have the foreign readers in St Petersburg believing in old fashioned Russian 'skaska's, or fairytales, rather than finding out about any privatisations. Just to be on the safe side he was thinking of different forms of leverage which he might acquire over the newspaper's editor and its main reporter who was listed in the paper as a 'Mike Leigh'.

One of his phones rang again. It was a call he had been waiting for all day. He snapped his finger and his assistant ran over. Roman Felixovich mouthed to his assistant to pick up all his papers and briefcases and to bring his car and driver to the front of the restaurant. He never spoke back down his phone but quietly ended the call. He wiped his lips with a napkin from the table and took out several dollar bills from his pocket which he put down next to his half eaten meal. He did not want to be late. Through several contacts he had been offered a ten minute meeting with the official tasked with preparing the papers for a list of companies to be privatised. The official was technically low ranking – a bureaucrat in the St Petersburg Property Fund, but his pen possessed more power than anyone could imagine. Anyone except, of course, Roman Felixovich who had the vision to see how he could use the opportunity of privatisation together with the funds he was building through his trade in consumer goods to acquire substantial and much more profitable businesses. It would be the opportunity not of a generation - but of a century!

Twelve

ADAM'S suspension of his judgement indeed turned out to be the best approach as Victor Nikolayevich explained the company's history in a rambling tale jumping across centuries and places without stopping for breath. Hampton managed to signal to Adam for him not to make notes of this and he mouthed that he would have Anna write up the company's history from the information they already had, if it were needed. Victor Nikolayevich banged the table and jumped to his feet on several occasions. The lawyers sat tight and smiled as often as they could. They might as well have been watching a comedy show and with or without translation they understood very little. Victor Nikolayevich finished by enunciating the word 'privatisation' several times as if he was referring to a UFO from outer space. Leonid Marlenovich smiled broadly and spoke next.

"Perhaps I can explain more about our current activities to our guests, Victor Nikolayevich? You have covered our history in such a dramatic and colourful way."

Victor Nikolayevich beamed and took out a greyish handkerchief with which he wiped his brow and nodded to Leonid Marlenovich.

"As Victor Nikolayevich explained," began Leonid Marlenovich, "our company was founded by Peter the Great himself and its first shipyard was run by a Scottish engineer who became part owner of the company as it expanded. His name was John Berd, if I remember correctly." Leonid Marlenovich spoke in very good English and despite the General Director's 'colourful' and detailed history, Leonid Marlenovich repeated the key events in the history of the company. The Peter the Great Shipyard was one of several in St Petersburg and it played a leading role in shipbuilding throughout the Eighteenth and Nineteenth Centuries. Its ownership history was complicated and the company was run for two centuries by two wealthy Russian families, the Baronskys and the Yusupovs, until it was nationalised by the Soviet State after the Revolution of 1917. After the Second World War the site they were on had been redeveloped. Part of the old offices had been damaged during the Siege and two new office blocks had been built in their place. As they could see though much of the old interior design of the original offices had been either restored or rebuilt inside the new building. The building nearest the river had survived and as it was the oldest part of the site it was decided that it should not be demolished. At that time the company had also faced two major challenges.

"The first," explained Leonid Marlenovich, "was a debate over which ships we should build. After the war it was decided to prioritise new ships for the Soviet Navy and especially submarines. The Cold War had started and that is where our shipyard lost out. The berths in our yards here were not deep enough for the work the Soviet engineers wanted to do on new submarines. Work they wanted to undertake in total secrecy. There were deeper and less visible shipyards than ours."

"What happened, Leonid?" asked Hampton. His ears had shot up on the mention of the Cold War.

"We – how do you say – 'diversified'?" Hampton nodded. "We took the lead in all types of non-naval ships and vessels. You may have noticed some of the models in our reception. These are mainly the old and large ships we used to build. If we take you to our showroom next door you will be able to see some of the more modern crafts we build." Leonid Marlenovich then continued to describe many of the ships built by the company from ice breakers and trawlers to ferries and speed boats. He then returned to the second challenge. "As you will remember the Cold War meant that we were not able to sell our ships and boats in many countries abroad but we needed to earn whatever hard currency we could by selling abroad. Our second solution was to diversify again and this time geographically." Leonid Marlenovich stood up and went over to the map of the world behind Victor Nikolayevich's desk. He pointed to the pins in the map and explained how the company had built a network of operations in cities around the Baltic and Northern Europe and one as far away as Cuba which was the Soviet Union's communist ally on America's doorstep. "In one way or another these operations allowed us to sell boats to these countries and from these countries on to many other countries."

"I would never have thought that a Soviet company could have been so successful abroad especially during the Cold War," remarked Hampton. "This will certainly make the company appeal to foreign investors."

"Perhaps that is something to discuss later," said Leonid Marlenovich very quickly with a smile to Victor Nikolayevich who understood very little English. Leonid Marlenovich had also moved back to the map and was pointing to the pins stuck this time in several Russian cities. "And of course," he continued, "we are immensely proud of the repair yards and small factories we were allowed to build in key cities in Russia. Very few Soviet companies were allowed to own factories in other cities."

"Was that because of the centralised economy under Communism?" asked Adam.

"Yes," replied Leonid Marlenovich. "Production of most goods was centralised in one region and normally in one place. We were allowed to work in these other cities as it was more efficient to make repairs there and there had always been historical links to these cities from our company." Leonid Marlenovich continued to explain the cities on the Volga River which flows from the north west of Moscow down to the Caspian Sea, cities on the Pechora River which flows from the Ural Mountains to the Barents

Sea in the Artic and cities around Lake Baikal, the deepest lake in the world, which is in southern Siberia.

To Adam and Hampton it was an education. The sheer size and vastness of the country and its rivers, lakes and sea ports were fascinating. The struggle with Russia's climate and the bravery of those who sailed its rivers and seas was impressive indeed. They felt privileged at being some of the first non-Russians to hear about these activities. At times Adam almost felt akin to an explorer himself. He also watched Victor Nikolayevich as much as he could and started to see the occasional sparkle in the old man's eyes as he listened intently to Leonid Marlenovich's descriptions and picked out the English words he could understand and acknowledge.

As Leonid Marlenovich finished his descriptions Victor Nikolayevich stood up and pointed to several of the pins on the map of St Petersburg behind his desk. He spoke quietly to Leonid Marlenovich who nodded and then explained to Hampton and Adam that Victor Nikolayevich wanted to add some comments which he himself would translate. Hampton had the distinct impression that Leonid Marlenovich wanted to control the flow of information by acting himself as the interpreter.

"We sell to all the major towns in the Northwest of Russia," began Victor Nikolayevich through Leonid Marlenovich. "We have always done this. Do you know when was the only time when we could not sell our boats and the other equipment we made?" He asked as he pointed to the pins on the map. His tone was sad but thoughtful.

Adam looked at Hampton. "During the war?" ventured Adam slowly.

"No, almost. During the Siege." He paused and looked at each person in the room with a little nod. "Yes," he continued, "the Siege of eight hundred and seventy-two days when the city was surrounded by the Germans and no-one could get in or out. Except for some of us." A mischievous glint had now appeared in his eye. "And we provided more than boats. We used our foundry and workshops to make more useful products." He went over to the window and looked out with a deep sigh.

Hampton looked with raised eyebrows at Leonid Marlenovich who just motioned to him to wait. After what seemed like several minutes Victor Nikolayevich finally turned back round. "Shall we talk about what will happen now and how you can help us? Is that correct, Leonid Marlenovich? What advice and help can foreign lawyers give us?"

Hampton seemed to check mentally and then he looked at Victor Nikolayevich with a large smile. "Do any parts of your workshops or berths need new equipment?" he asked quickly.

"Always," shot back Victor Nikolayevich. Lack of investment in production. Lack of modern equipment. These were his daily gripes. These had been the staple complaints of everyone operating in the command economy where a company was given the equipment that the central planners decided was required whether it was needed or not.

"Well, what if we can find a way to raise funds to invest in new equipment as part of the privatisation of the company?"

It was Leonid Marlenovich's turn to raise his eyebrows. Privatisation was going to be a battle for control of the company and he did not see how this could be linked to raising money for the company itself. If the city was selling some of its shares in the company then he had no doubt that the city would take whatever was paid for the shares and keep it all.

"What if you were able to set up a new state-of-the-art boat production unit?" Hampton paused for a split second. "Perhaps it could be put on the site of the old building we could see near the river, for example, - the building which Leonid Marlenovich said had not yet been developed since the war. If that was a possibility then you would not to have to redevelop the existing workshops and yard." Hampton smiled at Adam who started to scribble down notes. Leonid Marlenovich frowned slightly.

"Fanatastic idea. Leonid Marlenovich, what do you think?" Victor Nikolayevich asked excitedly. "Can this be part of our privatisation?"

"If the lawyers think there is a way to raise money for the company at the same time then we must look into it," replied Leonid Marlenovich now with a smile to Hampton. The smile was a clear challenge. "Though we do already have some plans for the old building you mentioned."

"Yes, yes of course, we do," interjected Victor Nikolayevich. "But that will not cause any problems will it if we have new machinery? I'm sure we could fit in some new equipment."

"Let me look into this," replied Leonid Marlenovich sitting up in his seat and looking intently at Hampton. Adam had picked up on Leonid Marlenovich's body language. He had also been mightily impressed at his boss' quick thinking. He must have had some form of plan.

"That's great, Leonid," continued Hampton, "and I must mention, if I may, that we have close links with an investment fund which might be interested to invest in such a project. They have over thirty million dollars to invest and they want to do it as quickly as they can."

A large smile spread across Leonid Marlenovich's face. Rather than reply he spoke quickly and quietly in Russian to Victor Nikolayevich. They had a brief and heated exchange with Victor Nikolayevich looking with puzzled and then wide-open eyes towards Hampton. Hampton moved slightly in his seat.

"Thirty million dollars, that is impressive," beamed Victor Nikolayevich after a slight pause. At the same time the young woman came back into the room with two bottles of vodka, "and something to celebrate," added Victor Nikolayevich

"And in return for investing what would you expect a foreign investor to want?" asked Leonid Marlenovich.

"Possibly some form of representation in the company. And of course they would like to be able to check that the money is spent on the new equipment as agreed."

"I'm sure it can be considered," replied Leonid Marlenovich. "And can such investments be arranged as part of our privatisation?"

"Well," said Hampton. "I am glad you asked. That is where good lawyers come in. We have been studying all the ins and outs of privatisations. The laws are still being developed. We think there are ways."

"How convenient," replied Leonid Marlenovich again with a big smile. He now knew what was driving Hampton. Even if he himself did not yet know how this privatisation was going to work out, he now knew how to control the process after all.

Meanwhile Victor Nikolayevich had stood up. The young woman had quietly placed glasses of vodka in front of each of them. They picked up the glasses and joined Victor Nikolayevich on their feet. He raised his glass. "To co-operation between the great countries of England and Russia, allies in war, in peace and now in privatisation!" And with that he downed his vodka. The others followed him. Adam managed to stifle a cough as the vodka burned his throat and his eyes watered. Before he could put his glass down it was being filled again. Victor Nikolayevich's cheeks were burning red and he completed the formalities of the toasting with vigour and aplomb.

As they left the office, Adam smiled at both the women seated behind their desks as Hampton thanked them and concentrated his flattery on the older woman, Adam tried again to look into the office of the Deputy General Director. As he was two steps away from the half open door it flew open and out came a large bear of a man who handed a raft of papers to the older woman saying that he had signed them all except two which required Victor Nikolayevich's signature.

"So what do you think of your first sight of a Russian company in St Petersburg?" Hampton asked Adam with a big smile. Hampton was clearly more than satisfied with their meeting.

"Stuck in a bit of a time warp, really. I mean all those ancient models in the glass cupboards. Victor Nikolayevich is obviously very proud of them."

"Ah, but that is just the rough surface, Adam. Can you not feel the weight of history and that raw instinct for survival?"

"Well Victor Nikolayevich did go on a bit about the war."

"You know it is remarkable that despite having the stuffing kicked out of them by the Germans and then abused for decades by their own leaders with their perverse sense of planning, not to mention the means of terror – that they are still here. And still building boats which sell. Victor Nikolayevich is not a spent force just yet even if he is so full of sentimentality. They say Victor Nikolayevich often weeps openly when he talks of the past."

"Did you know that they wanted some new equipment?" asked Adam.

"Did not have a clue," replied Hampton with a smile, "just thinking on my feet and what company anywhere in the world - let alone here - does not want new equipment!"

"You're right," said Adam, "and it definitely worked here." He had already seen that his boss was very different from the other partners in Miller Lombard whom he had worked for. He was a swashbuckling lawyer, he thought, and then laughed to himself at the word 'lawyer' – they had just had a two hour meeting and never discussed any legal matters once!

"Adam, do me a favour as soon as you are back in the office," said Hampton. Adam nodded. "Arrange an urgent meeting with Dominic Corley before he flies back to London and let's think of the best venue, somewhere private." Again Adam was struck by the cloak and dagger tactics of his boss – and he had thought that they were just venerable lawyers!

"Leonid Marlenovich, what are we going to do?" Victor Nikolayevich was cradling his empty vodka glass in his hands. He had helped himself to several more toasts which

Leonid Marlenovich had declined. Leonid Marlenovich lit a cigarette and took a long puff. "What do you think?"

"What do they know?"

"About what?" said Leonid Marlenovich becoming slightly irritated.

"About the new products you have started bringing in and sending out," whispered Victor Nikolayevich, his face now looking more like a guilty schoolboy.

"They won't find anything out," replied Leonid Marlenovich calmly.

"How do you know?"

"I'll take care of it."

"You said that Hampton was not just a lawyer," continued Victor Nikolayevich.

"He's not. We know he worked for the US military."

"So just like you he has turned into a new businessman."

"Our type never change."

"No, you just profit when the world changes."

Leonid Marlenovich was momentarily stunned by Victor Nikolayevich's insight. "Victor Nikolayevich, need I remind you of the work I do for this company?" he asked rhetorically.

"I know, I know. I just don't know what to think any more. Privatisation, new investments and foreign investment funds. These are all new and so complicated." He had a resigned look on his face. "It is not like it used to be."

"Don't worry. Just keep control as you always have. You are the General Director." He stubbed out his cigarette. "Anyway I don't think we need to worry about Hampton or his investors. I will be able to control them. There are some others who we may need to watch." He took out several sheets of paper from his suit pocket and unfolded them.

"Apparently some other people are watching all the notices on the privatisations and asking questions about us."

"Does this mean that we will have to defend ourselves against foreign invaders again? Or will they be Russian this time?" Victor Nikolayevich jumped up and walked to the large cabinet and touched the glass casing where the sword was displayed.

"Let's just wait and see. There is nothing to worry about yet," said Leonid Marlenovich unconvincingly. Events had started to speed up fast. He could already sense that some people had designs on the shipyard and possibly even their new special products and he, for once, did not yet have any fall-back plans in place.

Thirteen

ENTERING the entrance of the Home Anna took off her boots and donned a pair of her own shoes from her bag. It was now just past six pm and very quiet – the laughter of children she had always known in her own childhood especially in the summer time with her family, relatives and neighbours at the dachas, was rarely if ever heard in the Home. Valentina Alexandrovna had left a message at Miller Lombard for Anna to meet her in the Home when convenient for an update on the search for information on Sasha. She had stressed that it was not urgent.

Although the Home was a home to over one hundred children from new born babies to eleven year olds, there had never been a crueller irony in a name. Cries were also very rare. Although Anna normally only visited Sasha she did occasionally venture in to the dormitories. The best Anna could do when she met a room of children was to turn some of the sorry grim little faces into smiles and then giggles before she left. She would make them giggle if it killed her. And then she would leave immediately before the children realised because she herself could not cope with the look of blank despair that would spread across the faces whenever they knew it was time to say goodbye.

She went inside and headed for the Director of the Home's office. It was all so depressingly Soviet looking. She had the luxury of a new Western office and had often calculated that the cost of her desk and all the computer equipment on it could pay to refurbish one of the small dormitories which housed eight to ten children and provide then all with new beds and blankets. It was all so dark. She remembered the first time she had been on a dormitory and she had looked along the two rows of beds all occupied with children dressed for sleep even though on that day it was just after lunch time. She bit her lip and pledged to herself again that it would have to change and that there would be space, light, air, giggles, laughter and cries – noise, noise, and more noise.

Valentina Alexandrovna's update was going to surprise Anna in a way she could not have forseen. Anna found the Director behind her desk in her small office. Valentina Alexandrovna smiled as she waved Anna in. They exchanged greetings and Anna handed over a small carrier bag with some of her usual gifts of food and treats. The gifts were always different depending on what Anna could find and as always they were divided up for Sasha, some for the children and some for the staff to keep the delicate balance in place. As always Valentina Alexandrovna was effusive and genuine in her thanks.

"So are you ready for some news, my dear Anna?" smiled Valentina Alexandrovna. "It is not much but it is our first possible breakthrough."

"Please," replied Anna looking down at her hands and not knowing quite why.

"Well, the family name has turned up from the strangest source?"

"Strangest?" repeated Anna looking up at Valentina Alexandrovna and feeling her cheeks start to heat up.

"Yes, I spoke to a friend of my brother who works in the Mayor's office and he made some enquiries. He did not expect any replies but strangely and this is strange, Anna," Valentina Alexandrovna paused but Anna remained silent. After a couple of seconds she continued. "It is strange but he got a short note back from the FSB. The FSB!"

"The FSB!" exclaimed Anna, "you mean the old KGB?"

"Precisely."

"Why would they be involved?"

"I don't think they are involved as such," said Valentina Alexandrovna, "but that the family name of Tyublonski turned up in a search of their database."

"And what did it say about the name?" Anna could feel her heartbeat starting to race.

"The note says that an individual with that name was a Russian national and that he was last noted as under surveillance in a former Eastern bloc country."

"I don't understand," said Anna utterly confused.

"Neither did I at first, Anna. It took me a while to think what it could mean. And I did ask my brother who could only explain that there has been tremendous upheaval in the KGB's records and databases. This was after the KGB lost most of its control of the Eastern bloc countries a few years ago. In any case a man with the Tyublonski family name still showed in the records and must have been kept there for a reason."

"I still don't understand," said Anna.

"Well, if I am correct, this could prove that Sasha was part of a Russian family, the son of the Tyublonski on the database and that he was probably born abroad in the Easter Bloc and then brought back to St Petersburg as a young child turning up in the care of the old lady who was assumed to be his grandmother."

Anna was staring at Valentina Alexandrovna even more confused.

"So the next question is over to you Anna. I remember you explaining your family's history."

Anna's face was still blank.

"Anna, did you not say that your parents or grandparents lived for some time in the Eastern bloc?"

Anna's face lightened up and she stared at Valentina Alexandrovna. "When I was little my father had a posting to Prague and we lived there for two years. But my father was also in the Soviet Army and stayed in Poland for several years after the end of the war. My uncle was also in the Soviet Army during the war and stayed somewhere in the Eastern bloc afterwards as well."

"Precisely. The name is so uncommon. We might have a link."

Valentina Alexandrovna came round from behind the table and hugged Anna. Anna's brain was in overload as she thought through what she knew of her father and her uncle's postings. She would have to think how best to discuss this with them. For the first time her visit to the Home was ending really positively. She decided against asking to see Sasha. As she was leaving she whistled to herself a song from her childhood and it seemed as though the Home was coming alive. She stopped herself at the door and the silence of the Home engulfed her like a cold tomb. She looked behind her and all she could see were the cold, grey walls. She was cross at herself and at the selfishness of her happiness at this breakthrough. She would have to find ways to help more than just Sasha. She would really have to start thinking of ways to help a lot more of the children if she was truly to enjoy the chance of having Sasha as part of her life and out of the Home.

Fourteen

TWO other diners entered the Old Customs House restaurant later that day and were directed to a table in the middle of the restaurant. It was six thirty in the evening and still quiet.

"Quite impressive, John, this place. You could never tell by the outside."

"No, Dominic. Quite right. It has not been open long and it is building quite a reputation. What would you like to drink?"

"A gin and tonic would go down well," said Corley scanning the room discreetly whilst at the same time admiring the original brown brick walls with old paintings and the occasional stuffed head of an animal hung on them.

"Not a vodka lover?" asked Hampton with a broad smile.

"Only when I have to," replied Corley with a raised eyebrow.

"Now tell me what you have found? Adam was very insistent that we meet before I fly back to London."

"I'm glad he caught you," said Hampton taking the menus from the waitress who asked them in English, "to drink?" Hampton ordered a gin and tonic for Corley and a beer for himself and asked for time to look at the menu. He then continued to explain that they had met with a company which might interest the British Redevelopment

Fund especially as it had properties on the embankment of the river.

"Well, are you in a position to reveal the company's name?" asked Corley who had listened to Hampton patiently and paused when the waitress brought them their drinks.

"I am hoping that we will be appointed as their lawyers this week and I have already indicated to them that we know of several investors who might be interested," replied Hampton. "Cheers!" he added lifting his glass.

"Cheers," replied Corley fixing Hampton with a firm look. There was a moment's silence. Corley then put his hand in his suit jacket pocket and withdrew a folded up map. It had the Hotel Astoria on the front. He opened it up and placed it on the table. It was a map of the centre of the city which showed the main streets, buildings, canals and the River Neva. "I appreciate you maintaining client confidentiality, John. Admirable, especially in this country."

"I guess I will feel more comfortable as soon as I have a signed letter from the company appointing Miller Lombard as their legal adviser for their privatisation. But," he paused and looked at Corley with a firm look of his own, "I can give you some indication to test your interest."

"Let me make this easier for you, John," replied Corley quickly. "We have done quite a bit of research and there are parts of the city which we think will really prosper. Our investment fund has been set up in order to help the Russian economy transform to a market economy by making very risky investments in the hope of high returns if we invest early enough when prices are low. I, however, also believe that quite a few of the properties in the companies will turn out to be more important and valuable than the products the companies actually manufacture."

"So you are looking at having properties to underpin the investments in your portfolio?"

"Precisely. I could not have put that better myself. Shows why you lawyers are so good at writing documents and prospectuses for investments," smiled Corley who was sure that Hampton was starting to open up. He hoped he would not have to resort to any more heavy-handed tactics. Hampton was sure to 'play ball', just as his American countrymen would say.

"Well in that case," continued Hampton, "I think we may have come across a real prospect for you." Hampton took out a pen and pulled the map that was on the table closer to him. He looked closely at the River Neva and followed it. "Do you mind?" he asked motioning with his pen.

"Be my guest," replied Corley.

Corley watched Hampton draw a circle around an area on the south bank of the Neva and had to hold his breath. He picked up his drink and focused on his glass.

"The company I am thinking of has several properties right here on the river," said Hampton looking up at Corley.

"That looks like a very good area," replied Corley draining his glass. "Just out of the centre and on the river." He had to surpass a surge of excitement. "No name yet, though?" he said trying to sound nonchalant.

Hampton took a look around the room. "Nothing I can say at the moment," said Hampton with a big smile as he scribbled the name of the 'Peter the Great Shipyard' on the map next to the circle he had just drawn.

Corley was stunned. He put down his glass. "Perhaps some more drinks?" he said as he folded up the map. "I look forward to learning the name of the company in due course."

With the smile still on his face Hampton looked for and motioned to the waitress. Corley again scanned the room and then instinctively touched his suit jacket to feel the map. Hampton had come up with the company at the top of his list but he needed to be sure no-one else could have seen what had been written down. He looked around again and could only see two tables near them which were occupied and the people at those tables struck him as not the type he should be worried about. The surge of excitement was abating and he decided to change the conversation.

"The work at the Hermitage you mentioned briefly last time. How is that progressing?" he asked.

"Well like almost everything in this country we need to find a way to get things moving," replied Hampton.

"Bureaucracy still rules in places like that, no doubt."

"Definitely. Whilst our committee has the green light at some pretty high levels, we just don't seem to be able to move forward."

"And what is the committee's purpose?"

"To find the forgotten masterpieces and other works of art that the Hermitage and the other palaces in St Petersburg have either mislaid or locked away somewhere and then to retrieve them and put them back on view here. And also to exhibit them abroad in the future."

"Sounds very straightforward," said Corley.

"And it should be and it also is an area thankfully that is not attracting the mafia types."

"Presumably they have plenty of other targets than a Matisse or a Da Vinci," quipped Corley.

"Yes," laughed Hampton, "but I would not rule them out completely. What interests me," said Hampton lowering his voice to a whisper, "and it may interest, shall we say, some of the more enlightened new Russians, is that there are quite a lot of objects and paintings which are not recorded anywhere officially and which could be worth small fortunes if they were to be recovered here and then turn up somewhere in the West."

"War booty and the like?" asked Corley also in a whisper.

"There are a number of obvious times when lots of this forgotten art and treasure was stolen from the Russian State and perhaps more intriguingly stolen by the Russian State itself."

"Revolution, Second World War, fall of Communism and now perestroika," the words rolled off Corley's tongue as his imagination started to fire. Hampton nodded. They remained silent for a minute as the waitress brought their new drinks. Once she had left, Corley picked up his glass and Hampton followed.

"Cheers, old boy," he said. "Perhaps a financial donation from a British source might help unblock the bureaucracy around your committee?"

Hampton had not yet thought of soliciting funds from anyone not even his own firm. But clearly any funds from a reputable source such as a British company would undoubtedly open doors.

"Well, Donald," he said raising his glass again, "I guess one favour definitely does deserve another. Cheers!"

Fifteen

ADAM had spent long enough alone in his hotel room. He did not feel comfortable yet staying too long by himself because as soon as his mind was unoccupied it would yank him back to the events of that night of his Welcome Drinks. Plus any number of different sights, sounds and comments would likewise trigger flashbacks and a cold sweat would run down his back. A driver's eye or a pretty girl's face would set him off immediately. But with the passing of some time he could now cope with rerunning in his mind the sight in the bedroom. The colour of the hair meant that it must have been the blonde girl not the black haired girl, the 'Lena' not the 'Olga' – both very common names. He was convinced that the body was not breathing but so far he had not heard any rumours of any strange or unexplained deaths of any young women. He had thought about enquiring about such matters – after all who would be better placed that a local law firm like Miller Lombard? But he feared the questions that might be asked because he had deserted the scene. He would have to wait and see. He was avoiding all bars and especially the one in his hotel.

He went down to the hotel's main restaurant picking up a copy of the St Petersburg Times at the entrance. He ordered quickly and opened the paper. As he tucked into his food he started to read an article on the recent increase in unsolved crimes in St Petersburg; top of the list of which was the description of the bombing of the building across the street from his hotel. There were also mentions of five unsolved murders in the city since the beginning of the year – all of local businessmen! Men, thankfully, not young women! For the first time he was beginning to question why he was in the country. He needed something to occupy his mind and take it away from late nights and violent happenings. He finished his food quickly.

Back now in his hotel room he switched on the TV, muted the volume and took out his papers. All the papers he had received in the green plastic folder had now been translated from Russian into English. He laid them out in six piles on the bed with the translations on top and the Russian originals underneath. Although his Russian was still pretty basic he had spent plenty of time poring over documents in his last two years to become familiar with the Russian Cyrillic alphabet, technical legal terms and key words and short phrases. One of the easy parts was always checking dates as they were numerical as well as written. The task he had been given, which had now been prioritised by Hampton, was to summarise the list of buildings which the Peter the Great Shipyard used and to check their current ownership and status. Once he had identified for himself the key documents and any issues he would then pass the file onto the team of junior Russians in the office to do any outstanding legwork and draft the summary which he would then finalise.

He then split the six piles in two groups. He placed the first group, which related generally to the company where properties were involved, on the small desk putting the telephone and hotel bits and pieces on the easy chair at the side. He put the second group which were the deeds of title and assorted records for specific buildings on the floor. These were the documents for the main buildings which included the shipyards and workshops, the office block and showroom, an old foundry, a recreation building which he recognised as a dacha outside the city and properties in three other cities.

As was his working practice he diligently set about reading all the translations from cover to cover and highlighting all the key words and queries with a yellow marker pen and scribbling down any points that came to mind on a separate white note pad. He always preferred to immerse himself in a long session without any background noise and to go through for several hours at a time without a break until his cheeks flushed and his head start to gently ache. After just under two hours he stood up and stretched satisfied that he had a sound overview of the situation. He took a beer from the minibar, flicked through the TV channels and lazed on the bed.

The channels in English were just the news on CNN and old BBC programmes on BBC world. There was a selection of programmes in German, French and Italian all of which were showing old dubbed American programmes. He flicked through the Russian channels which were largely incomprehensible and seemed to be dominated by slow and quiet documentaries or bizarre quiz games. He watched one game for a while which seemingly had soap powder as the prize for the first of two blindfolded contestants able to undress themselves and then to dress a full size mannequin with their own clothes. The studio audience seemed to enjoy it.

He hit one channel which looked like news and just as he was about to switch over the face of the Prince of Wales filled the screen. Not a recent shot but clearly of the Prince. The following shot of Buckingham Palace confirmed that it was indeed the Prince. The next shot showed the Winter Palace in St Petersburg and a close up of an old boat. The newsreader then came on and spoke for several minutes from which Adam gathered zero. Next came some old black and white footage of troops marching and Adam recognised that they were German by the style of their uniforms. Then there were barricades and a city partly in ruins but with huddles of people hiding behind barricades pointing rifles. The next shot made him almost drop his beer. It was a close-up of a crying, dirty child trying to wake up its mother who was sunk in an old chair and showed no sign of movement. There was a moment of silence as this was showed, the child's cries not being broadcast. The mood then changed as loud military music boomed out and quick shots showed trucks and horses making their way across a frozen lake and final images of cheering crowds. The picture of the Prince of Wales reappeared, the Prince now shown in full ceremonial dress and handing out medals. He took another drink and made a note to find out how these dramatic pictures and the Prince of Wales were connected and what relevance it now had to St Petersburg.

He now needed a break more than ever and so he looked at the in-house video programme and saw that at eleven pm a recent film release starring Mel Gibson would be shown. It was now ten to eleven giving him time for a quick wash and possibly to tidy the papers away. 'What was he thinking of!' he thought to himself. The papers were originals and he should not leave then lying around on the floor at any time. He knelt down and carefully started to place the six piles into separate clear plastic folders. For the first time he started to appreciate the age of some of the documents; their yellowing papers, fading ink, flaking seals and general feeling of history. This was one of the aspects of being a lawyer that had always intrigued him - proof and evidence of ownership. Nowadays people's wealth was recorded on a bank's computer, which always made him feel nervous since at the touch of a computer a person's wealth could be either multiplied or erased.

Several of the documents looked particularly old. He picked up the file relating to the shipyards and workshops. It was the Property Register issued by the City Council of St Petersburg describing the properties and detailing its current and previous owners. He looked firstly at the translation and read that in 1918 the property had been registered in the name of the city of Petrograd as St Petersburg was then called, in 1946 the management of it had been given to the Peter the Great Shipyard Collective and in 1992 a claim had been made against it but had 'rejected' stamped on it. He then took out the corresponding Russian document which was two pages longer and had a gritty feel between his finger and thumb as he rubbed it gently. He put these documents back in their folder.

Next he took out the folder with the documents for the 'Old Foundry' and studied then carefully. The ink on the Old Foundry document looked more smudged than on the other documents. A frown started to cross his brow as he looked carefully at the word 'rejected' in Russian and saw that it had a long hand written note in the margin next to it which had been crossed out. He quickly grabbed the translation and found that the translator had added to the bottom of the translation a sentence which said that the handwritten markings are unclear but possibly indicate that there is an Appendix to the document which details the hearing in the international Court of the Hague but which was not accepted by the Superior Court of St Petersburg. He looked at his watch. Nine pm in The Netherlands. There probably would not be many people left in the Miller Lombard office there but, then again, lawyers are trained as night owls.

He called and when he came off the phone nearly two hours later the credits to the Mel Gibson film were scrolling up the screen. He had made a start. There had been not one but several claims upheld in the International Court of the Hague relating to the Old Foundry building. That had made him widen his investigations and convince a young colleague who had found the references to do some more investigating for him. What baffled him was that his colleague could only find additional claims relating to the Old Foundry and not to any of the other buildings of the company which were clearly considerably more substantial buildings.

Sixteen

ANNA and Adam had been happy with the division of labour set out for them by Hampton. Adam was concentrating on the properties of the Peter the Great Shipyard whilst Anna was to write a summary of the company's history and its business. Hampton had explained that this work was to form part of the documentation that the company would publish for parties interested in buying shares in the company through its privatisation. They would publish a document called an Information Memorandum and their firm would issue a legal opinion on the contents of the document to the effect that all the information in it had been checked and was correct. The actual terms of the privatisation and its timing would be a closely guarded secret and all they had been told was that Leonid Marlenovich would be in charge with advice from Hampton. It was widely expected that some twenty-five per cent of the shares in the 'Open Joint Stock Company Peter the Great Shipyard' - to give the company its full and correct legal name - would be put up for sale and that this sale could take a number of different forms. It was also rumoured that several parties were considering making bids.

The documentation to be prepared by Miller Lombard on behalf of the company was to be in both Russian and English which would allow foreign investors as well as Russians to considering making bids to invest in the company. As it was being written with the assistance of one of London's most prestigious law firms it would be a great feather in the cap for the company. The company would stand out amidst the myriad of privatisations of companies about to take place. Miller Lombard would be heavily rewarded for its efforts although the exact fees were known only to Hampton who had carte blanche from London it terms of fees. Miller Lombard wanted to make a name for itself. Adam had been given the properties as he had more experience in this area than Anna although Adam would have struggled with the other work as the source material was all in Russian and he would have needed much more extensive translation support.

On her desk Anna had a memo from Adam who had summarised what Victor Nikolayevich and Leonid Marlenovich had told Adam and Hampton at their meeting, various materials from the company and other publications her assistants had found relating to the company and shipyards in the city. She read through what she had written so far.

'The origins of the Peter the Great Shipyard can be found in a company set up in the reign of Peter the Great in the early 1700s to build the ships Peter the Great wanted to start the Russian Navy. He wanted to expand Russia's influence in the Baltic Sea and even further beyond into Europe. He is credited with laying the foundations for the start of Russia's own industrialisation, much of which was based in St Petersburg. The Peter the Great Shipyard was one of several ship building companies which flourished under private ownership until the Revolution of 1917. The company was nationalised shortly thereafter. Production at the company was diversified during the Great Patriotic War (The Second World War) for almost three years.'

'Eight hundred and seventy two days to be precise,' she thought, as she remembered the stern tones of her history teacher, 'due to the blockade or siege, she would have to check the better way to say it in English, of the city by the Fascist German Army.'

She stopped. Should she expand more, she thought, for foreign investors to fully understand the importance of the survival of both the city and the shipyard? Maybe not. The aim of document was to give investors an overview of the company today and the short description of its history was really there to make the story complete. No one would invest in a company because it so narrowly survived annihilation fifty years ago. At least in Russia, though, no one had yet forgotten. St Petersburg had suffered great devastation but today it was hardly visible in the centre of the city; indeed some were saying that the city had started to regain some of its Imperial Tsarist splendour and even she could appreciate the beauty of many of its buildings. It had an altogether lighter air and feel to it than Moscow where she had studied.

Though the city had recovered and its sticks and stones been rebuilt the scars of the blockade on her own relatives and their friends in St Petersburg were still visible. The years of near starvation in the city had killed many and left many, who were strong enough to survive on eight ounces of bread a week in the earliest, darkest days of the blockade, crippled or weakened for life. The generation which had survived the blockade were now fewer and fewer. Adam had told her of the look on the face of Victor Nikolayevich at the company during their meeting and she had picked up some comments on his renowned role as a boy during the Siege. She was partly curious about this but also reluctant to ask any questions because she knew that all those who had survived the Siege once they were reminded of it would eventually not be able to hold back the nightmares of those eight hundred and seventy-two days. The survivors would invariably cry and force themselves to recount the events so that the memories of those who had died would live on.

She returned to the summary and drafted a section on how the production of different vessels had evolved and how the company had built up its sales of boats abroad and set up its own repair yards in several key Russian cites. She decided she would suggest that they insert some maps to show the locations. As she considered the best form of maps her mind was struck by her conversation with Valentina Alexandrovna and Sasha's origins which were now believed to be in an Eastern bloc country. She was waiting to talk to her father and had decided to do this as soon as she could and in person. It would be a delicate conversation as she knew that her father had married after the war somewhere outside Russia but that his first wife had died. The subject was very, very rarely mentioned. Her father had then married her mother in Russia much later. Her mother was much younger than her farther and Anna had arrived when her father was in his early fifties and the family had not long after spent two years in Prague. Anna was conscious that there could be several potential links between her father and Sasha now. She had decided that her best option was to put the information directly to her father and see what he would or would not tell her.

She turned back to her writing. The next section on her list was to describe 'privatisation.' She sighed. Describing the process of companies being transferred from the State into private hands seemed very straightforward as a legal process. The ownership of companies was being split up and transferred to those who had a stake in the companies such as the workers, the management, the local government, the relevant ministry and the central government in Moscow. So far it was straightforward in essence and none of these parties had to pay any money for being allocated their shares. Where the process now became more complicated was when one or some of these parties wanted to sell their shares – then who would want to buy and what would be the price they would pay? Local and central government were keen to sell some or all of their shares to raise money. This is where the simple legal process of privatisation entered uncharted waters and each company's future was put up for grabs. Anna stopped and started to think long and hard. She was intrigued at the great efforts by Hampton to secure a role for his law firm in the process. She was equally as intrigued at the comments made by Dominic Corley and even the excitement the 'deal' evoked in Adam. She was also sure that Victor Nikolayevich and Leonid Marlenovich would be considering the implications of what was happening as they had effectively owned the company for a long time. They may not have had any legal ownership, as no-one did under the Soviet system, but they would consider the company to be theirs. Theirs to defend and theirs to use for their own benefit whenever they could as long as they kept the city on side. With so many possibilities opening up Anna decided to watch and listen to everything and everyone involved. Perhaps, just perhaps, there would be a chance for her to become involved in the process beyond simple paperwork. It was her city, her heritage, her people – surely the city's founder who brought in so many foreign experts in his day to take advantage of their knowledge and who could easily master the graft and greed of his own courtiers and nobles, would see this as a once in a lifetime opportunity. An opportunity to take control and make a difference to the lives of those who toiled and suffered through yet another turn of the wheel in the city's turbulent and dramatic history.

Seventeen

INSPECTOR Bushkin looked at the badly typed message on his desk and swore under his breath. The message was for him to go to a restaurant called Taganka Blues. There were several complaints about a late night disturbance. The Chief of Police was insisting that he investigate and he only. 'More nonsense,' he thought to himself but he wanted to remain on good terms with his boss. Although no one thought his boss was effective at running the police force he was very well connected in the city. On occasion, though, he could be unpredictable and Inspector Bushkin did not know who had the most influence over his boss. For these reasons Inspector Bushkin did all he could to keep his boss on an even keel.

He knew the restaurant well and its owner. It was one of several in the city that had been successful in appealing to the now steadily growing number of foreigners working in the city. Its appeal lay in the eclectic mix of entertainment acts it had on each night. The restaurant only had a small stage in one corner but it managed to squeeze in a range of acts including a top class violinist, a female contortionist and many different singers, musicians and dancers. It also sold vodka in half litre bottles with the lids thrown away on opening. As much as this was a Russian tradition it certainly helped the tips to flow to the acts from the foreign diners.

To keep his visit quiet he decided to walk there. The restaurant was on Literny Prospect and having telephoned ahead the restaurant's door was opened as soon as he walked up to it. It was ten am and the restaurant would not open for another couple of hours. As he stepped in through the door he was struck by a large pile of swept-up glass in the middle of the room. The tables were all bare and had not yet been laid for lunch. A small bald man came over to him. He had a dark complexion and was colourfully dressed even for relatively early in the day with a dark purple shirt with wide sleeves.

"Inspector, good morning," said the man. "I'm glad it is you who has come."

"Good morning, Yuri," replied Inspector Bushkin very informally. "How's business?"

"Very good generally, Inspector. They said there have been some complaints?" Yuri asked looking concerned.

"Yes, but I don't think you should be worried. The Chief wanted me to check them just as a formality."

"I see," replied Yuri with an exaggerated sigh. "I'm sure I can extend our hospitality to the Chief whenever he has the chance to visit us."

"I'm sure he will," said Inspector Bushkin. "Now the complaints were made of, let me see," Inspector Bushkin took out the message from his pocket, "of excessive noises at one am and again at two am."

Yuri frowned. "It was an odd night yesterday, certainly, but where were the noises heard, Inspector?"

"It does not say," replied Inspector Bushkin. He had only briefly looked at the message previously and as he looked at it again he realised that there were actually few details. "I presume," he continued, "that they mean outside. What do you mean by 'odd night'?"

"The acts were good and they played till about one am and then we had an incident but everything was inside the restaurant so I can't see how it was noisy outside."

"Well just take me through the evening. Can we sit down?"

"Of course. I'll just get someone to bring us coffee and some snacks. Take a seat anywhere." Yuri shuffled off to the back of the restaurant. Inspector Bushkin watched him remembering that Yuri had been a professional gymnast until a bad fall had damaged one of his ankles. He came from a family which originated in Uzbekistan, one of the former Republics within the Soviet Union. He looked around and decided to sit at a large round table in the centre of the room. Yuri came back and sat opposite Inspector Bushkin.

"It was an average evening to start," said Yuri, "and we had a new act of four gypsy singers."

Inspector Bushkin looked at him.

"A very distant relative sent them," continued Yuri, "they came dressed in traditional costumes and sang and danced very well. Went down well with the diners."

"Seems very normal."

"I guess it was and we had a couple of Americans who joined them and tried to dance but couldn't. We then had a visitor."

"Who?"

"Maria Petrovna."

Inspector Bushkin whistled quietly under his breath. This was why his boss had sent him.

"And she was in a state," continued Yuri

"Drunk?"

"Very. But the good news was that one of our waitresses managed to coax her into the ladies. She tried to give her coffee but she would not drink it. Eventually she did drink some water. The bad news though was that she had heard the gypsies singing."

"Why bad news?" asked Inspector Bushkin.

"I'll come to that. While she was in the ladies, the gypsies danced a final song. This was very loud and had all the restaurant banging on the tables so this was probably your first noise complaint."

Inspector Bushkin nodded.

"And then," continued Yuri, "the gypsies did a runner and left in a flash."

"Is that odd?"

"Well it was because I had agreed to give then five dollars each but they did not come for the money. They got some tips but still twenty dollars is something I've never known anyone turn down, especially gypsies."

"Was there any explanation?"

"None except one of the waitresses overheard them saying that they had been well paid in advance. I'm trying to call my relative to find out if there are any other reasons but no news so far."

"And Maria Petrovna was sobering up in the ladies during this?"

"She was till she came out and drank a bottle of vodka."

"Could you not stop her?" As soon as he had asked this Inspector Bushkin realised that it was a daft question. No-one would dare to try and stop her. She was the twenty-something-year old daughter of the Mayor of St Petersburg and she did whatever she wanted.

"I tried to," replied Yuri averting his eyes from Inspector Bushkin, "but she insisted. Made me drink with her. Said she was celebrating."

Inspector Bushkin frowned. Maria Petrovna and several other daughters of the most powerful people in the city were notorious for their partying which more often than not went out of control. They were reined in by their fathers on occasion but would always start again after a suitable break.

"What was she celebrating?" he asked.

"This is where it gets odd, Inspector."

"Go on."

"The saint's day of her new best friend – of an imaginary new best friend," said Yuri with a look of deep embarrassment.

Inspector Bushkin looked at him intently. He was not surprised that someone should be celebrating someone's saint's day. In Russia the feast day of the saint someone is named after carries as much significance for a lot of people as their actual birthday. He was concerned that the 'imaginary' nature of her friend could be leading towards Maria Petrova being under the influence of more than just alcohol. Should something happen to her a lot of people would be in serious trouble with the Mayor. A waitress had appeared with coffee and a tray of pastries.

"Ludmila," said Yuri to the waitress, "how bad was the girl last night?"

"Very," replied the waitress. "She was very, very drunk."

"Nothing else?" asked Inspector Bushkin.

"No, we were with her all the time and she had nothing with her. In the old days she would have been put in prison for years for the mess she caused," said the waitress as she left. Inspector Bushkin looked at Yuri who in turn looked at the large pile of swept up broken glass.

"Yes, she decided to dance."

"Still with her imaginary friend?"

"She stood on this table," replied Yuri, "and she seemed to be dancing with someone. She was certainly talking as if someone was holding her hands up and dancing with her."

"Did she not fall off?"

"No, that was the amazing part. She shouted for a peasant song to be played and then danced the whole song on the table. The few diners who were still in could not believe it. Kicking her legs up in the air. And then the finale"

"Go on."

"She pretended to kiss her imaginary friend and then she kicked every single glass off the table. Every single one. One by one. That is the mess swept up over there."

"What did you do?"

"Waited till she'd finished and then helped her down and put her in the car waiting for her outside. I think she finally realised she had gone too far."

"Did she say anything?"

"Bizarrely she walked out almost normally and thanked me for celebrating the day with her."

"What day?"

"The feast day of Saint Gregory, today the 12th March."

Inspector Bushkin looked blank.

"Her imaginary friend, Inspector, was none other than Gregory Yefimovich who she said was coming back to the city." Yuri held his hands up palms open. The blank look on Inspector Bushkin's face started to change. "Yes," continued Yuri, "Gregory Yefimovich Rasputin. Can you believe it? That is the most out of her mind I've ever seen her and yet she looked so peaceful and calm as she left."

Inspector Bushkin did not reply as the image of the wax figure in the museum shot through his mind. The figure seemed to smile at him.

Eighteen

THE phone rang in an elegant office overlooking the Mall in London. A well groomed man in his mid-sixties picked it up.

"Good to see you caught the early train to the office," said Corley. Corley was standing in a quiet corner of a hotel foyer smiling at himself for having arranged the call for nine o'clock Moscow time which was six o'clock in the morning London time.

"Old habits. Now tell me. Are you making any progress?" The man spoke with even greater precision and diction than Corley and was a master at being economical with his words.

"Yes," replied Corley confidently.

"Are you sure? There are other means," he said slowly.

"You sound a trifle unnerved. That is not like you."

"Concerned, dear boy. Slightly concerned. Need I point out to you that Her Majesty's relations with what's left of the Evil Empire are of great interest to a lot of people. This is especially the case with an historic visit to St Petersburg by a member of the Royal Family now on the cards."

"I seem to be slightly out of touch," replied Corley calculating how to unsettle the former Brigadier the most.

"Well if you will turn to finance as an alternative career," said Green with a touch of reproach.

"This is the modern world we live in."

"I do so remember your previous frustrations and our concerns about the pressure you were under."

"It was my choice to leave," said Corley sensing he was now losing the upper hand.

"Of course, it was, of course. Now do us both a favour, old boy, and explain what progress you have to report on the current situation."

"I think it will become clear shortly. I am putting the investment fund in pole position to engage with the company which I believe could hold the key."

There was a pause and then the man said, "do not test our patience, Donald. I want a full report by tomorrow on your project and specifically on how you are going to secure the situation and recover what is necessary."

Nineteen

THE Hamptons were spending the day at home. It was Sunday and Ellen had decided that they would all stay in. As normal the week had been hectic and the day before they had visited some American friends who rented an apartment in the city centre. It was now late March and the pristine snow was showing signs of melting. It had turned slushy in several parts of their garden. The spring thaw was coming and promised at least a week of melting ice and thick mud. She was not looking forward to it and had spent a good hour that morning sorting out the family's array of footwear and boots in preparation for the thaw. Hampton had spent some time in his study but promised he would spend the afternoon with Alex. Alex had watched some DVDs and was waiting for his dad who had an extra document case with him with books in which he was going to show him. They ate a light lunch. On the previous Friday Ellen had had a good shopping trip to the Swedish run supermarket where the variety of food becoming available was starting to increase. Shopping in the normal Russian shops was a foreign shopper's worst nightmare – you could not go with a shopping list, you had to go and grab whatever was on offer. The Swedish supermarket was beginning to resemble one in the West except for its prices which were two to three times higher than in the West. After she had tidied away their plates, Ellen said she was going to have a quick read in the bedroom and possibly a nap.

Hampton brought the extra document case to the table in the kitchen.

"I think these will have been worth waiting for, Alex," said his dad. "I was told that they are normally never let out of the curator's office in the Hermitage. There are very few copies left anywhere."

"But you are the Vice Chairman of the new art committee, dad," said Alex excitedly.

"You got it and that's why they are letting me borrow these," replied his dad taking out a pile of soft backed books. "Let's see what we have." He laid the four books out on the table. They were all A4 size or slightly larger. Several were old. "We have one catalogue here from 1902 and then three from the 1970's."

"What does it say on the cover, dad?" asked Alex excitedly.

"They are catalogues of exhibitions at the Hermitage. 1902 means before the Revolution. One thing the Tsars of Russia did was to collect art. Did you know, Alex, that the only place that has more French art than the Hermitage here in St Petersburg is the whole of France itself?"

"Yes, dad. You told me that before," replied Alex picking up one of the newer catalogues and flicking through some of the pages. "This one is all about Impressionist Art."

"Very good, Alex." The catalogue was in Russian only and Hampton guessed that his son had recognised some of the paintings.

"What I want to try and do is cross-reference paintings in the 1902 catalogue with the paintings in the newer catalogues," continued Hampton.

"What for dad?" asked Alex.

"To see which of the paintings in the old catalogue are not in the catalogues from the 1970's."

"Why would they not be, dad?"

"Some may have been taken away or gone missing during the Revolution of 1917 or more likely during the

Second World War. That is when many paintings and other works of art where either evacuated from St Petersburg or hidden somewhere. This was just before the Germans arrived and surrounded the city. It was all done in a massive rush."

"Why was that, dad?"

"The Germans surprised the Russians big time. The Russians thought that the Germans were heading for Moscow after Hitler broke his pact with Stalin and decided to attack Russia. Instead they went to cut off St Petersburg first and the Russians did not realise it until the Germans were almost here."

"Wow!" said Alex excited by the thought of troops rolling past the small town they were in before anyone had realised.

"Yes, so the Russians could only get some of the art safely on trains and out of the city. Some of it they hid or even disguised."

Alex's cheeks burned red but his father did not notice. The thought of the piece of amber he had in his room tingled through him. "So what happened to the works of art that were moved?" asked Alex.

"Most of them were accounted for and many brought back after the war. But no-one really knows how many are missing, Alex. Lots of the records were destroyed. The Committee that has been set up is going to try to identify and then to recover all the art and objects that have gone missing or in some cases stolen."

"Are there many of them, dad?" asked Alex. The word 'stolen' again burned his cheeks.

"No-one really knows for certain and that is what we are going to try and find out. You remember all the crates you saw in that room on your visit?" Alex nodded. "Well there have been rumours for a long time that when some of those crates are opened then the paintings that should be there may not be."

"Really?"

"Yes, and that is why some experts believe that there was a ban imposed from a high level on opening a lot of them up. That ban, though, is being lifted now that Communism is over. Work will start to make a full and proper list called an 'inventory' of all the exhibits and to check everything is original. The Hermitage needs some special equipment when it opens the crates to be able to preserve and restore some of the painting which may have been damaged in storage. A lot of work and a lot of money is needed to do this."

"Where will the money come from?"

"That's what the Committee is working on." Hampton proceeded to explain more about the Committee with Alex nodding as he flicked through the catalogues and enjoyed the colours and shapes of lots of the paintings and other works of art. Each image was locked into his brain like photographs on an old roll of camera film. He often looked at a picture from different angles slightly tilting his head to watch as shapes and colours changed ever so slightly. Each image gave him almost a physical sensation; as music can be to the ears of a musical virtuoso, so these objects were to Alex's eyes. They were alive in his mind. Hampton watched his son absorbed in the catalogues with a broad smile. Hampton had always loved looking at paintings but Alex seemed to go a step further and take the images deep into himself.

Alex put down a catalogue and asked, "so, dad, are we going to be like hunters for lost art?"

"Sure are. We are going to work with the Russians to find and to bring back all the works of art that have gone missing and to make the Hermitage the world's best art museum as it should be."

"Sounds great."

"And we are also including art that was in the other buildings when the Germans invaded."

"Other buildings?" asked Alex.

"And this might be the best bit for you, Alex."

"Why, dad?"

"Well you know that the Tsars built summer palaces?"

"The Hermitage used to be the Winter Palace, didn't it?" replied Alex.

"Precisely, it was. And then the Tsars built summer palaces to live in outside of the city in the summer. And now you might guess why I choose this house for us to live in."

Alex's eyes widened and he looked out of the window.

"Here in Pushkin we are right in between the summer palaces. The Alexander Palace and the Catherine Palace. They are both within walking distance through the woods from the compound."

"Wow!" said Alex. "What went missing from these palaces, dad? Do you have some more catalogues?"

"Quite a lot went missing and the sad thing is that some great works of art were also destroyed. The most famous is the Amber Room. Some people called it the Eighth Wonder of the World. A whole room full of amazing panels made from amber and jewels."

"Where was it taken from?" asked Alex the tingling feeling starting at the end of his fingertips.

"The Catherine Palace. When the Germans were invading there was not enough time to take the panels of the room down and so they were disguised at first by covering them with paper and cloth. Like redecorating the room."

"Did the disguise work, dad?" asked Alex thinking of the piece of rock he had hidden in his room.

"Sadly, no. The Germans found it. Hitler wanted the whole room to be taken to Germany and it was dismantled by the Germans and taken to a castle in Koningsberg which was the ancient capital of Germany. Then disaster struck." Hampton paused for a moment while Alex rubbed his hands. "When the Russians attacked Koningsberg and started to beat the Germans then everyone says that it was then that the Amber Room was destroyed in a fire in the castle."

Alex did not say anything. His dad continued to explain the works of art that had disappeared from the other palaces and then they returned to the catalogues and looked through them for a good hour. Alex then excused himself and said he would go back to finish watching a DVD in his room. His dad was happy to adjourn to his study to go through a pile of legal paperwork.

In his room Alex rushed to the plastic tub under his desk and took out the cloth bag. He decided to put both hands inside the bag and touch the piece inside. He closed his eyes. The piece felt hot but Alex kept his hands on it. And then he saw it. He was standing in a room and looking around at the four walls. The walls were a glow. The colour was warm. Small items sparkled. It looked to Alex as if the Amber Room had not been destroyed. He took his hands out and put the bag away.

Ellen had cooked as close a dinner to what she would have done on a Sunday in Chicago. She had to put up with chicken legs rather than chicken breast and improvise with some ingredients but her husband and son declared her cooking as 'real home cooking' in the middle of the Russian forest. In truth the apple pie was frozen and made in Sweden but to them it tasted American.

Alex's mind was spinning with the thoughts of the summer palaces and missing works of art. He could not wait for the thaw to come and to be able to walk through the forest. His parents were surprised by his sudden interest in the Russian weather and climate.

"They say the roads and sidewalks will be a mess for at least a week when the snow melts," said Hampton. "The drivers will also have to swap back to summer tyres so that the winter tyres with the metal studs don't damage the roads."

"I think the problem is more the pot holes in the roads than the tyres," commented Ellen recalling the bumps they had had with the pot holes that week. It had seemed like on every journey. The thought of the car triggered a mini flashback to the bullet that had hit the Volvo. Hampton had eventually been told by his office about the bullet but he had been told that the driver had been alone at the time. He in turn had told Ellen only on the condition that she agreed not to worry. She had agreed. She looked at Alex who looked back at her with a look of worry crossing his face. Ellen was sure he could tell what she had been thinking. Alex's mental state still concerned her and she made a note to make an appointment to see their family doctor back home as soon as they were next back in the States on leave.

Later that evening Alex had gone to bed and had fallen asleep with a note book at his side. Ellen could see a list of works of art and some scribblings. As she kissed him gently on the forehead she picked up the notebook and almost dropped it. Alex had scribbled the word 'Volvo' and next to it written 'other shootings but we won't die'. She left his room, took out her diary and called their doctor's office in Chicago. She did not care that it was a Sunday in the States. She left a long message.

Twenty

THE car that came to pick Sasha and Yelena Matrovna from Children Home No. 8. this time was not one of Roman Felixovich's cars. This car was an old Volga model, the staple of the Russian car industry. The Volga was a big sedan car modelled on American Ford cars of the 1950's. Although heavy and cumbersome to drive it was relatively comfortable for passengers. This car was also decorated inside with a plethora of religious pictures and plastic icons. It had been sent by Metropolitan Melnikov's office. The driver was a small spritely man who wore a cassock under his thick overcoat.

"Look at all these icons," said Sasha as he got into the car, "I've never seen a car with so many in before."

"They help to keep us safe on the roads," said the driver with a smile as he turned to Sasha and crossed himself. Yelena Matrovna did the same. "It should take us about half an hour," said the driver.

"Very good," replied Yelena Matrovna.

"Where are we going this time, Yelena?" asked Sasha.

"To a very special place, Sasha, where we can practice singing again. It is in the countryside and a perfect place to sing and worship."

"Sounds great," replied Sasha thinking back to his grandmother and his early life in the countryside and the time he spent in the chapel.

The driver for all his religious appearance drove like a madman clearly believing in the infallible power of his icons. They quickly left the city and headed south. As they drove through the countryside the first signs of the thaw were visible in fields and at the side of the road - black patches of slushy mud and dirty puddles. There were the occasional clusters of wooden buildings but very little sign of life. After some twenty-five minutes the Volga slowed down and turned off the road onto a very slushy track. The driver drove slowly letting the weight of the Volga occasionally slide the car forward. He picked out his route down the track with some skill to avoid the car becoming stuck. To Sasha and Yelena Matrovna the few minutes down the track felt like being on a mini roller coaster as they were thrown backwards and forwards. The Volga turned a corner and reached a gate. Behind the gate were several buildings which looked like the outbuildings of a farm. The driver banged on the car's horn three times.

"You won't be disappointed, Sasha," said Yelena Matrovna looking at the puzzled look on Sasha's face. Their first trip had been to the magnificent Cathedral of Our Saviour-on-the-Spilt-Blood which had enraptured Sasha and sent a chill down his spine whenever he thought about the singing. "Do you remember, what I told you about the olden days?"

"You mean about the persecution of the believers?"

"Yes, well this is why some of the places of worship had to be kept secret and I guess we have come to one of those today." She looked at the driver.

"Quite right," replied the driver. "You will soon see." He was about to use his horn again when a man appeared behind the gate. He was tall and dressed in a long white fur coat. He opened the gate and beckoned to the driver to drive in. The driver drove the Volga as directed and stopped at the side of a long wooden building. The tall man opened the door and greeted Yelena Matrovna and Sasha. He then asked them to follow him.

Yelena Matrovna and Sasha went into the long wooden building which was empty inside save for some bales of straw at one end. They could hear faint strains of music though they were muffled. Suddenly the music started louder and clearer. The man had opened a door in the floor. Light also jumped out of the door. The man quietly and reverently asked them to follow him. They descended a flight of wooden steps and gasped at the sight. The room was long and its walls all glowed with a warm light. At one end there was a small altar lit up by dozens of candles. In the centre of the room stood a group of ten singers and musicians. They were dressed in white and at first glance had a gypsy air. On closer inspection their clothing though bore the marks of religious attire and the people's complexions were Northern Russian rather than the more swarthy look of Russians from the Middle and Near East. Several had long hair tied at the back. The most striking feature about the men were their beards – they were deep black, long and trimmed so that they flowed down the men's necks and onto their chests.

"Welcome, dear friends," said one of the singers stepping forward. "You are most welcome. Let us greet you with a song."

Before Yelena Matrovna or Sasha could reply the group started a slow and soulful song which evolved into a slow chant and finished with the ten singers and musicians all bowing their heads in unison.

"Thank you for your kind welcome," said Yelena Matrovna. "My name is Yelena Matrovna and this is Sasha," she continued. She had brought Sasha in front of her and had her hands on his shoulders. "Sasha has the true gift of singing."

"Yelena Matrovna," began Sasha about to protest but Yelena Matrovna gently put a finger to his lips. "May we sing with you?" she asked.

"Of course. Please join with us," said the singer offering a hand to both of them. They both took a hand and joined the group in a circle.

In the cathedral Sasha had frozen at first until it seemed as though another voice had led him on. This time he joined the first hymn without a second's hesitation. During the second song, a slow chant, Sasha's voice became more and more pronounced and before he had realised he was chanting the lead section of the chant and chanting it alone. He finished with a subtle but loud vocal flourish and bowed his head with the others. A clap sounded, followed by another and then another. "Bravo! Sasha! Bravo!" said Yelena Matrovna. The singing continued for almost an hour until the majority of the singers' voices began to waiver. Sasha sang a final song by himself which again was applauded with feeling. As the applause subsided cups were passed round the group. The drink tasted of fruit but was bitter and strong. They had all sat down on the floor.

"Now some of us will dance," said the singer who had been the only person to speak. Six of the singers stood up, whilst four others picked up musical instruments and moved back to the wall of the room. Yelena Matrovna and Sasha followed the musicians. The musicians had a drum and three guitar like instruments. They began to play and the six others started to dance in a circle holding and then letting go of hands as their dance built up. Sasha watched mesmerised. He had seen dancing before, especially when he had lived with his grandmother, but none as skilful and expressive as this. The musicians gradually increased the speed of their playing and with a loud bang on the drum one of the six dancers leapt upwards and landed in the middle of the circle. She started to pirouette on one leg and spin. She thrust her arms out sideways and as she increased her speed her image seemed to blur. Sasha felt his eyes swim and his throat burn. With another loud bang of the drum the dancer dropped to the floor. Sasha looked at Yelena Matrovna. When the next dancer leapt into the middle as the drum banged Sasha watched Yelena Matrovna. She was swaying quickly and in time with the dancer. Sasha thought for a second that Yelena Matrovna was about to jump into the circle. Yelena Matrovna though caught Sasha's eye and she stopped and looked at him intently. A smile was beaming across Sasha's face and his eyes were dancing. Yelena Matrovna knew then for sure that they had both found their real family.

Twenty One

ROMAN Felixovich had been informed that the day before a car, an old Volga, had been to the Home and had taken Yelena Matrovna and Sasha out during the morning and had not returned until the evening. He was reluctant to push for information from his contact who was closely linked to the Metropolitan. He also wanted to avoid having to do favours for the Director of the Home, who to give her some credit, was using all the means she could to get help for the children. She was hoping that if the boy could really sing then the chances of him being adopted would increase. Rather than have to speak with the Director of the Home, Roman Felixovich decided he would instruct one of his drivers to bring Yelena Matrovna to his office.

He stepped out of his private office into the largely deserted office space where his assistant and his drivers spent their time. There were a couple of desks, a table and chairs, a sofa and a small kitchen area. He often used the table and sofa to meet with less important people to whom he did not want to show his real office. The room was bright as the windows were quite large. There were good views from this top floor of the building. To the left stood the impressive white domed Smolni Cathedral, one of the best Baroque style cathedrals in Russia. Its clean white domes and light blue walls always caught the day's light and gave the surrounding area a warm glow amidst the drabness of the other buildings.

Roman Felixovich motioned to the driver who was sitting at a desk to come with him. As he gave him his instructions, one of his other drivers walked into the office carrying a white envelope.

"Roman Felixovich," said the driver taking off his sun glasses. "They gave me this at the Property Fund."

"Very good," replied Roman Felixovich taking the envelope. "Get some lunch now."

"Yes, boss."

Roman Felixovich went back into his office and sat down at his desk. He opened the envelope and unfolded several sheets of paper. It was a list. He ran his eyes down the list and put the papers down. He smiled. His man on the inside of the St Petersburg Property Fund had proven his worth. He took out a mobile phone and dialled. He waited patiently until the number he had called answered. There were no greetings and he just said that the situation appeared satisfactory and that he hoped they would meet again soon. He ended the call and picked up the list again. The list had three columns. The first was headed 'Company' and had a list of names, the second was entitled 'Date' and had dates in it or occasionally was left blank and the third was headed 'Form of privatisation' and either had various words in it, or, again it was left blank.

Roman Felixovich had been working nonstop on two fronts. Firstly, he was amassing cash as quickly as possible whilst setting up his own bank to protect his cash. He was in advanced discussions with several partners locally. One of them was a senior official in the Soviet Union's former trade bank who had credible contacts with bankers in the former Eastern Bloc, in Switzerland and also a long list of contacts in banks in the more exotic tax haven locations. The best way to protect his cash was to control his own bank which in turn would put chunks of his cash in safe havens until he wanted to use it. Secondly, he was finding out everything he could about oil companies and oil reserves. He was convinced that the oil companies to be privatised would be the most valuable companies in Russia. The challenge he faced was that he was just not ready on either of these two fronts - cash and oil industry inside knowledge - to be able to bid to win them. He smiled as he underlined five companies on the list with a pen. They were the main oil companies in northwest Russia and they had not yet been given a date for privatisation as he had suggested. He was buying time which is what he needed desperately and luckily for him the price he was paying for this was next to nothing.

After a few minutes he went back to the list and checked the rest of the names. Several stood out but he was sure that these were earmarked for other parties. The paper mill would be taken by a group he knew well and who controlled a lot of the tree logging businesses in the region. He did not see too much value in the electricity or telephone companies because Russian customers simply did not pay for these services as they never had done under Communism. And now, why would they? The simple reason was that the use of electricity and telephones was not metered. When buildings had been built under Communism there was no need for meters because power, heating, water and telephone lines came with the apartments for which citizens paid a nominal rent from the nominal and nearly non-existent wages everyone was paid. The problem now was how could charges be calculated? The new mobile phone company, which in contrast charged customers as they made calls, had been set up with foreign partners but was effectively controlled by a local group with connections to the Mayor's team. Most of the industrial companies were in a right mess and struggling with the dislocation in their operations, supplies and markets caused by the breakdown of the Soviet command economy under which everything had been planned centrally with very little attention paid to what was wanted and then what was needed – the evils twins of 'supply' and 'demand' as Communism had declared the basic rules of a market economy. Some of these companies might survive, but why go through the pain?

He had been advised, though, by his source that he should take part in at least one privatisation, preferably a high profile one, so as to prove his credibility for when the targets he wanted to acquire came up for grabs. His source had suggested half a dozen names which it was known that the Mayor was keen to see go to safe hands. Russian hands, of course, and preferably local. Of these, his source had further explained, two looked the most vulnerable because either their management was weak or foreigners were already involved. The first one he could understand. It was the city's chocolate manufacturer which was very badly run and always in the shadow of its rival, the iconic Red October chocolate company in Moscow. The second one did surprise him. His source had edited the 'Form of privatisation' for this company and it now read 'to be determined'. This was to give Roman Felixovich the flexibility to work out how he wanted the company to be privatised in order to give him the best chance of making a bid to suit him. He, like almost everyone in the city, knew that this company was one of the most famous in the city and that its management was well respected, if die-hard Communist or as now termed 'Red Directors'. The newly established side-lines within the business were also very well protected with a very strong 'roof', or level of protection, which had strong links to the city's police force itself. The only explanation could be the threat of foreign involvement. He knew of Leonid Marlenovich but had never met him. He would have to start to work out his plans for his future ownership of the Peter the Great Shipyard. But what on earth would he do with it?

The final piece of advice his source had given him was for Roman Felixovich to contribute to one of the Mayor's projects for the city. This would open more doors for Roman Felixovich than he could currently open through his growing business activities and his own contacts. The city was finishing the building of a full sized replica of the ship in which Peter the Great had sailed to Europe on his Grand Mission. The ship was called the 'Standart' and its building had been largely financed before the collapse of the Soviet Union. It now needed sponsors to pay for its decoration before it was to sail once again to Europe to promote the city. The second was to contribute to a new committee based in the Hermitage which was tasked with reclaiming and rebuilding the Hermitage's art collections. Roman Felixovich did not like the sound of either of these projects and he decided that he would hold out making any contributions until it became make or break time for his bids.

He made a call on his phone and had started a conversation when there was a knock at the door and his assistant put his head round the door. Roman Felixovich waved at him to come in and put his hand over his phone.

"They have brought the singing teacher up," said his assistant.

Roman Felixovich signalled for her to be brought into his office. The assistant left and several moments later Yelena Matrovna was ushered into the private office and the door closed behind her. Yelena Matrovna was visibly impressed by the luxury of the private office and walked round touching the furniture and ornaments. With a flurry of brief commands and a curt 'goodbye' Roman Felixovich finished his call.

"Now I see why your private office is so special, Roman Felixovich," said Yelena Matrovna with a broad smile of admiration on her face.

"I try to have some comfort, Yelena Matrovna, when I am on my own," replied Roman Felixovich with a touch of embarrassment. He knew of the small flat Yelena Matrovna shared with an elderly relative and of her lack of money but he also knew that she never complained and that she cared little for material possessions.

"Where were you yesterday?" he asked.

"On a trip arranged by the Metropolitan. Did he not inform you?" Going by her abrupt summons today Yelena Matrovna was fairly sure that Roman Felixovich had not been told.

"I don't have an active dialogue with the Church," replied Roman Felixovich with a touch of curtness slipping into his voice.

"I thought you arranged the visit to the cathedral," replied Yelena Matrovna not responding to the curtness.

"I had it arranged," he replied, "a contact of a contact."

"I see," continued Yelena Matrovna. "Well I assumed, albeit incorrectly as it turns out, that you would have been told."

"Never mind," said Roman Felixovich, his impatience starting to show. He had his own reasons for treating Yelena Matrovna with care and more so now that the boy was creating interest. "Where was the trip to?"

"To a village church. You know one of the old types where we could practice singing in a proper way." She paused and looked at Roman Felixovich and then continued. "Sasha has a genuine talent."

Roman Felixovich looked at her without speaking. "He will soon become well-known," Yelena Matrovna continued, "and people will be interested in him and what he may be capable of."

Roman Felixovich looked at her again without speaking for several moments. Finally he sighed deeply and said, "and what are we going to do then?"

"That is something that we will have to wait and find out."

Roman Felixovich faced darkened visibly. He hated her coyness and yet he could not risk pushing her. Despite all his growing business power and the amount of cash he was amassing there were still forces that would not bend to money or to coercion. He had to be clever, very, very clever. "Very well," he said leaning back in his chair and putting his feet on his table, "then you must stay with him. You must see him every day and watch him and you must," he paused and sat back up. He looked at her with a steely determination. "You must tell me whenever he leaves the Home! Is that clear?"

"Crystal clear," she replied in a whisper as she carefully hid her smile.

Twenty Two

TWO shabbily dressed men were sitting and dozing at the side of the high wooden fence. The weather had shown promises of brightening up but there was still the chance of light rain. The melting of the snow had now largely finished with only the odd piece of dirty ice occasionally lying at the side of a road or under a tree. The men were not armed but their intent as security guards was recognisable, if somewhat comical. People occasionally walking by them paid them no attention. In this area on the outskirts of St Petersburg many traditional dachas had been taken over by new owners. The small wooden fences originally put up to keep out wandering dogs and to allow for neighbourly comings and goings were being replaced by two metre high wooden or brick barricades in a multitude of designs all with the objective of making casual visitors most unwelcome.

In the past the vast majority of the large dachas on the outskirts of cities in Russia were owned by factories in the cities and they were used by workers for spring and summer breaks. As well as providing a simple place to sleep in the warm summer months they become a hive of industry. All manner of vegetables and fruits are grown and harvested to then appear in preserved forms on Russian dining tables throughout the year, particularly treasured in times of shortages, and always the perfect accompaniments to vodka, chocolate and ice cream, the real staples of Russian life.

At the side of the men was a small gate. On its left hung a wooden sign with the words "Peter the Great Shipyard Collective" etched in the wood by hand. The men looked up as they heard the sound of a Jiguli, a make of the Lada car, built originally on the design of a 1950's Fiat. The Jiguli laboured up the lane towards them. The occupants made the men frown slightly. Two large Russian policemen were sitting in the front seats squashed in like two pickled cucumbers in a small glass jar. There was another man in the back seat.

The fence surrounded several buildings. The main building of two stories had been built from a variety of coloured bricks and had wooden balconies at the front and back and a metal roof. It also had a wooden deck at the back. The other buildings were wooden outhouses. Victor Nikolayevich and Leonid Marlenovich were emerging from a small outhouse dressed in light blue dressing gowns. A group of women were playing volleyball on a court in the corner of the grounds.

"How was the sauna?" briskly asked a middle-aged woman dressed in a white smock as they made their way to the wooden deck at the back of the main building.

"Excellent! Excellent!" beamed Victor Nikolayevich.

"What can I get you next?" continued the woman without any great enthusiasm.

Leonid Marlenovich plonked himself down on a lounger and started to light a cigar.

"I think you have worked enough for us today already," said Victor Nikolayevich, "the dacha is always well looked after and lunch was magnificent. Maybe you should take the rest of the afternoon off."

"But Victor Nikolayevich some of the women are still in their sauna."

"No 'buts'. You always do us proud. And you too should rest."

"And I'm sure we can manage without you for a while," added Leonid Marlenovich ensuring that this cigar was lit all round.

"I'll be upstairs if anything is needed," said the woman as she gathered up some empty glasses and took herself inside.

"You know, Leonid Marlenovich, how can there be any better life than this?" proclaimed Victor Nikolayevich himself stretching out on a lounger. "Winter over, countryside, fresh food, vodka and soon it will be summer. Russia is so well blessed."

"But don't forget Cuban cigars," replied Leonid Marlenovich theatrically taking his first drag on the cigar.

"Cuban? Has it all arrived? Why did you not tell me when the cargo from Cuba arrived?" Victor Nikolayevich sounded puzzled.

"Came in last night. I supervised the unloading myself. Wonderful cigars."

"Why did you not tell me before? I have been worrying all day."

"Worrying? Don't pretend. You enjoyed your lunch and sauna. You did not look like a worried man to me."

"Leonid Marlenovich, you know how much I worry about these things."

"Well don't. Everything is in order, everything cleared customs. And we are now preparing to send some of the products onwards with the next batch of boat orders to Riga."

"But they are all not ready, are they?"

"We'll soon see. Some documents still need finalising. Wonderful cigar. See there is nothing to worry about."

"I'm very happy for you, Victor Nikolayevich, not to have any worries these days," said an official voice cutting through the calm that had begun to settle on the two men.

"Inspector Bushkin, you arrive unannounced," answered Victor Nikolayevich standing up to shake hands.

"Your two guards are smoking with my men. You really should train them just a little," he said with a mild hint of criticism.

"I've said we should have guard dogs," said Leonid Marlenovich not bothering to look at the policeman or to get up, "much more loyal and obedient."

"Yes, yes," Victor Nikolayevich started to babble, "get some dogs, as you like, Leonid Marlenovich. Smoking, hum? Well, Inspector, as you are here perhaps you would like to join us for a cigar."

Leonid Marlenovich looked up as though he could not think of anything worse than to give one of his cigars away. "I'm sure the Inspector receives plenty of cigars and other benefits on his rounds," he said putting the box away.

"I'll pass, thank you, but perhaps a cold drink. I see at least your women have some energy." He looked over to the volleyball game which was continuing at a lively place.

"Young people have a lot of energy these days, Inspector," said Victor Nikolayevich siting back down.

The middle-aged woman appeared as if on cue and handed the policeman a drink.

"Cold enough for you, Inspector?" asked Leonid Marlenovich becoming much friendlier.

"Marvellous, Leonid Marlenovich. Your people are well trained at certain things which is what they should stick to." He looked unwaveringly at Leonid Marlenovich.

"Now, now, Inspector," interjected Victor Nikolayevich slightly confused at the mounting tension between them, "our people are very good at many things."

"Yes, you are excellent at making and selling...," replied the policeman.

"And providing your chief with a contribution," Leonid Marlenovich's tone was hardening again and warding the policeman away from getting into what he assumed would be a needless debate with Victor Nikolayevich. "You have a reason for coming out to us on such a nice afternoon?"

"A quiet chat," was the short answer.

"Maybe we should take a walk. Will you excuse us, Victor Nikolayevich, while Inspector Bushkin and I talk for a few minutes?"

"Well, if you don't think you need me."

"No, I'm sure I needn't bother you with this," said the policeman becoming more amiable. "The chief sends his best regards and thanks."

"Did he like the new sail boat we sent him on his birthday?" asked Victor Nikolayevich warmly.

"Delighted, delighted." The policeman cast his gaze towards the young women playing volleyball. "He really appreciates the boat," he added as he and Leonid Marlenovich slowly walked away.

Two middle-aged women were making their way from one of the other outhouses dressed in similar dressing gowns to the men. One of the women was plump and her face worn, the other in remarkable shape and with her hair tied up. Her face looked ten years younger than it was.

"That is so good for the skin," said the second woman, "you should do it more often and take more exercise. There is more to life than those endless accounts and book-keeping in the factory."

"I know, Natasha. Every time spring comes and I look at myself I have grown further outwards. You just stay so slim."

"Now, now, Larissa", said Natasha throwing her arm around her shoulder, "you have had a daughter and I have always had lots of time to look after myself."

"You ladies took your time," beamed Victor Nikolayevich.

"Victor Nikolayevich, why are you not playing volleyball? You know you can teach those youngsters a trick or two," smiled Larissa.

Natasha had reached the deck and whispered into Victor Nikolayevich's ear. "You would not like to admit that you are too old, my dear Victor, now would you?"

"Of course not," he said loudly, "especially when I have a chance to be on the same side as Alenka, the most beautiful Russian girl in the world." He was jogging over into the corner of the grounds and already reorganising the teams. The women sat on the deck and watched him throw himself about enthusiastically at every shot.

As she brushed through her long hair, Natasha asked, "tell me how did he ever make it to become General Director?"

"He was strong especially in the old days," replied Larissa.

"But everyone is now saying that he cannot cope with the pace of change these days. Some in the factory are comparing him behind his back to the drunken Yeltsin. They would never have dared to do that a year ago."

"I know and he knows too though he won't admit it. But he is a survivor and that is one thing at least that he shares with President Yeltsin. You know he lost all his family at the start of the Siege and then spent his childhood defending the city after being adopted by the shipyard. One way or another it has been his life and he has put all his life into it. Don't forget that he was very brave and he has helped a lot of people." Larissa had become very serious.

"Why did you never marry him?"

Larissa gazed over towards the group playing. "Everything would have changed," she said. "You're a fine one to talk about marriages! The last one was you third or fourth? And he is still alive?" she added jokingly

"Yes." She feigned a sulk. "But the second one got what he deserved and I paid the price for it. Five years in women's prison number 39 was no honeymoon."

"But since then you have never looked back," Larissa continued knowing that her friend regarded her time in prison as a small price to pay to break the vicious circle of drunken domestic abuse she had been caught up in.

"Just let's say I learned everything about human nature and its pitiful desires. They're not that pretty. Especially when you have to survive. Now I can show all our girls how to be tough and enjoy themselves whatever men throw at them. Especially the types like Leonid Marlenovich, our wonderful Director, and the Police Inspector over there."

A few minutes later Leonid Marlenovich and the policeman returned to the deck.

"Natasha Pavlovna, I was hoping it would be you in the sauna," smiled the policeman.

"I still have an occasional yearning for an enclosed space, Inspector," she replied with aplomb.

"That's long forgotten," replied Inspector Bushkin saluting her reply, "and I am so glad that business has really taken off since your release. Now if you will all excuse me I must be off." And with that he handed Leonid Marlenovich a package and turned on his heels. As he strode away Larissa quietly slipped from the deck and made her way over to the volleyball court.

"So Natasha, my darling, how are we doing?" asked Leonid Marlenovich sitting down and bringing out his box of cigars again.

"Fine," she answered without lifting her head as she looked through the documents she had taken from the policeman's package. "All the export documents seem to be in order. The next shipment to Riga should go through smoothly."

Victor Nikolayevich stumbled onto the deck pouring with sweat. "They almost killed me," he said hoarsely as he flopped into his chair. "What did Inspector Bushkin have to say?" asked Victor Nikolayevich once all the women had moved inside and he had got his breath back.

"Nothing to worry about with our new exports." He paused and then continued. "But there might be a tiny little cloud on the horizon."

"What type?" asked Victor Nikolayevich looking around for his drink.

"Someone else is making enquiries about our privatisation. You may need to go and see the Mayor this week."

"Straight away. I'll call his office on Monday and arrange to have a cup of coffee with him," replied Victor Nikolayevich. "Straight away!"

Leonid Marlenovich nodded and leaned back in his chair. This deep-rooted relationship with the Mayor was the only real reason he needed Victor Nikolayevich and he absolutely hated the feeling of powerlessness it gave him. Their new business lines were as well protected as they could be – the only risk was the people in power - and no-one stayed in power for ever.

Twenty Three

HAMPTON'S lunch was important and it had taken him the best part of two weeks to fit it into his diary. His objective was to explain to Vera, his secretary, that he was aiming to dedicate a lot of his time to his Art Committee work for the Hermitage and that for the time being he wanted it kept pretty much quiet from the rest of the firm. As secret as possible, in fact. He was going to ask her to be careful with what was written in his diary and in the files used for calculating time spent on legal work. This was the information that was used to work out the fees they charged their clients. It was not something he would have tried to do back in Chicago and definitely not in London but he had estimated that he probably had up to a year to establish the office in St Petersburg and so not many questions would be asked about what the office was doing for now. He had decided to explain it as simply as possible to Vera whom he knew was very intelligent and well educated and certainly overqualified for her role as a personal assistant.

They were entering White Nights. By night it was one of the city's hottest night spots, by day it was a restaurant frequented by some of the movers and shakers of the city and foreign businessmen predominantly from Scandinavia and Germany. It was also the haunt of several well-known local businessmen who were very easy to identify. They sat quietly in their uniform black polo sweaters and leather jackets, their entourages of thick set men with mobile phones and headsets occupying the tables around them watching for any attempt by any unwelcome guest to get within range of their bosses. The tall waitresses swanned in and out never bothering to ask the entourages if they wanted anything as their job clearly did not include being either fed or watered. Even though it was only lunch time a saxophonist sitting on a stool on the centre of the stage was playing slow melodies.

There were the occasional other guests. There was a group of American tourists. One of the tourists had gleefully taken out his video camera only for the maître d' to have been at his side in a flash and to have told him quietly that it was not allowed.

As he shrugged his shoulders and sat down the woman next to him whispered, "and why on earth not? This is no longer a police state, is it?"

The maître d' walked round to her and whispered in her ear quietly. "There are people here who are with people who they probably should not be with. We would not like to start any scandals." With that the woman stared around her and called her group into a huddle.

"Gee, honey, I think you better stop," she said her hands trembling.

Hampton and Vera had sat down in a corner. Vera looked as though she had walked off the cover of a fashion magazine; a startling yellow two piece suit aimed at looking business-like only served to accentuate her figure. She felt confident in her dress. She had spent five years working her way through Western fashion magazines and clothes. Russian men were easy to impress: the more on show the better. She had passed that. She had reached the stage like today when she went for it and she had Russian men debating which European country she was from.

They were finishing their lunch. Hampton's request had been fully understood and accepted. Vera would put down whatever Hampton told her and would guard his diary and files from everyone in the firm. She showed a very deep knowledge of art which impressed Hampton to the extent that he began to consider having her become involved. An idea struck him. Perhaps he could put her forward as a secretary and translator on the actual committee. It could help him tremendously. He could class this as a charitable donation by his firm and use his and her work on the committee as promotional work for the firm. This would put a key part of the work he had been intending to be clandestine on an official level. So much for his cloak and dagger thinking! He would clear the basics with London, put the project in general above board and then explain it to Vera. The lunch, like events on most days is Russia, turned out to be the opposite to what had been expected.

As they were about to leave Vera asked if she could be excused a moment. Hampton readily agreed and said he would wait for her in the car. Hampton stepped from the door and signalled to his office driver who was in a waiting car with its engine running. As Hampton took a few steps onto the pavement another car came alongside his, moved in front and a man leaned out of the passenger window. Hampton had no time to move as the man stuck out a revolver and fired at him twice. Hampton fell back slumped down against the wall dropping his briefcase. All around people stopped. In a split second the man who had a ski mask covering his face jumped from his car and grabbed Hampton's briefcase. Hampton's driver, who had watched everything without reacting, threw open his door in panic and the door hit the attacker as he was about to jump back in his own car. Hampton's driver dived down behind his wheel as the man fired another two shots at him.

The attacker's car sped off and as it accelerated it swerved to avoid a group of children crossing the road. Losing control the driver screamed out loud as the car mounted the pavement and careered into a wooden kiosk demolishing it and ramming into the building behind. The passenger ripped off the driver's ski mask and felt his neck. As he took out a knife he whispered calmly into the driver's ear. He then jumped out of the car and hobbled across to another waiting car.

The words from the Principal of the Anglo-American School had knocked Ellen for six. She had not collapsed but had had to sit straight down on a chair and she had clasped her stomach with one of her hands. The Principal who had come round from behind his desk to tell her had managed to grab her other hand and arm and steady her on the chair. She was speechless. The Principal shouted for a glass of water to be brought in which Ellen took without acknowledgement. She handed the glass back, took a deep breath and wiped underneath her eyes with her fingers. "Alex," she mumbled, "Alex!" as she left the Principal's office.

She arrived at Alex's classroom and looked in through the small glass window in the door. She could see him in the middle of the classroom listening to the teacher standing in front of the blackboard. She tapped on the door and opened it. The teacher smiled and Ellen asked if she might have a quick word with Alex. The teacher nodded to Alex who stood up and walked to the door. Ellen closed the door behind Alex and bent down so that her face was level with Alex's.

"What is it, mom?" asked Alex looking deep into his mum's eyes.

"Alex, you know what you wrote in your book the other day about..?"

"About the Volvo and bullets," interrupted Alex with a smile.

"Yes," replied his mum, "and what did you mean by the shooting?"

"Oh, that there will be another shooting but we needn't worry because none of us will die."

"That's what I thought you wrote!" she said bursting into tears and holding Alex in a tight hug, "and I only hope you will be right!"

Twenty Four

THE shooting of a prominent US lawyer working for a top London law firm in St Petersburg became world-wide news on CNN later that day. CNN despatched its Moscow correspondent to St Petersburg and by late afternoon he was reporting from outside the taped-off White Nights restaurant. Roman Felixovich was watching in his private office as was Leonid Marlenovich in his basement room. The staff at the Miller Lombard office had all stopped their work and were sat in their meeting room also watching CNN. The city seemed quiet.

"This is the first recorded attempt on the life of a foreign executive in Russia," stated the reporter. "Until now the shootings that have been taking place here and in Moscow since the start of perestroika have been of Russians. The foreign community here in St Petersburg is in a state of shock. John Hampton is a respected lawyer and his firm Miller Lombard is well known for the legal work it is doing in the country assisting both international and Russian companies. The motive for the attack is completely unknown and we are waiting for a statement from the police. John Hampton is said to be in a critical but stable condition." The reporter continued with some background on the city and then CNN cut back to its studio and ran summaries of previous murders in the city and in Moscow repeating the fact that the shooting of John Hampton was the first recorded case of an attack on a foreigner.

One of Leonid Marlenovich's mobile phones rang. He looked at it curious to know who could have been given the number of this particular phone.

"Yes?" he asked.

"Leonid Marlenovich?" replied the caller.

"Yes," replied Leonid Marlenovich. He did not recognise the voice but it sounded business-like.

"This is Roman Felixovich," said Roman Felixovich. "I was given this number by a mutual contact."

"Very good," replied Leonid Marlenovich.

"I wondered if we might meet?" asked Roman Felixovich. Roman Felixovich had his TV on mute but an image of a man on the screen made him look at the screen and almost drop his phone.

"Tell me where and when," replied Leonid Marlenovich.

Roman Felixovich gave the details and then quickly put his phone down and unmuted his TV.

"...and on a lighter note, whilst we wait for further news on the shooting and since we are in St Petersburg," said the CNN reporter who was now standing outside the Taganka Blues restaurant, "things have literally been going bump in the night in the city recently and it seems one of the city's most famous and disreputable figures is making a comeback." The screen cut to the museum on the Moika Embankment and the basement rooms were the wax figures were displayed. "Local rumour has it," continued the reporter, "that he always returns in time of crisis for the city. First, it was during the final days of the Romanov royal family on the eve of the Revolution when he was presumed murdered by a group of nobles although it took many attempts to actually kill him. Some people believed he had special powers and could never die. Next, he is rumoured to have returned during the Siege of the city in the Second World War and to have helped in the desperate fight for survival. And now in the last few months there have been disturbances in his museum on his birthday and visions of him here in the restaurant on the feast day of the saint he is named after. 'Why now?' you may ask. Well according to a lot of folk here this year many, many people in the city are struggling with the new Russia and all its changes. He has come back to help the city again." The report finished with a collection of images of Rasputin, the Romanovs, the Siege and Yeltsin on his tank.

The staff in the Miller Lombard office made a few half-hearted attempts at jokes about the Rasputin 'mad monk' stories and switched off their TV. Leonid Marlenovich tut-tutted at the puerile nature of the content of a supposedly serious news channel. The Americans for all their public moralising far too often seemed to turn to baseless sensationalism. Roman Felixovich shuddered. He did not want to admit it for a split second but it was starting to seem real. With a deep breath he snapped himself out of the thought and muttered under his breath, "stupid damn fairy tales again!"

Twenty Five

UNSURPRISINGLY not a lot of work was being done that afternoon in the Miller Lombard office. Vera had telephoned from a police station and Janna had been dispatched to go there and wait and provide Vera with whatever assistance she needed. A senior Russian lawyer was on standby to intervene if Vera was not released in good time. The phone line to the Miller Lombard offices in London and Moscow had been red hot and the Managing Partner in Moscow was flying into St Petersburg by early evening to take over running the office. No-one had any idea of how to react. Anna had frozen at the news and had sat in shock for a good five minutes. As if by instinct or some form of reaction she had telephoned Valentina Alexandrovna at the Home and asked to see her as soon as possible. Adam had addressed all the staff. He explained that he had spoken to the Moscow Managing Partner with whom he had worked for before he had come to St Petersburg. They had agreed to close the office early and switch all calls to their Moscow office. Adam was going to the airport to meet the Moscow Managing Partner. There would be a meeting with everyone at ten am the following morning.

"Hi, Adam," said Anna quietly as they were both nearing the office door. "How are you feeling?"

"Not sure," replied Adam with an exaggerated shrug of his shoulders. "I'm really not sure."

"No more news?"

"No. I guess we should just carry on for now. There is nothing else we can actually do."

"You are right," replied Anna, "I have been trying to carry on by writing about the company." She smiled meekly as it was an obvious white lie. Ever since the office had received the distressed call from Vera, she had not been able to concentrate on any work. There was a brief silence as Anna changed her office shoes for a pair of outdoor shoes and Adam started to put on his coat. "How far are you on with the description of the properties that you are drafting? Has the office been helping you enough?" asked Anna, trying to continue the conversation.

Adam was silent for a few more seconds and then asked. "Sorry, what were you were saying?"

Anna felt slightly puzzled. Adam still looked shook up but he must have understood her question. "I was just asking about the description of the properties, you know, including their history, who owns them now, any leases."

"Sure standard kind of things," replied Adam

"Exactly," said Anna glad that the conversation was becoming normal.

"Well, I still have some digging to do," said Adam with a brief smile and trying to establish a touch of seniority.

"Fine, well perhaps we can go through what you know as soon as you are ready and I can ask the team to do any further research for you."

At the mention of the properties Adam had become suddenly stuck between his duty to his client, which was the company, on the one hand, and the possible exposure to his firm in the work on the privatisation on the other. If any wrong information was written about the properties then his firm could be sued. His calls to the Miller Lombard office in The Hague had become more frequent and he was now sure that there was something more to the claims lodged against the properties than he had originally thought. It was a very delicate issue and he was not sure how, when and with whom to bring it up. Plus he did not yet have a full picture. The whole project also paled into insignificance with the shooting. He felt sorry that he had been off with Anna but he guessed that everyone in the office was in shock and needed time to think straight.

Given the early closing of her office Anna managed to visit several shops and pick up some interesting treats to take to the Home. She still had not yet had the opportunity to see her father to ask about his time in the Eastern Bloc and whether there was a link with Sasha. She had been able to talk her mother into coming to St Petersburg with her father for a visit and was waiting to see if it would be during the holidays in May or whether she would have to wait until June and the 'White Nights' – her favourite time of year in the city when they would have almost twenty-four hours a day of light. She was impatient and had thought of making a surprise trip to Moscow but then decided that it would make her questions potentially into a major issue plus she would have to spend two nights in quick succession on the overnight train which was doable but really tiring. She made good time to the Home and was soon seated in Valentina Alexandrovna's small office and drinking tea. Anna had spent the first ten minutes telling Valentina Alexandrovna everything she knew about the shooting. Valentina Alexandrovna had crossed herself on several occasions and become visibly emotional. Although daily life in St Petersburg saw its normal share of violent crimes, shootings like this were very rare.

"My, my," sighed Valentina Alexandrovna, "life can be hard enough here without such attacks. How are you coping, Anna?"

"I think the whole office is in shock. I can't concentrate. We have a meeting in the morning with the senior partner coming from Moscow and then I'll know more."

"Well, it is times like these when it may be best to just carry on with everyday life," said Valentina Alexandrovna wistfully. Anna just nodded. The shock of this attack, although very real, was nothing compared to the anguish she imagined Valentina Alexandrovna had to face every day when she looked at all those sad little faces.

"Have you any news yet, Anna?"

"No, I am waiting to talk to my father in person. It is delicate."

"I understand," replied Valentina Alexandrovna. "On my side, though, I may have hit a little snag."

"Oh?" replied Anna, her eyes widening.

"Yes. My brother's friend has received a warning."

"Warning!" gasped Anna. "A threat?"

"No, Anna – not that type of warning. I should have thought in the circumstances. Wrong word to use." She stopped and smiled at Anna and lent forward across her desk. "No, he was told by his boss in the Mayor's office that he should not access the database he went into."

"I see," said Anna. "For security reasons, I suppose."

"He's not sure. Anyway he is not the type to take kindly to being told what not to do and he had another look in the database."

"Was that not a bit risky?"

"No, he said he was very careful. And do you know what he then found?"

Once again Anna's heartbeat was racing. "I've no idea.."

"Nothing!" said Valentina Alexandrovna. "Nothing – I mean the name and the references to it had been deleted."

"Really?" Anna once again was confused.

"He came out of the database straight away and then made some very discrete enquiries."

Anna was looking at Valentina Alexandrovna, her mouth open.

"A clean-up of a number of databases had been made. No reasons were given. But, here again, is a very strange thing." Valentina Alexandrovna looked at Anna and became concerned at Anna's visible distress. "This order came straight after a meeting between the Mayor and Metropolitan Melnikov."

"The Church!" exclaimed Anna. "Why would the Church?"

"Anna, we have no idea. Is it a coincidence or is it a conspiracy?"

After further heated debate, they could not decide – for now though it looked like for one reason or another, that their searching might be being blocked. But why would anybody not want Sasha found?

Twenty Six

THE St Petersburg Times not surprisingly followed the CNN line and its front cover ran the headline: 'It was inevitable - attacks now on foreigners.' The article added little to what had been reported on CNN but its reporter, Mike Leigh, had been resourceful enough to access the private clinic where Hampton was being looked after. Hampton had agreed to a brief interview only on the basis that any quotes were to be vetted by his office. The newspaper had agreed not to mess with a law firm such as Miller Lombard. Hampton himself was now fully able to talk. A bullet had missed his heart by less than an inch but had punctured a lung. So far it had been decided that it was too risky to fly him out of St Petersburg to Helsinki and the Canadian run private clinic in St Petersburg was doing a very good job in such an emergency.

After various background questions Leigh asked what had been in Hampton's briefcase. "Nothing of any importance," replied Hampton.

"Then if it was not a robbery, why did they want to kill you, or at least perhaps warn you away from something?"

"I think an inch from the heart was hardly meant as a warning shot," replied Hampton with a smile.

"I guess you have been told by the police that the attackers were English speaking," continued Leigh digging.

"I'd go further and say that I'm sure that they were British," said Hampton slowly.

"How can you say that?" asked Leigh.

"I can recognise a Brit when I see one. It showed in his eyes. I've been on military assignments with NATO and British soldiers in my former profession."

"Did you hear him speak when he went back to the car?"

"By that stage I was unconscious, I guess, but as the shot hit me I thought it weird to be shot at by a Brit in St Petersburg. It was only when the press reported that they had shouted in English that it came back to me."

"And there's more than that to it as well," continued Leigh delighted at the direction of the conversation.

"How do you know?"

"One of the passers-by, a veteran soldier, swears that the guy who got away slit the throat of his driver who was injured as their car smashed into the wall. Said that he had not seen such an atrocity since the dark days of the Second World War. It was quite a conversation I had with him as he was being taken to the police station. Now they say he's resting in a home for the elderly and the police say he's no longer in a fit state for further questioning as a witness. I did not get the conversation on tape."

Hampton had been listening with great attention. "A veteran you say of the war or of the Siege?"

"Does it make any difference?"

"It might do. How well do you know your history of St Petersburg at that time?"

"Attacked as part of Hitler's attack on the Eastern front. 'Barbarossa', I think, the operation was called."

Hampton nodded. "Go on," he said.

"Stalin thought he had a deal with Hitler but it all fell apart when Hitler decided to fight everyone at the same time on two fronts. A classical error according to military experts. St Petersburg was then saved in the end by Hitler turning all his efforts to Moscow and overstretching his forces once more. Plus he lost narrowly at Stalingrad."

"Here he had the city sown up and was strangling it slowly to death," said Hampton.

"Hitler had some form of mad fixation to destroy every part of the city because of it being the cradle of the Revolution and the birth place of Communism," added Leigh.

"That also cost him dearly," interrupted Hampton. "He could have sued for surrender much earlier but wanted to bleed the city to death. And of course, the Soviet Union becoming a de facto part of the Allied Forces stopped the British launching a planned attack on Stalin which Churchill would have started by invading Finland. Would have been weird if it had been the Brits reaching St Petersburg. Churchill too wanted to wipe out the Communist threat."

"So where is this leading us?" Leigh was becoming more curious.

"I just thought that a revaluation of history now that we have so much more information potentially available in the new Russia might challenge the conventional wisdom on both sides," he emphasised 'both' heavily, "and it might make a good subject for a special report."

"I think my editor would rather I find out why you were shot," replied Leigh feeling that Hampton was just trying to put him off track. "The present is newsworthy enough!"

"Yes," said Hampton with feeling, "and I would dearly like to know who it was, too".

"As a lawyer you must be treading on plenty of people's toes here."

"Look, I can't answer that. I am bound by all sorts of client privileges."

"But there must be some who you should be able to identify as possible enemies."

"I'm starting to feel a bit tried now," said Hampton warmly. "Listen I promise that when we have some news you will be the first to know. Adam, take down all his contact numbers, can you?" He said as Adam entered the room. Adam shook hands with Leigh and they exchanged cards. The reporter left. Adam talked about how the office was shaping up without him and his contact with Ellen. Hampton wanted to discuss the office's workload but Adam told him that it was out of his hands now and that he was under the strictest instructions precisely not to talk about work with him. Adam asked what the reporter had asked and Hampton gave him a brief summary and they returned to discussing the attack.

"So what did they take from you, John?" asked Adam.

"Memos on the new Hermitage committee, newspapers."

"That's all?"

"Well, what else would I take to a non-client lunch?"

"Agreed, so what do they think you had?"

"No idea. My only meeting later that day was with Leonid Marlenovich who had called and asked me to come over to his office in the afternoon. This was to be separate from the meeting you and Anna were going to with the company to go through the draft information we are preparing. Something to do with a delicate issue that had come up. And in any case the office has the files relating to the company."

"So that doesn't make sense." Adam was feeling better that it seemed to have nothing to do with the Peter the Great Shipyard.

"Vera checked with the receptionist. There had been no strange calls while we were at lunch and there was nothing particularly confidential in my diary."

"Mistaken identity, then? Out to rob some Swedish businessman or something?" Adam ventured cheerily.

"That is unlikely. You know that they were Brits?"

"We heard that they had shouted something in English, but were they definitely Brits?"

"I am pretty sure," replied Hampton. "Have you noticed anything strange at all, Adam?"

"Me! Do you think that I would notice anything out of the ordinary?" said Adam.

"Not really," smiled Hampton.

"What are the police doing?" asked Adam.

"I have not had the pleasure of a formal visit yet. But that should be soon."

"Well I'd better leave you these," said Adam handing over a large box of chocolates with a picture of the Fortress of St Peter and St Paul on the front, "a selection of chocolates to commemorate the lifting of the Siege, no less."

"Siege?" said Hampton.

"The Russians in the office thought it apt given your survival from a foreign attack!"

"How thoughtful," replied Hampton with a touch of irony in his voice, "but unfortunately the doctors have banned all chocolates and sweets!"

"I'd better leave them, in any case," replied Adam. "A message has come inviting you to the first meeting of the Art Committee at the Hermitage next week," he said after putting the chocolates on a cupboard at the side of the bed. "Shall I ask Vera to see if they can rearrange it for a later date?"

Hampton thought for a moment. "You know, Adam, it has taken months to get these people together. It should really go ahead. If I brief you on the key points, can you deputise for me? This is work after all. Our contribution to the city."

Adam looked genuinely shocked. He would never have thought that his boss would want him to do something as important as this and his knowledge of art was pretty much zero.

"There are just a couple of points I want to get agreed at the outset. I will brief you fully. Vera is going to be the committee secretary so you won't be on your own."

It was a big step for Adam as he guessed the rest of the committee would be some of the most important and influential people in the city.

"Ok," he said, "but you'll need to tell me everything."

"Of course, I will," replied Hampton making a mental note to tell Adam as little as possible. "And there is just one other thing," he said, "I promised Alex that he and I would visit some of the paintings afterwards. Apparently there are a few new ones going to be on display."

"No problem," replied Adam mentally adding up all the brownie points he would be collecting. He was beginning to think like a Russian – he was adding up all the favours he would be owed.

"Oh, and Adam," started Hampton again, "there is one final, final thing."

"Not the office's work load?" questioned Adam with a smile.

"Not quite, but you know Dominic Corley already."

Adam nodded.

"You need to arrange for him to meet the Peter the Great Shipyard company as soon as possible. Take Vera to interpret for you both."

"Sure," replied Adam with a slight shrug of his shoulders and a smile. He knew his boss would revert to work as soon as he had the chance. It would take much more than a bullet to stop him. Most other people would have left Russia for good after such an attack. His boss was driven and nothing like any of the other foreigners Adam had come across in Russia. His boss was a 'man on a mission' and Adam had to admit that his boss' enthusiasm was infectious and that he needed to toughen and smarten himself up if he was going to keep up with him.

Twenty Seven

ADAM looked at the list of invitees to the inaugural meeting of the 'Committee for the Restitution of Works of Art belonging to the Hermitage of St Petersburg'. It was impressive containing the Deputy Mayor, the General Directors of the Hermitage and of the Summer Palaces, a Deputy Minister from the Russian Ministry of Culture in Moscow and several others from departments and Russian organisations which Adam did not recognise. Vera could not add much and just said that they were the types of bureaucrats you could never escape from. She said the real power lay with the Deputy Mayor and the Deputy Minister. Adam had been briefed to concentrate on two points namely to confirm that the Committee would include the works of art relating to the Summer Palaces and not just the Hermitage and to propose that non-foreign organisations be allowed to fund projects set up by the Committee. Adam had left Alex in the car with a book to read and said he would be back as soon as possible to take him to visit the new displays.

    Vera interpreted for Adam as he went round to shake the hands of the committee members who were sat around a marvellous long and wide marble table in the Hermitage's Leonardo Da Vinci room. The light shone brightly through the palatial windows. The committee members all greeted Adam warmly several asking about Hampton's condition and others thanking him for acting as a deputy committee member. Two members spoke excellent English and the others used Vera. Adam was offered tea and the meeting was opened by the Deputy Mayor with a lengthy speech. Vera summarised key points for Adam rather than translating word for word. She did the same for the Deputy Minister who seemed to time his speech to be a few seconds shorter than the Deputy Mayor. Each of the others then contributed a few sentences each only. The Deputy Mayor then turned to the agenda. The first items were procedural matters. They then turned to the actions the Committee would be taking and it was agreed that the General Directors of the Hermitage and the other palaces would meet separately to draw up a detailed plan for making an all-encompassing inventory list of every work of art that was and should be in the possession of the museums. The plan would be discussed and approved at the next meeting when the next steps in terms of validating the list would also be addressed. Thereafter specific actions for each work of art deemed missing would be put in motion. Adam was asked if he had anything to add and he requested official confirmation of the inclusion of all the other palaces which it seemed from the discussion so far was the case. This was confirmed officially by the Deputy Mayor. The General Director of the Catherine Palace then raised his hand and asked to speak.

"You raise a very important point, Mr Carter," said the General Director in very good English, "and I know that it is something Mr Hampton is very enthusiastic about."

Adam nodded. His biggest fear about the meeting was being asked to discuss the points in any detail.

"Yes," continued the General Director. "We at the Catherine Palace suffered some of the greatest losses of art during the Great Patriotic War and we have lots of projects. The Amber Room is, how do you say, 'top of the list'?"

"Correct," replied Adam grateful for being able to make a reply.

The Deputy Mayor moved the meeting on and they quickly came to the last point on the agenda. Funding. Adam listened as all the members duly complained about their own lack of funding and proposed a long list of names that they wanted to be approached to provide funding. The Deputy Mayor listened politely but only wrote down a couple of the names suggested. He indicated that there were two people in the city whom he thought that either he or the Mayor himself would be able to encourage to contribute. The implication was not lost on any of the other members and there were no questions. The Deputy Mayor turned to Adam and asked if he or Mr Hampton had any thoughts.

"Mr Hampton did ask me to clear with the Committee that contributions can be made by non-Russian donors or sponsors. Will these be permitted?"

"Of course," replied the Deputy Mayor speaking in English for the first time. "And who do you have in mind?"

At that moment Adam wanted the Hermitage to sink right into the River Neva and take him with it! One of the most powerful men in the city was asking him a question and he was not prepared. This would look terrible for him, Hampton and the firm if he could not come up with a credible answer. He did not matter but the firm did. He thought of what the General Director of the Catherine Palace had been saying about a famous room. He knew that it was widely believed that it had been destroyed by German troops. An idea hit him. He felt inspired.

"Well," he said slowly as he was turning the idea into a sensible suggestion, "John, I mean Mr Hampton, is hoping that you will allow him to approach several foreign companies with whom he has had a very preliminary and strictly confidential chat." Adam stopped as several of the members and the Deputy Mayor nodded. They seemed to be buying the notion of confidentiality and hopefully they would not press him. "And he is thinking in particular of approaching several large German companies through the German consulate here for whom we do legal work about," he stopped to allow Vera to translate and to let his idea crystallise, "about financing the rebuilding of the Amber Room. After all it is widely believed that it was German soldiers who were responsible for it being destroyed by fire under their guard." He had slowed down during the last few worlds and he watched as Vera finished the translation and the idea sank into the committee members. There was a silence. Adam looked to the window. Forget the Hermitage sinking, perhaps he should jump straight out of the window now! And then a clap followed by several more.

"Bravo, Mr Carter," said the General Director of the Catherine Palace. "What a splendid idea. To right one of the cruellest wrongs of history and in such a memorable way. Bravo. Please write this in the minutes."

The meeting ended on a high note with Adam being congratulated by each member as the meeting broke up. Vera smiled at him too. He had surprised everyone and no-one more than himself.

Alex could not wait to tear around the Hermitage to where they had been told some new works were being exhibited. Vera had asked Adam if she could leave and Adam had agreed. She said she would do the minutes of the meeting in both Russian and English. Adam had a job to catch up to Alex. He came into the Pavilion Hall and saw Alex in front of a glass case in the middle of the room. In the case a stained glass window was suspended from the ceiling with steel wires. It was a large window split in four sections with different coloured glass in each section. Around the window and on the cross bars were lots of brightly coloured stones.

"Quite an expensive looking window, Alex," said Adam standing next to Alex in front of the case.

"It is from the Saint Sophia Cathedral in Kiev," replied Alex, "and I found it."

"Really?" asked Adam puzzled. Although Alex was still a relatively young boy, Adam did not think he would still be making up fantasies.

"Yes. It was all wrapped up in a store room. No labels on it or anything. I was the one who discovered it. If it was not for me the Russians would not have opened it and would not have found what was inside. Could have been lost for years in the store room. There are hundreds of things in there."

Alex's story was sounding a little more realistic.

"Any others?" asked Adam. "We'll have to put you on your dad's committee at this rate."

"Has the committee started work yet?" asked Alex.

"Not yet but we have agreed some of the things it will do," replied Alex still flushed with the success of his quick thinking. "And I think they are going to rebuild some famous room out of amber. That was my idea at any rate," he said feeling pleased with himself still.

"The Amber Room?" asked Alex slowly.

"That's it."

"There's no need to rebuild it," said Alex.

Adam looked at him with a frown. "Why not?" he asked.

"There's no need because it is still here in Russia," replied Alex moving on to the next new exhibit.

"A likely tale," said Adam. "I met the guy in charge of the palace it was in."

Alex wasn't listening to Adam anymore. He had become engrossed in the next exhibit which was a huge Impressionist painting. Alex was developing a real interest in the style of the Impressionists and he often made his own drawings in their style. His dad had been really impressed with his last attempts. Adam decided to follow Alex and preserve his feeling of success by leaving their conversation where it was. He was still proud of his idea and was sure Hampton would be impressed as soon as he heard. Alex was just a young boy and what did he know!

Ellen rushed to the front door as soon as she heard the sound of a car. Their compound was quiet as always although with spring accelerating quickly after the thaw there were plenty of birds singing. Adam had gotten out of the Volvo with Alex.

"Thanks for bringing Alex back with you Adam. I know it is out of your way. Will a quick beer make up for it? And you can tell me about the committee. Vera called me to let John know that it went very well." She smiled broadly at Adam who smiled back.

"It was a bit daunting," replied Adam, "but I think we got what John wanted. How is he, by the way?" They went inside and after downing a glass of water Alex ran upstairs. Ellen took out two beers and gave one to Adam. Adam recounted the committee proceedings and told of his quick thinking in a very modest way.

Meanwhile Alex upstairs had taken out the piece of stone from its cloth bag. As he held it up to the light its amber glow intensified and Alex's hands tingled and felt warmer and warmer. He stood up and lifted the piece up above his head and placed it near to the window. The light from outside streamed through the rock and the glow became deeper and deeper. Alex closed his eyes and then there it was again – the room! The whole room was glowing around him. He felt himself turning and then all of a sudden his hands felt a burning pain and he dropped the piece with a loud bang.

"What was that?" shouted Ellen. "Alex!" She gave Adam her beer bottle without thinking and ran across the kitchen and up the stairs. The heat in Alex's hands had disappeared as quickly as it had come. He pushed the piece under his bed with his foot and placed the cloth bag over it. As his mum entered the room he picked up his bedside lamp. "Alex, what happened?" said his mum slowing down and seeing that Alex looked as normal.

"I knocked my lamp over," he replied looking embarrassed.

"Come here," said his mum cuddling him tight to her. "I guess I am just edgy after what happened to your dad. I think we are going to leave this place."

"No, mom," objected Alex, freeing himself from his mum's embrace. "We must stay. I know we must stay."

Ellen put her arms on his shoulders and looked at him intently. He was emotional. She really did not know what to do.

"I'll talk to your dad."

"And tell him we are staying," insisted Alex.

"I'll talk to him. One of the senior people from dad's law firm is coming here from London soon and we are going to talk about it. We are just waiting for dad to be in a good condition to talk and to have had time to think."

"Ok, mom," said Alex pushing himself against her and she put her arms around him. "But I know we will be staying."

Ellen squeezed him. She knew he was right most of the time but this time she was not sure. He was after all just a young boy and what did he really know.

Twenty Eight

ONLY very, very occasionally did the frustrations boil over. The hundred or so children were reduced to a state of silent compliance with the Home's rules for almost all of the time. Just occasionally, very occasionally did things get out of hand. Maybe it was the warmer weather and a desire to spend more time outside. On this occasion two rooms of young boys had not gone to their rooms after lunch and instead they had ran out of the canteen and headed for the entrance to the Home. Seeing the old woman at the door they decided to find another route out and one of them signalled to the others to follow him down a set of stairs. The stairs led down to the basements were none of the children had ever ventured before. The boys pushed a door and then forced their way in.

At that moment Sasha looked up from his watery ice cream with a start. He thought he had heard a bang. He closed his eyes and as if in a dream he watched as two boys came hurtling out of a building. They did not look as they ran into a street and were hit by a bus. He dropped his spoon and got up. He dashed out of the room which served as the canteen.

The boys in the basement were surrounded by cardboard boxes which they eagerly opened and looked into. Most of them had never seen such televisions, microwaves and other goods. "Don't take anything!" yelled one of the boys.

"Let's find a way out of here." He looked around a saw a door across the room. "This way!" he yelled again.

Sasha had reached the entrance to the Home and opened the door. The old woman watched as Sasha stepped outside and she walked to the door. Outside Sasha looked frantically down the street. To the right about five hundred metres away he saw a large blue and white single decker bus. It had stopped but Sasha looked on in horror as it started up again. There were no signs of any boys. He looked again and recognised the front wheels of the large black car which had taken him to the cathedral. It was parked in a road on the right side of the Home. He ran down the steps at the entrance towards the black car.

The boys were still in the basement and they were having an argument about whether they should take some of the boxes. They would be able to sell the goods they thought. The boy who had been leading them was adamant that they would not take anything. They were 'orphans not thieves', he shouted. "Let's just get out of here and find somewhere to stay. If we steal anything we'll be put in a worse place than here." The boys very reluctantly agreed as they ran out of the door and started to career up the road at the left side of the Home.

Sasha had reached the corner of the building and he could see into the large black car. The same driver as before complete with black sunglasses was sitting in the driver's seat. Sasha waved madly at him and then ran back to the entrance of the building. Rather than get out of the car the driver started the engine and moved the car forward. It turned into the main road and drove towards the entrance. In doing so it caused the bus to indicate and pull out into the middle of the road to drive round the car. At the same moment two of the boys came dashing out of the side road and managed to stop themselves in front of the black car by grabbing hold of the car's bonnet. The bus drove past them and its driver motioned visibly angrily to the two boys. The old woman was now at the top of the steps behind Sasha. She crossed herself and muttered, "thank God for the black car coming at that moment. If it had not come the boys would have run into the road and would have been knocked down by the bus." The driver had got out of the car and took hold of the two boys by the scruff of their necks. They complained at his heavy handiness but he replied that a small beating would be a small price to pay for them still being alive and for going into the basement which he assumed they had come out of. The boys nodded meekly.

As he passed the old woman she stopped him and blessed him. The driver for once took off his sunglasses. He then pushed the two boys in through the entrance and turned to Sasha. He had not known what had made him react the way he did to Sasha's waving at him but he had felt as though he was being given an order. He shook his head as he imagined what would have happened if the boys had gone under the bus. Sasha nodded to him as if to acknowledge that he had the same thought. "And, you, Sasha," he said gruffly, "you'd better come back in and don't tell Yelena Matrovna or Roman Felixovich about any of this." He did not know if he was more afraid of his boss finding out about the boys breaking into the basement or of this young orphan who seemed to be able to read his mind.

Twenty Nine

INSPECTOR Bushkin was sitting in small dark room opposite his boss, the Chief of Police of St Petersburg.

"Where are the FSB?" growled the Chief, a heavily set man with a bushy moustache and an ill-fitting uniform

"Should be here any minute," replied Bushkin who was marginally better dressed than his superior and physically in very good shape. A disjointed nose, the result of a violent encounter in his youth, marred what would have been a classically Slavonic face.

"I want to leave this to them," continued the Chief.

Bushkin gave him a questioning look. "They were foreigners," he said, "and shooting a foreigner. But it was on our patch. And it has nothing to do with anything we are doing."

"You said that about the bomb opposite the Grand Hotel. You still have not found anything," said the Chief asserting himself.

"It was the wrong street either by mistake or it was a warning. If they had not blown one of themselves up and the other had not panicked we would know by now. But everyone is sure that it was either a mistake or a warning. Nothing more sinister." Bushkin spoke authoritatively.

"How can you be so sure?"

"I know all the rackets in that area. It is a very friendly area. Everyone thinks the same."

"How do you know that?" The Chief had always preferred not to get to closely involved.

"There would have been reprisals by now. Big time. But all there is a truce and soon no-one will even remember that it happened."

"Ok, ok, but I still want to hand the shooting of this American lawyer to the FSB. Let them take the heat and answer the press' questions. Let's keep out of it."

"If we don't join it we will not know what they will find." Bushkin could feel his teeth gritting.

"But what will they find? They don't know the area. Let them go chasing off into Finland or even London. Work with Interpol for all I care. This is not a local matter." The Chief had stood up and pulled up his belt.

"I think it has a reason here," continued Bushkin firmly. "What kind of reason I don't know yet but I'm sure that there is."

The Chief sat down again knowing that he would have to compromise with his powerful deputy, if only to get some peace and be able to get out and enjoy the first days of spring. "Look talk to the street. Do what you want but officially this is for the FSB. Let them have the veteran soldier who witnessed it as well."

"He has not got anything more to say," said Bushkin without emotion.

"Don't tell me," sighed the Chief.

Thirty

IN St Petersburg the Mariinsky Theatre is second only to the Hermitage in the style and stature of its building. It is home to the Mariinsky or Kirov Ballet as its troupe of ballet dancers is better known around the world. The Kirov Ballet has been the producer of so many famous ballet dancers as well as so many acclaimed ballets. The Managing Partner of Miller Lombard from London had timed his visit to see Hampton in St Petersburg impeccably. Swan Lake was on at the Mariinsky Theatre on the evening of his visit and the St Petersburg office had impressed him by securing tickets. They did not tell him but it was very easy as Vera's sister worked at the theatre and produced three seats in one of the best boxes right at the side of the stage without any problems. Also they only had to pay the official rouble price which converted into a couple of dollars only. Outside the theatre black market tickets such as these could easily cost a hundred dollars each.

Miller Lombard's Managing Partner had touches of grey hair and he wore a dark suit. He had visited Hampton as soon as he had flown into the city and he was due to see him again the following morning before flying back to London. He was also keen to assess the state of Ellen and their son Alex and so the trip to the theatre was an excellent opportunity to have a quiet chat. He had lined up another partner in the firm who was currently in Dubai to replace Hampton in St Petersburg.

"What a fantastic place this is, Ellen," he said as they took their seats. There were six chairs in the box, three in front and three behind. Alex had taken a front chair at the end nearest the stage and Ellen and the Managing Partner sat down behind. The box was virtually on the stage. A young woman had sat next to Alex who was gleefully using the small binoculars that they had hired to look at everything in the theatre. "Your husband is certainly a brave man," he continued, "and from what I can see this is a challenging country."

"It certainly is," replied Ellen with a small laugh, "but John loves being a pioneer. Alex likes it here also." Alex turned round and nodded vigorously.

"Well, you are probably the bravest family in the whole firm," he smiled and patted Alex gently on the back.

"I guess here you just have to get on with it and put up with everything that comes at you."

"But surly a bullet is a step too far?" he said lowering his voice.

Ellen looked at Alex who was now leaning over the wall of the box. "Alex, she said tugging his sweatshirt. "You'll be on the stage if you keep leaning over." She did not know if anyone had told him about the bullet in her car. Alex turned around and shook his head as if to say that the Managing Partner had not been told. He sat back on his chair and Ellen continued, "of course, it is. I just wish they could find out why and then we would know if anything just like this could happen again."

"True," he replied, "we are putting all the pressure we can on the British and American embassies to get some sense from the Russian police. The good news, though, is that the investigation has been passed to the FSB so we might find out something. I'm told the local police are out of their depth."

"That is good news," replied Ellen as the orchestra pit right in front of them filled with musicians and the audience started to clap them in. The young woman had tears in her eyes and she had taken a tissue from her bag. Ellen tapped her on the shoulder and asked if she was alright. "My brother in the lead dancer," she said proudly through her tears, "and I have waited six months for a chance to see him."

Ellen patted her shoulders. "That's fantastic," she said.

"Thank you," replied the young woman as the orchestra warmed up and the squeaking violins fought with the deep brass instruments to see how much noise they could both make. Alex was enthralled and trained his small binoculars on musician after musician.

"Well, you and John can take as much time as you need to decide."

"Thank you," replied Ellen a small tear starting in her eye. She was grateful for the conductor arriving and instantly guiding the orchestra to start the mesmerising and iconic sound of Swan Lake. Slowly the deep velvet curtain opened and one beam of light lit up a small shape curled up on the ground in the middle of the stage. The music ever so slowly and ever so gently started to increase in volume and speed. The dark stage looked to be a lake and the whole audience immediately entered the magical scene of one of the world's most famous productions. The first half of the ballet passed in no time.

The second half of the ballet was more dramatic than the first, the music seemed louder and the dancing more energetic. Both the young woman and Ellen cried on several occasions. Alex watched the dancing in awe. As the final act was nearing its conclusion the male lead dancer leapt across the stage, landed and then shot bolt upright to pirouette round and round. The audience exploded in applause. Alex closed his eyes and watched the dancer whirl round and round into a blur in his mind. He opened his eyes as the dancer flopped onto the ground with a majestic sweep of his arms. Alex started to hum and sing very quietly. When the ballet climaxed several minutes later as the characters of Odette and Siegfried ascended into the sky the evil spell over them broken, the whole audience was on its feet. The clapping lasted a full five minutes with three bouts of 'Hoorahs' coming from the audience. The young woman's face was streaming with tears and Alex fell off his chair as the lead dancer leapt across the stage to their box to hug his sister. The Managing Director showed his sense of the occasion by shaking the dancer's hand firmly as the young woman turned round and hugged Ellen - it was if she wanted to pass her brother's hug on around the world! She then hugged Alex as he got to his feet and the Managing Director patted Ellen gently on the shoulder.

"Wow! What emotion!" said Ellen drying her eyes.

"I can see that there is a magic about this place every now and then," replied the Managing Director with a slight cough to disguise his own emotion.

"And that's why we will decide to stay," piped up Alex with a huge smile. He then started to hum and sing louder this time.

"Did you learn a new song at school today, Alex?" asked Ellen.

"No," replied Alex, "it just came to me in my head when I was watching the dancing."

"Is it a Russian chant, Alex?" asked the Managing Director to whom Ellen looked at in clear surprise. "I'm in a male voice choir back in London, Ellen. It's about the only hobby I have time for."

"Don't know," replied Alex, "it just comes round and round like the dancer did."

"It is like an old chant," said the young woman, "one they used to dance to in the old days. It was actually banned for many years because it was classified as being from a religious sect."

"Well, Alex," said the Managing Director, "I can see you are fitting well into Russia, almost like home."

"It is home," he replied with a smile. "Isn't it, mom?"

Ellen did not answer him but exchanged goodbyes with the young woman. If Alex could read her mind now, she did not need to reply, she thought as they started to make their way out of the box. It looked increasingly likely that they were going to stay.

Thirty One

IN the basement room thick smoke hung heavily in the air mingling with the scent of expensive perfumes. Two dark-skinned men wearing loose fitting brightly coloured clothes were being entertained by four young women with French champagne, black caviar and vodka. Leonid Marlenovich walked in with a concentrated look on his face and switched on the air conditioning.

"Hombre! How are you, my brother?" said one of the men as he jumped up and hugged Leonid Marlenovich warmly. The look on Leonid Marlenovich's face seemed to lighten up a touch.

One of girls looked inquisitively at them, 'brother?'

"What? We don't look alike?" said the man his accent becoming more obviously Caribbean.

"Blood brothers, Winston and I," said Leonid Marlenovich.

"And bosom pals. We go back a long way. Lenny, this is my cousin, Jean," he said introducing the second man.

"A long way," smiled Leonid Marlenovich embracing the second man.

The young women had left.

"Nice pad you now have here, Lenny," said Winston.

"Thank you," replied Leonid Marlenovich, "it serves its purpose."

"And a great location," added Jean.

"Yes, being on the river and inside the shipyard means it is secure and out of sight."

"What was it before?" asked Winston.

Leonid Marlenovich paused for a moment and looked at Winston. The way he had reconstructed the long abandoned iron and coal store beneath the disused Old Foundry was his business and known to very, very few people. He had had the various different parts of the work done by different people so that no-one would know how he was using it other than a handful of people in his 'special projects' team. He decided though to answer the question to a degree. "It was part of the original shipyard founded by Peter the Great himself and it used to store materials for a foundry above. After our offices and showroom were rebuilt after the war and our yards, workshops and docks redeveloped the building above was left to preserve its historical value as a survivor of the Siege. It was just used to store bits and pieces and this basement was closed up."

"You can still feel a lot of history in the walls," commented Winston taking a long drag on a large cigarette and studying the décor of the room. For the most part it was very modern but the areas around the doors and the ceiling showed signs of much older decoration and several old brown bricks could still be made out above the windows here and there at what was the ground level of the building. After a short pause Winston sat up. "But much more importantly," he said fixing Leonid Marlenovich with a glazed stare, "how is the boat building business these days?" he asked.

"Steady as ever. Despite the changes, people still go on buying boats. More pleasure boats than shipping boats at the moment. Lots of smaller sizes." Leonid Marlenovich had poured himself a large drink of vodka. The others were enjoying the champagne.

"Have you seen our latest product, Leonid? We put a sample in the last shipment," said Jean looking at Leonid Marlenovich with a broad smile.

"You did what?" said Leonid Marlenovich startled.

"He, he!" boomed Winston, "don't worry! We marked the bag and put your name on it. Did you not get it yet? It was delivered to your office. Did your secretary not see it and open it?"

"You better not be serious," said Leonid Marlenovich realising he was being set up.

"Serious? Man, we are always serious in Cuba." Winston's eyes were watering from the laughter.

"Good joke," said Leonid Marlenovich who gave a short half smile.

"Don't worry. We don't take any risks. We were just thinking of all the practical matters of how to get the product through to you." He leaned forward and looked intently at Leonid Marlenovich, "but there are two big questions facing our joint operation right now and we need to be sure that between us we can handle them both."

"What are they?"

"The routes and the man," Winston said empathetically.

"What about the routes?" Leonid Marlenovich was sounding a touch irritated.

"You had such a reputation in the good old days of the Soviet Union for sending cargoes all around the world. Your official importer and exporter status meant that no-one ever bothered you. Now it is the protection and security of the routes all the way along that has to be in place. There is so much thieving going on you would not believe it! And Russian customs are real small time now."

"We have the routes under control here. We've owned them for a very long time," said Leonid Marlenovich.

"Look, it's not Russia that anyone is worried about. It's getting the products to some of the places in the Baltics which are no longer under the control you had during the Soviet Union."

"So what is the problem?"

"There are rumours that a group out of London is looking to step up its own activities in our area."

"Rumours from where?"

"Good sources. One of your boat carriers was shadowed from Riga to Amsterdam by a merchant ship and a trawler. It was very obvious, apparently."

"We'll need more than that."

"Look, Leonid. We all know that the goods are well protected on our boats into here and that you can send them on with the boats you sell as export. But it is the security on the boats in countries neither of us control which might be at risk."

Leonid Marlenovich nodded but did not speak.

"The problem is," Winston continued slowly, "that these rumours are making our suppliers in some of the South American places nervous. Some are starting to talk about alternative sources and transport."

Leonid Marlenovich still did not speak.

"Now you understand our mutual dilemma. Should we consider doing parts of the routes over land instead of by sea?"

"Of course not!" Leonid Marlenovich flared up, "the costs are prohibitive and the goods are much, much easier to steal on land."

"So what do we do about the concerns over our routes?"

"We have to find out about the competition. And put the minds of our contacts at rest, of course," said Leonid Marlenovich firmly closing the first part of the discussion. "And the 'man'?"

"Hey, that is easier," said Winston, "You know that our bosses have great respect for Victor Nikolayevich."

"He knows nothing."

"Precisely so he cannot jeopardise anything." Winston's tone was warm. "No knowledge is a very safe thing to have as we like to say in Cuba. Everyone knows Victor Nikolayevich takes a little but he does not have your ambition. Fidel's people love him for the new boat he sends every birthday."

Leonid Marlenovich did not reply. He was thinking intensely about who he could use to find out about the competition.

"Man," continued Winston, "they're the only thing keeping the Russian flag flying in Cuba – all the cars are broken down and there are no spare parts anymore. Listen when can we see the old man?"

"Tomorrow afternoon," replied Leonid Marlenovich finishing his drink. "In the morning he's busy with a legal meeting and there are some people I now need to see."

Thirty Two

ROMAN Felixovich was having a very busy day. He had had a coffee with Leonid Marlenovich in the Old Customs House Restaurant. He had asked the owner to open it for him mid-morning and that had impressed Leonid Marlenovich. Before the meeting he had found out a lot about the Peter the Great Shipyard Company, Leonid Marlenovich and his boss. There was a strong relationship with the police which also extended into the customs office – and hence why he had decided on this restaurant as an appropriate venue. He insisted on the meeting being in private as he would not want to be associated in anyone's eyes with Leonid Marlenovich yet. He knew there was other business taking place alongside the sale of boats at the company but had not found out what it was other than that some 'other goods' were being shipped with the boats that were being sold into Europe. They had talked but spoken little. In truth the key objective for both of them was to take a measure of the other and both left with a lot to think about.

After the meeting he had his driver take him to an old and largely disused workshop along the bank of the River Neva where a full sized wooden sail boat was being worked on by a group of young people. This was the famous replica of Peter the Great's Standart but it was disappointing to look at. He had been given a list of items the builders, many of whom it turned out where volunteers, needed to finish the project. The items were mainly different colours of specialist marine paint. Roman Felixovich was following the advice of his contact in the Property Fund and was trying to find the cheapest way of helping one of the Mayor's projects. A quick look down the list and he was sure that he could acquire the items needed for a fraction of their cost on the open market. Whilst a foreign company, like Samsung, would be spending close to fifty thousand dollars to finance some refurbishment work which he knew was being done in the Mariinsky Theatre, he could acquire the materials for a tenth of that price. He would, however, put a 'price' on the Standart materials that should impress the Mayor.

His next meeting was much more productive. He had his driver drop him on a corner of a nondescript road and he walked several hundred metres to the entrance of a soulless six-storey apartment block. He shunned the lift and took the stairs to the fifth floor. The stairwell was dirty and unpleasant and he was glad he had put on a pair of his outdoor shoes before he had got out of the car. All the doors to the apartments were the same – grey steel and very few had numbers on them. He made his way to the fourth door along and rang the bell. An oldish but attractive blond haired woman opened the door. Roman Felixovich explained who had sent him and the woman let him in.

"Papa," she said in a loud but whispering voice, "you have your visitor."

Roman Felixovich had stepped into the small living room of the apartment. The furniture was old but had a look of substance about it. A very old man shuffled out of what should have been a bedroom and asked Roman Felixovich to follow him. Roman Felixovich took the few steps across to the door of the room and raised his eyebrows. He felt as though he was stepping into a military headquarters. All the walls of the small room were covered by maps with notes and stickers all over them. There was a desk against one wall, two steel filing cabinets and a bookcase full of books. There was no room for a table but there were two chairs. Roman Felixovich whistled softly. "Victor Alexandrovich, I think you have more information in here than there is in the whole of our once mighty Leningrad Oil & Gas Research Institute."

"Well as soon as they told me that I was being retired I had a year to build my own collection of research. Forty years in the oil industry brought a lot of information which the Soviet hierarchy seems to have placed little or no value on." He laughed gently and asked Roman Felixovich to sit on one of the chairs. "How are my colleagues?"

"Pretty much all gone now. Just a few turning up."

"And the research library and maps?"

"Long gone too."

"Into private hands I would guess."

"Yes, I have reacquired some of them and several of your former colleagues are helping me."

"Very good, very good, you seem very industrious just like your grandfather. Annushka, is our tea ready?" he said loudly.

Roman Felixovich looked at Victor Alexandrovich stunned. It had taken him several months to track down the former Head of the Institute and a chain of trusted contacts to finally meet him. He was stunned that this very old man knew more about him than he did about him. "Did you know my grandfather?" he asked feeling and sounding like a schoolboy. If they were playing chess Victor Alexandrovich would have him already in check and they had hardly started.

"I did. Our paths crossed in the rebuilding of the city after the war. He was determined to rebuild your family's fortunes. And now here you are. You have the look of him."

Roman Felixovich rubbed his chin and was silent.

"As soon as your name was mentioned to me," continued Victor Alexandrovich as the woman brought in a tray and put it on the desk. Roman Felixovich nodded in thanks to her. She must be his daughter he assumed, "then I knew you would be looking to seize the opportunities in our new era and then several of my former colleagues did some excellent research for me." He smiled broadly at Roman Felixovich and handed him a folder. "We were renowned for our research, you know, back in the Soviet days."

Roman Felixovich flicked through the folder and then handed it back. It made a KGB file look like a primary school report. Checkmate.

"Now how can I help?" asked the old man with a smile.

Roman Felixovich's head was a whir as he left the apartment block. Victor Alexandrovich probably had more knowledge than anyone about the vast oil and gas reserves under the ground in Russia. What was more he had piles and piles of data on test drills which was the crucial factor in deciding which oil fields were viable. Victor Alexandrovich was committing as much data as he could to sound. Every day he had been spending up to three hours recording the data on to a tape recorder. He feared, he explained, that he had the original and only copy of some of the files and wanted to preserve them. He had no means to make photocopies and would not let anything leave his room. None of his neighbours knew about his 'working' room and he was determined to keep it that way. Victor Alexandrovich had offered to let Roman Felixovich have the tapes once he had finished. He did not want any money for himself, just Roman Felixovich's word that his daughter, who looked after him every day, and her own two daughters would in turn be looked after by him. He would have trusted his family with Roman Felixovich's grandfather and so he assumed Roman Felixovich to be as honourable. They had shook hands without commenting further. Roman Felixovich's first action on his way to the car was to work out how best to safeguard Victor Alexandrovich, his work and his family. He knew the old man would not move and, in truth, if Roman Felixovich could discretely control the apartment building then Victor Alexandrovich was as safe there as anywhere else.

Back in his car he finished a call.

"Boss," said his driver, "you said for me to remind you about the Home. Yelena Matrovna is waiting for you, if you still want to see her."

Roman Felixovich had forgotten about the incident at the Home. His driver had thought better of keeping it from him knowing his boss' absolute obsession with information. His driver had given him an edited version. Roman Felixovich had said he wanted to see Yelena Matrovna. The Home was not far from where they were and the driver headed for the Home after a curt nod from Roman Felixovich who made another call.

"What did your driver explain to you?" asked Yelena Matrovna pointedly. They were in the Director of the Home's office.

"That he drove round thinking that I must have sent for him which is odd because he had dropped me for lunch and I had told him to come back at two o'clock," said Roman Felixovich, "and then he almost knocked two boys down who had been in the basement."

"It was a little more serious than that," replied Yelena Matrovna.

Roman Felixovich looked at her with raised eyebrows. It was becoming a day full of surprises and he thought this one was not going to be positive.

"Don't worry. They did not do any damage to anything in the basement. Everything there is in order," she paused. Irritating Roman Felixovich was a dangerous tack but she felt she had enough to say which would make him listen. "No, if your driver had not pulled out round the corner then the bus coming up the road fast would have knocked the two boys down for sure. Killed them almost certainly."

"So are you telling me, my driver, is some kind of hero? He was very nervous telling me. He is a tough guy and he would have been singing his own praises if he done something heroic."

"Well that's just it. You are right. He wasn't the hero," she paused again anticipating the effect of her next words. "Sasha was," she said quietly and firmly. Roman Felixovich stood up from his chair. "Moments before he had a vision of the boys being knocked over by the bus and he ordered your driver to drive round so that the bus swerved past your car and the boys were saved."

"Who knows about this?" replied Roman Felixovich a sense of purpose rising in his voice.

"Your driver, the old lady who looks after the entrance, Sasha, you and I."

"Not one more word on this, Yelena Matrovna, you understand. Buy the old woman's silence," he took out a roll of dollar bills and put then on the table. "I'll take care of the others."

"Of Sasha?" asked Yelena Matrovna concerned.

"Of course not. You will ask him not to tell anyone about this."

"Very well," said Yelena Matrovna relaxed again, "and he will stay as untouchable as he always is and always will be."

Thirty Three

CORLEY was in the Marriott Tverskaya Hotel in Moscow. It was one of the first Western luxury hotels to set up in Moscow after the fall of Communism along with a Radisson, a Sheraton, a Kimpinski and the lavishly refurbished National Hotel on the edge of Red Square and the Kremlin. The National boasted its Maxim's of Paris restaurant where the first thousand dollar bottle of wine had made it onto a restaurant's wine list in Russia. Corley preferred the Marriott which was a short walk to down to the Kremlin. He felt it was just far enough out of the way and yet had full Western comforts. It was a far cry from the austere and grubby Soviet hotels he had stayed in during the 1980's in Russia. His office in London had told him to watch CNN for a report on St Petersburg and he waited in his room. The report started with the 'news' that there was no news on the shooting of the foreign lawyer but then went on to explain that an historic visit to St Petersburg had been announced. The reporter was standing in front of the large statue of the Bronze Horseman, the monument of Peter the Great, which stares imperiously over the River Neva from its massive stone pedestal. The pedestal was hewn out of a giant granite boulder called the Thunder-Stone which was found on the shore of the Gulf of Finland into which the River Neva flows.

"The city of St Petersburg was entirely surrounded by the German troops when the last rail link was cut at the small town of Mga thirty kilometres south of the city on August 30th 1941. This created the Siege," said the reporter who continued, "or so thought the Germans. The one area which gave a slender hope of breaking the Siege was Lake Ladoga to the north east of the city which in time would become the lifeline of the city during the bitter Siege. This lifeline named by Russians as the 'Ice Road' or 'Road of Life' was the scene of many heroic acts as Russians built and maintained a road on the treacherous ice on which convoys started to move. It is to honour the people who built and who died on this road that the heir to the British throne, His Royal Highness the Prince of Wales, is to visit the city and to retrace the route in a symbolic convoy. But why is this of such interest to the British?"

The reporter turned to a man at his side whose intense demeanour immediately gave him away as a British diplomat. "Well as you know links between the great city of St Petersburg and England go back indeed to the period of Peter the Great himself who spent a lot of time in England during his famous Grand Mission to Europe. We were, of course, Allies during the Second World War and Britain provided much of the cargo that went along the Ice Road to the starving people of the city."

"According to local sources there are also stories of some British troops accompanying the convoy during the Siege. Will the Prince be honouring them?" interrupted the reporter.

"The Prince will be here to honour all who were part of the efforts to defeat the blockade."

"And the British troops?" repeated the reporter.

"I think that there may have been some British volunteers but no serving troops," the diplomat enunciated 'serving' very strongly.

"Official that is," repeated the reporter quickly. "Thank you. Well there you have it. Much interest is starting to be generated by the visit which we will cover for you extensively on CNN. We will be bringing you the full facts and tales relating to the tragic but fascinating Siege of St Petersburg. We understand that his Royal Highness will also be attending the launch ceremony of Peter the Great's replica boat, the Standart, which we will bring you news of in our next bulletin."

Corley muted the TV again and twisted a pen round which he had picked up from his bedside table. He wrote down name of reporter on a piece of paper and put a large question mark after the name. He left his room and went down to the lobby. He took a quiet seat in a corner and ordered a coffee. Five minutes later he was joined by a visitor.

"Donald, interesting times," said Leonid Marlenovich shaking Corley's hand and sitting down in the chair next to him.

"Coffee, Leonid?"

"Please. I understand that your fund is taking an interest in our company."

"Your information is as accurate as always. You always had good sources. And yes, I think that a shareholding in your company could be an excellent investment for our fund."

Corley looked at Leonid Marlenovich with a smile which was returned.

"And," continued Corley, "the lawyers you have appointed are arranging for me to meet with your General Director shortly."

"You too have good sources, Donald," smiled Leonid Marlenovich again.

"A smart move, if I may say so, Leonid. Appointing highly experienced British lawyers to handle such new and complex Russian legislation."

"Thank you, Dominic. You will understand little about our company from meeting our General Director but the lawyers are preparing what we should call some 'appropriate' information. An Information Memorandum they call it."

"I would assume that only you know the real picture?"

"And I will ensure that it stays that way."

"And who will make the decisions on the terms of the privatisation?"

Leonid Marlenovich paused and put down his cup on the table. He then smiled brightly.

"I see," said Corley with a knowing nod of his head. "Do I assume that we keep our relationship out of the discussions between the company and the fund?"

"I think that would be wise, Dominic. No point in confusing matters."

"No. And why raise any questions?"

"Precisely. I could not agree more," replied Leonid Marlenovich. "And while we are being so frank with each other and out of old-fashioned professional courtesy," he continued, "I am sure you will have no problem telling me something?"

"Of course not, Leonid," he smiled, "you just have to ask."

"With Miller Lombard playing a role in all this and no doubt acting in your favour, why would you then have someone like Hampton shot?" asked Leonid Marlenovich.

Corley gave a loud laugh. "I walked right into that one, didn't I? Defence right down! Isn't this one of the more old fashioned interrogation tricks from your KGB?"

"KGB? I thought you would have realised by now that the wonderful and once all-powerful committee for Government security is no more. It was abandoned to the four corners of our once mighty Soviet Union."

"Of course, I am sorry, it's the 'FS' something these days isn't it?"

"FSB. Like the FBI. If you can't beat them join them! That's the new motto. Hampton was attacked by British men you know."

"English speaking I thought which narrows it down to a large part of the world's population at the last count," Corley enjoyed his verbal sparrings with Leonid Marlenovich.

"Come, come you must be better informed than that. Even our local police have proof that they are British."

"How so?"

"The killer who escaped slit the other's throat while he was still alive."

"How dreadful."

"A technique perfected by your British Special Boat Service I believe. Although there is a school of thought that it was actually the German SS who pioneered the technique."

"I'm not an expert any more on the finer techniques of assassination but that again is purely circumstantial evidence."

"Maybe. But, just so that you know, fingers will be pointing at London from Moscow. Might not help your image here. Possibly even affect potential investments in a negative way."

"Well, I trust that this is where our relationship," Corley stressed 'our' heavily, "might just come into its own."

Leonid Marlenovich's smile was the widest it had been during their conversation.

Thirty Four

"YOU have a visitor," announced Leonid Marlenovich's secretary as Inspector Bushkin marched passed her.

"I have been summoned to a special briefing in Moscow but I thought I had better see you first," he said sitting down.

"Honoured I'm sure. But what's it got to do with me?" replied Leonid Marlenovich taking out a large cigar which he rolled underneath his nose.

"What do you know about criminal gangs in London? There are rumours that one of them has started to finance a Russian group?" Bushkin was speaking rapidly. "A group which has its eyes apparently," he continued, "on the same type of goods that we are moving!"

"It's the global economy we have now joined, Vladimir," replied Leonid Marlenovich with a smile, "and money now moves around at the click of a button. Money has no home, no loyalty anymore. And I guess there are lots of people looking at our markets now that the old controls have gone."

Bushkin leant over the desk, "I am serious, Leonid, we need to increase our security especially now that the FSB from Moscow is investigating the attack on Hampton. They'll be all over our city in the next couple of days!"

"Better chance if you sent for the FBI," quipped Leonid Marlenovich.

"I think you should take this seriously, my friend, this could become very serious and damaging to all our interests." Bushkin's face was darkening.

"Let me check things out and get back to you. Don't forget that John Hampton is a – how do we say? - a 'personal' friend of mine. And we can still all rest easy as they never got anything valuable from him in the attack."

"What do you mean?" asked Bushkin

"I mean his wallet was still on him!" Leonid Marlenovich's coyness was infuriating Bushkin.

"His briefcase, I mean," stammered Bushkin.

"I understand that it was pretty much empty with nothing of significance in it. But if you would like some rumours to start to send the FSB off track?"

"Don't complicate matters any more. Hold off. You had better be sure that you're not connected with this and that the FSB don't start looking at you or the boats." Bushkin was regaining his discipline.

Leonid Marlenovich mockingly held his up hands, "Vladimir, relax this is quiet St Petersburg. We are still a backwater. What could possibly be going on here? But be careful in Moscow, though, I hear it is full of bandits."

Bushkin looked at him sternly and stood up. In his day job he was the one in charge – the frustration with moonlighting was the attitudes from others that he had to put up with.

"That's if you believe all you hear," Leonid Marlenovich shouted after him as he left. He put down his cigar and his brow furrowed. So the rumours of another group looking at their operations were spreading and he could no longer ignore them. He would have to start some real investigations of his own. 'More FBI, than FSB!' he laughed to himself. It really felt like different forces were assembling to attack them from all sides. Maybe Victor Nikolayevich in his emotional ramblings was actually right for once! Some bizarre form of siege could well be looming again and they would have to defend themselves in whichever ways they could.

Thirty Five

ROMAN Felixovich had thought long and hard about where to meet his contact from the St Petersburg Property Fund which was carrying out the privatisations of companies in St Petersburg. The Mayor of St Petersburg had the ultimate responsibility for all the privatisations in the St Petersburg region except those ring-fenced by Moscow as being of 'national strategic interest'. Defence companies had obviously been ring-fenced but in many other industries the ring-fence was very blurred at the edges. The major struggle it was now widely believed would be for those companies which control Russia's phenomenal natural resources of oil, gas, metals and minerals. The St Petersburg Property Fund was taking care of the process and details of those companies selected in its region. It was a new official body but comprised bureaucrats from the Mayor's office and the City Council's large sprawling departments which in Soviet times controlled everything in the city and surrounding region. As with many new bodies instigated by Moscow on the advice of a plethora of international advisers from organisations such as the World Bank, the bodies where fluid, their longevity questionable and their competency above all debatable. It often felt as if the great and good of the Western world, having delighted at the fall of Communism, were hell bent on teaching the Russians how to play chess: in a game of chess there is only ever one real winner – the Russian.

The meeting took place in the office of one of Roman Felixovich's business associates. The office was in a nondescript small building at the back of a small factory which made wooden products on the outskirts of the city. Roman Felixovich and his contact had been left alone in the small office and were sitting on two chairs with a low coffee table between them. Roman Felixovich had laid an envelope on his side of the table and his contact had taken an assortment of papers out of an old leather briefcase.

"The privatisation of the Peter the Great Shipyard has been signed off by the Mayor," started the contact. He was relatively well dressed and spoke in an educated way. "I understand that he has a relationship with the General Director."

Roman Felixovich nodded.

"The next step is to decide what form the privatisation of the company should now take."

Roman Felixovich nodded again. His contact then explained that twenty-five per cent of the shares of the company were to be sold in this privatisation process. Forty per cent were expected to be in the hands of the management or some outside shareholders depending on how the on-going exchange of vouchers for shares finished. The balance of thirty-five per cent would be kept by the State to split between relevant governmental bodies or to be put up for sale at a later date.

"What power then does twenty-five per cent of the shares give?" asked Roman Felixovich.

"To have basic control of a company you need over fifty per cent but actually you need over seventy-five per cent to have real and full control."

Roman Felixovich looked at him questioningly.

"What this means is that if you have twenty-five per cent," he continued, "then you can stop a company doing certain actions. You can vote against various important actions."

"So it is a kind of secondary control?"

"Yes, in other countries they call it 'negative' control."

Roman Felixovich laughed slightly. "And I guess though that you can then do deals with other shareholders."

"Exactly."

"This is going to be messy."

"It is. In other countries privatisations have been more logical, more controlled and done over many years. For us it was decided by the World Bank and others that our privatisation should be as quick and as widespread as possible so that there can be no going back."

"There is a lot at stake."

"There is. The problem is," he paused as Roman Felixovich looked at him intently, "the parts we are privatising require cash to buy the shares. And that's why the Mayor is worried about foreigners because it is the foreigners who have all the cash."

Roman Felixovich smiled.

Thirty Six

VICTOR Nikolayevich was in a very jolly mood - the thought of meeting the envoys from Cuba every three months or so was one of the highlights of his work. The spring visit was the time of year when he hoped they would be bringing with them him his annual invitation to spend two weeks in Cuba as the honoured guest of the Cuban Sailing Association. The two Cubans arrived. Victor Nikolayevich hugged them warmly and then handed out glasses already filled with vodka.

"So here's to all the crops on your island this year. May they be as bountiful as Cuba is beautiful." They downed their glasses which Victor Nikolayevich immediately refilled.

"Here's to the Peter the Great Shipyard which is as solid as the city whose name it proudly bears," toasted Winston. As Victor Nikolayevich was filling the glasses for the obligatory third toast, Jean said, "Victor Nikolayevich, before we forget we have a letter for you."

"Really and what can this be about?" said Victor Nikolayevich eagerly opening the letter. "I am deeply honoured," he said. "Look, Leonid Marlenovich, an invitation from the Cuban Sailing Association to be their guest for two weeks in September."

Leonid Marlenovich looked at the invitation and nodded.

"This really is too generous," smiled Victor Nikolayevich.

"Of course not! You are our biggest supplier and now an even bigger customer," smiled Winston.

"Customer? Supplier? That is a little too formal is it not?" asked Victor Nikolayevich a little confused. "We are partners. Partners standing together, no matter what happens around us."

"Of course," interrupted Leonid Marlenovich, "and as long as we keep up with all these events around us and watch out for the competition wherever it may come from."

"That's right in these changing times business knows no borders and you never know who might be waiting around the corner," added Jean.

"Victor Nikolayevich, you must assure our partners from Cuba that we are their only choice here," continued Leonid Marlenovich.

"But of course. What could ever change that?"

"Victor Nikolayevich, the third toast, I believe," said Leonid Marlenovich raising his glass.

"Of course."

"To partnership!" said Leonid Marlenovich.

A wry smile lit up the faces of the Cubans. "To partnership!"

They downed their vodkas.

"Leonid explained to us that you are looking at big investments in the company, Victor Nikolayevich," said Winston.

"Indeed," said Victor Nikolayevich proudly, "we are going to expand into new business."

Jean looked at Leonid Marlenovich with a slight frown.

"Yes," said Leonid Marlenovich with a big smile on his face, "by building smaller and faster boats which we can sell into bigger markets and which are easier to deliver. We are looking at some great new innovations in design and in areas such as on-board storage."

"You must show us," said Winston also smiling.

"Let's take a tour before lunch," said Victor Nikolayevich enthusiastically, "and we can explain all about it!"

"You seem a little more confident, today, Lenny," said Winston quietly to Leonid Marlenovich as they were leaving.

"Let's just say," replied Leonid Marlenovich also quietly, "that we are putting some measures in place."

"Great to hear. I know we can always rely on you."

"Have a safe boat journey back," said Leonid Marlenovich with a smile.

"It'll be a blast, Lenny. We have just kept a few samples to use ourselves. To speed up the journey so to speak!"

"Very funny, Winston, and be very careful. After all you never know who you might meet on the route these days," said Leonid Marlenovich with an even bigger smile.

"Of course," laughed Winston, "we just love your Russian humour!!"

Thirty Seven

"ADAM, what's this fuss that you are causing all about?" said Hampton. He had recovered much of his professional drive and was frustrated by his physical condition and need to rest in the private clinic.

"What fuss?" asked Adam

"Missing documents."

"What?"

"I've had two of our legal assistants in here this morning complaining about missing documents."

"I thought you were supposed to rest?" said Adam trying to work out what his boss was going on about.

"I am. But Leonid Marlenovich called also. He is pretty irritated."

"Really?" Adam started to feel himself sweating.

"The documents came from him and you were supposed to make photocopies and let him have the originals back. Have you lost your senses leaving originals lying around? Where? In your hotel room?"

Adam's gaze dropped to the floor. He looked deeply embarrassed.

"No wonder the office has gone crazy trying to find them. The day I was shot we were supposed to give them back. Leonid Marlenovich had called but with what happened I was hardly in a position to remember." Hampton's tone was softening as he realised that he was partly at fault.

"Do you think that they were what caused the..?" Adam felt sweat pouring down his back.

"Don't be ridiculous," said Hampton briskly. "Do you think I would have had them with me in a restaurant?"

"Russians probably would not know that. They would not know about our rules about the confidentiality of documents. What goes on..."

"Neither do you by the way you are behaving. You are supposed to uphold office standards not disregard them," said Hampton with feeling. He did not like to talk to Adam like this but he owed a duty to his firm and to all of his staff.

"Honestly I did not think. My fault," replied Adam defensively, "I wanted to work on them in the hotel in quiet."

"You should have copied them. Where are they now?"

"In the office," replied Adam.

"Call one of the team now and tell them to copy them and put them in the safe. Then I will call Leonid Marlenovich and tell him to send someone round for them if he wants to put them back in his own safe."

"Do you think someone really wants them?" asked Adam.

"Not really and what for? They are just documents on properties."

"But everyone seems to be getting excited about them."

"They just do not want them lost. Can you imagine the problems the company would have if any originals were lost?"

"No, sure, sure I understand."

What would anyone want with them? For a moment he had a horrible flashback. The night of his Welcome Drinks. He was with the blonde haired girl outside the nightclub. "Your hotel. Which is your hotel?" "No not there." "Why not, why not?" But she had already known which hotel because she and her friend had met him there in the first place! That was when he had gone down for a quick drink with the Russian lawyer. It was then that they had got into a car, a black Mercedes - he saw it crystal clear in his mind for the first time. He shook his head at the flashbacks which still made him sweat - the thought of the driver's small black eyes and scar above his eye made him flinch. There had been no reports of any strange deaths and he had finally started to venture back into bars but only with clients. Despite himself he was hoping he might meet her friend again. He shook his head.

"Are you alright?" asked Hampton

"Yes, just thinking. Are you sure they're not connected to this?" Adam sounded worried.

"I can't think of a reason why."

"You should tell the police, though in case it helps them."

"It's not the police anymore," said Hampton.

"Oh?" said Adam swallowing hard.

"The famous FSB who incidentally seem totally useless. On and on about the nationality. As if I am to blame by being a foreigner. As if I caused it. The partners in London have contacted the Foreign Office and the Americans to complain."

Adam felt a shiver shoot through his body and he sat down again. "As they should," he said again not knowing how he could sound so calm.

"And the Foreign Office say that they offered to put MI6 on it but the Russian have refused. National pride and all that."

"So what's next?" asked Adam

"Don't know yet," replied Hampton.

As instructed Adam called the office and then fetched them both a coffee. They then moved on to talk about Hampton's plan for convalescence back in the States.

"Three months you expect to be out, then?" said Adam

"That's what the doctors reckon currently."

Hampton's next visitor that day was his secretary Vera. He had arranged for her to visit him each day before lunch. He had agreed with the senior partner in Moscow that he would only look at urgent matters or ones that only he knew about so that the office would run smoothly. He would not take on any project work other than top level advice if, and only if, it were genuinely needed. The Canadian doctor in the private clinic was very pleased with Hampton's progress and was weighing up the best options for Hampton's convalescence. The facilities in the St Petersburg clinic were sufficient for critical care but not really suited to long periods of care. Patients were often sent on to Helsinki or back home to the countries they came from. Hampton so far had shown little interest in where he would be going. His family normally visited him in the afternoon after school had finished. Apart from the occasional ad hoc visit from one of his staff, such as Adam, Hampton received no other visitors.

"Good morning, Mr Hampton," said Vera as she came into Hampton's room. It was a standard issue hospital room and Hampton could have been anywhere in the world. He was still on a drip and needed assistance to sit himself up and walk the few steps to the bathroom.

"Vera, please call me 'John'," replied Hampton.

"Good morning, 'John'," said Vera sounding uncomfortable. "How are you?"

"Good," replied Hampton with a slight wince, "the doctor thinks I am improving every day."

"That is good," continued Vera handing Hampton a file of papers. "I have opened all the letters to make it easier and I can translate any of the Russian ones if you need me to. There is nothing urgent." She sat down on a chair as Hampton quickly scanned the letters. He returned all but one to her and they discussed some replies to then briefly. Hampton then dictated a quick letter to the German Consul General in St Petersburg. Hampton knew him personally and so he 'took the liberty' of addressing the subject of his letter directly. He explained the work of the Hermitage committee and the thought he had had as to whether any German companies might consider a contribution to the restoration of some of the works of art including the world famous Amber Room which he fully appreciated might be a highly delicate subject. Hampton asked Vera to show the typed up letter to Adam who could then initial the letter and have it sent.

"This last letter in Russian, I presume," continued Hampton smiling, "is a list from the Committee?" He handed the last letter back to Vera.

"No, it is from the Head Curator at the Hermitage," replied Vera. Hampton winced as he tried to move forward to take the letter back. Vera could not tell but the wince was at the thought of what the list might contain and not his injuries. "It is strictly private and confidential and only to selected members of the Committee," said Vera pausing for a moment. "From doing the minutes it looks as though it is only to the members from the Hermitage itself and the Deputy Mayor. It does not include the representatives from the Ministry of Culture and anyone else in Moscow. You are included."

"Seems like we have a committee within a committee," said Hampton with a gentle laugh. He looked at the letter and, although, the opening two paragraphs were in Russian, the rest of the two pages were lists. "I think we have to act quickly on this Vera but in the strictest confidence." He paused and waited for Vera to nod which she did with a very serious look on her face.

"Can you ask the clinic's receptionist to let you use the fax machine? I have agreed this with Doctor Faulkner."

"Who do you want me to fax it to?" asked Vera.

"I'll write down the number on the top of the letter and you can fax it directly," said Hampton. It took him some effort to write the numbers down but Vera checked them and could read them all. "When you send it," said Hampton,

"I would expect a reply straight back." Vera nodded but could not hide her puzzled look. She left to do as requested.

Vera returned five minutes later and handed Hampton four pages. The first two were the two pages she had faxed. The clinic's receptionist had been very helpful and had shown Vera how to dial the number as it was international. Vera recognised the number as being in Chicago as the code was the same as to the Miller Lombard office in Chicago. The second two pages were the same pages that had been sent but which had been faxed back with a tick against several of the items on the list. Vera could see Hampton studying the tick-marked items intently.

"Excellent," said Hampton with a large smile, "thank you, Vera. Now can you please shred the pages that were faxed back as soon as you are back in the office and then send the original two in a sealed Miller Lombard envelope to my house with a note to say 'please put on my desk.' Thank you, Vera." Hampton closed his eyes as Vera stood up to leave. He would not be able to sleep again now for quite some time.

Thirty Eight

VALENTINA Alexandrovna reread the three pages of thin paper. They were old style carbon copies which would have been made by putting dark blue copying paper underneath the original document so that a copy was made on the sheet of paper beneath. She smiled and smiled. Very seldom did information on the children make her smile. She smiled again at the thought of the look that she was sure would appear on Anna's face when she passed her this information. Her brother's friend had certainly not given up digging after he had been told to stop. Maybe he was exploiting the disarray in the city's secret police and the KGB. These once all-powerful and feared bodies were not immune from the changes sweeping through the city. Loss of privileges and non-payment of salaries were enough to test the resolve of the most hardened operatives in the murky world of post-Soviet internal security. There were plenty of examples of former KGB staff now working for private security firms and Valentina Alexandrovna smiled again at the thought of the remaining heads of the security forces having to beg for funds from the city just as she had to. How the mighty were falling and thankfully how easy it seemed to be becoming to uncover information that in the past would never, ever have become available. She was looking at a carbon copy of an internal KGB record which had probably been traded for the price of a carrier bag of shopping!

With spring in its full but brief flow the Home allowed small groups of the children to spend time outside in a makeshift park behind the Home's main building. The area comprised several dilapidated wooden buildings, some benches, a rope swing and a tiny improvised sandpit. There were no toys and yet the ten or so children played as if they were in a Disney theme park. Their imaginations which were so crushed by being inside the Home went wild and for fifteen minutes or so they would play like normal children in any park anywhere in the world. They became pirates, they became princesses as their minds broke free from their daily existence. Anna who had quietly entered the Home after a call from Valentina Alexandrovna was startled by the high-pitched shrieks she heard as she walked down the corridor. She found a window that looked out of the back of the main building and was shocked to see the small group playing outside. She had not realised that the jumbled up pieces of wood and small old buildings were a play area for the children! She quickly counted the number of children and then sighed – it was only a tiny fraction of the children in the Home. What a difference a proper and larger play area would make to the Home! She made a determined note in her mind to prioritise finding the resources to install one.

Valentina Alexandrovna greeted Anna with her normal warmth and Anna handed her two bags without comment.

"My dear Anna," began Valentina Alexandrovna, "it seems as though someone is on our side, even if it is not the Church!"

Anna looked at Valentina Alexandrovna with a faint smile. Valentina Alexandrovna always liked to surprise Anna with her cryptic openings.

"Yes," continued Valentina Alexandrovna, "we have some real information this time." Valentina Alexandrovna lifted up the three pieces of thin paper and handed them to Anna. "This is the copy of the report on the entry into Russia of Sasha and his so-called grandmother."

"Really?" said Anna looking up from the papers.

"Yes, it is a report by the border guards at the railway station of a town called Druzhba."

"It has passport details and visa information," said Anna who had quickly scanned the three pages. "It looks as though the papers are carbon copies."

"Yes, and they have been extracted from the file which they were kept in. At that was in Moscow."

"Moscow!" said Anna with clear surprise.

"Yes, as I understand it the originals stayed at Druzhba whilst the copy was sent for filing in the central records for all border crossings which are kept in Moscow, of course."

"How on earth?" started Anna.

"Many records are now available if you have the right connections," smiled Valentina Alexandrovna, "and for a very low fee. After all who is really interested in border crossing in obscure places?" She laughed and Anna could sense a genuine feeling of satisfaction in Valentina Alexandrovna. "Files on people who were under supervision in Soviet times are much, much more sought after."

"I can imagine," said Anna with a huge smile. "So what does this report tell us?" She started to read the report much more slowly this time.

"They crossed the Russian border with the Ukraine just about five years ago. They were travelling under the Tyublonski family name."

"I can see the name. I can see the name," repeated Anna. It was her family name.

"So as I guessed," said Valentina Alexandrovna, "even if the papers were fake, the family name we can now assume is genuine."

"And how did they get a visa?"

"It was granted in Kiev, the capital of the Ukraine. It was a tourist visa and so probably it was just paid for."

"And," said Anna looking at the report, "the address in Russia they were visiting is given as the Fedorovsky Monastery!"

"Yes, the monastery is in the Pushkin village just outside the city!"

"Wow," said Anna jumping up, "so we have them! Fake documents or not!"

"Precisely," replied Valentina Alexandrovna ecstatic at the smile on Anna's face. Anna was positively beaming. "And now you can help, Anna."

"How?" asked Anna.

"We need to use this copy to re-register Sasha with his name and as a minor with residency in St Petersburg. The old documents of his supposed grandmother were not accepted. But now we have a formal Soviet record allowing him to enter Russia and with his name on it. We can start the legal process. Sasha can now officially exist."

"And with our family name!" Anna was beside herself with excitement until her lawyer training kicked in. "But we still need to find a link to our family," she said looking at Valentina Alexandrovna her smile turning to a look of consternation.

"Yes," replied Valentina Alexandrovna still smiling. She was not going to let anything spoil her breakthrough. "And the crossing helps us."

"How?" asked Anna slowly, Valentina Alexandrovna's cryptic way puzzling her once more.

"If Sasha is related to your family then by the location of the border crossing it is most likely that the former Eastern bloc country they would have come from would have been Poland, Hungary or Romania. We have no further information about which country the Tyublonski was being watched by the security services other than a country in the former Eastern bloc. We can rule of the Ukraine because it was part of the Soviet Union at that time and not the Eastern bloc."

Anna sat back on her chair. It was now up to her to look into her family's past. Sasha's identity was tantalisingly close. Anna's mind was suddenly jolted by the sight of the other children she had seen in the makeshift park behind the building. She immediately made a pact with herself – she would not help Sasha without also helping the other children and helping them in a serious way. Valentina Alexandrovna caught the wistful look on Anna's face. The breakthrough would change a lot of things and it was all for the cost equivalent to a bag of shopping.

Thirty Nine

ST PETERSBURG like many parts of the vast Russian land masse can experience strong storms with high winds and dramatic thunder and lightning. These normally occur in late summer when the land masse has heated up for several months. Tornadoes are rare but do sometimes occur. Spring which lasts for two months at most is normally calm with light breezes. This made the strong winds on a late April morning seem unusual. The workers painting the replica Standart boat were taking heed of the local weather forecast and had decided to finish their work for the day and have an early and extended lunch. The boat was made out of oak, larch and pine exactly as the original. The painting of the outside of the boat was almost complete. The top deck was painted in green along its sides and then there was a layer of yellow paint as if a large ribbon had been tied around the boat. Below this there was a deep red layer with the rest a natural dark wood colour. The main mast which stood twenty meters high was still to be finished and the boat's sails had yet to be fitted. As the Standart was in a makeshift dry dock on the quayside if it sails caught the wind it would not be able to move as on the water and the sails or the masts could be damaged. The dry dock was shielded from the road inland by a small forest of pine trees.

As the workers made their way to the wooden cabin a short distance from the boat which served as office, workshop, kitchen and canteen, a gust of wind rattled across the quay and the workers expressed their relief at their decision. A small storm could very well be on its way. This was confirmed several seconds later by a dull roll of thunder. Spots of rain then fell on the roof of the cabin as the workers filed in and sat down at a long table with benches either side. They discussed their painting efforts and all agreed that the paint would have dried and should not be affected too much by a shower or two that afternoon. They had been told that the paint supplied was of Western manufacture and that it was top quality marine paint.

A short while later a police car stopped at the main gate to the quayside. Inspector Bushkin got out of the back of the car and indicated to the driver to open the gate and park inside the small boat yard. Inspector Bushkin looked up at the darkening sky as he pushed a side gate and entered the yard. He took out the message he had received and read it again:

'There are reports of night time activity at the Standart boat yard – please investigate.'

As the Standart was a high priority of the Mayor the Chief of Police had insisted that Inspector Bushkin be the one to check out the information. Another prank, no doubt, mused Inspector Bushkin as he walked across to the wooden cabin. He would obey the command to keep the Chief of Police happy but he would make it known that such work by the city's top criminal investigator was pretty much just another PR exercise and that he would want something in return. He now had a growing list of projects that he needed the police and other authorities to steer clear of.

He walked into the cabin and announced his arrival. The foreman stood up and offered Inspector Bushkin a seat at a small table in the corner which was effectively the office for the yard. The table had diagrams and papers all over it. The foreman attempted to tidy them up and then went to fetch some coffee. As he walked away a loud bang sounded on the roof of the cabin and the workers stopped talking for a moment. There was a second bang and then a flash of lightning. The workers started talking again and laughed. There was going to be a short storm as forecast. Again they were happy that they had come inside. Lunch was bread, cold meat and some vegetables which had been laid in the middle of the long table. The workers started to help themselves.

Inspector Bushkin went back to the door of the cabin and looked at the Standart. The wind was increasing and the trees in the pine forest were swaying. The boat was rocking slightly. The sky suddenly darkened, the wind picked up again and Inspector Bushkin had to take a step back into the cabin as a gust of wind shot across the yard picking up small pieces of wood, swirled around the mast of the boat and smacked into the side of the cabin. The workers stopped talking again as Inspector Bushkin brushed tiny pieces of wood and leaves off his jacket. He went back to the door followed by several workers. The foreman had put a coffee pot on the table and joined the others at the door.

"Looks like quite a storm, Inspector, stronger than forecast," said the foreman.

"A bit early for this time of the year," replied Inspector Bushkin as a zigzag of lightning illuminated a line of trees behind the boat and a clap of thunder boomed across the yard. The wind was swirling faster and faster and the mast of the boat was rocking more and more.

"This boat seems to be attracting all sorts of strange happenings," replied the foreman.

"That is why I am here," said Inspector Bushkin quietly, "there are reports of some disturbances."

Before the foreman could reply one of the workers shouted "Wow!" and stepped back from the door. He had bent down slightly and was covering his head with a hand. "It feels electric!" he said. Inspector Bushkin pushed past him and then did the same shielding his eyes. The foreman had joined him and both of them were framed in the doorway as another massive bolt of lightning hit the trees with an almost instantaneous roar of thunder. The wind was now almost gale force and both men had to hold onto the doorway to avoid being blown inwards.

"Wow! Look at that! Can you believe it!" shouted the foreman over the noise.

"What?" shouted back Inspector Bushkin trying to move further out of the door to look. Inspector Bushkin was now in front of the foreman and only he could see what happened in the next few seconds. He had his hand shielding his eyes from the wind and rain which was lashing down and being blown almost horizontal. He managed to look at the mast of the boat. It was rocking side to side, the wind had picked up more leaves and pieces of wood which were been thrown and whizzed around the mast like a mini tornado and there at the top of the mast, standing with his feet on the rails of the crow's nest, was a figure in a black coat. Inspector Bushkin watched his mouth open as the figure threw off its hood to reveal a mass of black hair and a long beard. The figure was being lashed by the wind and rain but it seemed to be roaring with laughter. Inspector Bushkin tried to lift his hand up to see better but the wind and rain would not let up and he strained to see. With the next flash of lightning the figure swayed holding onto to the mast with one hand and with the next clap of thunder the figure jumped into the air. The wind picked up to a frenzied speed and Inspector Bushkin was blown back through the doorway. The foreman grabbed the door and closed it. Everyone in the cabin stood still and looked to the wooden roof of the cabin. The storm made a final surge, the whole cabin shook and then silence. No-one spoke.

Inspector Bushkin went back to the door and pushed it open. It had become eerily quiet and the sky was starting to brighten. He looked at the boat and frowned. A black shape lay at the side of the boat in a puddle of dark red liquid. The foreman had joined him at the door and he whistled under his breath.

"Has the storm killed someone?" he asked. "Looks like something strange has really happened, Inspector."

"Wait inside," said Inspector Bushkin as he walked over to the boat. He arrived at the shape and he crouched down. The red liquid was dark but looked too thin to be blood. He took out a pen and dipped it into the liquid and then smelt it. It had a chemical odour. By this time the foreman and several of the workers had stepped out of the cabin. Inspector Bushkin then turned to the shape and recognised the black coat with a hood that he had seen on the figure up the mast. No body parts were visible and he slowly lifted the hood with his pen. There was no head. He took hold of the coat with a hand and gave it a sharp tug. The coat lifted up easily to reveal a large piece of wood stuck underneath. Inspector Bushkin got to his feet. He would have to start a search. He was sure that he was the only one who had seen the figure and he was beginning to doubt what he had seen. He looked along the side of the boat and saw two further puddles of liquid. One was green and one was yellow. As he looked up the side of the boat he heard a collective loud moan as the foreman and workers ran towards the boat. The puddles were pools of paint. The paint on the boat had run and been washed off the boat by the storm. The workers started to argue and swear amongst themselves. They must have been given cheap imitation marine paint! They were looking at the paint cans. They thought they had top quality German paint. There would be a lot of work to be done to repaint the boat. Heads would roll. The Mayor would not be impressed. Ignoring the arguments Inspector Bushkin moved away from the boat and set out to determine how to carry out a very quiet and discrete search of the yard.

The yard was not particularly well maintained or kept tidy and there were piles of wood and other materials dotted across the five or six acres that the yard covered. It had a high metal wire fence around it except for the side that bordered the river. The construction of the replica was being done mainly by volunteers who had been given the yard to use. It had been disused for a long time and it showed. Inspector Bushkin made a mental calculation that a proper search of the yard would take a large team and probably more than a day. He did not have that amount of resource to use on what was feeling more and more like a wild goose chance and the sight he had seen during the storm more like a scene from a dream or a nightmare. He would, though, do a survey of the yard and look at anything that seemed out of place. He called the foreman over and was given four workers to assist him. They set off in a group to cover the yard in a methodical way starting along the inland fence which had the pine forest on the other side.

After an hour they had covered almost a quarter of the yard. They had found lots of pieces of old materials and rubbish but nothing out of the ordinary. They stopped for a short break and then continued again. This time Inspector Bushkin walked more briskly and instructed the workers not to lift up things which they had seen before and only stop if something looked different or unusual. After about half an hour they had covered a further quarter of the yard and were about to stop for another break when one of the men swore as he stood on something that made a cracking sound. He bent down and picked up part of a broken bottle. Inspector Bushkin walked over and the four workers gathered around. They lifted up several planks of wood and some old sacks. One of the workers who was carrying a spade shovelled out several spades full of debris and dirt. There were lots of broken bottles.

"Perhaps there has been some night-time drinking in here, after all," said Inspector Bushkin.

"Have we found what you were looking for Inspector?" asked the worker with a spade.

"Well it's something. Why don't you guys take your break? You have been very helpful. Let me borrow the spade."

As the men walked back to the wooden cabin, Inspector Bushkin dug out several more spadefulls of broken glass. He also established that the glass was in several crates which had been buried in the ground and covered over by the sacks and planks. He pushed the spade into the ground in several more places and felt resistance. More crates he was pretty certain. He crouched down and examined several of the broken pieces of glass. The pieces were of clear glass and looked to be from bottles. It was odd that they had no labels on any of them and from a large piece he determined that the shapes of the bottles were old fashioned. The bottles then could not have been used by youths drinking at night recently as he first had assumed. Something tugged at the back of his mind and more so when he saw four numbers on a piece of glass. It was a year. 1943. As he looked at the glass something was stirring in his memory. He heard a familiar noise, like a deep laugh, coming from the small forest of pine trees. He looked over to the trees across the yard. A black shape was disappearing into the trees. He looked frantically at the boat. The black coat had gone. The sight during the storm flooded back into his mind. The laughing face was smiling straight at him again. Despite himself and his forensic police mind he knew that it had been him again. It was him again. But what was he up to?

Forty

ALEX and his mum had had an enjoyable half an hour with Hampton in his room at the private clinic. No formal decision had been made on their future yet but the Miller Lombard partner in Dubai who had been lined up as Hampton's replacement had been informally stood down. Hampton had been given as much time as needed to convalesce as he was sure to make a full recovery. He would fly back to the States as soon as he was able to fly and Ellen and Alex would complete the school year before joining him. A late summer holiday for the three of them was being planned by Ellen with the emphasis on the 'relax' in the American 'R&R' of holiday 'relax and recreation'.

After they had gotten out of the car in the compound Ellen went to the front door to go through the rigmarole of opening the large padded door and shove it open with her shoulder. The driver had picked up an envelope which had been on the passenger's seat and was about to get out of his car as Alex closed his door and walked to the front of the car. Alex spied the envelope. "Can I take that?" asked Alex.

"Yes," said the driver handing Alex the envelope and grateful for not having to get out of the car. He did watch though as Alex followed his mum into the house. Vera had insisted to the driver that the envelope had to be delivered to the house and not be left anywhere else.

"Mum, Yuri gave me a letter from dad's office," shouted Alex to his mum as he dropped his school bag on the floor. "On the front it says 'please put on my desk'."

"Well put it in dad's study and then come for a drink and snack," replied Ellen who was now in the kitchen.

Alex stepped into his father's study. It was a small room off the hall way with a small desk, a filing cabinet and a large metal cupboard. As he went to put the envelope on the desk he felt a sharp burning in his fingers. He put both his hands on the envelope as the heat disappeared as quickly as it had come. The envelope seemed as though it did not want to be put down. The envelope was sealed but a gentle pull opened it without tearing or any other signs of damage. Alex took out the two pages of paper. It was mainly a list and some of the Russian letters started to take shape in his mind. He instantly knew what this was about. He stared at both pages for several seconds and then put the sheets back in the envelope without resealing it. He put it down on the table. He had better join his mum. He was confident that she would let him look at the Hermitage catalogues which were also in his dad's study once he had done his homework. Then the lists would be clear, crystal clear.

Forty One

YELENA Matrovna had changed her attire completely. Gone was the black dress she wore every day that befitted her role as a teacher. Gone was the hair pinned up with a clip and gone too were the reading glasses she had on her chain. Instead she was all in white with a yellow belt and red boots. Her long black hair was flowing onto her shoulders. She sat in the back of the small car as Sasha climbed in beside her. As Sasha's eyes lighted upon her she put her index finger to her lips. Sasha smiled. Yelena Matrovna did not need to speak. He could tell that she was warning him not to say anything. Once the car had driven for a couple of minutes, Sasha looked at Yelena Matrovna again – the journey would not be long and Sasha's eyes widened at the thought that Yelena Matrovna would be meeting her master!

"Yes, Sasha," Yelena Matrovna finally spoke, "today you will understand so much more. He will be there." Sasha frowned slightly. He could not make out in Yelena Matrovna's mind who the 'He' was, but he had an idea. He thought he had seen him at the Home.

The journey this time was quite short. They had driven largely in silence for about fifteen minutes and then turned down a small road. Sasha could see that they were not far from an embankment and they stopped next to a high wall and a gate. They got out and Yelena Matrovna thanked the driver who nodded solemnly. Yelena Matrovna pushed open the gate and they walked into an overgrown garden. A small cupola on the building in front of them glistened through the trees and bushes. They were outside what appeared to be an abandoned church. Sasha followed Yelena Matrovna who seemed to know the way as she walked confidently through the bushes. They quickly reached a door which Yelena Matrovna opened. Inside it was definitely an abandoned church. It was empty and bare save for some faded paintings on one of the walls. The roof was full of cobwebs. Sasha felt a pang of disappointment. His previous trips out with Yelena Matrovna had included singing in one of the city's most famous cathedrals and then visiting the underground church in the country. He was about to ask Yelena Matrovna why they had come to such a place when a loud beat of a drum rang out behind them. The sound was pure power and resonated throughout the small church rippling with tiny echoes in the domed roof. Sasha jumped and turned round. A man dressed the same as Yelena Matrovna and with long hair and a long beard was advancing towards them. He banged the drum again and two more drummers dressed the same and also with long black beards appeared behind him. Sasha felt like putting his hands over his ears to stop the deafening noise but as if on cue the drumming softened to a low rhythm as three women entered again dressed in the same way and the door to the church was closed shut. A key was turned in the lock. Yelena Matrovna took Sasha by the arm and led him to the side of the room. Again she put her index finger to her lips and Sasha nodded.

For the next ten minutes Sasha stood transfixed as the men beat their drums and the women danced. Their dancing went beyond dance. Sasha had seen this type of dancing in the country. The women would form a circle and then as their movement speeded up they linked arms and began to whirl. Their feet spent more time airborne than on the ground. Suddenly the drum beat would change, the women would reverse their direction and gradually unlink their arms. Then a thunderous drum beat and one of the women would leap into the middle. She would start to twirl in the opposite direction of the others. The air became thick with dust whipped up by the women's feet. The drumming reached a frenzy and only stopped when the woman in the middle dropped to the floor. Sasha could hear some quiet noises and work out some of the words. The language was ancient. They were praying. Eyes were shut.

The next dance was Yelena Matrovna's turn. Sasha again watched spellbound as Yelena Matrovna seemed to soar as she leapt into the air and then twirled. The dance lasted longer than the others and as Yelena Matrovna dropped to the floor, the voices around her were louder than before. Sasha stepped forward to have a closer look at Yelena Matrovna. She was being held by one of the men who had sat on the floor. He was supporting her head. Sasha could see that Yelena Matrovna's eyes were open but she did not look conscious. There was no light in her eyes.

"Sasha, our son, do not worry," said one of the other men who was now standing behind Sasha and had put his hands on Sasha's shoulders. His voice was calming and melodic. "She is dreaming."

Sasha resisted his desire to go to Yelena Matrovna and turned his head to look at the man. He had a long black beard and his eyes were deep blue. "Our master is with us," said the man again with a sweet melody in his voice that sent tingles through Sasha's body, "and you have just seen the power he has over her. It is a power that can demand total obedience but it is also a power which protects."

"Where is the master?" asked Sasha his voice barely audible and shaking. This was the first time he had spoken in the church.

"You will be able to see him when you recognise the sign he has left for you and only for you."

Sasha thought for a second. He smiled at the man. He had thought that the master was the man who came to the home and who he had seen talking with Yelena Matrovna several times. He had arranged for them to visit the cathedral and the boys in the Home whispered that he was one of the new businessmen or mafia even. But now he understood. He smiled again at the man who nodded calmly at Sasha but this time with a faint flicker of fear in his eyes.

A look of concerned obedience almost. It was if the man was treating Sasha as his superior. Sasha finally understood that their master was much more powerful than the new businessman. The man bowed to Sasha as Yelena Matrovna was lifted to her feet.

Yelena Matrovna took a few minutes to recover all her faculties and shortly thereafter she and Sasha left the abandoned church and found the same car and driver waiting for them outside the gate. Before getting into the car Yelena Matrovna spoke softly to Sasha. She just wanted to make sure that Sasha realised that very few people even in the new Russia understood the religion of the Old Believers, that many would dismiss it as a sect and call them 'whirlers' and 'khlysts."

Sasha just smiled and replied with his own melody flowing through his voice. "I have always known," he said, "and it is he who has always protected me."

Forty Two

ANNA had arrived at the offices of the Peter the Great Shipyard with an assistant and she had met with the company's book-keeper, some of the staff in the company's sales office and the Head of the company's legal department. She was putting the final touches to her description of the company for the privatisation documentation and had been given free reign by Victor Nikolayevich to talk to whomever she needed. This was on the condition that she report all her findings back to Victor Nikolayevich and that Leonid Marlenovich would have the final edit on all the documentation before it was released to any potential investors who might be interested to bid for the shares in the privatisation. As the work was very much under Anna's remit, Adam had remained in the office to prepare a proposal to a potential Swedish client on assistance with an acquisition in Karelia, the region north of St Petersburg.

Anna found most of the company's employees very helpful. She was careful to explain that she had the permission of Victor Nikolayevich and that what she was doing would help attract new finance for the company. Most of the employees were very keen to discuss their working at the company. Only the Head of the legal department was reluctant to say very much. He was setting up the company's first Share Register where the owners of all the newly created shares in the company were recorded by name and number of shares owned. The Share Register was the only legally valid record of ownership of shares in the company and as such was going to become arguably the most important document in the company. There were no printed share certificates. Anna was not sure whether the Head was not prepared to answer many questions because he himself did not know the answers - as a lawyer Anna knew most of the answers before she asked the questions - or whether the Head was reverting to a Soviet-style position of silence being the best answer to a question - so as to avoid potentially compromising oneself, that is.

In any event the Head of the legal department reported directly to Leonid Marlenovich whom she would ask. The only thought that struck her as she left the Head's small office was that whoever physically controlled the entries in and out of the Share Register would have the opportunity to perhaps alter entries. She shook her head and made a note to ask Leonid Marlenovich directly how the integrity of the Share Register would be maintained. If Share Registers were not foolproof than the whole of privatisation and the investments it could bring would be in jeopardy.

Anna passed through the turnstile in the office entrance after showing the old woman who manned the turnstile a piece of paper granting her permission to enter. Anna also handed the woman two further pieces of paper granting the same access to Mr Corley and Vera from their office. Anna explained that they would be arriving shortly. Anna made her way to Victor Nikolayevich's office and took a seat in the waiting area outside. It was very rare for her to have a few moments of peace and quiet and she closed her eyes. As she sat two intertwined images ran through her mind – the makeshift playground at the Home and a magnificent sailing ship. These must have come to her after her visit to the Home and from the company's brochures of its top yachts which she had been studying. The contrast was heart-breaking and she opened her eyes. Her mind was clearly being very stretched at the moment but she still managed to smile slightly to herself – there must be a reason for her mind to be working this way.

Corley and Vera joined her a few minutes later. They spoke about Hampton's progress since the shooting and how quickly life had gone back to normal. Corley joked that their office and work was probably much more efficient without Hampton. Anna understood the English humour in the comments and smiled. Vera, however, could only frown. Before Anna could explain to Vera, the office door was thrown open wide and Victor Nikolayevich bounded out.

"Anna, my dear Anna! How good to see you!" Victor Nikolayevich was about to greet Anna with a hug and kisses to both cheeks but sensing Corley's presence he stopped up short and turned to Corley with a huge smile. As usual his collar was open and his tie seemed to be strangling him. "Very pleased to meet you, Mr Corley!" he said excitedly in heavy accented English and grabbed Corley's hand which he shook vigorously.

"The honour is all mine," smiled Corley as he then pronounced 'Victor Nikolayevich' in a strong as Russian as accent as he could muster.

"Thank you, thank you, Mr Corley," continued Victor Nikolayevich as he ushered his three guests into his office. Leonid Marlenovich was standing near the window. He came over and shook Corley's hand without speaking. As was customary neither Leonid Marlenovich nor Victor Nikolayevich offered to shake hands with either Anna or Vera. Anna quickly introduced Corley to Leonid Marlenovich who commented that he had heard a lot of positive things about Mr Corley from Hampton. Corley said he was very pleased that Hampton had spoken so positively about him. Anna also thanked Victor Nikolayevich for seeing them and apologised for the absence of her boss John Hampton and her colleague Adam Carter. Victor Nikolayevich expressed his concern over the shooting and said he was very happy to hear that Hampton was on the way to a full recovery. Tea was offered to everyone and readily accepted. As the discussions started Anna could not help feeling that the meeting had already somehow achieved its objective. Everyone was smiling. Victor Nikolayevich showed none of his normal nervousness and even Leonid Marlenovich was making light-hearted remarks. It felt as if everyone had known each other for some time. As the senior figure from

Miller Lombard she decided to move the meeting on to its agenda.

"Victor Nikolayevich," began Anna, "perhaps we can present the company to Mr Corley. Mr Corley can then explain to you about his fund."

"Excellent, Anna. Of course. Perhaps as Leonid Marlenovich speaks much better English than I do, he can make a small presentation for Mr Corley."

Everyone agreed and for the next twenty minutes Leonid Marlenovich spoke about the company's history, its products and how the company expected to develop in the future. Corley asked a lot of questions. Anna kept notes. Corley then explained the objectives of the British Redevelopment Fund which Leonid Marlenovich summarised for Victor Nikolayevich who in turn nodded and smiled. Anna again took notes. After his explanation Corley paused and the meeting took a short break. Victor Nikolayevich and Leonid Marlenovich excused themselves indicating that they were in need of a short 'smoke' break. Corley explained that he did not smoke. While the others had left Anna asked Corley to what extent he wanted to discuss the company's privatisation. Corley responded that he wanted to discuss it in as much detail as they would allow and that he was in a position even to make them an initial offer. Anna was stunned but quickly composed herself. Yet again she felt that a deal had already been done and yet her boss was in hospital and this was the first face-to-face meeting between the company and the fund. She made a note on her pad which she underlined – 'check with Adam what has already been agreed.' As Victor Nikolayevich and Leonid Marlenovich were coming back into the room Anna warned Corley that they would unlikely be able to leave without Victor Nikolayevich talking about the war, especially if they started to drink vodka. Corley rolled his eyes but with a friendly smile. Victor Nikolayevich then surprised everyone present by starting in English.

"Until now we were afraid of privatisation," he said still with a heavy Russian accent, "but now it is an opportunity. This is true." He stood up and walked to the window.

"You are most correct, Victor Nikolayevich," said Leonid Marlenovich with a smile to Anna and Corley. "Perhaps I may continue in English and explain our plans to Mr Corley?"

Victor Nikolayevich nodded and remained by the window. "Our plans, please," he said as he looked out of the window.

For the first time Anna sensed a tenseness in the meeting as Corley shifted in his chair. Anna thought he wanted to stand up and join Victor Nikolayevich at the window.

"Mr Corley, I presume you were briefed on the discussions we had with Mr Hampton about the options for our privatisation," said Leonid Marlenovich.

"A little," replied Corley. "I am most keen to hear about possible investments that your company wishes to make and whether our fund might be able to provide some finance for them. And then whether," he stopped and threw a quick glance at Anna, "this can be done as part of your privatisation."

"Thank you, Mr Corley. Let me explain," replied Leonid Marlenovich who then went on to describe the potential investment in a new state-of-the-art production line for small pleasure boats. These were the type of light vessels very popular now in the United States and which the company anticipated would sell well throughout its own markets. The company had received quotes for the machinery and plans were being drawn up to put a new line on site.

"Well that sounds excellent," commented Corley as Leonid Marlenovich paused, "and do have some idea of the costs?"

"They are being calculated as we speak. The machinery we will need to purchase will be in the region of five million dollars and the total cost of the project could be twice that."

At the sound of the word 'dollars', which of course is the sound known worldwide pretty irrespective of language or accent, Victor Nikolayevich beamed and returned to his seat. Together with Leonid Marlenovich he began to draw plans with a thick pencil on a piece of A3 paper he produced from his drawer. Corley joined them and all three men were soon on their feet bending over the piece of paper, pointing, nodding, adding suggestions and rubbing out. To Anna the three relatively old men looked like young boys poring over the design of a new boat or a train. Language had ceased to be much of a barrier and the English and Russian words merged into one another as the plan took on a life of its own. Finally Victor Nikolayevich picked up the piece of paper and held it up. The paper was a mass of lines and numbers and to Anna it made no sense at all. Nevertheless she and Vera clapped politely. As she looked closely Anna could make a large question mark over what looked like the area on which the line was to be built. Leonid Marlenovich caught her eye.

"We are not sure where exactly to put the new production line," he said quietly in Russian.

"I see," replied Anna. The question mark seemed to be over the Old Foundry building.

"Now Anna," continued Leonid Marlenovich switching back to English, "it was Mr Hampton who first came up with the idea of investment as part of the terms of the privatisation. Are you able to explain any further?"

"Yes," said Anna finally relieved that the meeting had returned to its agenda. "We have reviewed all the rules on privatisation from a legal perspective and I can confirm that Mr Hampton was correct in his original assessment that the privatisation of a company may include investment conditions as part of the price to be paid for the shares sold in the privatisation."

"That is interesting," interrupted Corley. "When the UK privatised its State-owned companies back in the 1980s, it was just shares sold for a price that was set." He paused and everyone looked at him to continue. "And so in your case," he continued, "this would presumably mean that there can only be one buyer of the shares on offer."

"What do you mean?" asked Leonid Marlenovich.

"Well in our case lots of private individuals and investment funds, similar to my fund now, were all able to buy shares and just to pay for example five pounds per share."

"But I think, Mr Corley, in your case there were lots of individuals and funds who had plenty of money to invest. This is not the case here in Russia. Don't forget that we are going through a crash course in market economics and mass privatisation in one go. We are literally smashing up the system built by communists since the Revolution. We are putting most of the economy back into private hands and there is very little cash yet in our system to pay for it."

"Your analysis is very profound, Leonid Marlenovich," replied Corley. "Anna, how then will this Russian form of privatisation actually work?"

"You are correct in your analysis, Mr Corley," replied Anna. "In this form there will only be one winner for all the shares put up for privatisation. We expect this to be twenty-five per cent." At the mention of 'only one winner' Victor Nikolayevich jolted in his seat almost as if he had been woken from a sleep which he should not have fallen into. He looked at Leonid Marlenovich who motioned at him to hold any comments.

"Only one?" said Corley.

"Yes, because the winner as well as paying an amount for the shares also agrees to invest an additional amount of money into the company. This is what is called the investment condition."

"And if the winner does not invest?"

"Then the terms are not fulfilled, the shares go back to the Government and the winner loses the money he has paid for the shares in the first place."

"Ah-ha!" said Corley, "this is something I need to think through."

"I think we all need to, Mr Corley," said Leonid Marlenovich. "Maybe we can take another break?"

The break lasted a good fifteen minutes. Corley discussed many of the possible issues around this form of privatisation with Anna while Victor Nikolayevich and Leonid Marlenovich chain-smoked. Leonid Marlenovich agreed with Victor Nikolayevich that he would push Corley as far as he could to see if he was serious about investing. In turn Victor Nikolayevich insisted with Leonid Marlenovich that he would set the scene by explaining his personal history at the company. Leonid Marlenovich could not dissuade Victor Nikolayevich and had to take the view that if Victor Nikolayevich did not put Corley off now, then no-one would! Corley was surprised by Victor Nikolayevich's choice of topic but sat and listened.

"I was here that night, you know. Here in this factory," Victor Nikolayevich spoke quietly.

"Which night, Victor Nikolayevich?" asked Anna.

"The night our city was finally liberated from the Germans." Victor Nikolayevich moved to the map behind his desk. "The speed with which the Germans had moved at the beginning was breath-taking," he said and made a large sweeping hand gesture pointing to the map. "We were not ready of course, but, Boom! Boom!! Boom!!!" his voice got louder and louder, "then they blew up the train station and railway tracks at the village called Mga and we were cut off. It was like lightning. They say there were no-one on the inside to help them and, if that is true, then it was a truly amazing feat. If anyone did then they were surely killed by the Germans or..," he looked to both walls and lowered voice and said very conspiratorially, "or else by the resistance. By us." His voice had become a whisper. "But in swept the Germans and the city was faced with a slow and painful death." He stopped.

"But you had the convoys," said Corley.

"The convoys," Victor Nikolayevich went and looked out of the window. "They were my escape too. I was only eight years old. The shipyard had become my home. I lay on the roof at night waiting for the bombs to drop and if they did not explode I would throw them off the roof. I kept this roof in one piece. Threw off forty nine bombs into the river. And you know what we made in the factory?"

Corley looked at Victor Nikolayevich.

"Grenade launchers and booby traps. Yes, we made them however we could from whatever materials we could use. We would do anything to kill those Nazis."

"Victor Nikolayevich has a great passion for the company, Mr Corley," said Leonid Marlenovich, "he sees our privatisation as just another step in the struggle we have always fought. Hopefully this time the struggle will be a lot less dramatic and certainly not violent."

"I would assume so," replied Corley with a smile. "So, Anna, can you give me an idea of the type of terms?"

Anna looked at Leonid Marlenovich who nodded very slightly to her.

"It is very hypothetical at this point," she replied, "but, for example, there will be an agreed amount of investment into the company and then an auction for the price to be paid for the shares."

"I see," said Corley, his tone more serious that it had been, "so this means that it will really be competitive bidding?"

"Yes. For example the opening bid may be set at a price and then bidders put in bids above that with the highest bid winning."

"You forget a few points, Anna," interrupted Leonid Marlenovich, "the bidders will need to agree the investment amount with the company and then it depends how the bidding is done."

"You are right, of course, Leonid Marlenovich, and we do not know yet how these two points will work."

"Well that is for the company and Miller Lombard to determine," Leonid Marlenovich smiled at Anna. Anna felt Leonid Marlenovich's eyes on her and blushed slightly. "Although it will clearly help if we have the backing of our preferred winner." This time Leonid Marlenovich smiled brightly at Corley. Anna could not be sure but she sensed a wave of conspiracy passing between the two men but she brushed it away.

"May I make so bold, Leonid Marlenovich," replied Corley, "and ask that Anna, or rather Millar Lombard to be more correct, draw up a legal agreement, a Memorandum of Understanding perhaps, between the company and my fund in which we can agree how much we will invest and how much we are prepared to pay for the shares?"

"Donald, I thought you would never ask!" said Leonid Marlenovich jumping to his feet and motioning to Victor Nikolayevich to do the same. The men all shook hands. Anna and Vera remained seated. Leonid Marlenovich's use of Corley's first name all of a sudden like that had knocked her for six and she was utterly confused at the sudden and newly found level of familiarity between the two men who had only just met.

Forty Three

ADAM had taken a decision. The flashbacks were now affecting his work. He had picked up on the looks from some of his junior colleagues and support staff in the office. They were all well used to the drunken antics of most business people and the resulting morning after hangovers but they had started to nod to each other or whisper quietly whenever Adam had left his desk to take a breath of fresh air or spend time in the bathroom. He had considered feigning an illness but then thought that that would have meant an appointment with the local private clinic. The problem was whenever his mind became idle for more than a couple of minutes, the black Mercedes, the sofa, the door to the bedroom would come back to him invariably followed by the scene he had seen in the bedroom. As he would close his eyes the young women would be there talking to him, tempting yet terrifying him at the thought of what might have or what actually did follow. He would have to sort himself out.

He thought of asking Vera, his boss's secretary, who herself had experienced a traumatic event with the shooting, to perhaps go out for drinks with him and a few others from the office. He might then start some casual conversations about people they all knew, unexpected things that had happened, gossip – anything that might lead to information. Putting himself in solitary social confinement, as he had, was only making it worse for him. As a first step he was going to venture back down to the bar in his hotel. He had not attended the day's meeting between the Peter the Great Shipyard and the British Redevelopment Fund as he had had to work on a proposal to a potential Swedish client but he had taken up Corley's suggestion of a drink in the early evening in the hotel bar before Corley left St Petersburg to fly to Moscow.

He had a short time before going down to the bar and so he used the time to look through various papers he was working on which he had brought from the office. After flicking through several memos and the meeting note he had written on his meeting that day his eyes settled on a draft list he was compiling on the owners of the Old Foundry. His colleagues in the Miller Lombard office in The Hague were still researching the various claims for him and he expected to have their findings in several days' time, although the deadline he had tried to set kept being pushed back. He had also asked one of his colleagues to formally request all the information on the property held by the authorities in St Petersburg. He looked at his list which simply had two columns with five years and five names written all in pencil in them. The years were 1726, 1788, 1852, 1918 and 1946 and the corresponding names against the years were Berd, Baronsky, Yusupov, City of Petrograd and Peter the Great Shipyard. As the history of the company was now well-known to the Miller Lombard team there did not seem anything amiss or of note in the ownership pattern. Berd was a Scottish engineer who was known to have been given a stake in the original company, the company had then been owned by two wealthy Russian families before falling into state control after the 1917 Revolution before then being managed by the current company configuration after the Second World War. Analysing the claims once he had the information would be interesting but above all he hoped it would give him the chance to confirm the current ownership of the building within the company once and for all and that there were no valid ownership claims from other parties against it. Properties were all too often the last piece of a deal to fall into place and he did not want to be the lawyer responsible for a loose end which could potentially undermine the company's privatisation. He put the draft list and other papers into his briefcase.

Shortly after six Adam entered the bar and looked around. Immediately he could see the Russian lawyer and the two girls laughing and sitting in the same seats as the night of the Welcome Drinks! He stepped back and shook his head. He opened his eyes and the bar was empty. Hardly exorcising a ghost. Coming to the hotel bar was bringing them back more vividly than ever! He walked over to the bar, sat on a stool and slowly looked around. Apart from a man in a chair near the window, the bar was still empty. A bartender appeared and Adam ordered a beer. He drank most of it in two long swigs and the bartender without asking put another beer next to his first one. Adam smiled a 'thank you'.

Just as Adam was starting the second beer, Corley walked up to the bar. Adam turned to greet him and watched as a group of young women walked past the entrance to the bar. He could see short skirts and hear high-heeled shoes clicking louder than the laughter the women were making as the young women went out of view. They were carrying their coats and on the way to the hotel's cloakroom on the left side of the hotel lobby. He got off his stool and almost lost his balance.

"Adam!" said Corley warmly, "great to see you. How are you?"

"Great, Dominic!" replied Adam shaking hands and turning back to the bar. "What can I get you to drink?"

"A beer would be nice," said Corley, "where do you want to sit?"

Adam would have liked to have positioned himself to watch the entrance to see if the group of young women appeared again but decided to take a more neutral position. "Anywhere you like, Donald. I'll bring the beers over."

They sat at a table in the middle of the bar.

"I hear the meeting went well," said Adam.

"Excellently," replied Corley, "yes, excellently and your colleague Anna is a bright young thing."

Adam nodded.

"We've been invited to invest in the company through the privatisation and Miller Lombard is to draft a Memorandum of Understanding between us."

"We're already on to it," smiled Adam. "John is really pleased."

"Good and how is he? Is he still looking to restore these long-lost works of art he keeps going on about?"

"Oh, yes," laughed Adam, "there is no stopping him! Shooting or no shooting!"

Corley also laughed. Then as they drank their beers they talked about Hampton, the Hermitage and Adam's success on the Committee. Gradually the bar started to fill up with other business people and, as Adam started to notice, the occasional young woman but most of them were accompanying men who looked predominantly Russian.

"I would love to stay for dinner, Adam," said Corley finishing his drink, "but I'd better take the eight o'clock flight back to Moscow. I am sure you won't be short of pretty young women to take to dinner! Much more fun for sure!"

Corley tried to pay for the drinks but Adam insisted on paying and Corley left after a warm handshake. Adam then went to the bar and paid. He was not sure what to do next and so decided to go up to his room and fetch a book to bring back down to read. He left the bar and crossed to the lift. As he did so he caught sight of a young woman taking off her coat and handing it to the cloakroom attendant. She had long black hair in a ponytail half way down her back. The lift door opened and Adam went to step in. He could not resist a look and as he turned his head he saw the young woman's slightly large nose and the wide smile she had spreading across her face. Adam pressed the button in the lift with a hand that was physically shaking. He stayed holed up in his hotel room until the following morning.

Forty Four

VERA handed Hampton an envelope marked for his attention only. It had been passed to her by Adam and she knew that it originated from Dominic Corley who had brought it personally from London which probably meant it was cash. Foreigners were allowed to bring in as much physical cash as they wanted as long as they declared the amount at customs and then on leaving the country took back less and declared the lower amount. Hampton opened it and tipped out a note and a small thick plastic wallet. He smiled. The generosity of Corley's fund was greater than he had anticipated. He looked at Vera and smiled again. He was putting a lot of faith in Vera but since the shooting and their daily meetings in the clinic there was undoubtedly a strong relationship between them. Vera seemed to understand well enough how they were having to operate and he had to admit that fixing situations, albeit on a small scale, was clearly Vera's forte. He wondered how effective she would be as a secretary or personal assistant in their London or Chicago office where daily life and situations were much simpler but he had to admit that she would probably be even more effective.

"This is the financial sponsorship sent by Corley's fund," said Hampton, "and a note wishing me a speedy recovery."

"Has the doctor decided anything yet?" asked Vera.

"Not yet," replied Hampton, "there will be a discussion in a couple of days. Did London send you the details of the company's medical insurance evacuation policy?"

"Yes," replied Vera. She opened her bag and passed Hampton a file.

"Thank you," he said, "I'll read that later. Now back to this donation and the Hermitage Committee. This is what I propose to do."

Hampton then handed Vera the small plastic wallet with US dollar notes in and instructed Vera to deposit five thousand dollars into the Miller Lombard's office bank account and then transfer it to the Hermitage Committee's bank account. She nodded and said that she would ask for the bank details and make sure the transaction was completed and documented. Hampton then asked Vera to send the remaining five thousand dollars in cash to the Head Curator at the Hermitage. This was to be done in person and to his private address. Hampton did not need to explain anything more.

Alex finally had his wish. He was being allowed to visit the Catherine Palace without having to go on an official accompanied tour. He was now the proud possessor of two guide books in English on the Catherine Palace and he had managed to read about some of the history of the Amber Room. He had badgered Adam into finding information for him. He said to Adam that he did not want to bother his father, that his mother did not have any contacts and that he, Adam, was now himself on the Hermitage committee. Adam had given in and had asked Vera to get hold of whatever she could. With a small dip into office expenses Vera had materialised the guide books and some history books. She was surprised at Adam's growing interest in the palace but his idea of asking foreign companies to help finance the Amber Room was probably the reason. The Soviets had decided to reconstruct the room in the late 1970's and some preparatory work had been done on the room itself in the early 1980's but the real work had ground to a halt through the lack of funding. She was not then surprised when Adam asked her next to arrange a visit for him to see the palace for himself along with Alex. She offered to go with them but Adam said that they would be fine and would use one of the Hamptons' drivers. The palace was very near the Hampton's rented dacha.

Just before leaving to get in the car Alex went to his room. He told his mum and Adam who were chatting in the kitchen that he needed to pick up his guide books. In his room he went straight to the plastic tub under his desk. He took out the piece of amber from its cloth bag. The piece seemed to sparkle. He felt the usual tingling in his fingers and for the first time felt a little scared. If this small piece had such an effect on him, then what would large pieces do? He put the piece away quickly, grabbed the two guide books from his bed and bounded down the stairs.

Adam and Alex were shown into the Great Hall or Hall of Light as it is also known by a very old man. The old man spoke little English. Vera had told Adam that they would have two hours by themselves and that a retired curator would take them between the rooms but otherwise they would probably be on their own. As the old man pointed to a clock on a wall Adam agreed the time they had and the old man shuffled off towards one of the doors.

"Wow!" said Alex excitedly, "this place is amazing."

"And we are probably the first people, especially foreigners, to be let in by ourselves for many years. Shall we explore? Can I look at one of the guide books?"

The two of them walked around the Hall commenting on the paintings and elaborate decorations on the walls as they passed. Adam smiled at the massive fresco called 'Triumph of Russia' on the ceiling which depicted a battlefield strewn with bodies and the Russian flag flying triumphantly. Would Russia ever triumph again at anything, he thought to himself. Even the current privatisation of iconic Russian companies seemed set to revert ownership to foreigners and not to Russians. Russia's economy was so badly dislocated that many doubted that it would ever recover. Alex for his part was enthralled by the artistry. For a young boy he showed an appreciation of paintings and other forms of art far beyond his years. Even Adam was picking up on the fact. Adam also noticed that Alex paid little attention to his guide book yet was full of facts and recognised virtually every major painting of sculpture. Must be his father's genes!

The old curator did as Vera had explained and kept the pair moving through the rooms.

"Adam, how long do we have left?" asked Alex all of a sudden.

"About twenty minutes and only a couple of rooms to go," Adam replied. "Vera did say that some of the smaller rooms would be closed. Renovation work apparently."

"Really?" asked Alex. He had not reckoned with this. He was saving the best till last and savouring the magnificence of the palace on the way. He would have to change plan. He opened his guide book. "Which room is next?" he asked.

Adam opened his guide book. "Looks like the Painting Hall," he said, "with plenty of painting by European artists. Just up your street."

"No, not really," replied Alex closing his books. "The paintings in the Painting Hall are famous for being more decorative than masterpieces. You can have a look though! Here comes our curator."

"I shall study them all, Alex!" said Adam closing his guide book. "More decorative than masterpieces, I'll bet!" he continued as he turned round to see the old man shuffling along the corridor towards them. Shielded from the curator's view by Adam Alex quietly moved past the Painting Hall. He waited till Adam went into the Painting Hall with the curator and then quickly went to the next door.

He could read the sign above the door written in Russian letters. He had seen the name in English and in Russian so many times. The letters were etched on his brain. He felt his heart starting to beat. He could not touch the door to the room for fear of the heat, for fear of what might happen to his fingers. He closed his eyes and ever so slowly pressed the index finger of his right hand onto the door. The door was heavy, its surface polished but it was cold. One by one he pressed the fingers from both of his hands on to the door. Same feeling. Nothing. He then jumped backwards as the pressure from all of his fingers pushed the door open slightly. He could hear the slow footsteps of the curator who was about to come out of the Painting Hall. In a flash he pushed the door wide enough open to slip inside and pull it to behind him. He closed his eyes and stood perfectly still.

Alex could hear only the faintest of sounds. His mind had gone blank. He had waited so long to be in this room that he dared not open his eyes. He had read all the history of the room being built, its panels being hidden behind paper and cloth as if the room had been redecorated. The Germans, though, finding them straight away. The panels then being dismantled and sent to Germany, the panels being in a fire - and yet he had felt the room, he had some of its amber. He knew that it had not been destroyed. And now a horrible thought was dawning on him. The panels might not be here. He opened his eyes quickly. His brain calculated the different sights that hit him and quickly rationalised them. The walls were all draped in large white dust sheets, the floor had been relaid in warm wood and the ceiling had been decorated in a wonderful amber colour. The light in the room was bright with the tiniest hue of amber reflecting from the ceiling. He understood. He had been meant to see this. The ends of all his fingers throbbed with a faint tingle. The room was prepared for the panels to be put back in their rightful place! The sound of his name being shouted loudly startled him and he turned to the door. He almost fell over. The old curator was standing at the door looking at him with a deep smile. The old man put his finger to his lips and smiled again. He stood back and opened the door motioning for Alex to step out. His name was now ringing down the corridor. Alex stepped out quickly but not before the old curator could grab Alex's hand. He pressed a small object in Alex's hand and smiled again. Alex nodded, his eyes wide open with tears welling up. Alex took a deep breath and shouted to Adam that he was coming. The small object was burning in his hand but the heat was warm and causing him no harm at all.

Forty Five

HAVING established an identity for Sasha, Valentina Alexandrovna had relented on Anna's request for writing and language lessons for Sasha to make up for all the basic schooling he had missed. This was done through twice weekly classes given by a retired teacher who Anna had found. The retired teacher was a nearby neighbour and was delighted to help the children. Anna insisted on paying the teacher a small amount per lesson from her own pocket. So as to avoid accusations of favouritism a group of children were taught each week with the composition of the group changing regularly. Only Sasha remained permanently because of the help he so obviously needed and none of the other children complained. Any attention was lapped up and savoured. Sasha wrote very slowly and always wrote in large letters. He could read a music score by sight but still struggled with a page of written text. The lessons though had an immediate impact and Sasha was quickly able to read simple stories. He had also started to write simple sentences of his own or to copy small passages from books and other sources.

Anna for her part was having difficulties in arranging for her parents to come from Moscow to visit her in St Petersburg. Her mother had suggested she could come without her father but Anna had dissuaded her. She was fairly sure that her mother would not know many of the details of her father's and her uncle's time in the Soviet Army in the Eastern bloc after the end of the war. It was a time when the norms of civilised behaviour would have taken several months if not years to re-establish themselves after the many, many atrocities committed across Eastern Europe during the war. She would have to be patient with her father if she was to find out what she needed. She had explained that the investigations around Sasha were throwing up possibilities and that she would like to explain some of these to her father but that was as much as she had said so far. Her father's slow response to visit did indicate to Anna an unwillingness to engage but he would not be able to hold out for much longer. Anna had to be patient.

Valentina Alexandrovna had moved more quickly and sent requests for information on the birth of Sasha to the authorities in several countries and received negative replies back from all of them. Sasha's birth had not been registered. This did not surprise her and led her to follow up with requests to the authorities to ask if Sasha had been resident in any orphanages at any time in the five years before he had turned up on the Russian border at a town called Druzhba. The only problem here was that some of the orphanages in some of the countries were run by religious orders and not all the children would be registered with the relevant authorities. Replies here were slower but after several communications Valentina Alexandrovna was narrowing down the search to Poland and Romania. She had called Anna and asked her to come and see her the next time she came to the Home so that they could see what progress they were both making.

The retired teacher was delighted at the progress the children in the Home were making and especially Sasha to the point that she had asked Anna if she could do more lessons and to do more on her own account. Anna had smiled and explained how desperate she was to help as many children as possible and how she saw the effect that the slightest interaction had on the children. Anna said she would come up with a plan. Anna asked about Sasha and the retired teacher was delighted to recount how avidly Sasha was now taking to writing down his own sentences. This had really taken off when Anna had given him a notebook. The notebook had Miller Lombard, the name of the law firm she worked for, on its front cover. The teacher said Sasha slept with it under his pillow and hid it where he also hid his few prized possessions. Anna made a mental to note to give every child in the Home a notebook. Her law firm was full of notebooks and she was sure they could spare enough for the Home. She would see what Vera could do on the next stationery order.

Forty Six

VICTOR Nikolayevich has pestered Leonid Marlenovich nonstop about the 'products' which had arrived from Cuba and were to be sent on to destinations in the Baltic and Europe. Leonid Marlenovich had intimated every time the subject was brought up that Cuban cigars were widely sought after in the West. Very few were being exported officially from Cuba and so those which they were adding discretely to the market were easily absorbed and without anyone taking any notice. As they and their partners were avoiding certain taxes and the ridiculous US embargo on Cuban goods, however, the operation was kept quiet and off the books. Victor Nikolayevich had no objections to the secret nature of the trading but just wanted reassurances that they would not become involved in any scandals. He readily swallowed the cigar line, but did not believe it. There had to more to it, but he accepted what he was being told for the time being.

Victor Nikolayevich had joined Leonid Marlenovich to inspect a shipment of four boats that were bound for Riga. They were being transported on a barge which had docked off the company's slipway. They were both on the barge together with Natasha who was responsible for the company's export sales. To put Victor Nikolayevich's mind at rest the best he could Leonid Marlenovich had engineered for Victor Nikolayevich to find a large packet of cigars on one of the boats and for it then to be restored in a compartment which would not be suspected nor discovered unless the boat was stripped into pieces. Victor

Nikolayevich nodded to Leonid Marlenovich and the subject was dropped for the rest of their inspection. They left the barge and a group of workers stopped and greeted Victor Nikolayevich as they walked through the main shipyard.

"Off to Cuba soon I expect, eh?" said an old man giving Victor Nikolayevich a knowing wink.

"Well it's not automatic you know, it does not happen every year," replied Victor Nikolayevich.

"Nothing is automatic around here anymore," continued the man and the group of workers with him agreed.

"Well your lives will soon be much easier," said Victor Nikolayevich with a genuine smile.

"That is what you say every year," moaned one of the workers.

"This time it's true," said Victor Nikolayevich continuing to smile. "We have a plan for a brand new state-of-the-art production line!" His enthusiasm was met with blank faces.

"How?" one of the group asked eventually.

"Well, through our privatisation we are raising the money to buy some brand new equipment and install a line to make small fast boats. Brand new models which are in great demand all around the world!"

"Well where would a new production line go?" again asked one of the group. "The yards are pretty full and we always need more space for what we are doing now."

"We are looking at redeveloping the Old Foundry building, is that not right, Leonid Marlenovich?" said Victor Nikolayevich turning to Leonid Marlenovich.

"Possibly," replied Leonid Marlenovich, "the basement has been partly redeveloped but there are still some areas that have not been used for a long time."

"Is that not because the building belongs to someone else?" asked one of the group who looked at Leonid Marlenovich with the faintest of challenges in his eyes. "There are some rumours, Victor Nikolayevich." Most of the workers knew that something was going on in the building and there had indeed been growing rumours about it being used by someone rather than the company itself.

Victor Nikolayevich momentarily looked stunned. He hated the fact that one of his workers might know something he did not. Plus he hated their capacity for rumour mongering and conspiracy theories. "Well if it is someone else who might own the building then it will certainly only be the city," he said firmly. "Leonid Marlenovich, remind me to talk to the Mayor. Nothing will get in the way of the new line." Victor Nikolayevich moved away smartly, the secretly hidden cigars long forgotten already.

Leonid Marlenovich motioned to the worker who had brought up the subject of the Old Foundry's ownership and had him accompany him across the yard. It was agreed that the rumours should stop and Victor Nikolayevich not be bothered any more with such idle gossip.

Forty Seven

THE Standart finally looked like a three-hundred-year-old boat. Its second painting had dried well and it had had several days of good weather to acquire a slightly weathered appearance. The afternoon of the mini storm had passed into local folklore despite Inspector Bushkin's attempts to hush up the strange events. Opinion was divided between those who believed that the paint was a cheap Russian imitation of a German marine paint and those who thought the boat was cursed and had been interfered with by a supernatural force intent on sending a message. Roman Felixovich had supplied the paint which he knew to be genuine and he had been put out by the actions of the boat's main sponsor, Samsung. Samsung had had new paint flown in specifically from Korea to redo the painting. Roman Felixovich had let it be known that something untoward had happened to the paint he had supplied and he had made it clear that he would find out who had been involved. He believed that someone was trying to sabotage his contribution to the project and embarrass him with the Mayor.

The Standart was having an unofficial visit from the Mayor and staff from the main departments in the City Council. They were boarding the vessel and having friendly conversations with the experts and volunteers about the project. For his part Roman Felixovich slipped into the disused yard unnoticed and inspected the new paint. Without a word to anyone Roman Felixovich then left and got into the back seat of his Mercedes which was parked just outside the boat yard. He then shook hands with the well-dressed man already seated in the car. Roman Felixovich motioned for his guest not to speak and ordered his driver to drive to the nearest spot where he could park up unnoticed. After about five minutes the Mercedes turned down a leafy side road and several hundred meters later stopped. Roman Felixovich ordered his driver to wait outside the car which his driver duly did.

"I see that there are many of the officials from your Property Fund visiting the boat," said Roman Felixovich.

"A good day out for my colleagues," replied his guest. "The Mayor enjoys an entourage. Please take a look at this." He handed Roman Felixovich a folded piece of paper from his suit pocket. Roman Felixovich opened it and read it quickly.

"Who has proposed this?"

"The company."

"Can it be changed?"

"It is now up to me to make a recommendation to the Mayor's office. I have the final say in the Property Fund. Therefore, indeed, it can be changed."

Roman Felixovich looked again at the paper and started to make some mental calculations. More importantly he played out various scenarios in his mind. It would not just be about the sums involved but how they were to be paid and crucially how the bidding would be done and controlled. He made a final calculation and then took out a pen and a small notepad. He wrote down two numbers and two phrases. He showed the pad to his guest and motioned to which sections of the paper they referred to. His guest nodded understanding full well what was meant and also the fact that there could be no evidence that the paper had been interfered with - a new paper would be produced by his department. Roman Felixovich put his hand in his pocket and took out an envelope which he handed to his guest. Roman Felixovich then tapped on his window for his driver to get back in the car. Without any further conversation they dropped the guest at the first metro station they drove to.

Forty Eight

ADAM had developed a routine emboldened now by the sighting of one of the girls in the hotel lobby and by the hope that sooner or later the memories of the night of his Welcome Drinks could very well metaphorically be 'put to bed'. He would go to the hotel bar as soon as he arrived from the office and have two beers. The bar was normally quite empty and the beers settled him. He would then spend a few moments in the hotel lobby looking at notices or browsing in the very expensive little shop before going to the lift. Several times this had gone to his plan and he had caught sight of the young woman with long black hair. Olga, as he remembered. He had then taken the lift hoping that she too had seen him. If she had not appeared he would venture back down fifteen minutes or so later and again loiter in the lobby before going outside for a short walk. More often than not in this case he would see her sitting in the bar. Each time he saw her, however, she had been alone. Only once had she seen her talking to a group of other young women. As of yet, though, he had not seen her with the other girl, the 'Lena', of his flashbacks. With the passing now of several months since his night of horrors, as he mentally now termed the night of his Welcome Drinks, the flashbacks did not make him sweat. He could watch and analyse them more. The final missing piece remained though what had happened to Lena.

On the last occasion, however, Olga had turned the tables on him without any warning. As he had crossed to the lift and pressed the call button he looked towards the cloakroom as the lift doors opened. As he turned back to step in the lift, Olga had stepped out of the lift! With a long and deliberate smile she had taken his hand and put a copy of the St Petersburg Times in it. "Thank you," she had said quietly and walked into the bar. Adam had literally trembled as the lift had gone up the five floors to his level. Only when he had entered his room and paced back and forth a dozen times did he open the newspaper. A small pink piece of paper fell out. It had a number written in elegant handwriting and three words. "Call me, Olga."

Forty Nine

IT was now June and Green was at his desk in London on a call to Corley. The line he assured Corley was scrambled.

"So you said you had a plan. To bid in a privatisation is hardly the type of move we would expect, even from you Donald. Very novel. We know you are into money these days but surely you can find a better way to make some than that. There must be some brilliance in it somewhere but so far no-one in the department has been able to fathom out where. I am sure there is some logic in it somewhere." Green was being deliberately dismissive. "Anyway to things that matter, you know your real job."

"My extra-curricula brief is to assist, when requested, in the protection of Her Majesty's interests," he said as if quoting from text, "and frankly I do not know yet what I am looking to protect."

"In good time, old boy, all in good time. You know the form. And we prefer it to be when 'required', not 'requested'." There was a slight pause and then he continued. "We would not want to put you in jeopardy now, would we? What with all these nasty attacks going on."

Corley changed track. "Is this connected to the Prince's visit?"

"Why on earth should it be?"

"Does it affect the timing?" he continued rapidly.

"Well, there you may have something. We would not want to get the Prince mixed up in anything now would we?"

Corley's training had taught him to be doubly suspicious whenever the other side started to sound reasonable and make the first concessions. He knew he had something.

"When is the visit scheduled for?"

"If you kept your eyes on the press you would see."

Corley pressed the mouse on his computer and on his screen flashed text from the Times announcing that the Prince of Wales trip to St Petersburg was confirmed for 21st and 22nd of July. "I find the FT more intellectually challenging," he said as he continued to scroll down the screen, "and it is free from court gossip."

"He is due to travel to St Petersburg on 21st and 22nd of July," said Green. Corley nodded to himself becoming more and more suspicious; there had to be a connection. "And who is taking care of the security arrangements?" he asked

"The Foreign Office and the Royal Protection Service, naturally."

"Have they been out here already?"

"I would presume that they have been talking with their Russian counterparts as the normally do. Donald, old boy, you know all the procedures. Nothing has changed since you left. You really should not get too caught up in the financial world. Now tell me please how on earth this privatisation bid is going to help us."

Corley could detect a nervousness in his voice. Now he was sure there was a connection. "If I understand from your fax of the satellite maps you are estimating the site to be somewhere under the buildings of the Peter the Great Shipyard?" he asked.

"Yes, along from that grotesque monument over the entrance in a building which looks like being next to the quayside," replied Green quickly. "Why are you not taking control of the company instead of asking for a lot of funds just to buy a part of it? Many questions are being raised about that."

"Firstly, I doubt we will have to pay much of that but I want to guarantee the funds to convince the company to do it our way. I want to have an agreement that makes us the company's preferred investor. A memorandum to show good faith."

"Good faith!" Green sounded angry. "A memorandum! What kind of soft option is that? A number of people are beginning to think this is just one large financial scam on your part. Now that would be a highly dangerous road for you to set off on."

"Secondly," interrupted Corley ignoring the comment and its veiled threat, "I want to be part of an open bidding competition to make this whole strategy legitimate to the outside world so that no-one starts to ask questions. Now if you prefer covert storming of buildings, there are certainly precedents for that in St Petersburg!" Corley's tone had turned acidic.

"We are hardly thinking of re-enacting the Revolution." Green had become much calmer and almost humorous. Corley thought it better to break off discussions.

"After the privatisation bidding is done I will be able to ensure that the contracts for redeveloping the site we are interested in go to a company controlled fully by us."

"Now why did you not say so before?" Green sounded relieved. "Your plan may finally have some merit. But be careful and no slip-ups."

Corley had hung up and was eagerly scanning through newspaper articles on his screen. After a few minutes he called Miller Lombard's office and was put through to Adam. After some general chit-chat Corley came to the point.

"Adam, in the draft you are preparing for the privatisation what is said about the use of the money?"

"Exactly what you wanted. To redevelop the Old Foundry buildings and install the new production line."

"Very good," replied Corley, "have you heard if there are any other parties interested in bidding?"

"There are rumours of several and we are using all our contacts to try and find out who they are."

"Excellent, but don't worry too much," said Corley sounding very upbeat.

"Really?" replied Adam sounding puzzled.

"Oh yes. The more real investment interest growing the better." Corley leaned back on his chair smiling. "And don't forget we will shortly tie the company down with an agreement. Speak soon."

Adam hung up. Corley's confidence had surprised Adam. Not one of the deals he had worked on in Russia in two years had ever gone to plan – maybe this would be a first. Once again he suspended his judgement.

Fifty

IT was a Tuesday and Alex knew that the Catherine Palace was closed on Tuesdays. It did not make any sense why it was closed on a Tuesday but then many things were different in Russia. He could still, though, walk in the palace's grounds. Very few people ventured in the grounds when the palace was closed but the fact that he could see the occasional person gave Alex some comfort and his parents did not object as long as he kept away from the ponds. He knew the grounds well from his guide books and the several walks he had taken recently with his mum and Adam. The first time he had been in the park was with his mum and dad and that had been in the winter. Then the grounds were a snow-covered landscape with deeply frozen ponds. The bridges and monuments then were also snow-covered but still distinctive and magical. It was now early summer and the grounds were coming to life and they were stunning. Alex had a plan. He had had a short dream which had been very unclear other than to show the windows of the room he had been in. He had decided to see if he could see through the windows from the outside.

He approached the palace from the back and walked around the Great Pond. He could tell where the room was by counting the windows to the left of the large windows which he knew were windows of the Grand Staircase. He then climbed up one of the large flights of steps which led up to the back of the palace from the Great Pond. The fountains which were in the centre of the flights of steps had been switched off because it was a Tuesday. He kept his eyes now fixed on the windows to the room and continued to walk towards the building. He soon reached the windows to the room and felt a wave of disappointment. The windows had the large white dust sheets covering them. When he had been in the room on his visit with Adam the sheets were on the walls and not the windows. He put his hands on the glass and then jumped back as he heard a crashing noise. For a split second he thought he had smashed the window but the glass was intact. He looked all around him and took several steps back. Everywhere was quiet and peaceful again. He felt a tingle in his fingers.

He took a deep breath and stepped back to the windows. He lifted his hands up gingerly and gradually closed his eyes as he pushed his fingers onto the panes of glass in the window. The glass felt warm. As all his fingers made contact he heard the sound again. He kept his eyes tight-shut and the crashing sound continued. Images swirled in front of his eyes and it seemed as though he was watching movements in the reflection in the glass but his eyes were still tight-shut. The movements and the sounds came into focus. His heart jumped but he kept his fingers on the glass. He could see soldiers! The crashing sounds were shells landing in the grounds of the palace. There were distant screams and then shouts, sounds of car engines and then a deep roar as a tank appeared at the side of the pond. People were now running out of the doors at the back of the palace. Footsteps were crunching frantically on the gravel. Gunshots were zinging around him. And then his hands felt red hot but he could not move them! The glass in the windows was melting and turning into an orange like colour. And then the white sheet was pulled back from the window and Alex sank to the floor.

Alex studied his hands. There was nothing on them. He touched his face with his fingers. Apart from a heart that seemed to be beating like crazy he was just the same. The grounds at the back of the palace seemed the same. The fountains were still not on. The only difference was that he could hear the faint sound of voices. These were not the maniac sounds he had just experienced but adult voices and they were very near. Slowly he knelt under the window and raised his head several inches at a time. He passed the window sill and then peered into the window just for a fraction of a second. He sank back down and closed his eyes. He could see the reflection again but it was fading fast, he could see men in long black coats pulling paper and cloth off the walls in the room and shouting loudly. As the reflection faded out, its place was taken by just three men. He had just seen the three men in the room. Men in dark suits. They had been pointing at the walls. He shook his head and again knelt up. This time he raised his head in one movement and stared in. Three men in dark suits were still pointing at the walls. They had their backs to him and as one started to turn round Alex took off from the window running as fast as he could and not caring to mask the loud crunching noise his feet made on the gravel. He ran and ran and headed round the palace. He stopped briefly at the start of the large lawn in front of the palace to look behind him. Everything was peaceful. He jogged to the gates and went through them. Outside there were several benches and he sat down on one of them. He closed his eyes but saw nothing and could only hear his own blood pumping through his ears. A few minutes later he heard the sound of a car engine in the distance and then he saw a large black car coming through the gates. It stopped only very briefly and then accelerated off quickly. Its windows were blacked out. The one part of the car, though, which stood out to Alex was its number plate. It was red indicating it was a diplomatic car and the letter 'D' on its bumper was the real giveaway. They were Germans. But why were the Germans here again? The last time they had been there was in 1941 when they had discovered and dismantled the Amber Room just as Alex had seen in the reflection. Why were Germans back in the room again?

Fifty One

HAMPTON had received a bag full of papers from his office. They were hand-delivered by the office receptionist, Janna, as Vera had not been able to make it as she was assisting Adam in a meeting with a potential new client. Hampton took a brief look though the papers and told Janna that she would not be needed and that she could return to the office. Hampton preferred to wait for Vera. He opened the letters making mental notes of replies. He laughed quietly to himself as he read the reply from the German Consul General. After wishing Hampton well the Consul General went on to explain that he thought the idea could have significant political value and he had taken the initiative to visit the room himself. He had arranged to visit the room yesterday as it was a Tuesday and the Catherine Palace was closed to the public. He had been able to do this because he was fortunate that an old contact had managed to arrange a private visit for himself and two prominent German business leaders whose names he thought it best not to reveal yet. In the room itself all three of them had felt the weight of history upon them and indeed one of the business leaders had also remarked that he had also felt the eyes of the world watching him. He looked forward to discussing the next steps with Hampton as soon as he was fully recovered.

Hampton's reading was then interrupted by a visit from the clinic's Canadian doctor. Hampton's progress was now officially 'excellent'. The prescribed rest was working and

Hampton's good physical shape prior to the shooting was proving to be the key. The wound had healed quickly and his lung was nearly back to full breathing capacity. The doctor also went so far as to suggest that Hampton could leave the clinic in a matter of days and was probably in a position to fly directly to the States for the final phase of his convalescence. He could even consider a normal flight rather than an evacuation so long as adequate comfort could be arranged. Hampton's response slightly disappointed the doctor. He seemed subdued and not excited by the possibility of flying back to the States so soon. Hampton said he would discuss with his wife and asked if they could delay the decision for now. The doctor nodded as he left.

Hampton now faced his first real challenge for several months. In amongst the letters he had not read was one from the Head Curator and the Hermitage – he had recognised the stamp on the back of the large envelope. He opened it quickly and scanned the document inside. It was a dossier and largely in French. He needed to send a fax urgently. He took a deep breath – he would have to wait till Vera came the next day. The stakes had just rocketed sky-high.

Fifty Two

VICTOR Nikolayevich could not have felt more uncomfortable. The room he was in was so tidy and clinical. The large wooden table, rectangular yet with smooth oval edges, was made of a dark wood and heavily polished. He counted twelve wooden chairs with light blue seat covers arranged around the table. There was no obvious place for a General Director to sit. No place to sit and dominate proceedings. A cabinet in the same wood was along a wall. On the cabinet was a tray of glasses and bottles of water. He had picked one up to check it was water. Sadly it was just water. The only other items in the room were a telephone on a side table and three large photographs on one of the walls. They were photographs of London, New York and Tokyo. Impressive shots of the iconic views of the cities with the name of each city embossed in big letters below its photograph. Despite the photographs Victor Nikolayevich felt as though he was on a different planet and yet he was only a few kilometres from his factory, his fortress for the last five decades.

"Welcome, Victor Nikolayevich, to Miller Lombard," said Adam entering the room with Anna and Vera. "Leonid Marlenovich and the Head of your legal department will join us shortly. Vera, can you sort out some drinks?"

At the sound of the word 'drink' Victor Nikolayevich's eyes had lit up. In a low voice he entered into a long conversation with Vera, made a mock begging gesture with his hands and ended by giving Vera a quick hug. Anna spoke to Adam about the whereabouts of Dominic Corley and Adam excused himself to make a quick phone call. This was partly to distract Adam from Victor Nikolayevich's antics. Victor Nikolayevich had managed to sweet-talk Vera into preparing him a large coffee with three fingers of brandy in it which Anna had approved with a discrete nod of her head. Victor Nikolayevich had asked for four fingers but Vera had battled him down to three.

"Dear Anna," said Victor Nikolayevich with a big smile, "this is a different world in here, don't you think?"

"It is," replied Anna also with a big smile, "but we are still in Russia. It is still our country."

Victor Nikolayevich was struck by the feeling in Anna's voice. She was one of the few people he had met who seemed to be able to handle the foreigners. He was about to launch into a speech about how much he loved his country when the door opened and Leonid Marlenovich walked in finishing a call. He was followed by a short man carrying an armful of documents. It was the Head of the company's legal department and Anna had met him before when she had been at the company. She had grown very wary of him because of the silence which had greeted most of her questions to him. Leonid Marlenovich had told Victor Nikolayevich that he would go ahead to the lawyers to finalise the 'Memorandum of Understanding' which they were going to sign with the British Redevelopment Fund.

"Is everything in order, Leonid Marlenovich?" asked Victor Nikolayevich.

"I think so. Do you agree, Dimitri Alexandrovich?" replied Leonid Marlenovich addressing the short man.

"I think we should ask that question to our international lawyers?" replied Dimitri Alexandrovich avoiding eye contact with his senior colleagues.

"Come, come, Dimitri Alexandrovich," said Victor Nikolayevich in a very jovial voice, "you are still our legal Head. We all need to learn new things. Especially with all the changes."

Dimitri Alexandrovich nodded. Victor Nikolayevich was about to continue when the door opened and Vera entered with a tray of drinks followed by Adam and Corley laughing loudly. Corley slapped Adam on the back as Victor Nikolayevich eagerly took the large cup offered to him. The men then all shook hands as Anna showed then all to their seats. She put the company executives on one side, Corley on the other side and then positioned herself next to Victor Nikolayevich and Adam and Vera either side of Corley.

"As I discussed with both Leonid Marlenovich and Mr Corley," began Adam, "we have arranged a surprise for the meeting."

Anna sat up in her seat and was about to comment when Adam stood up and continued quickly. "I just need to bring the phone onto the centre of the table," he said as he picked up the phone and placed it in the centre of the table. He pressed several buttons and then asked for the call to be put through. He sat down smiling.

"Good afternoon, gentlemen and ladies," said a voice over the phone's loudspeaker. The slight American accent was unmistakeable. Victor Nikolayevich jumped up and nearly split his drink. Everyone smiled.

"Good afternoon, Mr Hampton," said Victor Nikolayevich loudly in his heavily Russian accented English. "How are you?" he continued looking at Anna and whispering in Russian to her.

"I am recovering very well, Victor Nikolayevich," said Hampton. "Vera, can you translate for Victor Nikolayevich and I?"

"Of course," replied Vera. For the next twenty minutes Victor Nikolayevich and Hampton had a very animated call as Victor Nikolayevich who was on his feet throughout asked Hampton to take him through all the details of the shooting and everything that had happened since. Victor Nikolayevich expressed his outrage and Vera had to avoid translating a plethora of inappropriate adjectives used by Victor Nikolayevich. Hampton for his part tried several times to steer the conversation back to the privatisation but

Victor Nikolayevich would have none of it. Amongst a long list of actions he promised to do was to meet with both the Mayor and with the Chief of Police to demand they redouble their efforts to catch the would-be assassins.

During the conference call Adam, with Leonid Marlenovich's nodded permission, passed Corley the Memorandum of Understanding for him to read through. It was a two-page document and there was a Russian original with an English translation. Corley read it several times and Anna was intrigued to see him read both the Russian and English versions. He had spoken very little Russian but from the ease with which he scanned the Russian text Anna guessed that his Russian must be relatively good. She herself had prepared the document which Adam had added to but changed very little. Leonid Marlenovich's input had been on the figures and form of privatisation whereas his legal colleague had spent an inordinate amount of time fussing over the language and punctuation. Anna thought that he did not actually understand what the document was about and had merely sought ways to try to prove his importance.

The conference call wound to an end with Hampton wishing everyone well in the rest of the meeting and said he hoped to be back in person as soon as possible. As the call finished Victor Nikolayevich sat down, drained the rest of his drink and took out a handkerchief. He wiped his eyes and looked at Anna who passed him a copy of the Memorandum. To avoid Victor Nikolayevich's clear emotion becoming the centre of the meeting she asked if she could read out the Memorandum in Russian and then in English point by point to make sure it was clear to everyone. If there were any questions then they would deal with them there and then. She also asked Vera to arrange some more drinks and signalled that Victor Nikolayevich should have the same again. This was lost on everyone except Leonid Marlenovich who gave Anna a fleeting and knowing smile. He too was beginning to appreciate Anna's handling of people, both foreign, and indeed, Russian.

The first lines of the Memorandum were straightforward and defined the two parties to the agreement – the full names, legal status and addresses. Anna then read out the first key phrase. "In this Memorandum the two parties hereby agree the terms of their mutual co-operation in the privatisation of twenty-five per cent of the Company's shares which are to be offered for sale in an auction." She paused and everyone nodded. Anna then went on to read the actions that the parties would take which detailed all the potential steps both parties would take for the British Redevelopment Fund to win the auction. She then turned to the terms of the privatisation and everyone looked at the papers as Anna said, "the auction will be based on a minimum price for the shares of 1 million dollars and an investment in the company of 10 million dollars to be deposited in the company's bank account." She paused as the amounts sunk in – such figures pronounced in a meeting like this seemed vast. Most of the Russians in the room had never seen more than handfuls of dollar bills, including Victor Nikolayevich. To the foreigners, the figures were indeed just that - figures.

"I must congratulate you Victor Nikolayevich and Leonid Marlenovich on such strong terms," said Corley. "I can assume that no-one else will have any such funds at their disposal?"

"We hope not," smiled Leonid Marlenovich, "but to be on the safe side it does say a 'minimum' of 1 million. Please continue, Anna."

Furthermore," continued Anna, "the British Redevelopment Fund is prepared to bid up to 2 million dollars for the shares if necessary." Leonid Marlenovich looked at Corley who was about to say something but Leonid Marlenovich motioned for him to listen to the rest of the clause. "The Fund will also deposit the 10 million dollars into the company's bank account at the same time as it ownership of the twenty-five per cent of the shares is recorded formally in the company's Share Register." Anna looked up at Corley who nodded for her to continue. "The ten million dollars of investment are to be used only to purchase and install the new production line and the Company hereby commits to allow the Fund to have sight of all documentation relating to the line and all plans to redevelop the site. The Fund will have the option to appoint the contractor for the installation of the line."

"Excellent," interrupted Corley who smiled at Leonid Marlenovich. "It is only an option, Leonid. I am sure we will be able to agree on a local contractor but the option does give the Fund the required level of security for investing such a sum."

"I fully agree, Mr Corley. We will value your input and advice as much as we do the funds you are providing."

Adam beamed. The meeting could not be going any better. Victor Nikolayevich had finished his second cup and nodded intermittently to Leonid Marlenovich and to Anna. Anna explained that there were just two more points of substance to the agreement. "Clause three," she said, "says that the auction will be made via sealed bids. Clause four says that that this agreement is exclusive to the two parties." She sensed a look of concern on Victor Nikolayevich's face and explained further to him that this only meant that the agreement was between the Company and the Fund, no-one else. And that neither the Company nor the Fund could make any other agreements with other parties for the privatisation. Victor Nikolayevich looked at Anna and then nodded. Dimitri Alexandrovich, who had not made a single sound throughout the meeting, stood up and walked round to Victor Nikolayevich. He whispered in Victor Nikolayevich's ear that such clauses were not usual in Russian legal agreements. Anna overheard him and shook her head. Victor Nikolayevich asked Dimitri Alexandrovich to go back to his seat.

"Leonid Marlenovich," said Victor Nikolayevich, "are you happy with the agreement?"

"I am and I am sure that the terms will be successful, Victor Nikolayevich."

Adam was about to add that the terms had not yet been formally set by the Property Fund but then he assumed that they had been agreed behind the scenes by the company and the Property Fund. Instead he asked when the auction was expected to be announced.

"My information is," replied Leonid Marlenovich, "that Dimitri Alexandrovich was told by the Property Fund, that the terms will be published on Friday 30th June. Is that correct, Dimitri Alexandrovich?"

Dimitri Alexandrovich nodded and smiled sternly at Adam and Anna.

"Excellent!" said Corley standing up. "I will have the funds ready to be sent! Should we now sign the agreement?"

Following Corley's lead everyone stood up. After several minutes the Memorandum was signed and then toasted ceremonially with copious amounts of vodka. Vera materialised the vodka and glasses from the cupboard in the room. During the closing of the meeting Victor Nikolayevich felt as if he was now truly once again back in Russia, his country.

Fifty Three

SHORTLY after the meeting with the company Janna brought Adam a thirty-page fax from the Miller Lombard office in The Hague. Adam had decided not to bring up the subject of the company's properties in the meeting as he had been assured first thing in the morning that the information from The Hague would arrive that afternoon. He had also decided to wait until he had all the information he was waiting for on the Old Foundry building from both the authorities in St Petersburg and his colleague in The Hague. He checked that the main meeting room was now free and went in taking his draft list of ownership of the building, the fax and a large light green envelope with the grand logo of the St Petersburg City Council embossed in the top right hand corner and the back sealed in wax which had been delivered the day before.

He opened the envelope and took out three leaves of almost translucent paper. He studied them carefully and could make out that this was as he had expected a copy of the Property Register and on the second page a list of owners in chronological order. The document he had received from the company had only been one page long. He took out a dictionary looked up several words and then painstaking transliterated the names of the previous owners of the building against the dates. The Register confirmed his draft list with a minor correction to one of the dates:

1726	Berd
1789	Baronsky
1852	Yusupov
1918	Petrograd
1946	Peter the Great Shipyard Collective

The third and last page contained the dates of court claims and a short description. With his limited Russian he could just make out some of the names which he wrote down together with the dates of the claims:

1946	Claim by Yusupov, FA
1992	Claim by Berd, WC
1992	Claim by Baronsky, DA
1993	Claim by Yusupov, FR

He needed to have the descriptions of the court claims translated fully but he reckoned that the claims had been rejected. He then turned to the fax from his office in The Hague. There were copies of court filings which were in Dutch and English. It took him a while to start to work out which claims had been filed. His colleague had given him a briefing on the processes at the Supreme Court for Arbitration and Restitution in The Hague. This court could investigate a claim and then forward its findings to the court in the country concerned which in this case was the court in St Petersburg with its recommendation but the final decision remained with the country court. Adam knew that in reality filing a claim in The Hague in this way was really to try to apply pressure on the St Petersburg court. The court in The Hague's real function was to settle major restitutions of property following conflicts and wars and not to settle individual cases but as his colleague had said 'why would lawyers complain when good fees were to be earned?' Adam was becoming less interested in the pros and cons of filing in this way and much more interested in the parties involved. One thing for sure was the fact that the company had not provided him with all this information and once again he decided to suspend his judgement on the motives of those involved. He added another column to his list of court claims and added the title of 'law firm'. He would study the fax in great detail and work out which lawyers were involved in the claims. Unfortunately it would take some time.

He picked up the phone in the meeting room and dialled an internal number. "Anna, hi," he said, "there is something I would like you to look at when you some time."

"What is it?" asked Anna.

"It's a list of claims on one of the buildings at the Peter the Great Shipyard. It is from the Property Register and it is in quite technical looking Russian."

"Can't I have someone translate it for you?"

"Probably, but you will probably understand it more."

Anna agreed to Adam's request. Adam put the three pages back in the light green envelope. He had told Anna he would have them photocopied and dropped off at her desk. Despite his previous experience with original documents something made him decide to keep these pages in his possession day and night.

Fifty Four

THE colourfully decorated twenty-metre yacht was moored in the West Harbour of the Port of Helsinki. The yacht flew a Dutch Antilles flag and only a keen boat watcher would recognise the yacht's Russian 'Neva' brand, which was a direct copy of a popular American yacht. A man dressed elegantly in a tweed jacket and with a soldier at his side was standing at a high point along the quayside. Through his binoculars he watched as the crew members on the yacht looked to be making to leave the yacht. He spoke into his phone and a couple of minutes later two Finnish police cars arrived at the yacht's mooring their lights flashing but their sirens off. The police boarded the yacht. The man kept his binoculars trained on the yacht and watched the police move through the yacht lifting up seat covers and searching in cupboards. They left ten minutes later with a salute to the yacht's captain. They also left empty-handed.

Shortly afterwards the crew decided to leave the yacht. Emboldened by the failed search they soon found the nearest bar in the port and started to drink quickly and loudly. Thirty minutes later a fight broke out between one of the crew and a huge bearded Finn over who had knocked over whose drink. All the crew found themselves accompanying their fellow crew member to a police station.

The soldier and the man in the tweed jacket having witnessed the arrest from a discrete distance had returned to the quayside by the boat. The soldier was eager to board the boat.

"We can search the boat again ourselves this time," said the man, "but the Finns won't impound her unless we can prove that any goods found on it belong to the crew."

"But, Mr Green," said the soldier, "we know this boat and what it must be carrying from St Petersburg."

They boarded the yacht. Green was eager for them not to spend much time aboard lest anyone return. They made a cursory search without any result. "Best to send her on her way," he said as he climbed back onshore, "but check it is wired ok. We do not want any mistakes and the Cubans must know nothing."

"I guess at least they will cool off on their trading for a while," said the soldier joining Green on shore.

"I'd guess that they'll switch ports out of St Petersburg from Helsinki to Riga or somewhere similar next time so we must keep track of the boat all the time."

He took a small computer with a large screen out of his pocket. The computer had a map of the world on the front. He pressed a button and a small red spot started to flick at the bottom of Finland. "There she is. There's nowhere she can go without us knowing. He pressed another button and a video screen came up. He adjusted the buttons at the side and picture came up of inside the captain's cabin. He then pressed a rewind button and replayed a scene showing four crew members opening a bag and passing round a white powder.

"Why do not you want the Finnish police to have this as proof?" asked the soldier

"We have much bigger fish to catch than some recreational substances," said Green.

"But why go to the effort of this raid and arrest on shore and let it all fail?"

"Appearances, appearances," said Green with a smile, "and to send these Cubans home with heroic tales of avoiding capture on the high seas. We need them to keep their bottle. My intelligence is that they and their backers have been getting somewhat nervous."

"All the same it will look as though we failed and it will not impress the Finns."

"Dear boy, our ops never 'fail'. Well they never fail in their real goals. Keep up the good work."

"Donald, have you read the Times today, page 17?" Green asked. They were speaking on a pre-arranged conference call a few days later. "Boat raided in Helsinki."

Corley flicked through the internet screen on his desk.

"Yacht had come from St Petersburg, I think," Green continued. "One built by the Peter the Great Shipyard in fact. Perhaps the company should be more careful who they sell their boats to."

"Why are you so interested in the actual boats that the company makes of all of a sudden?" Corley was becoming irritated by Green.

"Just getting the hang of this business thing and these investments. It must pay to understand what such companies actually make."

"I see that the Prince of Wales is awarding some medals," said Corley changing the subject, "and taking a journey by road and by sea on something called the Road of Life. He is then going to christen a replica boat called the Standart."

"How interesting," replied Green.

"The replica boat does not sound that interesting," said Corley. "Its site on the other hand is very interesting."

"Where would that be?" asked Green.

"Its site is an old disused boat yard on the bank opposite the Peter the Great Shipyard," said Corley quickly.

Green laughed loudly. "What? Do you think something bad will happen to him when he visits this replica boat? Maybe there by a sniper on top of that monstrous statue in the Peter the Great Shipyard who will fire all the way across the Neva." He continued to laugh.

"Why do you find this so amusing?"

"I love the way you dig, dear Donald, but you will have to do much better than that. Much, much better."

Corley smiled to himself as he put the phone down. He knew it was ridiculous but he was intrigued at how Green had reacted so dismissively to such an obvious line of questioning. It made him even more convinced that behind the smokescreen of the visit something major was being stirred up, or perhaps that the visit was being set up as a cover for some unfinished business. It was so like the dark factions within the secret services to have two plans, to have two set-ups with no-one knowing which one of the two was really going to happen. These factions were much feared for operating in the twilight area with their own agendas which they could readily put before the national interest; some of these factions thought nothing of linking up with undesirable elements in other countries to achieve their own agendas. He was going to have to walk on a number of tightropes to work his way through the coming weeks – he was even beginning to wonder which side he was supposed to be on.

Fifty Five

INSPECTOR Bushkin despite his private ventures was still a good detective. He had kept the finding of the smashed bottles in the Standart boatyard under wraps. He had the area covered over with tarpaulins and cordoned off. He had it done in such a way as not to attract any attention. He had also taken a selection of the smashed glass to have it analysed by one of the curators at the Hermitage whom he had known for many years. The curator was an expert in Russian jewellery and Inspector Bushkin thought he would be able to help identify the smashed glass and to do so off the record. A thought still tugged at the back of his mind and he hoped that the curator would provide him with a starting point as to the origins of the glass. He would then try and work out why there was so much of it where it was and if there was anything else to investigate. Illicit vodka production was an obvious possibility but why leave so much evidence if this were the case? Why smashed bottles? He was a good detective and did not like it when something remained a mystery. He was also still doing his upmost to uncover who was behind the strange events which the press enjoyed reporting about so much. This really irked the Chief of Police who bemoaned the constant jokes about ghosts and 'that peasant' who the police could not catch. Inspector Bushkin needed to keep a calm and rational boss.

Inspector Bushkin was shown to the curator's office which had changed little in well over a hundred years. It was still largely Pre-Revolution in its furniture, cabinets and workbench. It had a computer but its screen was switched off. Papers and pieces of jewellery were everywhere. The men greeted each other warmly and chatted about people they knew whilst the curator ordered some coffee. Inspector Bushkin recognised some of the pieces of glass which he had had discovered. They had been labelled and laid out in an organised fashion on a board on the curator's large wooden desk.

"Don't worry, Vladimir," said the curator as he sensed Inspector Bushkin was looking at the pieces. The request has been for an 'off the record' analysis. "That is just my way of examining the pieces. Don't worry I am not making them into an exhibition."

Inspector Bushkin nodded and smiled. "Thank you," he said.

"Although they have some potential."

"How so?" asked Inspector Bushkin.

"As, how can I describe them? As folklore, perhaps."

Inspector Bushkin stared at the curator and frowned.

"I thought that the bottles never existed. That is was a myth of the Siege. But maybe the 'bottles of life' were not a fairy tale, after all." The curator was beaming. "You see I had the inside of the bottles examined and they are still tiny traces of fruit juice in them. Very faint after fifty years but enough to provide enough evidence to show that they were real."

Inspector Bushkin's frown intensified. That was what had been tugging at the back of his mind. He had heard the story of the 'bottles of life' when he was a small child although the story had been 'lost' when the official history of the Siege had been written and the heroics of the men and woman who worked on the Ice Road or Road of Life had become the focus of the history.

"Yes, Inspector," continued the curator, "you probably heard some of the same stories as I did when we were children."

Inspector Bushkin stood up and paced up and down the small office. "Yes," he said, "the story was that people who were starving would be woken by a sound in the middle of the night.."

"Of a man laughing," interrupted the curator.

"Yes, of a man laughing," continued Inspector Bushkin concentrating hard, "and they would follow the sound until they would find a bottle and take it home."

"The bottles were full of concentrated juices made from all kinds of fruit and as such they were very high in calories."

"People would hide the bottles and then destroy then after drinking because anyone caught with the juices would have to hand them over to the authorities and never see them again."

Inspector Bushkin sat down. "The strangest thing," he said quietly, "is that there must be thousands of them in one place."

"Really? That would be interesting to see."

"Well, I will see what I can do later. The place will be easier to visit in a few weeks' time."

"And so they are real, after all," smiled the curator. "It is not a fairy tale or a mirage or even a vision brought on by starvation as some people used to say."

Inspector Bushkin looked at the curator with his frown returning. He remembered what people used to say in the story when they were asked about the laughter – it was always if Gregory Yefimovich Rasputin was back to help them and that he had invited them to a party where the laughter would never end and the drink would flow on throughout the night like it did at the famous wild parties before the Revolution!!

Fifty Six

ADAM had finally cracked all the information buried in the thirty page long fax from the Miller Lombard office in The Hague. He had found the identity of the law firms representing the claims on the Old Foundry building. It had not been easy because each specific claim had been officially filed by a Dutch registered law firm as is the requirement of the process. He had had to track correspondence further back to glean which law firm was really behind each claim submitted by a Dutch law firm. He looked at the amended list he had compiled:

		Law firm	Location
1946	Claim by Yusupov, FA	Zorin	Moscow
1992	Claim by Berd, WC	Malborough & Co	London
1992	Claim by Baronsky, DA	White & Grace	Detroit
1993	Claim by Yusupov, FR	Antiopolis	Cyprus

He folded the list and put it in the light green envelope which contained the originals from the St Petersburg Property Register which he put back in his briefcase. The London law firm had jumped out at him and it made some sense as Berd was a Scottish engineer. Rather than speculate or investigate he decided to call Anna and see if she had looked at the Property Register. He dialled her internal number but was told that she was out of the office.

Adam then looked through his large A4 sized diary on his desk. As he did several times a day he flicked to the back inside cover which had a two page planner for the following year - 1996. There was nothing written in the planner but it had the small piece of pink paper with the telephone number and request to 'Call me, Olga' stuck in the top right hand corner. Several times a day he would go through what he would or would not say on the call. Should he suggest a drink? Should he come straight out with it and ask her where and even how her friend, Lena, was? Should he ask her why she had given him the note? No, that was inviting more than he was prepared to contemplate and would probably lead to a straightforward financial proposition. This was an area he avoided. There were plenty of stories. He closed his diary with a rather louder than necessary noise as Vera, his boss' secretary came over to his desk. He was convinced that the girls in the office thought he had no interest in girls whatsoever – comments about English public schools were often made with a giggle or two. But what did they know!!

"Adam," smiled Vera. With the work that they were now doing together, especially at the Hermitage, Adam felt that he at least was on the way to a normal and grown-up relationship with Vera. He suspected that Vera had her sights set much higher – more than likely on his boss, but, as was his way he had suspended his judgement. After all what did he himself actually know!! "Adam," smiled Vera again, "are you free tomorrow night?"

Adam looked at her with a slight frown but then put on a more serious face. "Let me check," he replied opening his diary. As he did so the piece of pink paper fell out of the inside back cover of his diary. Adam's heart jumped. He tried not to react and heaved a massive sigh of relief as he looked at the piece of paper. It had landed on the floor written face down. Before Vera could sense what was up with him he said quickly. "Yes, actually I am free." He closed his diary this time very quietly.

"Very good," continued Vera, "tomorrow is Janna's birthday and all the office is going for a drink at six thirty at the Senate Bar. Because John is not here he wants you to be in charge."

"Great," replied Adam with a big smile. Vera looked at him with a faint look of surprise. She had expected him to find a way to object. "Can you sort out a birthday card and some flowers?"

'We are having another drinks party tomorrow at six thirty at the Senate Bar and you are welcome,' Adam had said down the phone in one breath. After his conversation with Vera, Adam had stepped outside the office for some fresh air and dialled the number on the pink piece of paper without another thought. All the girl had had the chance to say had been 'Da?' when she answered the call followed by a 'good' after Adam's invitation. The 'good' had had a surprised, but at the same time, a seductive ring to it. Adam had not said anything else and ended the call. The 'good' would not leave Adam's mind in peace.

The Senate Bar was relatively empty at six thirty the following day as the Miller Lombard staff entered. Adam put his credit card behind the bar and the bar quickly came to life. Adam busied himself making sure everyone had at least one large drink and he fussed over Janna. At the same time he kept an eye on the entrance to the bar. To make sure everyone could enjoy themselves without any lingering office formalities, Adam decided to make a quick speech as soon as possible and present Janna with the flowers and card. As he finished and proceeded to give Janna a hug and kisses on both cheeks which provoked an outburst of surprised applause, Adam caught sight of the girl he had invited entering the bar. Adam disengaged from Janna, pecked Vera on both cheeks without any warning which sent her face blushing smartly and then raised his glass in a loud English, 'Cheers!' As the commotion and applause settled back down, Adam quietly made his way to the end of the bar and ordered a double whisky. As he did so the girl joined him at his elbow. "What would you like to drink?" asked Adam.

"A B52 bomber," she replied with a smile at the bartender who nodded. Adam gulped and nodded his consent to the bartender.

"And I'll have another double!" he said downing the drink the bartender had put in front of him.

"Very good," said the girl with a big smile at Adam. The words sent a shiver down Adam's spine like he had never felt before.

Olga it quickly emerged knew one or two of the girls at Adam's office. She left the bar with another smile at Adam and went over to greet them in a very low key way. No-one seemed to pick up on the fact that Adam had invited her. In fact one of the other girls in the office had kissed Olga on the cheek and whispered in her ear. Adam guessed correctly that the girl was explaining that there was a credit card behind the bar and that she was sure no-one would mind if Olga joined Janna's birthday party. Adam came over to them both and asked if they would like another drink. The other girl smiled at Olga with a conspiratorial look and with it Olga had officially joined the party. From this point on Adam relaxed visibly. He talked with several of the staff and then manoeuvred close to Olga. He learned that Olga worked for one of the largest companies in the city and he in turn explained a little of his background in Russia. The bar was noisy and the atmosphere became friendlier and friendlier. Adam was working up to asking Olga about her friend but needed to visit the bathroom. He excused himself and made his way towards the toilets. He turned back round at the door and saw Olga put her hand in to her small handbag on the bar and take out her mobile which must have been ringing. She looked animated as she started to speak on the phone.

When Adam walked back over to the bar a few minutes later he could not see Olga or her handbag on the bar. He took a quick look around the room but could not see her. The music in the bar had become louder and lights were flashing in a corner of the bar as the disco was warming up. No-one paid any attention as he walked to the door of the bar and stepped outside. He looked both ways on the road and froze. Across the road was a black Mercedes with a dent in its bumper on the driver's side. He could see a young woman in the back seat talking on a mobile phone. As the car set off the woman looked across to the bar. It was Olga. She looked straight through Adam without acknowledging him. For the second time that evening Adam felt a shiver down his spine like he had never felt before.

Fifty Seven

ROMAN Felixovich did not like surprises. He had learned since his first forays into the black market that it was the trading in information and favours which was much more important than the buying and selling of actual goods and services. The Soviet economy had bred a system that worked on permissions – permissions which were traded as smartly as stocks and shares were traded on the stock exchanges of the capitalist markets, albeit the permissions were traded in the dark. Those who controlled the permissions worked with such opaqueness and dissimulation that only those operating in the same manner could tell who they were. In the past a high rank in any sector of Soviet life opened many doors and yet the doorkeepers to the black economy could come from any rank in Soviet society. The secretiveness was greater than any Masonic Lodge and more akin to that observed by the Magician's Circle! Two pieces of information about the Peter the Great Shipyard had surprised Roman Felixovich despite his meticulous planning and manoeuvring.

On the surface the first piece of information was very concerning. He had been informed that the company had just signed an agreement with a party which was being called the company's 'preferred bidder' for the forthcoming privatisation. This information had come from a source within the company. A source which was said to be unhappy with the arrangement but which still required suitable compensation for providing the information on this confidential agreement. Roman Felixovich's reaction to this news was mixed. On one hand it showed that the company, as he had been told, was in need of support from one party or another and was in negotiations – the company could not survive on its own and hence was vulnerable to an outside party taking control. On the other hand he needed to find out who the 'preferred bidder' was. The agreement had been arranged by a foreign law firm called Miller Lombard. Roman Felixovich had several options on how to take this forward.

The second piece of information was more puzzling and potentially really problematic. The company had put in a request to the St Petersburg Property Fund to finalise the terms of its privatisation. Roman Felixovich assumed this must have a direct relationship to the agreement which was being rumoured. The request was proposing that a minimum amount of ten million dollars be invested directly into the company by the winner of the auction for the shares. The real problem was that it was being proposed that the ten million dollars be in cash deposited in the company's bank account. This was not how he had thought the investment conditions would work! Ten million dollars in cash today could buy him control of half of the companies in the whole of the city! He had not expected anything like this – it could be a knock-out blow, a full house or even a fatal checkmate. He now realised why the Mayor had highlighted this company as one at risk of being taken out of the city's control. Some other parties clearly had their reasons for trying to take it over and they were either very daring in taking on the company's local protectors at the top of the city's police force no less, or stupidly naïve! His counter attack would have to have greater force or subtlety than he had assumed. He needed time to think.

Fifty Eight

WITHOUT really noticing Anna had started to spend some time with other children in the Home and not just with Sasha. She had thought up a game to help the younger children to learn to count. She used a selection of coins from different countries which she managed to collect from contacts within her firm. Adam had been very useful in arranging for coins of low value to be sent to St Petersburg from some of the firm's larger offices. She would sit a group of children in a circle and start some basic counting games. As the game developed she would ask one of the children to guess which country a coin she picked up was from. Then she would launch into a story of foreign lands where there were all kinds of different landscapes and wonderful animals. She would imitate the animals and then have the children make the same noises. After the first story all the children would rush to pick up a coin and ask, "which country? Which country, Anna? Please tell us."

On one occasion a little child had ran over to join the game. "Tell me which country, which country?" she said excitedly. Anna picked her up. "Australia," she said turning the child upside down. "Can you see? Everything is upside down in Australia."

"Kangaroos! I can see kangaroos!" the little girl shouted in a fit of giggles. Such moments were a rarity but Anna managed to make them magical despite the overwhelming feeling of depression that the Home had on her. It was not the children nor most of the staff – it was the simple fact of life that a once great superpower had collapsed into a vast country in economic and social meltdown with the result that the least cared for sections of society were bearing the brunt of the dramatic upheavals. Something, however small, would have to be done – to be done by those who cared and by those who could find a way. Society itself had too many deep-rooted issues to resolve with itself and with its traumatic past.

Anna for once had her own troubles. She had become very angry at her father when her mother had called to cancel their trip to St Petersburg planned for the last week of June which was the most perfect time of year to visit the city. It was when the days were virtually twenty-four hours' long and the nights became the 'white nights' – only a few minutes of actual darkness in the middle of the night and otherwise hours and hours of wonderfully pale but enchanting light. The city hardly slept during the white nights and its inhabitants were free to spend hours and hours outside. The news had been in a rushed phone call from her mother who said that her father was very sorry but felt very unable to travel at the moment. For a man who had spent most of his working life travelling and who was still in good health, this sounded like a definite excuse. Anna became less angry when a man arrived at her office and asked for her in person at reception. He had a huge bouquet of flowers for her and a message from her father. Anna accepted the flowers as Janna and Vera joined her and made a huge fuss over the bouquet. As he was leaving the man turned to Anna and handed her a parcel and explained that he had to leave immediately as he was taking the next train back to Moscow as instructed by Anna's father. Anna was stunned. She and the women in the office had assumed that he was a local courier delivering flowers and not, as it now appeared, that he had come all the way to St Petersburg from Moscow on the train to deliver the bouquet and a parcel to Anna and then to go straight back again. Anna put the parcel in her bag and neither Janna nor Vera asked her anything about it.

For once Anna had reversed the tables and called the Director of the Home to ask for a meeting as she finally had something to show her in relation to Sasha. As Anna entered the Director's office she saw that her neighbour, the retired teacher, was in the office. She had just handed Valentina Alexandrovna a folded-over piece of paper and explained that it would be useful for Valentina Alexandrovna to look at the progress that Sasha was making with his writing and to see what he was now writing.

"Is he doing well?" asked Anna with enthusiasm as she entered and greeted both women.

"Remarkable. It is as if a light has been switched on in his brain," replied the retired teacher. "Now if you will excuse me I have the last session to do today. It is such a privilege to see how quickly these children respond."

Anna smiled at the word 'privilege'. The children were the most underprivileged in Western society! What would she do for them with a just a small pot of resources!

"So, Anna, you have some news?" smiled Valentina Alexandrovna.

Anna frowned as she took out an old leather bound book from her bag. "I'm not sure exactly what I have," she said as she put the book on her knees. "You know I was expecting my mother and father next week."

Valentina Alexandrovna nodded.

"And I was hoping to ask him about the family past even though I suspected that there are things in the past that he might not want to tell me. Especially what went on after the war."

Valentina Alexandrovna nodded again.

"Well at the last minute he cancelled the visit. But before," Anna had raised one of her hands to stop Valentina Alexandrovna speaking, "you say anything, he sent me this book instead. He had it delivered by hand from Moscow."

It was Valentina Alexandrovna's turn to frown as she looked down at the old leather bound book on Anna's knees.

"I came straight here with it," continued Anna with a slight tremor in her voice. "It is an old photo album which I have only looked at for a second. I did not want to look through it by myself."

"I understand," said Valentina Alexandrovna softly, "shall we look through it together?"

"Please," replied Anna.

Valentina Alexandrovna moved her chair behind the desk as far as she could to one side and motioned for Anna to come round to her side of the desk. There was not enough room for another chair so Anna leant on the back of Valentina Alexandrovna's chair and looked over her shoulder.

"There is no name on the album or dates but the photographs are all black and white," said Anna as Valentina Alexandrovna turned through the first pages. The first pages were photos of men in smart uniforms. Most of the men were smiling and by looking at the backgrounds Anna and Valentina Alexandrovna decided that the photos were pre-War. There was then a blank page and then the photos took a grim turn. The backgrounds of the photos were of destroyed buildings, burnt-out vehicles and smoke. The men in the photographs looked decidedly unkempt with beards and ripped uniforms. Most shots showed the men smiling and laughing wildly. Occasionally they were holding objects in the air as trophies. "The spoils of war and the dehumanisation of the civilised human being," said Valentina Alexandrovna quietly and with a deep sadness. The last few pages provided some relief. The shots showed family pictures. The backgrounds were back to more normal settings. Buildings had signs with letters which looked not to be Russian. The men were dressed smartly in civilian dress.

"These pictures, Anna," said Valentina Alexandrovna, "sum up the effects of the Second World War especially on our men. Just a few pages can tell a huge story."

"I'm glad you saw then with me," replied Anna. Her face was pale and her voice was very low. "I can now look at them without worrying."

"And without judging," said Valentina Alexandrovna, "these were horrific times and no-one can really judge. And now we have the chance," she paused and smiled at Anna, "to put some parts right."

Anna looked at her blankly.

"To find out who Sasha is related to," said Valentina Alexandrovna. "I presume your father is in the photos?"

"And my uncle," said Anna with a deep sigh. "I need to look to see where they are and especially at the back. I am pretty sure that I recognised my father's first wife in one of the pictures as he still has one photo of her in Moscow. She died when she was still quite young."

"I know you told me before," said Valentina Alexandrovna standing up. "Now why don't I make some tea while you look through? And then I have an easy way to solve this?"

"Really?" asked Anna in a mixture of surprise and excitement.

"When you are ready I'll ask for Sasha to be brought to us and we can see if we can find the family resemblance. What do you think?"

'Yes,' nodded Anna with tears welling in her eyes. Valentina Alexandrovna gave her a hug as she squeezed past her.

Anna spent the next ten minutes looking through the photographs and was beginning to pick out her father and her uncle. Many of the photos in the first parts of the book were group shots of soldiers before and in the aftermath of the war. Her father and uncle looked similar especially when they had beards. Her uncle though was taller and this helped when they were both standing in the same photo. She did think that if there was any doubt she could now telephone her father. She would not have to discuss the backgrounds to the photos now that he had sent them and she could just ask to confirm who was who in some of the shots. The final photos had only her uncle and father in and appeared to be in two different locations. These must be their post-War assignments in the former Eastern bloc. Given the civilian dress, beards once again and poor quality of the printing, she could not quite tell who was who. One of them had a distinctly long beard – perhaps it was an attempt at a new look or identity? Perhaps their family name had been in the KGB database not for surveillance purposes but for the opposite reason - as an agent! She took a deep breath. Maybe she had found out more than she was intended to. How would her father ever think she would be given access to KGB records! Her mind was a whirr with possibilities and she closed the book quietly and firmly. She had a crucial few minutes coming up with Sasha and she needed to focus. Focus on finding the link and nothing else.

Sasha came bounding in, grinning and with his Miller Lombard notebook under his arm. Anna hugged him and Sasha could not wait to show her the pages he had written in his notebook.

"That reminds me, Sasha," said Valentina Alexandrovna, "your teacher has given me some of your writings to look at which I won't forget to do. Now, Sasha, as you know we are trying to trace your family and we are hoping," she paused and briefly smiled at Anna who had suddenly acquired a faintly nervous look, "that there may be a link to Anna's family."

"There must be!" said Sasha smiling. "We are so much alike and my grandmother promised me that my family would be here!"

"Now, Sasha. I hope too, but we need to find the proof."

"I know," said Sasha, "grandma told me to be as patient as I need to be. My family will be here even if it takes a long, long time."

"You are such a sensible boy, Sasha," continued Valentina Alexandrovna, "now what I want to do today is to take a photograph of you so that we can compare your picture to some records we will be looking at." Valentina Alexandrovna opened one of her filing cabinets and took out a Polaroid camera. Sasha's eyes widened and he pestered Valentina Alexandrovna sufficiently to let him hold it. Valentina Alexandrovna explained that the camera was very expensive to use as it produced the photo there are then. Sasha could not wait as Valentina Alexandrovna took two photos. She promised Sasha that she would let him have one of the photos when they had finished their work. Sasha said he preferred to take a photograph of the special cross he kept which his grandmother had given him and Valentina Alexandrovna agreed that she would do this as soon as she had some spare time. After several hugs Sasha left them and sang to himself as he left the Director's office.

The two photographs of Sasha were pretty identical. Anna put one in her bag and they placed the other on the desk and opened the photo album again. There were no photos of either her father or uncle as a boy so they concentrated on looking at the facial features. After five minutes of slowly turning the pages they both were breathing heavily and they agreed that Sasha looked very similar to both men! The family lineage was clear to see. They had looked at some twenty photos of each man and the facial similarities to Sasha were striking. Anna could feel tingles up her spine as they turned each page. Valentina Alexandrovna had taken out a handkerchief. As they came to the photos at the back Valentina Alexandrovna squeezed Anna's shoulders. Neither woman dared speak at the risk of not being able to hold back their tears. Then the image struck them both with a flash. The photo of the man with the long beard had Sasha's eyes. They both looked backwards and forwards at this photo and at the Polaroid photograph of Sasha. For a split second the eyes in both photos seemed to sparkle at them. This was a genealogical match if ever there was one! Anna gave a sob and Valentina Alexandrovna wiped her own eyes with her handkerchief.

They drank tea and slowly calmed down. Valentina Alexandrovna then became all action and set up various meetings to start the processes to formalise Sasha's identity. Anna had returned to the album and could now look at the photo of the man with the beard objectively. It could be either her father or her uncle. Whilst the eyes matched Sasha's however she looked at them, the beard did hide much of the rest of the face and the relative height of the man in the picture was impossible to gauge. She had felt increasingly reluctant to call her father. Now as much for her father's sake as anything else she wanted to find another way to identify the man in the photo. She looked again at the face and once again the eyes seemed to sparkle. They seemed to know. Without a further thought she touched the photograph and then calmly lifted it from the page. Like the rest of the photos in the album it was held on the page by four small corner holders. She turned it over. There was writing on the back and a name, date and place. Sasha she now knew descended not from her father but from her father's brother – her uncle! She clasped her hands together and prayed. Nothing on earth could be better than this! She felt as if her own child had been born and she thanked God vowing with all her being to help as many children in the Home now as she could to show how thankful she really was.

Valentina Alexandrovna joined Anna in an embrace which was as joyful as it was tearful. They both had heads aching from the emotions they had been through. An hour later Anna finally left and Valentina Alexandrovna quickly attended to the masses of paperwork on her desk and rearranged the day's meetings she had missed for the next day. She packed her bag and before she set off on her rounds to check on the children before she left for the evening she unfolded the paper which the teacher had given her. It was Sasha's handwriting. The first lines were elegantly written in large letters. It described the work his grandmother used to do. The second paragraph threw Valentina Alexandrovna. It was not in Russian. It was a Latin script which she could not quite place. The third and final paragraph was back in Russian. The handwriting was shorter and thicker than the writing in the first paragraph.

Valentina Alexandrovna recognised it as an inscription. Sasha must have copied it from somewhere. She scanned it and stopped abruptly. Where could Sasha have seen something like this? He was only a young boy. Valentina Alexandrovna had only ever seen such wording once before. It was a religious inscription which contained what could only be described as an evocation or even worse a kind of curse. She screwed the piece of paper up and made a mental note to check on Sasha. As she dropped the ball of paper in the bin she felt a twinge in her hand. At the same time she realised that the middle paragraph of the writing was in Romanian. It was also not lost on her also that the place written on the back of the photograph of Anna's uncle had been Bucharest, the capital of Romania. She felt a shudder as she closed the door to her office. For once she did not feel like talking to Sasha. She would just quickly look in on the dormitory where he slept.

Fifty Nine

THE public notice boards outside the office of the St Petersburg Property Fund were being watched more and more with each day as the final terms of the privatisations of different companies were steadily being announced via large paper notices pinned up on the boards. This was a throw-back to Soviet times when official notices and daily newspapers were stuck up on noticeboards in factories and in the centres of cities, towns and villages for everyone in theory to have access to. Officials could rightly state that everyone had seen the information because it was literally posted in front of their eyes in their workplaces or their places of leisure. It was one of the lesser draconian tools of Soviet propaganda and information control.

In the basement of the building opposite the office of the St Petersburg Property Fund a small café had opened and several tables had been set up on the pavement. The tables had a clear view of the large noticeboard outside of the Property Fund and the tables were occupied from the early morning until late afternoon when the Property Fund closed. All those drinking the over-priced drinks took their time and as soon as a notice went up they would leave their chairs and saunter across the road. On most occasions they would saunter back but every now and again notes would feverishly be taken and mobile phone calls made. Two young legal assistants from Miller Lombard were working a daily routine and they were pretty indistinguishable from the dozen or so other young people all moderately dressed who were keeping watch on the noticeboards.

Shortly before lunch the watchers at the café had finished most of their drinks. This time and the last few minutes before the Property Fund closed in the late afternoon were the usual times when the more interesting privatisation notices were put up. The smaller and lesser interesting cases were put up steadily throughout the day. As if on cue most of the watchers gathered up their papers, bags and mobile phones as two officials from the Property Fund walked towards the noticeboards with large pieces of paper held out in front of them. With their usual nonchalance the two officials pinned a large notice each on the boards. The notices were set in the middle of the boards over the top of ones already there. As had become the official-watcher routine the watchers stood well back allowing the officials time to pin and adjust the notices until with a parting glance and small smile the officials were happy that the notices had been correctly issued. The law on open publication had been fulfilled correctly. There could be no complaints later that the notices had not been made available to everyone. What physically happened to the notices afterwards was not the officials' concern.

The watchers had also developed an unwritten rule amongst themselves. They would jostle for position and make good use of shoulders and elbows. The Russians were after all world leaders in the art of queuing and queue-jumping. This was an unfortunate national by-product of the command economy and lack of goods through most of the Soviet era. This had transformed queuing into an industry in its own right and a career for many a robust and forceful Soviet housewife. Here however they would let everyone enough time to copy down notices without any jostling or pushing and notices were not removed until several hours after being put up. The watchers from Miller Lombard worked efficiently and had the key terms written down in a couple of minutes. They both wrote down the terms separately and then they compared. With a few minor corrections and a final look at the notice they nodded to each other. They then flagged down a passing car.

Several minutes later a black Mercedes pulled up several hundred yards from the Property Fund. Its driver got out and walked to the noticeboard. The watchers were dispersing and the driver walked up to the noticeboard with purpose. Without looking round he pulled the two latest notices from the board tearing them each into two pieces as he did so. He folded the pieces up. As he walked back to his car several of the watchers stopped and looked at him, muttering loudly. The driver ignored them and got back into his car. His boss was not taking any chances.

Back at the Miller Lombard office Anna was looking at the notes handed to her by one of the assistants. It was pretty much the announcement verbatim of the terms for the privatisation of the "Open stock company Peter the Great Shipyard". She read the terms several times. She had no option but to call the company. Adam had gone to lunch with a foreign guest and calling Hampton was still in emergencies only. She would talk to the company and then have Adam call Corley once he was back from lunch. It took her five minutes on the phone to the company to establish that Victor Nikolayevich was also at lunch and not to be disturbed. Using all of her native insistence she won a commitment from Victor Nikolayevich's secretary to try and get Leonid Marlenovich to call her as soon as possible or failing that Victor Nikolayevich to call her after lunch. Having finished the call Anna could not sit down. She would go directly to the company. It would only take ten minutes or so. As she packed her bag her phone rang. Leonid Marlenovich was in reception.

Leonid Marlenovich read the piece of paper without sitting down. Like Anna he read it several times. His face remained passive. Finally he smiled. "Well, well, well," he said, "someone is clearly taking an interest in our privatisation, Anna. What do you think of the terms?"

"They are clearly very different from those in your agreement with the British Redevelopment Fund," replied Anna, "and from those submitted to the Property Fund."

"Have you told the British Fund?"

"Of course not," she blushed slightly.

"They will soon find out in any case," smiled Leonid Marlenovich. "So let's work out what they mean. The amounts are less than we wanted."

"Correct," replied Anna, "the starting bid for the shares is five hundred thousand instead of one million but as this is only the starting bid the Fund can still bid higher."

"Yes, so that does not make any real difference. It is the investment amount which changes things."

"It does," said Anna, "the amount has been reduced from ten million to five million."

"So we can only build half-size boats!" laughed Leonid Marlenovich.

"And," continued Anna, "the amount is to be made up of investments into the company during the course of three years and not all in cash at the start." She looked at Leonid Marlenovich who seemed to be making mental calculations. "This will not please Victor Nikolayevich."

"I know," replied Leonid Marlenovich, "but leave him to me. We must also tell the Fund that five million will be enough."

"Really?"

"Yes, we tell them that it will be still be the ten million as in our agreement – the five million through the auction and then an additional five million on top from them to be sent separately."

"Will that work?"

"We will make it work," said Leonid Marlenovich with a strong sense of conviction. Anna recalled how surprised she had been when Leonid Marlenovich had called Corley 'Dominic' at the end of their first meeting. There was clearly a relationship that she had picked up on but which no-one else had. "But," continued Leonid Marlenovich, "the real problem we have," he stopped at looked intently at Anna, "is the type of auction." This was indeed the term which had worried Anna when she first read it and why she had been about to go straight to the company. An auction by sealed bids, which was what they had wanted, could by its nature easily be manipulated to ensure a preferred winner. Envelopes can be swapped as easily as playing cards.

"An open cry auction," said Leonid Marlenovich, "this will be our first real challenge."

Sixty

CORLEY was upbeat on his call to Green. The terms of the privatisation had been faxed to him. Adam had called him to explain that the company had thought it prudent to reduce the starting bids to build in flexibility in the auction. The agreement between the Fund and the company did not need changing as it looked as though all eventualities were still covered and ten million was still the amount to be invested. The one point Adam did raise was that the Fund would have to appoint a Russian national to make the bid under a power of attorney as the auction would now be live. Corley had asked if the change in type of auction was something he should be concerned about. Adam had explained that in Miller Lombard's view a public auction would be more transparent than sealed bids which might be tampered with. Corley agreed and suggested Anna be appointed to act in all relevant matters on behalf of the Fund if she was willing and if it was ok with the company and with Miller Lombard. Corley explained the terms to Green.

"Very well, Dominic, just as long as everything remains calm and under control," said Green, "and we do not want to have any surprises what with the Prince's visit. The Mayor's office in St Petersburg, we hear, still has its doubts about investors. One minute pro-British, next pro-American, next anti-all-foreigners. They really do not know what they want by all accounts."

"And we want them pro-British?" probed Corley.

"Now more than ever," came back the response.

"And the real reason?" asked Corley probing further.

"The real reason, as you know, is to show how we are supporting the great changes in the Russian economy, helping companies to adapt and then to grow." Green could have been reading from the Fund's publicity material which made Corley even more suspicious.

"So you are fully in favour of the plans for us to finance the new production line for building new boats?"

"Keep going to plan. Build your new line. What we do not want is anyone making any unexpected changes at this stage."

"So how do we do this?" Corley asked quietly.

"Donald, dear, dear. It is quite obvious." There was a moment's silence. "Pay whatever you need to, dear boy, to ensure we have control."

Corley was confused. Until now Green had always been against spending anything but the bare minimum.

"Ok," he replied, "how much money can I have?"

"Let's say you come back and tell us. It would have been much simpler if we had done this from the start."

"The company would never have accepted it. Now there might be an opportunity." He was thinking on his feet. "Perhaps I will propose that we redo our agreement to strengthen our cooperation as a back door way of taking control. They do not seem that knowledgeable about agreements. The law firm is officially the company's adviser but they are effectively working for us as we are the ones paying all the fees in the deal."

"Well there you are, Donald, excellent! Your old skills are coming back to the fore once more. Time, I think as you say in business, to consolidate. I think that's what you say."

Corley was staring out of window. He might be playing the company to get what he was after but he now had a horrible realisation that Green was playing him with even greater effect.

"Yes, consolidate, dear boy."

Corley's naturally suspicious mind was for once dumbfounded.

Sixty One

CORLEY had come to the Miller Lombard office as soon as his plane from Moscow had landed in St Petersburg. Anna had readily accepted to be the Russian national acting on behalf of the Fund and her position as such had been cleared with the company and internally with Miller Lombard. It was part of the execution of a transaction agreed in principle between the company and the Fund and so there was no longer any potential for a conflict of interest. Anna had spent an hour going through the various papers which the Fund would have to formalise. They included powers of attorney for Anna to act in the name of the Fund and bank mandates for her to sign to transfer funds. They had stopped for a break and been joined by Adam.

"Victor Nikolayevich does seem to be under more stress than ever, don't you think?" asked Corley looking at Anna and Adam. "During our last meeting he became even more emotion than usual."

"What was he saying?" asked Adam.

"Going on and on about the way they survived the Siege of the city during the war."

"What do you think, Anna?" asked Adam.

"I think it was a horrendous tragedy that could have been avoided," replied Anna with a short sigh. It was a subject that was never far from many people's minds in the city. Despite the passing of some fifty years it was easily brought to the surface by any number of remarks or references in conversation especially amongst the elderly.

"How could it have been avoided?" asked Adam, "surely the only way would have been for the city to surrender and then it would have been razed to the ground no doubt!"

"I think we should have been better prepared at the beginning," continued Anna.

"Nobody was prepared for the Blitzkrieg of the Germans," added Corley with an unusual softness in his tone as he picked up on Anna's sadness at the topic.

"How did it actually happen?" said Adam.

"The Blitzkrieg is what the Germans call it - a lightning strike. In this case it was the immediate and crucial disabling of the railway system," said Corley who seemed to know his history very well.

"On our side," said Anna quietly, "we learned at school about the bravery of our men heroically defending the railway stations."

"But sadly," said Corley, "I think you might find that some either ran away or defected over to the Germans."

"What makes you say that?" said Anna with a slight challenging note in her voice. It was unusual for her to challenge other people and especially a client but this was a topic which could not be treated slightly. Corley would have to understand what the Siege meant for people and especially the likes of Victor Nikolayevich if he ever was going to have any kind of meaningful relationships in the city.

"Because the Germans could not believe how easily the stations were taken." He paused and looked at Anna with a look of an old university professor. "Only the station at the village of Mga held out for more than a few hours. Had Mga not been taken as quickly as it was, then the Siege may not have actually happened. It was the most critical moment of the lightning strike." Corley paused as did Anna – the name of the small village of 'Mga' was always greeted sadly and silently by those who knew its significance.

Adam was the next to speak. "The TV reporter from CNN is really getting into the history what with the Prince of Wales coming," he said trying to redirect the conversation. "I first saw it a few of weeks ago on Russian TV but could not understand a word of it. There were some horrific pictures of the starvation, though."

"Do you know, Adam, how many people starved?" asked Anna, who despite herself, was now starting to become a touch emotional.

"No," replied Adam softly.

"The official Soviet figure was six hundred and fifty thousand but a further million still remain unaccounted for even after you count those that were evacuated along the Road of Life," said Anna her normal calmness beginning to return.

"What was the population before?"

"About three million."

"Really!" Adam threw his eyes upwards. "Now I can understand why you would never forget."

"And it was the Road of Life which saved many of them?" Adam was willing Anna on. "Tell me more about this Life Road," he said.

Anna sighed softly. "The Road of Life was probably one of the genuinely real heroic acts of the war."

"Go on," continued Adam

"The only route back to Russia was across Lake Ladoga to the north east of the city. Small boats could make it across in the autumn but as the lake froze in November it was decided to build a road across the ice."

"That must have been risky."

"At the start very risky and many of the horses which pulled the first sleds across the ice died on route. People started to drive trucks across in late November and many were lost."

"Should they have not waited?"

"The city was starving to death."

"Sure, sure, go on."

"The key thing at first was to show it was possible and enough trucks eventually made it to prove it, said Anna"

"And then?"

"And then a long road was dug out by soldiers in two weeks when the city's food was down to six days left."

"That was cutting it close," said Adam whistling softly under his breath.

"It was and the road was not well built. With the heavy snow falling it was a real battle to make it passable and only a small amount of supplies were actually getting through. The city was down to one day's food." Anna paused.

"So what happened?" asked Adam after a few seconds.

"The general in charge was removed, the road building improved and order put into the weight of the cargoes and in defiance of our Soviet tradition, large bonuses were paid to the successful drivers," said Anna.

"So it took near starvation and a world war to bring back financial rewards as an official way of incentivising workers," said Adam surprised at the depth of his own analysis.

"For a short time under extreme circumstances, yes. Don't forget that the behaviour of some of those starving in the city was less than heroic when survival is the only motivation."

"I would not want to imagine," said Adam genuinely. "So the road worked?"

"Slowly but surely, yes, and towards the end of the winter on the return journeys the truck started to take out people from the city."

"Really?"

"Yes over half a million made it out."

"A real story of heroism. But so little is talked about it," said Adam.

"Maybe that is why your Prince is coming. Even though we won in the end the blockade was a disaster for the city and many who survived were ill and suffered for the rest of their lives."

"If only, as you say, your troops had been better prepared in the beginning."

"Yes. So you see a lot of the way Victor Nikolayevich behaves is because surviving the Siege marked him for life."

"But surely the defence of the company can be nowhere near as dramatic as the saving of your city," said Adam.

"In Victor Nikolayevich's mind it is a nightmare of similar proportions."

"Really?"

"Really. You will see," and at that for the first time since their meeting began she smiled at Adam and at Corley. It was a smile though of sympathy; she knew that they could never really understand.

Sixty Two

HAMPTON was quick to go through the normal daily greetings and enquiries over his health from Vera as she sat down as normal in the seat next to his bed the following day. He even took time to ask how the meeting with Adam and the potential client had gone but before he turned to the letters he needed to dictate from the previous day and the new pile Vera had handed him, he asked Vera to fax the contents of the dossier to the same number as before. He also suggested that Vera bring something to thank the clinic's receptionist the following day. Vera smiled and was intrigued by Hampton's clear agitation.

"Hermitage committee business?" she said with a smile. Hampton just nodded. This was the first time that his incapacity was putting matters beyond his control. Physically he did feel much better as the doctor had said but he was determined to be evacuated out of the country on a private plane and this was not just for effect or sympathy.

"This package was also delivered just before I left the office," continued Vera with a bigger smile as she bent down and pulled a two foot long tube shaped package from her bag. Hampton almost jumped out of his bed but managed to stop himself and wince. He was not that well yet.

"Thank you," he said taking the package. Vera stood up and left the room without further comment. Hampton's even greater agitation was a sign that she ought to leave him alone to examine the package.

Hampton took a deep breath. 'He was behaving like Alex on one of his birthdays!' he thought to himself. He smiled to himself as his composure slowly came back. He closed his eyes and the images of Alex opening presents on his birthday in recent years span round like a kaleidoscope in his mind. He opened his eyes again and studied the package. He shook it and then removed the layer of brown paper it was wrapped in. He was right. It was a cardboard tube for storing maps or documents. It could also be used for storing a canvas. He undid one of the ends and lifted the tube up to look inside. He gently put a finger into the tube and breathed out heavily as he felt the grainy texture of canvas. His mind started to race with the possibilities but one thing was sure, the Head Curator was true to his word. There were hidden works of art starting to resurface. He would stick to his plan and set the date for his evacuation. He would have Vera reseal and repack the tube and send it to his home as she had done with the envelope. It was a risk but it was just the sample; the rest would be moved with the upmost secrecy.

Sixty Three

NOW that the terms of the privatisation of the Peter the Great Shipyard had been published and the date of Friday 30th June set for the open cry auction there was intense internal pressure at Miller Lombard for the team to sign off the information they had prepared on the company so that it could be given to parties interested in bidding for the shares of the company in the auction. As Adam had feared the only item with a question mark over it was the ownership of the Old Foundry. In the opinion of Miller Lombard having studied the relevant documentation did the company own the property and was it free from any charges or claims? On the surface it could be stated that the company did but internally at Miller Lombard they had to be sure that none of the claims by other parties on the property were valid under Russian law. If they were to highlight the claims in the information then it was certain that they would be opening a can of worms and a barrage of questions.

Adam was sitting in the main meeting room with Anna. Anna had studied the information of the Property Register from the City Council and had had several conversations with other Russian lawyers in their firm. It boiled down to which law they applied in this case. On balance Anna said that the view of the firm should be that the Property Register was the evidence which they should rely on as proof that the company did own the property. The fact that the four claims on the property had also been rejected in the court in St Petersburg was further proof especially as the claims had also been made under the previous and different systems of law which existed in Russia before and after the Revolution. Adam had not thought of this and was extremely pleased that he could argue that this was the conclusive verification that they needed although he was also very embarrassed that Anna had seen this pretty much straightaway and he had not. He prided himself on thinking outside the legal box but this time he had been stuck squarely rooted in the box. They also decided that in the spirit of transparency they would put in a brief note to the effect that there had been some claims on one of the company's properties in the past but that they had been declared invalid.

"The note should not bother anyone, will it, Anna?" asked Adam, "but I think it best that it is mentioned somewhere especially for the likes of Corley's fund."

"Probably not," replied Anna. She had a suspicion that Leonid Marlenovich might object in which case it would probably be left out of the Russian version of the information as an irrelevant detail.

"Great," said Adam with a smile, "such a lot of fuss over what is the least used of the company's properties. Derelict by all accounts."

"But necessary for the new production line," added Anna.

"Of course," replied Adam embarrassed once again that he was missing a basic point. "I'll send the final version of the information to London," he said quickly, "with a brief note for the record explaining our work and conclusion here. I would hope to have our legal opinion that all the information on the company including the ownership of its assets and properties is 'true and fair' from all legal perspectives issued in a couple of days."

"Very good," said Anna.

Adam felt a strong need to show he was better than how he was performing at the moment. Anna was looking at him slightly quizzically and he could sense she was trying to figure out what was going on with him. "I know that we have settled what we will say in the information and what our legal opinion is, but the law firms who made the claims," he said brightly, "make interesting reading, Anna, if I can show you?"

Anna nodded as Adam fumbled in his briefcase and dug out a sheet of paper. He was making very discrete enquiries about the four law firms but had had nothing interesting back. As he handed Anna the paper, Adam watched as Anna's eyes widened and then her brow furrowed. Not again, thought Adam to himself, what have I missed this time?

"Isn't Detroit next to Chicago?" she asked.

It was Adam's turn to nod. "Let me find out more about these law firms," he said, "and let's see if that tells us anything."

Anna handed him back the piece of paper and smiled. "Let me know what you find."

"Why did you ask about Detroit and Chicago?" asked Adam.

"Nothing really I just remember John mentioned once that it was his father who inspired him to become a lawyer."

"Really?" asked Adam.

"Yes, and his father was the head of a law firm in Detroit."

Adam went pale. This time he was not embarrassed because he did not know something. Rather he felt a shot of fear that the property issue, although it was to be signed off without anything controversial being said, was not over at all and that is was the centre of everything that was now swarming around in his mind. Was it linked to the bullets that had been shot at his boss? Why was he now carrying the original documents from the Property Register in his briefcase? Anna had stood up and walked to the door of the meeting room. Adam looked at her and smiled meekly. Anna looked as though she was about to say something but she just nodded and left the room. Adam closed his eyes and the vision he saw was as vivid as the one he had had when he woke in that strange apartment. For it to go away he needed answers, a lot of answers.

Sixty Four

LEONID Marlenovich was in his office when he heard shouting outside coming from the main shipyard. He switched off his phone and went into Victor Nikolayevich's room from where he could see down into the yard. A crowd was gathering outside one of the workshops. He went over to Victor Nikolayevich's desk and called down to the guard at the entrance to the yard.

"What on earth is going on down there?" asked Leonid Marlenovich.

"Somebody has been caught stealing," replied the guard.

"Stealing, so what is all the fuss?" He shrugged his shoulders. "People have to live."

"No, not tools or parts or anything," replied the guard, "papers and documents from the legal department."

Leonid Marlenovich put down the phone, went back to the window and saw Victor Nikolayevich striding to the crowd with his secretaries trying to catch him. As he approached the crowd Victor Nikolayevich picked up a piece of wood. Leonid Marlenovich ran from the office and down to the building's entrance. As he reached the crowd a hush had descended. Victor Nikolayevich was standing over a man on his knees with his head touching the floor and his hand protecting the back of his head. In a low controlled voice Victor Nikolayevich said, "you have betrayed all your comrades." He raised the stick without any signs of trembling.

"Victor Nikolayevich, please, please let me," Leonid Marlenovich reached over slightly out of breath and took hold of Victor Nikolayevich's arm. Victor Nikolayevich calmly removed Leonid Marlenovich's hand and landed a blow on the man's back.

"Victor Nikolayevich! For God's sake! He is the Head of our legal department not some useless worker!"

Leonid Marlenovich's attention was caught by the guard at the entrance waving wildly at him as two men forced their way past him. One of them was carrying a camera with a large lens.

"Victor Nikolayevich, for God's sake!" repeated Leonid Marlenovich who then continued in a whispered hiss, "do this somewhere else!"

Victor Nikolayevich was aiming for a second blow but Leonid Marlenovich wrestled the stick off him. "Victor Nikolayevich, there is a camera coming here. Somewhere else, please."

The two men were crossing the yard quickly.

"Let the world see how we treat traitors," said Victor Nikolayevich calmly.

"Victor Nikolayevich," Leonid Marlenovich looked at him in the eyes. "Victor Nikolayevich, not here."

They stared each other out. Leonid Marlenovich blinked first. "Somewhere else, please." He passed the stick behind his back to one of the men in the crowd.

"Get rid of that!" ordered Leonid Marlenovich as he kicked the man on the ground. "Get up now." A small group of workers pulled him up and lead him away towards the far end of the yard which led down to the river.

"Mr Leigh from the St Petersburg Times! How kind of you to come and make a report on our shipyard," said Leonid Marlenovich.

Leigh was straining to look past Leonid Marlenovich and towards the small group now moving to the river. "What is going on with that man?" he asked.

"Mr Leigh, did we plan a meeting for today or perhaps an interview?" asked Leonid Marlenovich

Leigh motioned to his photographer to move and follow the group. Victor Nikolayevich stood in his way with a curious look in his eyes – one of defiance mixed with a sense of uncertainty. His eyes had started to water.

"You know our General Director, of course, Mr Pulgarkov, Victor Nikolayevich."

"Yes, yes of course," said Leigh looking at his photographer. "Can you not get past?"

"Mr Leigh, can I remind you that unless you and your colleague can show me your passes you could be seen as trespassing in our yard," said Leonid Marlenovich. At the same time the guard from the entrance had arrived and was tugging at the photographer's jacket indicating for him to go back to the entrance to sign in.

"Fine. You win. Jack, let's go back to the entrance." The photographer put down his camera.

"We will win," said Victor Nikolayevich in low quiet voice wiping his eyes on the sleeve of his jacket, "we will win."

At that moment a muffled shout came from the direction of the river followed by a splashing sound.

"What was that? Jack, did you see that? Did you get that? Sounded like someone being thrown into the river. Did you get it?"

"Sorry, Mike," replied the photographer. 'Camera was off' he signed.

Leigh switched on a Dictaphone he had taken out of his jacket pocket. "Victor Nikolayevich, can you comment on what has just happened? Why was a man just thrown in the river? Has there been some dispute? Was he one of your workers?"

"I am sure that no one has been injured," interrupted Leonid Marlenovich with a faint smile.

"But he was just thrown in!" said Leigh the pitch of his voice rising.

"I think we will find that it was a minor accident or something but we will investigate it fully," said Leonid Marlenovich. "Now I presume that the reason why you have come is to ask some questions about our privatisation. Why don't you switch that off, put your camera away and we can do a proper interview. Victor Nikolayevich will give you a tour of the yards, our workshops and our showroom. We could speak exclusively and on the record this time."

Victor Nikolayevich was now beaming. "We will give you plenty to write about for your newspaper," he said with enthusiasm and rubbing his hands together, "there is so much we can tell you!"

The crowd was dispersing. Leigh and the photographer followed them into the entrance to the offices. Leonid Marlenovich was grateful for this unexpected diversion. He had just had a coded message from the Cubans about an incident that they themselves had had in Helsinki on their own way home and they had only been carrying samples for their own use. It had convinced them that Leonid Marlenovich's way of moving product hidden on the company's new boats was considerably safer. The powers that be in South America had asked for Leonid Marlenovich to take control of the next two shipments 'personally'. They had stressed 'personally'. Leonid Marlenovich did not think too long about what that really meant! The next shipment would be the most valuable to date and prove to all the parties involved that his way of transporting the goods into Europe was by far the safest and the one to use for the future and the one that they would all invest significantly in. He needed to prepare for the shipment immediately and make a number of key telephone calls. Leonid Marlenovich knew that once Victor Nikolayevich started talking he would be fully occupied for several hours and that his own presence would not be missed and he would be able to make the critical arrangements. He would return for the end of the interview and then he would make sure that the reporter had got the right story!

Sixty Five

"DONALD, perhaps it's time we brought you into the picture a touch more," said Green on the phone.

"Not before time," replied Corley flicking through files on his computer.

"You remember that the visit is getting nearer," Green paused and then continued, "and that there are – how can I put it? - certain interests which would like to put His Royal Highness in a difficult position."

"How difficult?" asked Corley.

"Let's just say front page news, perhaps," replied Green curtly.

"With the final aim of what?" Corley's tone had hardened.

"That is not for us to wonder why," replied Green calmly.

"But you want to prevent it?"

"I want to flush out some of these interests that may wish it," answered Green remaining very calm.

"Whilst potentially endangering the heir to the throne," said Corley quietly and with an undertone of clear provocation.

"Donald, please give me more credit than that! My aim is to protect all of Her Majesty's interests and subjects."

"Her Majesty," Corley emphasised 'Her'.

"She is our monarch, Donald to whom we all owe our allegiance." Green's voice was assuming a superior attitude as he tried to mask an underlying nervousness. "And to all our future monarchs just as much."

"Are you sure that you are not in some medieval fantasy?" quipped Corley

"Very good, Donald, very good, as always," laughed Green quietly. "You know as well as I do that our democracy only stands because of our long history of strong values and unwavering commitment no matter what is thrown at us. Our moral upper hand is our strongest weapon. It is the bedrock of our high standing throughout the world."

"You are losing me," responded Corley. He was becoming somewhat bewildered at Green's comments on democracy and morality.

"Don't worry," replied Green. "Let's get back to the task at hand."

"Please."

"The issue is that the Prince's visit is stirring up forces which we had hoped had gone to sleep permanently." Green was sounding more assured.

"And?" asked Corley quietly again.

"And they may use this visit to embarrass us," said Green.

"So? Double his security," replied Corley

"It is not he who will necessarily be the direct centre of attention," continued Green.

"So it's getting back to the site then again," said Corley with a touch of triumph almost in his voice.

"Yes. We need to ensure we have control of it," continued Green quickly, "so that nothing is disturbed and only we can remove things if it becomes necessary."

"Has the satellite confirmed the position once and for all?"

"Yes, twice and it is costing me a small fortune to use the American's equipment at NASA to verify it. Now more critically where are you up to in ensuring you can control the company?"

"The privatisation auction has been announced and I should soon gain a significant amount of control over the assets we want," replied Corley.

"Good. You need to close this as soon as possible. Tell me about the state of play in this privatisation process. Or actually tell me what is really going on behind it."

Sixty Six

ADAM had decided not to tackle Hampton about the possible link between the Detroit-based American law firm and the Old Foundry building until he had worked out as much as he could about the other three claims and the law firms involved in those. He now had quite a lot of the relevant information and he was sat again with Anna in the large meeting room. They were having a quick coffee.

"The London law firm," Adam was saying, "has its office in Pall Mall and do you know who else also has an office there?"

Anna smiled at Adam. She had guessed straightaway but did not want to steal Adam's thunder. She had been intrigued by the whole property conundrum and the importance it had to Adam but she had much weightier matters to concentrate on.

"That's your country, Adam, so I am sure you can find out," she replied sweetly.

"You are almost there," said Adam with a grin. "The British Redevelopment Fund!"

"Of course!" said Anna with a smile.

"It makes total sense and shows why Corley had such an interest in the company from the beginning!" Adam was sounding as if he were patting himself on the back. "My guess is that the Fund must have found out about the company from a descendent of the Berd family or more likely from a Professor of Russian history."

"Why would Corley be in contact with people like that?" asked Anna.

"Obvious," said Adam lowering his voice, "Corley has to be ex-MI6 and most MI6 officers are recruited from Cambridge or Oxford by the professors in the Russian departments. My guess is this is the most likely way that Corley picked this up."

Anna was confused but took what Adam had said to be plausible. "What about the other claims?" she asked.

"The first claim was by a Russian law firm and my findings show that it is most likely on behalf of one of the rich Russian families which owned the company in the past."

"The Yusupov family?"

"Correct. And then the fourth claim which was made in a similar name but this time from Cyprus is, I bet, on behalf of the same family or a relation."

"Why do you say that?"

"Well, where does all the money go from Russia if it is sent abroad?"

"Where?" asked Anna.

"Cyprus, of course!" said Adam excitedly. "There is a special Russian-Cyprus tax treaty which makes Cyprus the easiest place to send money and lots of Russians are setting up legal entities there which all require Cypriot law firms. So my bet is that it the same or related party to the first claim."

"Any idea who?"

"Nothing that far yet," replied Adam slightly deflated. He had hoped that Anna would have been more impressed by what he had worked out.

"And the American firm?" asked Anna with a challenging look at Adam.

"Time to ask John," he replied quietly. "I just have to find the right moment."

For once Adam was looking at the property mystery calmly – the claims all appeared related to previous owners of the company who were trying to recover a property which they had most probably been owners of before. The obvious reason now was the value of the building on a prime waterfront location. His flashbacks were also fading. Now only a slight sweat trickled down his back on occasion but it still did happen and when it did it still seemed to place some doubt still in his mind over whether the claims were just about the value of the building.

Sixty Seven

THE St Petersburg Times had done precisely what Roman Felixovich had wanted the newspaper not to do. The newspaper had an exclusive interview with the Peter the Great Shipyard ahead of what was now described as 'its eagerly awaited' privatisation by an open cry auction. The article was full of well taken photographs and the interview with Victor Nikolayevich even made sense. He sounded like a highly knowledgeable General Director – quite the opposite to what he was thought of locally. 'Leonid Marlenovich's words, no doubt,' mused Roman Felixovich. If it were bad enough that attention was being drawn to the privatisation, then the public revelation of an agreement with the British Redevelopment Fund was even more of a serious blow. The newspaper stated that an agreement had been made and that the British Fund was the company's preferred bidder. The Fund was therefore widely expected to win the upcoming auction and become a significant shareholder in the company. The only saving comment in the article was that the Mayor's office had not been prepared to comment on anything ahead of the privatisation auction.

Roman Felixovich thought long and hard at how the article had come about. Perhaps it had been arranged by the British Fund itself. Classic old style propaganda, of which Pravda, the communist newspaper which had controlled so much of the information reported to the citizens of the Soviet Union, would have been proud. The newspaper being an English language addition might have links to the Fund. Perhaps the Fund was trying to put off other foreign parties from looking at the privatisation. Roman Felixovich could not see how the company could have done it. Perhaps the law firm involved. In any case now it did not matter. The privatisation was now fully public. He looked at the pile of crumpled paper on a chair in his office. His driver had said that he had torn down the notice of the announcement of the privatisation within minutes of it being put up on the noticeboard. He would have to take a much more direct route.

"Congratulations on your publicity, Leonid Marlenovich," said Roman Felixovich later than afternoon. Leonid Marlenovich had returned Roman Felixovich's call without too much of a delay.

"Thank you, Roman Felixovich," replied Leonid Marlenovich. "Victor Nikolayevich naturally enjoys talking about our company to anyone who is prepared to listen, that is."

"I see you have already done your privatisation," continued Roman Felixovich, the touch of irony in his voice clear to Leonid Marlenovich.

"I am not sure the newspaper understands the reality of the situation sufficiently. They are foreigners after all."

"I am glad," said Roman Felixovich, "that you see it that way." He paused. The next exchange of words would be crucial to them both. Roman Felixovich decided to continue to be direct. "Perhaps, we should continue our conversation in person?" he asked. His voice had lost its edge.

"I am sure we can come to an agreement of our own," replied Leonid Marlenovich. "There are certain sensitive parts of our business which I have to take care of personally."

Roman Felixovich paused. For a moment he thought Leonid Marlenovich's words had been said too quickly, automatic almost but then he decided to take them as said. "I am sure we can," he replied briskly. They agreed to meet that evening.

Sixty Eight

ELLEN still always shuddered when see and Alex got into their car in the morning to go to school. She rotated their seating plan with one of them each day sitting in the seat which the bullet had struck. She was banking on the theory of lightning never striking in the same place twice. Although, in Russia she had to admit she felt very unsure! Every morning she would ask herself why on earth she had let her husband and son talk her into staying. But she had accepted that they would stay until the end of this academic year, see how well Hampton recovered and then the sit down as a family to discuss for a final time where they should be in September when the next school year would begin. Hampton would shortly be leaving the clinic to fly back to the States for his final convalescence. Ellen had won the battle with the clinic and her husband's firm, or rather their insurers, over how Hampton should fly to the States. He was going in a private jet as a medical evacuation. There was no way he was going on a commercial flight, comfort or no comfort arranged! No-one had argued with her and arrangements were being made. Her husband had visibly brightened at the news and the clinic had relaxed its no mobile phone rule to permit Hampton to be involved in the arrangements. He particularly insisted on having space on the jet for boxes of files which he said were essential for him still to be able to undertake a light case load in a remote location as he returned to full health. Adequate provision had been made on the private jet for whatever he or his office wanted to send.

On this particular morning Alex was sitting in the back seat of the Volvo and in 'that' seat as Ellen called it. They had set off as normal. Alex gave a little yawn as they set off which his mum caught. Alex did spend a lot of the time in the evenings reading, which Ellen had to be thankful for both in terms of his strong academic progress and because it took his mind off his father's absence. Before he went to sleep, Ellen would read with him and mix up the types of books adding her own variety to the tomes and tomes of history books and art books which Alex favoured.

"Alex, why don't you have a little snooze on the way if you are tired?" she said.

"I'm ok, mom," said Alex as he felt his eyelids heavy and he yawned again. A minute later he was asleep. The car left the dacha area and quickly went past the Catherine Palace through the town of Pushkin and onto the M10. Alex murmured and lay his head against his mother's shoulder. He had fallen into a deep sleep but as the car accelerated Alex felt his fingers tingle. He tried to open his eyes but they were tight shut. The tingle intensified. This time he did not try to open his eyes as he could already see! He watched as lines of soldiers were walking at the side of the road. He was in a car alone in the back seat. The driver was hunched over the steering wheel and whistling frantically under his breath. Alex could detect a great nervousness in the driver and then he saw why. The car was driving wildly and in parallel with a train on a track. The train was a freight train with wooden carriages. The train and the car were heading for the same crossing point up ahead. Alex shouted as the driver accelerated hard. The driver was trying to beat the train. Alex tried to close his eyes but he could not. He tried to take hold of the driver but his hand passed straight through the driver's shoulder. And then a violent bump as the car reached the crossing first and shot over it. The car braked hard and swung round to watch the train. The train kept on coming but as it reached the crossing it flew off the track, rolled on its side and slid down a small dip to a crunching halt. Two of the wooden carriages had split open.

Smoke was rising and soldiers were screaming. Alex looked at the carriages and his eyes widened in a mixture of disbelief and horror at the sight of several crates. The colour of the contents was unmistakeable – it was amber. He tried to move forward but felt an arm tight around his shoulder.

"Alex," said a voice softly, "did the braking wake you? It looks like there has been an accident ahead on the road."

"What!" replied Alex sitting up and opening his eyes wide.

"You must have been in a deep sleep," continued his mum, "dreaming probably!" she smiled at him and kissed the top of his head.

Alex did not reply. It was not a dream. It had really happened and now he knew that the room could not have been taken to Germany in a train as everyone believed.

Sixty Nine

ANNA had finally had a long conversation with her father. Once Anna had said that she wanted to ask about her uncle, her father's floodgates had opened up. He had spoken in full flow for ten minutes and Anna had faced an immediate overload of information. Since Anna and Valentina Alexandrovna had identified her uncle as the family link to Sasha, progress on formalising Sasha's identity had been slow. This was inevitable at a time when the now defunct Soviet bureaucracy, which had sprawled across the fifteen countries of the former Soviet Union, was morphing into a new Russian system and a system which was adding computer-based records to its vast labyrinths of paper-based files. Valentina Alexandrovna had been asked to provide more details on Sasha's uncle. Anna slowed down her father's flow of information and asked him to simply summarise all he knew of his brother's life after the war and the names of any women he had had as partners. Her father confirmed that his brother had had several partners in Bucharest after the war and he would look through the old letters he had. He would write down everything he could find about his brother's relationships in a letter. Anna remembered several figures at her uncle's funeral in Moscow when she was a young girl whom she had not recognised and she asked her father to include what he knew about these in his letter. Valentina Alexandrovna had put all her own enquiries on hold until this letter came and they could decide where and how to seek out the proof of

Sasha's family they needed. It appeared that the proofs would have to start in Romania as her father had confirmed that as far as he knew all her uncle's partners after the war where local women from Bucharest, the capital of Romania.

There was also another link to Romania which Valentina Alexandrovna has mentioned in passing to Anna. She had seemed reluctant to talk about it but had felt it necessary to let Anna know. Sasha had taken to wearing his small cross-like wooden icon on a chain around his neck. It was normally kept under his clothes but occasionally he wore it on the outside. Valentina Alexandrovna had noticed that the chain bore a strong resemblance to one of the chains Yelena Matrovna used for her reading glasses. When asked about it Yelena Matrovna had simply nodded and smiled. Sasha's new teacher also confirmed what Valentina Alexandrovna had thought about the writing on the icon – it was in Romanian. Anna was delighted by this piece of information since Sasha had whispered to her that the icon had come from his 'grandmother' who had said that it had been in his family for many, many years. For Anna this was certain evidence of Sasha being the grandson of her uncle and of a Romanian woman. For Valentina Alexandrovna the wording she had seen that Sasha had written down troubled her more but she did not want anything to get in the way of identifying Sasha. She and Anna had agreed to await her father's letter before doing anything else.

Seventy

IT was decided at Miller Lombard that Anna and one of the legal assistants would go the company to look at the final papers for the privatisation which were being issued to the company by the Property Fund. The meeting was to check documents and would be most efficient just in Russian. There would be a final pre-auction meeting the day before the auction to make sure everyone was up to speed with everything. As Anna and one of the assistants entered his office, Victor Nikolayevich and Leonid Marlenovich were standing by the window with vodka glasses in their hands.

"It was down there you know, Leonid Marlenovich, right down there," said Victor Nikolayevich quietly.

"He did not survive for long though did he?" asked Leonid Marlenovich rhetorically. Anna sensed that the story had been told often. Leonid Marlenovich motioned to them to sit at the table.

"No just long enough to repeat a few words," replied Victor Nikolayevich with a heavy sigh.

"Was that a relative who passed away?" asked Anna sensing the emotions in Victor Nikolayevich's voice.

Victor Nikolayevich, though, did not reply.

"No, Anna," said Leonid Marlenovich. "Please excuse us. We are steeling ourselves for the auction," he said lifting his glass to indicate the way in which they were preparing, "with vodka and memories of our leader's heroic deeds."

Victor Nikolayevich looked at him with a tear welling up in his eyes at this rare moment of camaraderie. "In those days we were all in it together," he said, "and there were such bonds between everyone. We would do anything to help each other."

"And at times we would even help our enemies," said Leonid Marlenovich slowly and delicately.

"Really?" asked Anna just about managing to conceal the genuine surprise in her voice.

"He was badly injured and drowning in the river," said Victor Nikolayevich slowly, "I had to try and save him. By the way that the others were shooting at him I was sure that he was coming over to our side."

"An enemy soldier?" asked Anna in a whisper.

"Yes," Victor Nikolayevich nodded deeply, "right here outside the shipyard. He was trying to tell me what was happening but I could not understand any foreign words at that time. He tried to tell me ten times using the same words."

"What exactly happened?" Anna had sat down and was now showing her surprise that Victor Nikolayevich should have tried to have helped what was assumed to be an enemy. An enemy determined to destroy the city and all of its people. This was a new dimension to Victor Nikolayevich.

"I saw him swimming in the river trying to escape from a group of enemy soldiers on the quay over there firing everything they could at him. I jumped in the water and dragged him to the shore. He was trying to tell me what had happened but I could not understand. I tried to warm him and shouted for help but no-one else would dare come. After about five minutes he started to shake and then he died. Then the people came."

"And?" asked Anna very quietly after a few moments. The room had fallen completely silent.

"Our local militia thought it best to bury him quietly in case the authorities found out that I had tried to help him. So two old men took his body and buried it."

"What happened to you?"

"The old men said I had been brave and that one day I would be repaid but for my safety I should never mention it. For many years I never said a word."

"Until the body was found," added Leonid Marlenovich.

"Two years ago after all the political changes in the world and as part of our perestroika and glasnost his family finally came for the body."

"So they knew he was here?" said Anna.

"Yes. And they gave me a reward for trying to help him."

Anna looked questioningly.

"A thousand dollars," said Victor Nikolayevich slowly and finishing the last drops in his glass.

"Which Victor Nikolayevich donated to the Church," said Leonid Marlenovich.

"Yes, I did not want to take their money."

Anna nodded. "Maybe through this privatisation you will be repaid for your act of heroism," she said still not able to digest all of the story. Victor Nikolayevich and Leonid Marlenovich looked at each other and then moved to sit down.

Sensing the mood was returning to normal Anna asked, "did you receive the documents from the Property Fund?"

"Yes," replied Leonid Marlenovich. He walked over to Victor Nikolayevich's desk and picked up a large envelope. He passed it to Anna. It had not been opened.

"Thank you," she said as she passed it to the assistant who opened. "We will check the terms."

"Please," said Leonid Marlenovich picking up the half empty bottle of vodka from the table and turning back to Victor Nikolayevich.

Anna went through the documents quickly. The terms were as announced. The auction was set for Friday 14th July and there were instructions on how the auction would be carried out. Anna also noticed a small white envelope which was addressed to Victor Nikolayevich and was handwritten. The mark at the top corner of the envelope was the official crest of the office of the Mayor of St Petersburg. She passed it to Leonid Marlenovich without comment. Anna raised her eyebrows as Leonid Marlenovich opened it himself. Leonid Marlenovich smiled at her.

"We have a special message from the Mayor, Victor Nikolayevich," he said showing Victor Nikolayevich the handwritten note. "It says, 'I send you my personal best wishes for a successful auction and for the continued success of the Peter the Great Shipyard, one of our city's greatest enterprises,' from Anatoly Borisevich."

Victor Nikolayevich took the note, his eyes filling up. Anna herself now had to stare down at the papers to hide her own emotion.

Seventy One

HAMPTON was being driven in a private ambulance from the clinic to the airport. It had been arranged that he would pass through the VIP passport and customs area in a wheelchair and then be taken straight onto the private Lear jet. Ellen and Alex were being picked up from their dacha to be driven to wave goodbye at the airport. Ellen was finishing packing Hampton's suitcase when she heard the sound of cars at the gate to the dachas. Alex was waiting outside and he waved at the drivers as they parked up. Both of the office Volvos had come and the drivers got out, said 'hello' to Alex and then headed off for a smoke. Alex walked up to the cars and looked inside. He opened the boot of the car he and his mum were driven in and saw a couple of cardboard boxes with files in them. He tried the door to the other Volvo but it was locked. Alex looked again into the car windows and saw a large crate style box on the back seat. It was wide, high and about a foot wide and must have been wedged in with some effort looking by how tightly it fitted. Alex waited till the drivers returned and as they did he tried the back door of the other Volvo again. Still locked. He thought for a moment and then went back to the dacha. Five minutes later Alex and his mum were on the way to the airport.

The journey to the airport was short and as they drove up the main entrance road the drivers took a different route to normal and soon they were parked up next to an ambulance outside a small building. Alex raced out of the car and soon spied his father in a wheelchair. Vera was with him and filling in forms.

"Alex!" shouted Hampton, "how does it feel to be a VIP?"

"Great!" replied Alex hugging his dad.

"Mr Hampton," said Vera, "sorry to interrupt but shall I check all the files and boxes in the cars and have them taken to the plane. I have filled in all the forms for you. The officials here want the plane to be loaded as quickly as possible."

"Please do, Vera," replied Hampton with a big smile and motioning for Alex to hug him again. "Alex," he said, "why don't you investigate the VIP lounge while I talk for a minute with your mom?"

"Ok," replied Alex pulling himself away from his dad and following Vera as Ellen arrived.

Instead of exploring the lounge Alex moved to the door. Outside the drivers were having a tough job pulling what Alex now saw as a large wooden packing crate out of the Volvo. Vera was remonstrating with them to be careful and after several prolonged pushes, the drivers managed to extract the crate and place it on a baggage trolley. The cardboard boxes of files were piled up in front of it and Vera did a count of everything and then instructed one of the drivers to push the trolley directly to the plane which was parked some fifty metres away. The driver seemed to be questioning where to push the trolley as he pointed to the lounge. Alex looked behind him into the lounge and a small baggage inspection area and an x-ray machine. Vera told the driver to stay where he was and she walked purposefully past Alex and into the lounge.

Alex took a step outside and then moved towards the trolley. He felt a strange sensation, not a tingling, but the hairs on the back of his neck rose and his eyes hurt. He squinted and then crouched down. He looked at the crate and his eyes spun. The colours were bright, the shapes smooth, he could see lines and then figures. As he went to touch the crate he heard footsteps behind him. He turned and blinked up at Vera. Vera gave him a puzzled look and then spoke with authority to the driver who shrugged his shoulders, took hold of the trolley and set off to the plane. Alex followed Vera back into the lounge. He could not wait to find pencils and paper and draw as much as he could remember. He would really surprise his dad.

The goodbyes were very tearful. Hampton praised his wife and son immensely for staying on. Ellen was having another fit of doubts but Alex's serene smile and blazing eyes were counteracting her feelings. The end of the school's summer term was only weeks away and then they would join Hampton in the US for two weeks with another two weeks holiday in the Caribbean. Hampton's sadness at leaving them was painfully clear for all to see as he hugged Alex and then Ellen. Ellen's face was streaming and Vera handed her tissue after tissue. The VIP area had never witnessed such emotion and even the hardened officials were talking to each other with slight breaks in their voices. Hampton's mind was also ecstatic with anticipation. The crate had been loaded. The crate which would surely prove his own very Russian coup!

Seventy Two

VERA read out a message to the meeting from John Hampton. They were once again in the meeting room at Miller Lombard. Victor Nikolayevich had come by himself and availed himself of a large coffee, 'specially' made. Leonid Marlenovich was expected later but apologies were given on behalf of the Head of the company's legal department, who was on sick leave. Dominic Corley was scheduled to join the second half of the meeting when they would talk through the practicalities of the open cry auction. The message was one of good luck to all involved and it assured all those present from the company that Miller Lombard had been extremely diligent in its work in preparing for this crucial stage of the company's privatisation. The most senior figures in the law firm's Moscow office together with experts on international corporate law in London were all on standby should any points arise which the team in St Petersburg needed assistance with. Hampton again reassured the meeting that the legal team in St Petersburg was fully able to advise on the process. A legal opinion had been issued by Miller Lombard to confirm formally that all the information which had been prepared about the company was complete, true and accurate and that it had been verified in accordance with all relevant legislation.

Victor Nikolayevich was very thankful for the message and for several minutes returned to the scandalous shooting. Vera noted down everything he said and said she would send the reply to Hampton. Anna gave Adam a brief smile. To her it was pretty obvious that Hampton's note had been written by Adam and she doubted whether Hampton had even seen it. The highlighting of the legal opinion was definitely written by Adam!

The next twenty minutes of the meeting were spent on the details of the terms of the auction and on the procedure for bidding. Victor Nikolayevich then raised his hand and asked if he might show the meeting something. Anna looked at Adam and was about to try to prevent Victor Nikolayevich from launching into a speech, when she stopped as Victor Nikolayevich took out several pieces of paper.

"I have here another agreement," he said with a wink to Anna.

Adam took the papers. They were in English and Russian. It was an agreement. Adam looked very puzzled and he handed the Russian pages to Anna. Anna looked up at Victor Nikolayevich who was smiling broadly.

"What do you think, Anna?" he said quietly. "No-one would expect this."

"Who knows about this?" asked Anna.

"No-one," replied Victor Nikolayevich almost in a whisper, "not even Leonid Marlenovich yet. They were only signed this morning. All hush-hush and helped by our friends in the Mayor's office. A back up plan!" Victor Nikolayevich drank a large mouthful of his coffee, draining his mug which he pushed over to Vera. Without commenting Vera leant over, took the cup, stood up and left the room.

"Is this what I think it is, Anna?" asked Adam slowly. He rubbed the top of one of the English pages. He thought that correction fluid had been applied but the surface was flat. Correction fluid must have been applied to the original which then must have been photocopied. The result was a change of name, address and looking at the final page – a change of signature.

"Yes, Adam," replied Anna realising that the same had been done to the Russian pages.

"But," said Adam turning to Anna and looking at her sternly, "the original agreement is exclusive, this won't work," he said in English.

"Leave it to me," replied Anna. "Victor Nikolayevich," she continued, "this is a surprise. The same agreement you have with the British Redevelopment Fund you now have made with a Russian company called," she looked at the first page again, "St Petersburg Consumer Products. Is that correct?"

"Yes," replied Victor Nikolayevich in a low voice and leaning over towards Anna. His eyes were sparkling. "And we used the exact same words."

"I can see," replied Anna masking a tone of growing reproach. Copying and using someone else's agreement went so blatantly against all legal practice in any country including Russia. It was tantamount to forgery and yet that is exactly what Victor Nikolayevich was intending.

"Apparently Roman Felixovich was delighted by the idea and asked for it to be signed in the name of one of his private companies! There are some very clever people in the Mayor's office!" Victor Nikolayevich concluded with a small tap on the table as Vera returned with a second 'special' coffee.

"Victor Nikolayevich," continued Anna, "this is quite a change. I'll need to discuss this with my colleagues. May we have a five minute break?"

"Of course, my dear," smiled Victor Nikolayevich enjoying a sip of his coffee. "And I must give you these to check as well," he said taking out an envelope from the battered briefcase he had brought. "These are the documents you wanted from the company."

"Thank you. Can we check these later?"

"Of course, my dear Anna."

Adam was beside himself and Anna took most of their break to calm him down. She took a less excitable view. The Peter the Great Shipyard Company was their client and therefore they were legally bound not to tell the British fund about this 'second' agreement regardless of whether it was valid or not. Adam protested and said that there would never be any deal if it were not for the British Fund. Anna suggested that Adam discuss the situation with Hampton whom he was still obviously in contact with. Adam bit his lip and had to agree. They agreed that they would recommend to Victor Nikolayevich that he keep his doctored agreement confidential. Victor Nikolayevich readily agreed to this with a conspiratorial smile. He also agreed that the meeting with Corley would concentrate on how the bidding in an open auction would take place and that agreements would not be on the agenda.

Going back into the meeting Anna had to smile at Victor Nikolayevich's actions, legally naive and wholly inappropriate, but cunning. She was beginning to have doubts though about becoming the key person in the process with the power to sign the documentation in the privatisation. She suspected that events would bring further surprises and she after all was just a simple lawyer amidst a battle that could have long lasting effects on lots of people. Did she want to be such a pivotal figure?

Seventy Three

ADAM tracked Hampton down to a nursing home on the shore of Lake Michigan. Hampton had only been there a couple of days. He was very happy to take the call from Adam. Adam heard a slight clicking noise on the line as he was put through to Hampton's room which he assumed was to do either with an international connection or the nursing home's switchboard.

"Adam, great to hear from you? How are things?" said Hampton after the click.

"Hectic as usual," replied Adam, "but more importantly how was the flight and how are you?"

"I'm definitely on the mend now and the flight was excellent," replied Hampton with great enthusiasm, "I would definitely recommend a private jet but not perhaps in such circumstances! No passport controls or customs. Now what can I do for you?"

"Sorry to bother you but I wanted to check a case that might create a conflict for us," said Adam in his normal upbeat self.

"Yes, go on," replied Hampton warmly. His normal enthusiasm had also returned.

"It's about the properties belonging to the Peter the Great Shipyard," said Adam slowly.

"Has something new come up?" asked Hampton clearly putting his lawyer hat on.

"Well, we have been researching some ownership claims over one of the buildings."

"Yes?"

"I have been talking to our office in The Hague," said Adam.

"Very good. Great initiative as always!" It sounded almost as if Hampton was beaming down the phone. "And what did you find?"

"There are four disputed claims on the property. Two by a 'Yusupov', one by a 'Berd' and another by a 'Baronsky'." Adam said the last word slowly.

"Yes, the names are vaguely familiar," replied Hampton, his voice still full of enthusiasm.

"Well, the Baronsky claim was made by a firm called White & Grace in Detroit in Michigan."

"Well done, Adam! As I've always said you can certainly think out of the box and you can put two and two together to make five!"

"So, the law firm is connected to you?" asked Adam relieved that his boss had not reacted badly to the probing by a much junior lawyer and a direct subordinate at that.

"Fraid so!" Hampton's voice had not lost any of its joviality. "And you are right in thinking that it puts us in a very tricky situation."

"Conflict of interest?"

"Precisely!" replied Hampton. "I was asked very confidentially to make a claim for the property through The Hague in 1992 which was actually before I joined Miller Lombard and it was done through my dad's law firm in Detroit. It was also well before we started to work for the Peter the Great Shipyard."

"But could it not have stopped us working for the Peter the Great Shipyard in any case?" asked Adam who had started to wonder at his boss's actions. He knew his boss was very different to most of the partners in the law firm but to Adam it appeared inappropriate to be claiming back a company's asset for someone else on one hand whilst becoming the same company's legal adviser on the other.

"No, it was cleared by our conflicts and ethics committee in London before we became legal advisers to the company."

Adam sighed with relief and was immediately upset with himself for ever doubting his boss. "So who were we acting for before?" he asked aiming to close out the matter.

"Adam, that is something that I cannot tell even you!" Hampton laughed. "All I can do is point you to the official papers relating to the case if you can find them anywhere."

Adam was dumbstruck. "Of course," he spluttered.

"Anyway, I think it is all left well alone until this privatisation auction is settled and we can all get back to normal. The legal opinion, as you know, was signed off by our London office and we have verified that the company owns all its properties in accordance with Russian law." He paused briefly and then asked with his good spirit undiminished. "How are the rest of the staff in the office?"

They chatted for five more minutes and then Adam excused himself. He immediately dialled Anna's mobile. As he listened to the recorded message explaining that her phone was not switched on he heard the same slight clicking sound on the line as he had when he had been put through to Hampton. The conversation with his boss had only partly clarified the claim. His boss' reluctance to disclose who he had been acting for before could obviously be seen as professional etiquette yet a doubt was hardening in Adam's brain. Not able to reach Anna he decided he had to try and make some progress in the almost parallel universe of visions and strange encounters which he still fell into whenever a sight or sound reminded him.

Now that the sharpness of the image of the black Mercedes with the dent on the driver's side speeding away with Olga in the back had dulled, Adam resolved to dial Olga's number again. This time when he had met her he had only had a few drinks and her behaviour made no sense. He went through a range of permutations and scenarios in his mind and none of them seemed to be credible. She had contacted him. He had called her. She had come to the drinks. So far straightforward. He put together the images from the first incident when the driver of the Mercedes had taken hold of her in the nightclub with the image of the second incident. The driver clearly was involved. Was it he who was stopping Olga from being in touch with him? There had to be a lot more to it. He decided against asking the girls in the office who knew Olga to help him. He decided it was time to call her again. He took a deep breath. He dialled the number from the note she had given him. The number was no longer in use.

Seventy Four

THE auction room in the building that housed the offices of the St Petersburg Property Fund was quaint and old fashioned. It had wooden panels on the walls and velvet skirting boards along the bottom of the walls. The ceiling was high and the windows on the side of the room opposite the door were long and narrow with internal wooden shutters. Prior to the Revolution it could have been a reception room in a wealthy merchant's house. The only furniture now in the room was a long narrow table with three chairs behind it near to a wall and then a dozen rows of seats arranged in front of the table. On the table was a large hourglass, an abacus and a gravel – all three looked to be Nineteenth Century and definitely Pre-Revolutionary.

At a quarter to eleven the door opened and three men walked in carrying various papers and several wooden objects. They were the officials who were running the auction. They sat down in the chairs behind the table placing their papers in several piles. The wooden objects looked like small paddles and had numbers on them. Two large security guards then appeared in the doorway. As one of them walked over to the windows there was a large noise as one of the internal wooden window shutters banged against a window. The officials behind the desk all stood up and joked with each other as the guard with a strong shove pushed the shutter back and checked the window. It was locked and had not been the cause of the shutter moving. He checked all the windows to make sure they were shut.

The locks on the windows were old but firm. One of the men behind the desk pointed to a plaque high up on the wall opposite. It was old and looked like a faded painting of a man's head. By the animated conversation between the officials the plaque was the object of their conversation which ended with a loudly uttered pronouncement that 'it could not have been a ghost because ghosts had been banned by Stalin.' It was well documented that Stalin suffered from disturbing and hellish nightmares replete with the ghosts of the millions of people he had had executed. Although Stalin had publically banned all forms of ghosts his vast powers as a dictator could only be wielded against the living!

One of the officials looked at his watch and signalled to the guards to open the door. People then started to enter. Most went and took seats in the rows of chairs whilst several approached the officials behind the table and had various documents checked. Four people were given the wooden paddles with numbers 1 to 4 on them. They were to be used to make bids. Anna had approached the table with a young man who was one of the legal assistants at Miller Lombard. Although Anna had the powers of attorney in her name from the British Redevelopment Fund it had been decided that the physical bidding would be done by one of her male colleagues. The bidding, as with so many other features of Russian life, was decidedly a male pursuit.

Leonid Marlenovich had decided to stand at the side of the rows of chairs rather than sit. He wanted to watch the audience as much as the four men about to bid who had taken seats in the middle of the front row. No-one else was allowed to sit on the front row. Victor Nikolayevich had been invited to take coffee with the Mayor. This was a deliberate political move and took the General Director out of the process to give an appearance of impartiality. Victor Nikolayevich with two agreements stuffed into his jacket pocket was only too happy to oblige the Mayor. He took the precaution of a mid-morning 'constitutional' large brandy in case the Mayor's coffee perchance contained nothing stronger than caffeine.

Leonid Marlenovich nodded to Dominic Corley who had taken a seat on the third row with Adam. Leonid Marlenovich then motioned for Adam to come over to him which he duly did. "Good morning, Adam?" he said quietly. "Has the bidding been organised?"

"Yes, Leonid Marlenovich. Our colleague has number 2. He has his initial limit after which he will have to refer back to Donald."

"Very good. Who are the other bidders, do you know?" asked Leonid Marlenovich who knew full well that number 3 was Roman Felixovich and that the other two had been put up by the company to drive up the price to a sensible level.

"We believe that they are local brokers. Perhaps looking for some publicity."

"Most probably. Let's see."

As Adam returned to his seat there was a commotion at the door and a scruffily dressed man with a long beard pushed himself passed the guard. The commotion was silenced by three loud bangs of the gravel. The official in the middle of the table then put down the gravel and stood up. The scruffily dressed man sat on a chair at the end of one of the rows. He tried not to draw attention to himself but his old style coat and long dishevelled hair drew many eyes towards him.

"Comrades," said the official who had stood up, "or should I now say 'citizens' in the new order our country is now in? I am Judge Oserov and it is my task today to oversee the auction by public outcry of twenty-five per cent of the shares of Open Joint Stock Company Peter the Great Shipyard. The winner must pay the winning price bid for the shares and fulfil the investment condition of five million dollars." There was a general murmur of satisfaction at the figure. Feet scraped against chairs and then the room quickly quietened again. "My colleague will now explain the procedure." He sat down as the man on his right stood up. He explained that the bidding would start at five hundred thousand dollars and increase at increments of fifty thousand dollars. At each figure every wooden paddle raised would constitute a bid and the auction would continue until only one paddle was left by itself having bid on a number which would then be the winning bid. During the bidding at each figure all the remaining bidders would be given a small amount of time by the auctioneer to decide whether to bid or not. When the auctioneer was satisfied that there was a winner he would bang the gravel three times to signify that the auction was complete. The auction would last for fifteen minutes which would be timed by the hourglass. There would be no breaks.

As the official finished a visible buzz of excitement spread around the room. The Miller Lombard bidder was the youngest of the four bidders. He looked nervous and held his paddle tight in his right hand. Number 3 to his left was an intense little man who sat slightly hunched up and rarely looked around the room. The two other bidders were excited and could not keep still as they continually looked around the room and signalled to various people. To Adam it looked for all the world to be the start of a horse race with the four riders readying themselves for the starter's gun. He remarked this to Corley who was seated with his legs crossed and who exuded an air of grand insouciance. Corley readily agreed and reckoned that his jockey had by far the fastest horse and was definitely the clear favourite. As he said this Corley caught the eye of bidder number 3 who had turned round for the first time. The bidder seemed to be looking for Corley. Their eyes crossed but with a deft flick of his head Corley managed to avoid their eyes locking. Corley felt a quick shiver up his spine. The little man had a determined if hollow look in his eyes. Corley had seen that look before. He made a short joke to Adam about the abacus and hourglass to take his mind of the little man. A few of those seated in the audience were becoming restless as the Judge and two other official were conferring together. They were pointing to the shabbily dressed man with a long beard who had moved from his original seat and had moved to the end of the front row which was reserved for bidders only. The man had taken out a string like object and was muttering quickly under his breath and rocking slightly backwards and forwards on his seat. He now seemed to be wanting to create attention.

The Judge looked at his watch, frowned deeply and the stood up. He picked up the hourglass and turned it over. "The auction has started," he announced as his colleague on the right also stood up, picked up the gravel and shouted, "five hundred thousand!" All four bidders quickly raised their paddles and the audience applauded. Just as he was about to open his mouth to announce the next figure the shabbily dressed man stood up, stepped forward, moved across and turned around directly in front of the four bidders. As the Judge motioned frantically to the guards the man dropped to his knees between the Miller Lombard bidder and the little man and shouted several words. The guards grabbed him at either side and hauled him to his feet. They looked to the Judge who just motioned for them to take him to the back of the room and keep him under control. There was no time to deal with him at this moment and the auction could not be stopped. "Five hundred and fifty thousand!" shouted the official much louder this time as the audience started to point to the shabbily dressed man in fits of laughter as much as surprise. Again all four bidders raised their paddles. With a pointed stare from the Judge the official then shouted, "six hundred thousand!" as quickly as he could. The Miller Lombard bidder and the little man put their paddles up straight away. The other two bidders followed a few seconds later.

Corley lent over into the row in front of him and Adam and tapped Anna gently on the shoulder. "What was that all about?" he whispered quietly. "I think it sounded like an ancient Russian curse," replied Anna also whispering. "On us?" asked Corley barely concealing his incredulity. "No," replied Anna, "on bidder number 3."

"Six hundred and fifty thousand!" shouted the official as the audience attention focussed back on the auction. Again the Miller Lombard bidder and the little man put their paddles up straightaway. After nearly a minute one of the two remaining bidders raised his paddle but the other bidder with a large shake of his head put his on the table. He raised his arms and put his hands together in a quasi-wave to the audience who applauded him warmly. At eight hundred thousand only the Miller Lombard bidder and the little man remained. Adam calculated that the grains of sand in the hourglass had gone down by a good two-thirds and that they had entered the last five minutes of the auction. At nine hundred thousand the bidding pattern took a strange turn. The little man was now sitting on the edge of his seat and as soon as the Miller Lombard bidder started to raise his paddle, the little man raised his paddle in exactly the same way and at exactly the same time with his paddle almost touching the other paddle. It was if he wanted to bid at exactly the same fraction of a second.

Leonid Marlenovich had noticed the manoeuvre and exchanged glances with Corley. Anna had also turned to look at Leonid Marlenovich and all three of their eyes locked. Was it because they were two bids away from the million dollar bid? Time was running out so there would not be many more bids. The official moved quickly to the million dollar bid and the little man did the same action again. Instead of applauding the audience had gone very quiet. As the last grains of sands poured into the bottom half of the hourglass, the official rapidly increased the bids and the little man did exactly the same. He was acting with a specific purpose – he wanted to bid exactly the same as the Miller Lombard bid. He was sweating and did not take his eyes off his fellow bidder's paddle. He did not even blink. As the hourglass emptied the little man stood up, nodded to the Judge and made to leave. A deep throated roar shot from the back of the room and the sounds of a brief struggle echoed around the room. As the audience turned round the two guards were falling backwards each landing heavily on the floor. There was a gush of wind from the windows and a whirl of dark light. Then silence broken by the moan of one guard and a mouthful of expletives from the other. The gravel sounded once and the audience turned back round again. "There will be a short break for consultation," said the Judge loudly as he and his two officials quickly left the room.

The Miller Lombard team, Leonid Marlenovich and Corley rearranged some chairs into a small circle in a corner of the room.

"Uh hum," said Corley as the first to speak, "where does all that now leave us?"

Everyone looked at each other in puzzlement.

"Can I assume," continued Corley, "that we must now be in unchartered waters?"

"These auctions are quite new," said Adam, "shall I call our office in Moscow to see if they have taken part in one like this?"

"I think we can wait for the judge to come back first," said Leonid Marlenovich. "I am sure that it will be up to him to decide."

"So I guess the result then was that no-one actually won?" suggested Corley.

"Bidder number 3," replied Adam, "seemed intent on bidding exactly the same as us. And he seemed satisfied at the end. Bizarre."

"A curious little fellow," commented Corley. "Anna, did you say that strange man tried to put a curse on him?"

"He had some rosary beads and it sounded like an old Russian curse?"

"How so?" asked Corley.

"It would translate into something like – 'may their curse be your curse'," she replied.

"And where did he go?" asked Adam. "He did not go out of the door and I did not see anyone open the windows."

"I think in the confusion no-one paid him any attention," added Corley not sounding fully convinced. "Anyway back to business. Where is the Judge?"

After almost half an hour the Judge returned by himself and asked everyone to be reseated. He explained that the auction had not been completed in the correct manner. He had checked with the Property Fund in St Petersburg who had also checked with their counterparts in Moscow. The auction had been classified as 'annulled'. The audience erupted with a barrage of questions. The Judge raised his arm until the questions stopped. "I have decided," he said, "through the executive powers granted to the Commercial Court in St Petersburg in accordance with the laws on privatisation that the auction of twenty-five per cent of the shares of Open Joint Stock Company Peter the Great Shipyard will take place again on the same terms, here, one week from today and on the open outcry basis. This time, however, there will be no time limit other than the working hours of this court. The auction will conclude when there is one bidder left!" He finished his announcement with a raising voice and for good measure banged the gravel on his table twice. The cheers of relief that filtered through the corridors of the main building could easily have been mistaken as a sign of a successful auction. As the cheers subsided a final deep sound echoed around the room which no-one could work out what it was or where it had come from.

Seventy Five

THE CNN reporter was standing at the edge of a lake and speaking rapidly into his microphone. "It will be from this spot on the edge of Lake Ladoga that his Royal Highness the Prince of Wales will retrace the route of the so called Ice Road or Road of Life. This man-built road saved the lives of so many of the inhabitants of St Petersburg during the German Siege. To give you an idea of how difficult it would be to build the road when the ice had set and the snow was falling, the original plan for the remake of one of the Twentieth Century's greatest but little known acts of mass heroism, was to make it in the winter, but both the Russian authorities and the local army declined to attempt to rebuild the road even with the more modern equipment of today. It was truly an act of undaunted courage which first saved the city from starvation and then was used as an exit route to evacuate over half a million people to safety further reducing the threat of starvation for those left behind. The route this time will be by boat initially and then by road for the final few miles. I have with me again the Deputy Ambassador from the British Embassy. As we discussed last time there is a great British interest in this road. Who actually came up with the idea for the Price of Wales to honour those who died building and travelling on this road?"

"The initiative came we believe," replied the Deputy Ambassador, "from regiments within the British army who helped by providing supplies for the convoy during the Siege and I believe that the Prince of Wales is a patron of one of the regiments."

"And he will be accompanied by members of the regiment?" asked the reporter.

"Absolutely. There will be a number of military ceremonies at the beginning and end of the road and then there will be a final service of remembrance at St Issac's Cathedral the day after," said the Deputy Ambassador.

"Is there any truth in some rumours we are hearing," continued the reporter, "that the British Army is here to tighten up security for the Prince?"

"Good God, no!" replied the Deputy Ambassador brusquely and giving the impression of swatting the suggestion away like he would an annoying fly. "We have full confidence in the security arrangements which have been put in place but which of course I am not at liberty to discuss."

"Quite," said the reporter realising he had no chance of taking his line of questioning any further. "And what else will the Prince be doing?" he asked.

"The Prince has a number of official engagements," replied the Deputy Ambassador with a forced smile, "including launching the famous Standart boat and visiting a project for young people supported by the Prince's Trust and where there is a group of British volunteers."

"We are looking forward to it all, Deputy Ambassador. Thank you," finished off the reporter with a breezy smile to match that of his interviewee's. "Back to the studio."

Seventy Six

ANNA was having quite a day. The 'annulled' auction had set off all kinds of rumours and counter-rumours. There were lots of names suggested for the identity of the investor behind bidder no 3. These included large foreign companies and a list of local businessmen. The rumours could die out as quickly as they sprang up. The excitement at the deliberate stalemate or 'rigging' as some people were describing the odd bidding outweighed the stir caused by the old-fashioned dressed man whose antics had filtered their way into the local press. Now thankfully the rescheduled auction was only a day away and she hoped that the auction this time would be conclusive and in their favour. She had been given a new and much higher upper bidding limit by Corley and updated powers of attorney to act on the Fund's behalf. She had also been given the power to transfer the Fund's money as and when necessary. Corley had said he would appreciate a call from Anna to confirm any payments made but that he had complete trust in her regarding any payment. This had both flattered and worried Anna but again thankfully Anna was so busy that she had little time to think about it in any depth. Adam had wanted to meet with her as soon as she came to the office that morning to go through some further points before the auction but Anna had delayed the meeting as she had an urgent matter to attend to. She was sitting in an old car with Sasha next to her. They had just left the Home and Anna had just left Valentina Alexandrovna's office. In the office Anna and had handed Valentina Alexandrovna the letter from her father. Anna had read it only once when she had received it earlier that morning and again had not wanted to dwell on it. Valentina Alexandrovna had scanned the five pages in under a minute.

"Wonderful," said Valentina Alexandrovna quietly under her breath, "my dear, Anna, you see what this means?"

"Yes," said Anna also quietly, "Sasha must be our relation."

"Yes, your father gives very convincing details about your uncle's time in Bucharest and the names of his partners. Shall I follow up on this or will you?"

"Can you, Valentina Alexandrovna, I am so busy today and for the next few days?"

"Of course, Anna," replied Valentina Alexandrovna with a huge and warm smile, "I'll contact the authorities in Bucharest and request all the records on your uncle and these women. There might be a marriage certificate and if we are really, really lucky a birth certificate for Sasha with your uncle's name on or the name of one of these women. We are so close."

Anna looked at Valentina Alexandrovna with tears welling in her eyes and did not reply.

"But there is one quick thing you can do for me," said Valentina Alexandrovna, "and it will only take an hour."

Anna looked at her watch and made some mental calculations. If she was out for another hour then she would have to work like crazy for the rest of the day and she would have to meet with Adam as well at some stage but she nodded at Valentina Alexandrovna and took a deep breath.

"I have just had a call from the Metropolitan's office," Valentina Alexandrovna paused as Anna looked at her, her brow furrowing. "And," she continued, "they have asked for Sasha to sing a song for them to see if he is ready to sing at a public service in the Kazan Cathedral."

"Really," asked Anna, "that would be a great honour for him. Is Yelena Matrovna not here?"

"That's just it. I have tried to call her but I cannot get hold of her at such short notice. I just want someone to go with Sasha. I would go myself but.."

"Not at all," said Anna standing up, "of course, I can go."

And now Anna was sitting next to Sasha chatting idly about the buildings they were passing. Sasha said that he knew the car and the driver from a previous trip and that he had also been to the cathedral they were on their way to before. It was the Cathedral of Our Saviour-on-the-Spilt-Blood. His time there before with Yelena Matrovna had ended a little spookily, Sasha had said, but he had loved singing in there. Before they knew it they were inside the cathedral. Sasha excitedly took Anna's arm and gave her a quick tour. Anna had been in the cathedral herself twice before and had studied the fabulous mosaics in great detail but she did not want to spoil Sasha's abundant enthusiasm and pride in being able to describe everything to her. Several minutes later two men dressed in black cassocks entered, the first priest who was shorter than the second approached Sasha and Anna. Anna recognised the second priest who had stood back as the Metropolitan Melnikov himself. She was surprised that he did not address either Sasha or herself nor offer his ring for her to kiss. She felt a clear signal that he was simply observing so she lowered her eyes from him and turned to the first priest kissing his ring as did Sasha. He spoke in a whisper to them. He was clear and to the point. He wanted Sasha to sing a slow chant which he knew Sasha sang often and wanted Sasha to stand under the central spire. He did not mention the Metropolitan's presence.

Sasha sang beautifully and controlled the volume of his voice with such skill that it echoed up and down the spire with multiple vibrations and sounded as if a whole choir was singing. Halfway through the chant Anna risked a brief glance at the Metropolitan. His eyes were closed tight but his whole body seemed to sway ever so slightly. Anna looked back down to the floor. Sasha's voice was clearly electrifying to those who succumbed to its sound and rhythm. As Sasha finished the second priest clapped very reverently and beckoned Sasha to him. He put his hand on Sasha's shoulder and spoke very quietly to him. Anna looked back towards the Metropolitan but he was nowhere to be seen. She had not heard the sound of the cathedral door being opened and could only assume that the Metropolitan had left before Sasha had finished singing. She stepped over towards Sasha and the priest and stopped still. The priest had hold of Sasha's icon which he was holding up. It was still on its chain and around Sasha's neck. To Anna's complete surprise the priest then proceeded to put his lips to the icon and kiss it. He then made a sign of the cross over the icon and over Sasha who had immediately genuflected on one knee. As Anna then took another step the priest span round and fixed Anna with a powerful look. He put his hand back on Sasha's shoulder.

"Sasha must sing tomorrow at eleven thirty in the aisle of St Simeon in the Kazan Cathedral. It is a special celebration for one of our holiest of saints. A car will come for him at ten thirty."

Anna could not speak. She simply nodded and took Sasha's arm as the priest left them. Her head was spinning and she frowned as the timing dawned on her. Tomorrow was the rescheduled auction which she could not miss. She had all the powers to control the bidding and make any payments. The company, the Fund and her own firm would all be looking at her to make everything work! She would have to make sure Valentina Alexandrovna and Yelena Matrovna went with Sasha. There was too much happening now all at the same time. She needed to think straight and the last thing she needed was to have to talk to Adam about a building. Sasha had taken her hand and squeezed it. He had not said anything to her yet but had watched her as she had digested the instruction from the priest and what it meant. They stepped out of the cathedral and walked over to the car.

"Your singing was simply beautiful, Sasha," said Anna as they got into the car.

"You must sing, too, Anna," replied Sasha, "I know you can!"

Anna smiled at Sasha and then patted his knee. She had just remembered that her father and her uncle had both been accomplished singers when they were younger – before the horrors of war and the destruction of innocence. The early photographs of the album her father had sent her showed her father and uncle singing on many of the shots. Sasha was bringing everything back and with what beauty and power! She put her arm around him and could feel the warmth in his body. Sasha looked out of the car window and started to sing quietly. Before Anna knew it they were back at the Home and she was ready to tackle the next manic few days with complete composure and a determination to see what benefits she might be able to conjure out of them!

Seventy Seven

ALEX kept the folder in his school bag. The folder had a list of paintings and some drawings of his own. His mum had let him look at the catalogues from the Hermitage as long as they were put back in his dad's study after each time he looked at them. He was also told not to put any drink or food on the table when he had them out so as not to risk spilling anything on them or damaging them. He had to be extremely careful when turning the pages over – even though the catalogues looked new they were from 1902 and the 1970s. From the catalogues Alex had worked out the list of paintings which had been on the typed list which had been sent from his dad's office in the sealed envelope and which had been in Russian. He found them in the oldest catalogue. He had also finished his own 'masterpieces' – inspired by touching the crate which had been sent on the private jet with his dad. He had closed his eyes and drawn five pictures in coloured pencils. When he studied what he had done he quickly realised that the pictures were very much like some of the paintings in the catalogues. One was in the style of Matisse, another like a Picasso. He was sure his dad would recognise them. He found very similar paintings in the oldest catalogue as well and finished the drawings off with final touches of his own. What he needed now was a way to send them to his dad – there was no way he could wait until he and his mum went back to the States when school finished. He wanted his drawings to be a surprise so he did not want to ask his mum. He then remembered the lady who worked in his dad's office and who had gone to the Hermitage with Adam. She would be able to send them to his dad. He would have to find a way to go to his dad's office.

Alex's opportunity to go to his dad's office luckily came up a few days after he had finished his drawings. After school his mum had asked their driver to pass by the Miller Lombard office so that she could pick up some post which had arrived for her. They used the office address for all their correspondence as there was no postal service to the compound where their rented house was and they would not have trusted the Russian postal system for a second. In Soviet times all international post was opened and censored, now the Miller Lombard Russian staff had advised, all post was opened not to read but to be relieved of anything remotely valuable. Ellen had happily agreed for Alex to go into the office with her and in response to Alex's question she had answered that 'Vera' was the name of his dad's secretary.

Once in the office Alex quickly recognised Vera. He went straight over to her desk whilst his mum went into his dad's office to go through their post. Alex had taken his school bag in and he took out the folder as soon as he had said 'hello' to Vera.

"Can you fax these pages to my dad, Vera?" asked Alex in his politest voice.

Vera smiled and took the five pages from Alex. "I can," she replied, "but," she paused and looked at the five drawings, "the fax machine only works in black and white and these pictures may not look quite right."

Alex's face dropped. The idea of faxing had excited him but as he had not done any faxing himself he had not thought about the colours and now when he thought about it, Vera was right, he had only ever seen black and white pages on the faxes he had seen in his dad's study. He looked at Vera with the sadness on his face plain to see.

"But, what we can do," said Vera lowering her voice and speaking softly as she thought Alex was on the point of bursting into tears, "I can photocopy them in black and white to see what they look like and I will still then fax them, and," she paused and looked at Alex with a broad smile, "I'll also put the originals in the office post. I'm sure then that it will only take a few days to get them to your dad."

"Brilliant!" replied Alex, "that will be great and if you are photocopying can these pages also be photocopied in colour?" He had seen a colour photocopier in his school. It was very new.

"We don't have a colour photocopier, here in our office yet," replied Vera smiling again, "but I can send them to a special printing shop and have some copies made."

"Really?" said Alex with a huge smile.

"Who will the copies be for?" asked Vera.

"A set for me and one I'll give to my mum once dad has got the originals," replied Alex.

"And anyone else?"

Alex had not thought of anyone else but the idea of surprising people was taking hold of him. "Do you think dad's committee or the lady we met on our tour might be interested?" he asked. These were the people who knew so much about paintings.

Vera was struck by Alex's enthusiasm and by his innocence. She could not see how any of the experts at the Hermitage who were some of Russia's, if not the world's, most famous art experts would be interested in the drawings of a young boy, but she did not have the heart to disappoint him. "I'll make plenty of copies," she said.

"And then you can give them out at the next committee meeting," said Alex with glee. "Can I come to the Hermitage next time you and Adam go? I am sure Adam will say 'yes'".

"As soon as I have the colour copies why don't I give them to Adam and let him take care of them?" she replied with another broad smile. At least that way, she thought to herself, she was not being entirely untruthful about who might see Alex's drawings and Adam should be able to find a way to keep Alex happy. Alex thanked Vera in his best Russian pronunciation of 'spacibo!' the Russian word for 'thank you'.

Seventy Eight

UNLOADING the products as they arrived from Cuba was never a problem for Leonid Marlenovich to arrange. The products were safely enclosed within dozens of crates of tropical fruit and other exotic produce such as coffee beans and cocoa beans. The crates along with a set number of boxes of the best Cuban cigars passed unhindered through customs on their arrival into St Petersburg. Unhindered that was as long as three boxes of cigars were unofficially impounded at customs to be disposed of by the custom officials themselves and a further three boxes set aside for the police department. A further three went to Leonid Marlenovich for his person consumption and a final three passed through customs with duty paid to be put on sale, mainly to the city's top restaurants and several private individuals. Leonid Marlenovich was not greedy. He did, indeed, keep one box to enjoy at his leisure but the other two were sent care of Victor Nikolayevich to the Mayor's office. The crates of fruit and other produce were then delivered to Leonid Marlenovich's basement rooms where they were sorted, 'checked' and inventoried before the fruit, beans and other exotic ingredients were sent on to the city's chocolate factory. The delivery this time, it was soon discovered, was significantly more substantial than usual and shipping onto Hamburg hidden in a delivery of eight new small crafts was looking like being much more difficult than Leonid Marlenovich had envisaged. And this was the run he had personal responsibility for.

Leonid Marlenovich had called Inspector Bushkin as soon as his special operations team had discovered that several crates were crammed full with large bundles of the product rather than one or two bundles being hidden in the middle of a crate as had been the case before. They were both watching one of the last crates being carefully unpacked.

"Did the Cubans say how much they were sending for this run?" asked Inspector Bushkin.

"They never give a precise figure," replied Leonid Marlenovich as he knelt down and picked up one of the bundles, "we knew that this run was going to be big but it looks as though we might have five times more than on the previous shipments."

"If they don't tell you how much is coming how does anyone control how much is being sold on?" asked Inspector Bushkin who had also picked up one of the bundles.

"Let's just say that we have a system between the Cubans, ourselves and our partners in Hamburg," said Leonid Marlenovich smiling, "and the system is something that can never be revealed."

Inspector Bushkin looked at Leonid Marlenovich and weighed up the situation. He knew enough about how the majority of the criminal and black market businesses in St Petersburg operated and how little of any of it could be traced on paper. He decided not to probe any further - he was happy with the sum building in a bank account in Cyprus that was in the name of his elderly mother and which sooner or later would be his unexpected 'inheritance' to retire on.

"This time, though," he said to Inspector Bushkin with another smile, "we may have a few complications."

"Because of the amount?" asked Bushkin.

"Yes," replied Leonid Marlenovich, "I may need to look at the schedule of our boat deliveries to Europe and split the delivery."

"Is that wise?" asked Bushkin, "you told me that this was the big one, the test run."

"It is," replied Leonid Marlenovich his smile disappearing.

"And this other group out of London is still rumoured to be looking to interfere with this route?"

"It is," replied Leonid Marlenovich again. He paused and put down the bundle. "Even the Cubans had an incident on their way back. But as this run seems to be make or break for us we are going to have make the one delivery and take care of the interference all at the same time and once and for all. I will need some support."

"What kind?" asked Bushkin.

"When we leave," said Leonid Marlenovich, "I can arrange support once we reach the Baltic."

"I can get a police boat," replied Bushkin.

"Try and make it unmarked, will you," replied Leonid Marlenovich his smile returning, "or do you want to make it obvious to everyone."

Inspector Bushkin did not reply.

"Come with me," said Leonid Marlenovich after a few seconds. He had decided he would have to show Inspector Bushkin how he was going to send the delivery off, if his protection was going to be of any use. He doubted it would but it might provide some useful cover if the departure could be timed at a moment when the city's attention would be elsewhere.

Leonid Marlenovich took Bushkin out of the basement rooms, round passed the showroom and into the main shipyard. They then went to inspect the final touches being given to the light crafts destined to be delivered to Hamburg. Leonid Marlenovich explained that the eight light crafts would be lifted onto a small yacht carrier which looked similar to a barge. The carrier was one of the company's own carriers and it would shortly be moored outside the Old Foundry building. Once it was loaded with the eight light crafts the carrier would stay there until it was time to depart. Leonid Marlenovich did not need to explain to Inspector Bushkin that it was while it was moored and fully loaded near the Old Foundry that the additional cargo was added out of sight of the main shipyard. Leonid Marlenovich spent a good ten minutes looking at one of the light crafts in discussion with one of the shipyard workers. He then signalled to Inspector Bushkin that their visit to the yard was over and patted him on the back. His smile had returned.

"Do I suspect that you have a plan?" Inspector Bushkin asked Leonid Marlenovich smiling himself.

"I need to do some final calculations once all the crates have been sorted but with a modification to the storage area on these boats, I think we should have enough space."

"Great," replied Inspector Bushkin, "but that just leaves the risk of interference."

"I think that your suggestion of a police boat is an excellent idea," beamed Leonid Marlenovich.

Inspector Bushkin looked at him with a scowl.

"If we time our departure correctly then an unofficial police escort along the Neva and into the Gulf of Finland would be ideal. Our Hamburg partner with then take over in the Baltic. Delivery secured."

"What do you mean by timed 'correctly'?"

"In plain light of day, Vladimir! In fact when everyone in the city will be looking at the most famous boat ever built in St Petersburg and the whole world will also be watching on CNN!"

Seventy Nine

ANNA had tried to catch Adam in the office once she had returned from the Home after been driven back there in the car with Sasha. She so wanted to stay and talk to Sasha and to Valentina Alexandrovna but she had so much to do. No-one in the office knew of Adam's movements other than that he was out. Anna was a little cross but she buried herself in the final preparations for the next day's auction, checking and double-checking all the paperwork. She asked Vera to track Adam down and not to stop until she had located him. In the middle of the afternoon Vera came up to Anna with a relieved look on her face. Apparently Adam had spoken to their boss around lunch time and all he had said to one of the assistants was that he had to go to the Peter the Great Shipyard that afternoon. Anna thanked Vera and decided she would go to the company herself as soon as she had finished. If he was at the company he would be easy to find.

As it turned out the receptionist at the Peter the Great Shipyard had no record of Adam visiting that afternoon but she had heard someone from the showroom mentioning that a foreigner, whom Anna quickly deduced was an Englishman, had been seen on his way there not very long ago. Anna managed to hide her frown as she thanked the receptionist and headed for the showroom which was in the building next door. The showroom was in a Soviet-style grey building the same as the company's offices but the showroom itself was very modern and decorated to a high Western standard.

"Are you looking for Adam?" asked an assistant in the showroom, "then follow me."

Without replying Anna followed her through to the back of the showroom. This was an odd place for Adam to visit and there was something in the assistant's voice which Anna could not quite put her finger on.

"Adam!" shouted Anna with surprise as she saw Adam sitting on a chair. His shirt was unbuttoned and he looked in pain. Hearing Anna's voice he grabbed his shoulder and winced.

"He had a lucky escape," said a young woman standing at the side of him. She had black hair and Anna had a feeling she had seen her briefly somewhere before.

"She saved me actually," said Adam meekly looking at the young woman. The look that passed between the two of them was discomfort personified. The look was not lost on Anna.

"Well?" said Anna staring at both of them. "Tell me what happened."

"Adam," began the young woman.

Anna looked at Adam with a clear question mark over the young woman's familiarity with him. It seemed probable that there was some kind of relationship between Adam and the young woman. Anna was not jealous as such but she was feeling as though she had been left out of something.

"I was standing outside the showroom on my way to the shipyard entrance," intervened Adam, "I was early and looking in the window at the models of the boats and I saw Olga inside." He did not want to add anything else. His search for Olga had proved a failure ever since she had left Janna's birthday drinks. She never appeared in his hotel's bar since nor in any bar Adam had been to since. Her phone it seemed had been put permanently out of use. And then he had seen her as bright as day in the showroom of the company which he was doing legal work for! Just like that! After all his searching she actually worked at the Peter the Great Shipyard. She had mentioned in the bar that she worked for a well-known company in the city but he had not put two and two together or indeed just asked her!

"I had waved at him," continued Olga, "because I saw two men running up behind him to attack him."

"To attack him!" said Anna in a raised voice.

"Good job I took notice," said Adam having regained some composure, "I managed to turn half round and the piece of wood, or whatever it was, luckily hit me on the shoulder and not the head." He touched his shoulder and winced again.

"And?" asked Anna.

"That's it. It happened very fast. The girls ran out of the shop and chased the men off."

"What did they take?" asked Anna.

"My briefcase," he hesitated a moment and for some reason looked at Olga and then winced to cover up the look which she had returned with a firm stare, "with the file of papers," he continued slowly, "from the Property Register and the faxes from The Hague." Adam stopped. He finally had to admit to himself that he was beginning to suspect that it may not have been a random attack. "There was also a folder with copies of some drawings made by Alex."

Anna really could not believe that this had happened. "You are a liability, Adam," said Anna her voice softening. "First Hampton is shot and then you are attacked. I would have thought that professionals like you would be able to look after yourselves or at least take some better precautions."

"Anna!" replied Adam with visible emotion.

"He has had a shock," added Olga.

"Pour soul," replied Anna with a touch of sympathy mixed in with reproach. She was really struggling to accept that her boss and now her senior colleague should have put themselves in such situations. But maybe she too would have to admit that there was a sinister side to the events and that she too would have to watch around her more carefully. Was this all related to the company? She let the thought pass – everyday life at the moment for all Russians had its fair share of challenges and she had plenty on her mind with Sasha and the plight of all the children just in the one home.

"And I think he should see a doctor," continued Olga.

"No, I'll be fine," said Adam, "no worse than a rugby injury at school." He tried to smile at Anna as Olga walked behind him and gently pressed his shoulder. He winced and put his hand on hers. Anna looked at them bemused. "What about the police?"

"I'd rather not let anyone know," said Adam suddenly sounding serious. "I'm sure we can request other copies from the City Council and have the fax resent from our office in The Hague. Vera had a few copies of Alex's drawings." Adam also did not want to bring Olga into this. She had genuinely helped him. And there was the bonus that he now knew where she worked. She would not be able to disappear as easily again and he still had to find the final piece of the jigsaw from the night which still haunted him. He would ask Olga about 'Lena' as soon as he was alone with her.

Eighty

THE Kazan Cathedral is a huge memorial structure with wide pillars and marble facades beneath a mighty light green copper dome. Inside trophies of war hang side by side with religious icons. It has a number of side aisles adorned with elaborate decorations and centre pieces of simple paintings or statues. Each of these aisles holds an array of lighted candles. The services in the aisles proceed in tiny worlds of their own as tourists, locals and even vagrants go about their visits, worship and loitering in the cathedral or pass en masse down the wide centre aisle. The contrast with the intimate and magical feel of the Cathedral of Our Saviour-on-the-Spilt-Blood could not be greater.

As much as Anna had been disappointed by the cruel clash in timing of the auction with the service Sasha was to sing at, she had been delighted at the close proximity of the cathedral and the official building which housed the Property Fund where the second auction was going to take place just as the first auction had. The official building was next door and literally within spitting distance of the cathedral and the aisle dedicated to St Simeon. St Simeon is the celebrated holy ascetic and healer who was said to have been the religious inspiration of none other than Rasputin, or the 'mad monk' as his many enemies were want to call Rasputin, because of his dedication to St Simeon and his claims to have similar powers himself. For one moment she could see herself exiting the auction just in time to run into the cathedral and hear Sasha's first public singing but then the practical side of her brain kicked in – going by the manoeuvrings at the first auction there was no guarantee that this auction would finish even by the end of the day! If indeed there was going to be the same planned stalemate for each bid and the official day ended, then the auction would resume the next working day and again and again. It could give new meaning to a 'ground hog day'!

The unusual nature of the first auction had come to the attention of the St Petersburg Times. This had not come about in itself – the manipulation and minutiae of a privatisation process would be of little or no interest to the newspaper's readers – but because of the strange man who had uttered a curse and then seemingly disappeared into thin air. This is what had caught the attention of the paper's reporter, Mike Leigh. The fact also that the auction was part of the privatisation of the Peter the Great Shipyard, a company which had featured in an article in the newspaper recently, also gave Leigh every justification to attend and report on the auction.

The night before Valentina Alexandrovna had confirmed to Anna that Yelena Matrovna and hopefully herself would attend the service and Anna received a call from Valentina Alexandrovna at a quarter past ten to indeed confirm that they were both on the their way to the entrance to the Home with Sasha to await the car to come and take them to the Kazan Cathedral. Anna then joined Adam in Hampton's Volvo and they made the short journey to the official building. Anna had already spent a final two hours that morning checking all the legal papers and powers of attorney. Only she and Corley knew how much could be bid and she had briefed her male colleague on how she would signal the bids to him for him to make in the auction itself. Adam had arrived in the office with his arm in a sling but he had discarded it when they had left for the car. From his outward appearance no-one would be able to see that anything had happened to him. He had asked Anna to keep the matter confidential which Anna agreed to as long as Adam explained the attack to Hampton and let Hampton decide what actions should be taken.

For the second auction the officials were taking few chances. The chairs for the bidders were cordoned off with a guard sitting at both ends of the first row. Two guards were also positioned in front of the large windows and the wooden shutters had been pulled firmly shut. The officials were also much smarter dressed than the week before having gotten wind of the presence of the press. The hourglass to time the auction had been replaced with a much larger version but one which did not have any grains of sand inside. The four bidders had taken their places and their bidding paddles early. They were the same bidders as before with the exception of bidder 3. Gone was the small man with haunted eyes. In had come a much taller and younger man. He was dressed casually and had a black earpiece on his left ear. He had taken the step of conferring with the officials about the earpiece and had been given consent. As the audience started to file in the earpiece as well as the presence of the reporter and his photographer became the subjects of most of the comments. Victor Nikolayevich had arrived with Leonid Marlenovich. This time he wanted to watch the auction for himself rather than visit the Mayor and he had taken several large glasses of vodka en route 'for luck' he had said to Leonid Marlenovich as much as to calm his nerves. Otherwise the audience was largely as at the first auction.

As had happened in the first auction just as the officials were conferring and checking the time to start, a shutter flew open with a large bang. This time none of the officials or guards lost their composure. They conferred quietly and gave the impression that nothing untoward had happened. Two of the guards made a quick and perfunctory search of the room. Whispers of the room being haunted came from several individuals in the audience but these were met with polite rebuffs until a loud shriek of laughter rang through the room bouncing off the wooden panels on the walls. It was a mixture of deep guffaws with shrill screeches like glass shattering in a fireplace. This time the two guards in front of the windows jumped up and frantically threw open the wooden shutters as the laughter echoed around the room for a second time. The reporter and his photographer were first off their feet and they ran to the window followed by several others. As they leaned out of the window they looked down into the street below. It was a small side street and as they looked across they could see the imposing side of the Kazan Cathedral. "Look down there!" said the reporter, Leigh, to his photographer. They looked down and could see a tourist bus parked further back up the street and a group of elderly but large tourists standing close up to a street mime artist. As the mime artist completed his next routine, one of the men watching erupted in a deep belly laugh with high pitched wheezing. It was the same laughter. "Just a bunch of old tourists, Mike. Germans by the look and size of them," the photographer said turning to Leigh. Those at the window seemed to make a collective sigh and turned back into the room. The photographer could not resist his urge to take some photos and he trained his camera on the mime artist. As he zoomed in the white face painted artist turned his back and then in flash turned back round. This time the face was dark and bearded and the make-up had gone. The photographer did not flinch at the surprise and snapped away.

A few moments later the official banged his gravel on the table in front of him and called the proceedings to order. He began to explain the order of events as he had done previously. The clock above him was showing five to eleven and the auction would commence at eleven o'clock precisely. As the official continued Roman Felixovich was the last person to enter the room. He took a few steps into the room and spoke quietly into his hand which was concealing a small apparatus. Bidder 3 put his hand to his earpiece and made a small nod of his head. Roman Felixovich then left the room as quietly as he had entered. As he reached the door he turned round briefly and gave the smallest nod of his head that he could. Leonid Marlenovich who was sitting at the end of the second row returned the nod in similar fashion. Victor Nikolayevich and Corley who were sitting further along the row did not notice the exchange but Adam who was further along did. As Adam lifted his hand to get Corley's attention, Anna put her hand on Adam's hand and she motioned at him sternly to sit still. The official banged his gravel again and the large and empty hourglass was turned over. The bidding began.

In the aisle for the service to honour St Simeon a small congregation had gathered. Sasha was standing next to the priest who was dressed in a white cassock with a golden cross around his neck. Valentina Alexandrovna and Yelena Matrovna were standing with the rest of the congregation. Prayers were being said by individuals, several of whom closed their eyes and raised their hands in the air palms turned upwards. Yelena Matrovna did likewise but she also started to sing quietly. Valentina Alexandrovna had crossed herself several times but she kept her eyes locked onto Sasha who she could see had received instructions from the priest. A minute later the priest started a greeting and a prayer in a loud voice and silence descended on the small aisle for a moment. Yelena Matrovna's eyes flicked open as the sound of Sasha's voice started. He was starting with a low and quiet opening and Yelena Matrovna rocked gently on her heels. As Sasha's voice rose and filled the aisle Valentina Alexandrovna was shocked to see Yelena Matrovna turn and leave the aisle.

The auction was following the same pattern as the first auction only this time the audience was murmuring and occasionally laughing as bidder 3 religiously followed the Miller Lombard bidder. Bidders 1 and 4 dropped out at slightly higher values than the first time but clearly did not want to push their luck and each took a moment to milk the audience's applause as they dropped out. Both made straight for the photographer and reporter. The auctioneer now only under the time pressure of the day and of the 'empty' hourglass took his time at each fifty thousand dollar interval and even had brief exchanges with his colleagues. The officials did not seem to know whether to smile or frown as they like everyone else in the room had no idea where this constant stalemate was leading. At each bid Anna lent forward to signal approval to the Miller Lombard bidder whilst bidder number 3 would touch his earpiece before each replicating bid. As he did it this time the bidding had reached seven hundred and twenty-five thousand.

Yelena Matrovna had walked swiftly down the main aisle of the cathedral and turned left out of the main door and quickened her step. She was straining her ears and then she stopped and made a deep sigh. A bright smile lit up her face as she could once again hear Sasha's voice. He was building up into a crescendo and Yelena Matrovna's eyes lighted upon their target. Roman Felixovich was standing underneath the window of the building opposite the cathedral and the aisle where Sasha was. He had bent over and was frantically shaking a device in his hand. Sasha's voice was pouring out of the device which was amplifying the sound a hundred fold! Yelena Matrovna recognised the object as a new model of mobile phone and she guessed instantly that it which must be picking up the frequency of Sasha's voice. Roman Felixovich was visibly irate and had worked himself into a frenzy. He had taken out the phone's battery but Sasha's voice continued to sing out across the small street from the device. With all the physical force he could muster Roman Felixovich threw the phone onto the floor and watched as it shattered into pieces. The singing stopped for a split second then started up again. Roman Felixovich looked as though he was going to jump on the broken pits of the phone but he looked wildly at his watch and the time. He looked up to the sky and even though he must have seen Yelena Matrovna who was barley ten yards away as he was looking up, he did not recognise her. He looked down again at the bits of the phone. Sasha's voice was now fading. Roman Felixovich turned to the building behind him and began to run to its door. He shouted loudly. Yelena Matrovna did not hear the words clearly but it sounded to her that he had said that 'he must be destroyed for good this time.' Yelena Matrovna knew that despite all his growing powers this was the one thing that Roman Felixovich would always struggle to do.

Back in the auction room there was a stunned silence. Bidder 3 had not matched the Miller Lombard bid at seven hundred and seventy-five thousand. As the Miller Lombard bidder had raised his paddle, bidder 3 had grabbed at his earpiece and pulled it off. He was in some discomfort as if an electric current had shot through him from the earpiece. He had clasped his head in his hands and dropped his paddle. The official had raised his gravel and was staring at bidder 3 who then looked up at the official and shook his head clearly still in some pain. As the third bang of the gravel signalled the end of the auction and the winning Miller Lombard bid at seven hundred and seventy-five thousand dollars, Roman Felixovich pushed open the door to the auction room, took one look at his bidder who still had his head in his hands and then turned and left slamming the door violently behind him. The slamming door echoed down the corridor outside like a slow peel of laughter.

The audience in the auction room erupted. The officials clapped each other on the backs. One took out a handkerchief and wiped his brow. Victor Nikolayevich grabbed Anna in a bear hug as Corley, Leonid Marlenovich and Adam shook hands.

"My, my!" said Corley, "and we did not even reach our limit. Nowhere near,"

"Well, I am sure, Dominic, that your saving can be used as part of the additional investment you did agree to," replied Leonid Marlenovich as quick as a flash.

"I shall leave all the amounts and payments to Anna to sort out. She has all the powers and knows what I was prepared to do," said Corley with a smile on his face, "if that is ok with you, Adam?"

"Of course," replied Adam rubbing his shoulder which had started to ache, "and I'm sure Anna will check with our boss if she needs to."

"Excellent," said Corley as much to himself as to anyone else. "This is simply excellent."

Mike Leigh from the St Petersburg Times had confirmed the auction details with the officials and had photos taken of the empty hourglass and the official posing with his gravel. He had then moved Victor Nikolayevich and Leonid Marlenovich into a corner of the room. He began by observing that it looked as though the opposition bidder's use of modern technology had proven his undoing and that the old traditional form of bidding had won the day. Such a comment was right up Victor Nikolayevich's street who set off to wax lyrical about the traditional values of the company, the city and indeed of Russia itself. Thankfully for the reporter Leonid Marlenovich made highly abridged translations which the reported noted down sparingly.

Anna was anxious to leave to see if by any chance she might catch Sasha before he left the cathedral. During the auction she had thought for a moment that she had heard Sasha's voice in the distance but she had shaken her head and maintained her concentration on the bidding. She quickly agreed with one of the officials that she would come back after lunch to sign all the documentation and to instruct the payments to the Property Fund and to the company. She then turned to Adam who had been waiting to talk to her and she asked him to accompany her to the door.

"Well, what a great result," said Adam, "John will be delighted that we have pulled this off. It is a major success for us, too."

"It is," replied Anna, "I've agreed to finalise everything after lunch."

"Great," said Adam who paused for a moment but then continued. "Have you any idea who that person was who came in at the end and then slammed the door."

"I'm not sure," replied Anna with a quick smile, "but I have a suspicion that he might have a link to those property claims you were investigating."

"Really!" blurted out Adam who had hoped that the subject of the properties and all the related paperwork would be forgotten now that the auction had been won. A loud burst of laughter made both Anna and Adam stop and turn round. For once its source was clear for everyone to see. Victor Nikolayevich was rocking from side to side, his cheeks bright red and his chest heaving – he was laughing uncontrollably and in great delight at something. Anna caught Victor Nikolayevich's eye in between great guffaws of laughter and he winked at her. Adam, though, had stood still with his mouth half open – he had hoped that he had finally found his way out of the parallel universe which his flashback conjured up for him, but once again the mention of the properties and who might be involved sent him straight back in again.

Eighty One

ANNA had managed to catch Sasha and Valentina Alexandrovna on the steps of the cathedral. Sasha had seen Anna first and dashed over to her and threw his arms around her with such power that Anna was forced to pick him up and use Sasha's weight and flight to whirl him round twice. They almost fell over but with a couple of backward steps finally steadied themselves.

"How was it?" asked Anna. "I'm so sorry I missed it!"

"It was good," answered Sasha with a modest shrug of his shoulders.

"It was magnificent, Sasha," said Valentina Alexandrovna with a mixture of admiration and sternness in her voice as she gave Anna a quick hug. "His voice was perfect and could be heard throughout the whole cathedral. The Metropolitan himself said to me that it was the best performance he has ever heard."

"Wow!" said Anna.

"And what is more the Metropolitan is considering asking Sasha to sing at the concert to celebrate the launch of the Standart boat. He said he was going to propose this to the Mayor."

"Really!" said Anna. This would be a huge deal, she thought. "Do we have time for lunch?"

"I'm sorry, Anna, I have to go back to the Home and Yelena Matrovna is not here. I would love to leave Sasha with you but I think that until we have sorted out at the paperwork it is best for you not to be seen alone with Sasha in public. You know what people are like."

"I understand," replied Anna suddenly overcome by a wave of disappointment but one look at Sasha and she smiled brightly. "I'll come to the Home later this afternoon and maybe we can have a small celebration of our own and with some of the children."

"Wonderful," said Valentina Alexandrovna.

They chatted for a few more minutes and then walked over to the car waiting to take Sasha and Valentina Alexandrovna back to the Home.

The photographer from the St Petersburg Times had worked as fast as he could in the small improvised 'dark room' in the newspaper's cramped office. He had developed the roll of film with the photos of the auction and the mime artist as quickly as he could and had handed Mike Leigh an image which made them both look at each other with great excitement. Leigh had been running the 'Rasputin' story for several months now. It had even made CNN with the sudden surge of international interest in events in St Petersburg following the shooting of a foreign lawyer. This looked to be the strongest proof so far. Within minutes Leigh had penned his front page story and they added the photo. The rest of the week's edition was already in its final proofing stage so Leigh instructed one of their staff to take his new copy of the front page to the small print works on the outskirts of the city where the newspaper was printed and to wait for it to be added to the final proof of tomorrow's edition. He was to wait for the proof and bring it straight back that afternoon for final editorial approval. Leigh was sure this story would go global in no time and with his name all over it.

Anna arrived back at the Property Fund office at two o'clock. In their office Adam had relayed a conversation he had had with Corley at the end of the auction. Corley wanted Anna to call him as soon as the payments had been made as he would then contact the company himself. Adam suggested that Anna could call Adam himself if she wanted as Corley had invited him to the Old Custom's House for a celebratory lunch. Adam had looked somewhat embarrassed as he explained this to Anna. It was Anna after all who was doing all the important work. He did not try to defend his invitation by Corley and was relieved when Anna told him to enjoy his lunch without a hint of reproach or disapproval in her voice. He looked as though he needed a calming lunch. Anna herself was looking forward much more to another celebration later that afternoon.

The officials at the Property Fund fussed over Anna as she arrived with a heavy briefcase. She was offered tea and a large box of chocolates had been laid out in the office of the official who had run the auction. Anna listened patiently as the official read out the result of the auction which had been typed up. It was a formalistic announcement in keeping with the notices which had been put up to announce the terms of the privatisation. Anna nodded as he finished reading and then he and Anna both signed two copies of the notice which were then heavily stamped by one of his colleagues. Anna smiled at the stamping as she knew that the sole purpose of the official's whole working life was to stamp but then she stopped herself – so much of Soviet life had been formalistic and if you did not have the correct stamp a whole process could grind to a halt or even be stopped and potentially stopped for good. As much as such practices had become an anathema to the up and coming new generation of professionals she had to respect them and she would need a lot of approvals stamped, double-stamped and triple-stamped for her family to gain custody of Sasha. With a short and polite smile Anna then handed over the original copy of the power of attorney which gave her the authority to sign on behalf of the British Redevelopment Fund. The official then passed Anna a sheet of paper.

"This is a bank mandate," he explained, "for you to fill in. We will then fax a copy to your bank and take this to our bank. We trust that your bank will transfer the sum immediately."

"Yes," replied Anna, "the bank in London is on standby. As soon as they receive the fax they will transfer the funds."

"Excellent," replied the official, "and hopefully we all will not have to wait too long."

Anna did not reply but felt a sharp pinch of tension in the room. She understood that she would have to wait with them until the transfer went through. She after all was their guarantee. She felt a brief shiver down her spine and she crossed her legs. "I also want to instruct the bank to transfer the funds for investment to the company at the same time," she said.

"Really!" replied the official almost involuntarily. The five million dollars were due to be paid, but just like all the other officials in the room he had assumed that the winner in the auction would try all sorts of ruses to delay or frankly avoid making the investment.

"Very well," he said, "if you are sure?"

"I am," said Anna handing another bank mandate which she had already filled in. "I would like both mandates to be faxed at the same time."

The official looked at the second mandate and almost dropped it.

"This is the amount that company and the Fund have now agreed to," said Anna with a broad smile. "Is there a problem?"

The official simply shrugged his shoulders. This auction continued to surprise him – the uncharted territories of the new world of privatisation had now disappeared into the Bermuda Triangle and the Peter the Great Shipyard would soon be awash with cash!

"And while we wait for the confirmation that all the funds have been transferred, perhaps you can request that the company brings its Share Register here so that you can transfer the twenty-five per cent of the shares from your office to the Fund and I can take a notarised copy of the Register as proof that the Fund now owns the shares?" Anna's confidence and authority had surprised herself.

Perhaps it was the control she had over such vast sums of money which was intimidating the officials she was dealing with. It was affecting her to, she had to admit. Even after making these two payments she still had authority over a very large and unused amount. She stopped herself there.

Mike Leigh signalled to his photographer to join him in his office as he received a thick envelope from one of his staff. This would be the copy of tomorrow's St Petersburg Times for him to take to the newspaper's editor for approval for publication. He tore open the envelope and turned the copy over. The headline on the front page stood out in large black letters – 'Rasputin returns – exclusive picture captures the spirit of St Petersburg back in the city once again'. Leigh and the photographer then stared at the photo below. It showed a crowd of tourists looking at a spot. There was nothing in the spot. The image of the man in the beard, the image of Rasputin was gone!

"What the!" shouted Leigh, "where's the copy we sent?"

"It should be in the envelope," replied the photographer.

Leigh frantically emptied the rest of the envelope and the original type-set front page fell out. They stared at the photograph under the headline. The tourists were there but again there was no image of the man. "What is going on?" said Leigh his anger mounting.

"This is weird," said the photographer leaving Leigh's office. "I'll get the negative."

Ten minutes later both the photographer and Leigh were in the dark room. The negative was just as before. If anything the image of the man was more like Rasputin each time they looked at it. Every time they developed a photograph, though, the image did not appear. The photographer changed the chemicals but the image just would not appear on the paper.

"I hate to say it Mike," said the photographer, "but this just will not develop."

"This is just like being in some stupid film or fairy tale," said Leigh resigning himself to losing his world exclusive.

"There must be something in the atmosphere. Maybe we need a clean room or something."

"Let me put the negative in a cool box and have it sent to London for tests. They may be able to develop it there."

"Ok," replied Leigh, "and I'll work on a new front page story," he said screwing up the front page proof. He, for one, was now consigning the infamous Rasputin to the waste paper bin!

Whilst they waited for confirmation of the bank transfer to come through Anna remained in the official's office. A member of the Peter the Great Shipyard's legal team had arrived with the company's Share Register and sat quietly in a corner. The officials had stepped outside. Anna chatted with the middle-aged woman who had explained that her head of department was off sick, recovering from a fall. Anna stood up to stretch her legs and she wandered around the official's desk. She took a cursory glance at the pile of papers relating to the auction. Most were about the procedure for the auction and there was a list of registered bidders. She recognised the name of her law firm as bidder 2 and that it was bidding on behalf of the Fund. The other names were pretty innocuous and then a name jumped out at her and she remembered what she had said to Adam at the end of the auction. Bidder 3 was acting for a company with a nondescript company name but it had the name 'Yusupov' pencilled in by it. Two claims for the Old Foundry had been made in that name! As her mind started to work through the implications the officials came back in and Anna sat down. They were carrying bottles of Soviet champagne.

"The Mayor has instructed us to celebrate the success of our first privatisation," said the lead official loudly. Anna could detect that something stronger had already been drunk and she decided to insist on the share transfer to the Fund being registered and made legally valid before a bottle was opened. The officials started to demur but then did as instructed. Anna left with the notarised copy of the transfer and of the new entry in the company's Share Register showing the Fund as owning twenty-five per cent of the company's shares. It was now the company's largest individual shareholder.

Back in her office Anna immediately faxed copies of the extract from the Share Register and the bank transfers to Corley's office in London. She went to her desk and dialled Adam's mobile. It was now nearly five o'clock and she had fully expected Adam to be back in the office. Adam answered his phone and asked Anna to wait a moment. Anna could hear him excusing himself and the scraping of chairs.

"That's better," said Adam after a few more moments, "I can hear you now. How is everything?" Anna was struck by a touch of hesitancy in Adam's voice or was he slurring his speech.

"Are you still in the restaurant?" she asked quietly.

"I'm afraid so," replied Adam. "It has turned into quite a celebration."

Anna was becoming a touch annoyed. "Should you not have waited for confirmation that everything has gone through before celebrating? It only happened twenty minutes ago."

"We know," said Adam and Anna could visualise a boyish grin on Adam's inebriated face. "Leonid Marlenovich was with us and he got a call from the Mayor's office. The restaurant then sent a crate of champagne to our table."

Anna almost put the phone down.

"Wait, Anna! Wait!" shouted Adam. "They have saved a bottle for you and want Vera to come as well."

"I have another appointment," replied Anna deciding not to take it out any more on Adam. "I will try and come later and I will tell Vera."

"Great," replied Adam.

Anna was about to put the phone down but could not help asking one thing. "Adam, was Leonid Marlenovich invited to your lunch with Corley?"

"No, he came a bit later. Corley called him actually and Leonid Marlenovich came straight over."

"I see," said Anna sensing there must have been a reason.

"Leonid Marlenovich brought over the plans Corley wanted to see," continued Adam.

"For the new line?" asked Anna.

"No, they are still being drawn up. He gave Corley a copy of some old plans of the Old Foundry. It has been redeveloped several times and Corley wanted to see all the plans."

"I see," said Anna again, "enjoy the celebration," she said warmly. Adam clearly had had plenty to drink as he had not realised what he was saying. The Old Foundry was at the root of Adam's troubles and he was too far gone to recognise it – or maybe he wanted to forget all about it. The thought of the vast sums of Corley's money she had control over flashed through her mind but again she stopped it. She had her own celebration to enjoy and boy would she make it a good one for as many of the children as possible! For the same price as a crate of the best French champagne she would be able to buy a lot of party goodies and put them down as 'office expenses'!

Eighty Two

HAMPTON noticed straight away that the daily fax from Vera had more pages than normal which surprised him. He had not taken on any new work since the shooting and his assignments on the whole were being adequately taken care of by his staff. Vera had also improved her sorting and editing skills immensely in order to reduce the amount of information which was faxed each day. She now left a lot of material to be sent in the twice weekly internal mail between offices which was sent by secure courier. The message on the front of the fax though immediately grabbed his attention – it was a memo dictated by Adam on the successful second auction for the shares of the Peter the Great Shipyard. Hampton scanned the details on the page in a flash. He had had a very brief phone call from Adam as soon as the auction had finished so he knew the British Fund had won but he now slowly soaked up the details and smiled.

The successful privatisation of such a renowned Russian company was ground-breaking. This was a real first! A real legal 'coup'. This would make his and the firm's name in a market which, he was sure, was going to boom. His position would become stronger and stronger and the legal fees higher and higher – and that was just his day job, he laughed to himself. As he did he put his hand to his chest and then rubbed his shoulder. Barely a twinge. His consultant had said that his recovery had picked up significantly since he was back in the States and Hampton himself was confident that he would be fully on his feet in a matter of days. He had things to do and until his wife and son came back over he would have enough time to indulge in his first great passion without any questions. This would make one or two mega rich people very happy and several others very unhappy. In the process it would make Hampton and a couple of his contacts very wealthy in their own right.

But it was as soon as he had had this thought when Hampton's heart physically stopped. He had come to near the end of the fax and lifted up one of the last pages. His whole body froze. His arm and hand stopped in mid-air. He stared at the image. Then the blood started pumping again in his body. Pumping wildly as he looked at five pages and five drawings in a mad panic. They were near perfect images of the five originals paintings. Had someone photographed them? He had understood from what Vera had said the Head Curator had told her, that the only information anywhere on these five paintings was in the original 1902 catalogue of which there were rumoured only to be a possible half a dozen copies still in existence and two of those were in the Hermitage. And then it struck him and his pulse raced even faster. These were not photographs these were drawings. These were accurate but somewhat crude copies and they were in black and white – the colour versions might look even more different to the originals. He looked at the last page of the fax. There was a note from Vera in her elegant and elaborate handwriting. He felt a sharp pain in his chest. This could not be possible – his son's work was truly amazing, out of this world, but if anyone anywhere saw these drawings, then it would do immeasurably more damage to him than any bullet could do!

Eighty Three

THE Prince of Wales' itinerary in St Petersburg was finally made public. On the first day he was taking part in the retracing of the route of the Ice Road in the morning, holding a lunch on HMS Somerset and then officiating at the launch ceremony for the replica Standart boat replete with a twenty-gun salute. In the evening he would be guest of honour at a concert on Palace Square in front of the Hermitage. Day two was to consist of a service at St Isaac's Cathedral followed by an official ceremony in the City Hall. This was the first time in decades that the city was putting on such events. In the world of the new Russia and the jockeying of politicians for power and influence in the capital and in the regions the events were widely seen as a challenge to Moscow. The power struggle between Moscow and St Petersburg stretches back to the foundation of the city itself by Peter the Great. Russia's capital has been moved backwards and forwards between the two cities on several occasions.

For the average Russian on the streets of St Petersburg, however, the only interest in the events was the firework display after the concert and the extra availability of beer. Beer tents had been hastily erected in the centre of the city by Baltika, the city's main brewery. The British and Dutch navies had both sent sizeable warships to join their Russian counterparts in what was a tripartite Standart ceremony. Peter the Great had visited both Amsterdam and London on his Grand Mission to Europe three hundred years ago on the original Standart and both countries had been invited to send delegations to this historical remake of his famous vessel. The presence of several hundred foreign sailors carousing with their Russian counterparts was seen as an attempt to recreate a touch of the feel of the time of Peter the Great in the city and hence the large increase in the availability of beer. For the city the two days would be a new experience and another step on its progression back into the modern world after decades of highly organised and choreographed public events which always focussed on the virtues of Communism and were bereft of any celebrations or chances for people to party and let their hair down in public. Such behaviour was the preserve of the Tsarist times and something that the Soviet dictatorship had gone to great lengths to prevent.

The Ice Road convoy set off in the early hours of the morning and progressed by truck, boat and then by rail to complete the thirty mile route. Even though it was the opposite time of year from the when the road had actually been built and used, the cool clear water of the lake conjured up images of the frozen landscape which engulfed the lake in winter. The convoy was small and consisted of Russian military personnel and dignitaries from the city, Britain and The Netherlands and a small number of selected journalists. Russian historians and several survivors of the Siege provided commentaries. It was a low key event and the sheer challenge of the road impressed the British and Dutch dignitaries deeply. The press were passive in their approach and were saving their reporting more for the Standart ceremony. Little was discussed about the Second World War and its participants and not a single reference was made to Germany. The sheer courage and determination of the Russian people was the main focus of discussion. The assistance of British forces was noted but not emphasised. Those arriving back at HMS Somerset for lunch were simply in awe of such a feat of human bravery despite the horrific losses. Without the Ice Road the city's population would have been decimated to a point from which it may never have recovered. The heart of Russia would have stopped; its soul would have died. The Prince of Wales was rumoured to have said several prayers in private and to have listened to the Siege survivors with the same understanding and dignity as he had when he had met those who had survived the Nazi concentration camps.

Lunch was a private affair aboard HMS Somerset. The dignitaries and senior naval officers were served a range of fine wines and spirits but the crew as a whole was not allowed any alcohol. In exchange the crew were all given shore leave for the evening in order to meet with their Russian and Dutch counterparts and to sample the local beer, of which they were assured there would be plenty available. The crew was to be back on board by six am the following morning.

The disused shipyard which had been the base for the construction of the replica Standart had been transformed. Russian, British and Dutch flags were hanging everywhere. The yard had been tidied up and the workers' cabin converted into a small café. The boat itself, resplendent in its new and very shiny paint, had been moved to the edge of a newly built wooden slipway from which it would be launched into the River Neva. For the moment it was still on a large wooden stand with traditional wooden gangplanks on each side so that visitors could go on and off the boat and walk throughout the boat. A small high stand had been erected at the front of the boat with several microphones and speakers. The entrance to the shipyard was cordoned off and several other areas had been roped off. Three groups of officials stood near the entrance and they were greeting and vetting people as they entered. Those who made it in were given different coloured stickers. Several reporters and cameramen had taken up positions in front of the small stand. The Standart itself swayed slightly from side to side as people started to go on board. It was a very calm afternoon but the Standart's sails had not yet been unfurled. Several unkind words about the boat's seaworthiness could be heard above the squeaking of the boat's woodwork but these were light-hearted and probably the result of the very liquid lunch that a lot of the dignitaries had just enjoyed. By four o'clock the shipyard was full of some two hundred people most of whom who had been on board and inspected the boat. Except for a modern day diesel engine the rebuild had stuck religiously to the original plan which meant that its cabins were very small and most people struggled to navigate through the rooms and the boat's deck without bumping their heads or stubbing their toes. It was, however, decreed by most people as a bona fide replica of the original and a real success. Several people did comment though that the boat seemed to laugh as they were leaving it. This was put down to air circulating through the wooden beams and definitely not as the sound of the boat being haunted in any way!

A Vice-Admiral of the newly reformed Russian Navy introduced the day's two guest speakers as His Royal Highness the Prince of Wales and the Mayor of St Petersburg. The three men were on the small stand. Everyone else in the shipyard was standing quietly and politely as the speeches began. The contrast between the Prince of Wales and the Mayor of St Petersburg could not have been greater. The Prince read from a script which was then translated by an interpreter while the Mayor of St Petersburg spoke without notes in both Russian and English. The Prince's speech could not be faulted as it had been written in the very best Queen's English by the British Embassy but the way it was written with long over-elaborate phrases, contrived references and minimal punctuation meant that it did not translate easily into Russian for the majority of the audience. Having a surviving monarch from a major European dynasty on their own soil, the first for nearly over seventy years, though, was enough for most of the people there from St Petersburg. It was a mark, it was a sign of the changes that the Russian population were starting to believe in.

The Mayor, on the other hand, simply stole the show and mesmerised the audience. He took everyone back to the days of the original Standart and Peter's journey through Europe. He then fast-forwarded past the Revolution, the Siege and the fall of Communism to today. There could be no greater tribute, he proclaimed, to the founder of our magnificent city, than the rebuilding of his beloved vessel – the vessel that opened the city and the whole of Russia to the modern world and put us into Europe. What greater symbol could there be for the belief we are all showing in ourselves and in our city as we sail through the challenges buffeting us on all sides today? The Mayor spoke in both languages with such passion that many in the audience would rise up on the tiptoes, eyes would moisten and applause would break out spontaneously with every new sentence. The Mayor's oratory was so compelling that no-one took the news about the boat's condition as anything other than a minor timing setback. She needed a little more work before she could actually take to the water. A bottle of finest French champagne would still be smashed on her side by the Mayor and the Prince together but she would stay on land. The twenty-gun salute would be heard across the city today and its message of the relaunch of the whole city would resonate around the whole wide world in the days to come.

Eighty Four

THE Peter the Great Shipyard was closing early to allow all its staff and workers to join in the various celebrations in the city in honour of the relaunch of the Standart. Corley though arrived at the company just after four o'clock as most of the workers were leaving. As his taxi drove away a second car with two plainly dressed men stopped a short distance away and Corley signalled to the car just before walking into the entrance of the office building. Corley wanted to see the company's Share Register with his own eyes so that he could report back to London that everything had been formalised correctly. Inside the office building he was escorted straight through to the office of the legal department. He declined the offer of tea and at his request he was shown the Share Register immediately. He smiled brightly and told the staff who were there that he was pleased that everything was in such good order and that he did not want to delay anyone from joining the celebrations. The staff responded with smiles of their own and happily accompanied Corley back to the office entrance.

Outside the entrance Corley moved swiftly and walked past the showroom and turned down the side of the building. The two plain clothed men were standing at the door to the basement of the old building before the embankment. One of them was holding a holdall. Corley looked at the men who pushed the door open.

"The Old Foundry has been secured," said one of the men, "it was easy to break into."

"Very good," replied Corley as he followed them in. They went in and found themselves in a corridor with rooms off on both sides. Corley took out a piece of paper from his jacket and unfolded it. It was a plan of the building and he and the two men studied it. Corley pointed to one of the rooms on the plan and one of the men took out a small device out of the holdall. Several minutes late they broke their way into a room at the end of the corridor without much effort. Corley flashed a torch around the walls; they were red and blackened brick and as he looked closer he could see that they were original. The floor was covered in a layer of dust and obviously the room had not been used for some time; a few discarded crates indicated that storage was probably the room's function. Corley's breathing was getting deeper. He pressed another button on his torch and the intensity of the bream increased giving much more light. He placed it on the floor and spread out another large piece of paper.

Looking around at the walls and back at the paper he started to pace from one side of the room to the other. He repeated this several times. He then indicated a spot to one of the men who took out a spade and a crow bar from the holdall. The man firmly banged the spade onto the floor initially hitting concrete and then after adjusting his spot by a couple of feet he heard the dull thud of wood. He tore into the wood with the crowbar, splintering the wood and levering up the small planks. He worked quickly as the other man piled the small planks in a corner of the room. A large hole soon opened up in the floor and the gentle draft of cold air rose into the room. They had found the place. Corley shone the torch down and could see that there was a four foot drop down to another floor. The small device which one of the men was still holding started to bleep quickly. The man put it down and rolled down through the hole into the space beneath. He emerged a few seconds later with a bundle of what seemed to be old rags. It was an old and worn army overcoat.

The man unravelled the overcoat and presented Corley with a black metal box. Corley opened the box and took out a green folder. The words on the cover of the folder were in English and the faded sign on the cover was that of an Army regiment. There were several small objects in the metal box.

"Is everything in order, sir?" asked one of the men.

Corley was searching the box and an agitated look was spreading across his face. "Almost," he replied curtly as the agitation was replaced by a wave of pure panic. He tipped the metal box upside down but nothing else fell out. "Not all there," he whispered and as he did a loud bang rang out. All three men stopped still.

"Let's go," said Corley quickly.

"There's a dingy waiting for us here, sir. We will go down river in it to our boat," said one of the men who had scooped up the old army overcoat.

Corley did not reply as he followed the men out of the room and quickly out of the building and down to the embankment. He was trained to control his emotions in order to think rationally in the direst of situations but he had never known a feeling of frustration like the one building inside himself now. He jumped into the dingy and one of the men pulled on its starter motor as more loud bangs began to reverberate over the city. These were the large bangs of the twenty-gun salute. As much as they were meant to celebrate the relaunch of the Standart to the older inhabitants of the city they were more reminiscent of the haunting bangs of the darkest days of the Siege of their city fifty years ago.

The sounds also brought back to life an incident that had happened at the very beginning of the Siege – an event which could rewrite the history of how the Siege started and perhaps much of what followed - bursts of gunfire ricocheted off the walls as the boat beached outside the walls of the fortress. Dressed in camouflaged battlegear ten men jumped out of the boat and stormed along the fortress wall running straight for a boathouse. Six men also dressed in camouflaged gear were sitting inside the boathouse. At the sound of the fast running feet the men inside the boathouse anxiously grabbed for their weapons and as the intruders ran in with their machine guns blazing two of the men inside the boathouse were killed instantly. The six men had not expected an attack let alone such a brutal one. One of the men inside the boathouse did manage to climb behind an upturned boat to shield himself from the onslaught and he was able to return fire. There was a momentary stand-off as the intruders regrouped at the entrance to the boathouse. Seizing the moment one of the four men still alive inside made a sign for two of the others to follow him. Three of them then managed to make a dash out of a far window and started to run along the outside walls of the fortress. The intruders immediately split in two groups and one set off in pursuit of the fleeing men. A grenade was thrown into the boathouse followed by two men. The man remaining inside was standing behind the upturned boat but he quickly took a shot to the shoulder and dropped his gun. The intruders ran over and in one swift movement the lead man slit the injured man's throat from ear to ear without saying a word.

The small boy watched as three men who were being chased jumped onto a small boat and started to cross the river from the St Peter and St Paul Fortress to his shipyard. They disappeared out of view. He was used to the strangest sights as the city started to feel the dramatic effects of the German invasion. He spent his nights on the roof of the shipyard, his head buried under a sack waiting for the noise of the overhead planes to stop and give him the chance to search for unexploded bombs which he then tossed with all his tiny might into the depths of the river. He had been told that his parents had been able to get out before the Germans had cut off all the roads and railway lines to the city, but he knew that they must be dead. He was fortunate that the old women at the shipyard gave him bread and the occasional hug before he climbed up to the roof before nightfall.

He ducked just as the sound of gunfire reverberated across the water. Ducking instantaneously had become his sixth sense. Indeed at the sound of any bang he would hit the floor. As he gradually lifted his head and peered through his fingers clapped over his eyes he saw one man jump into the water from the boat and start to swim across. The remaining two appeared to put their arms in the air as a rope was thrown to the boat and the boat was pulled back to the quayside. The two men were then surrounded by a group of other men holding guns. They did not look like the local militia. From further along the quay he recognised several members of the city's makeshift militia now starting to run along and wave and shout at the men with the guns. The men with the guns ignored the shouting and calmly fired at the two men with their hands in the air at point blank range and then walked to the edge of the river. For a good ten seconds they emptied their guns into the water where the first man had started to swim. As the militia got within range of them the men turned smartly and were away.

The boy crawled to the edge of the river and watched the militia disappear past the side of the factory. He stared long and hard at the water with a strange wish that the man who had dived in had not been blown up by one of the unexploded bombs which he himself had thrown into the river! His wish came true as he saw the figure now two thirds the way across swimmingly slowly using just one arm. Without hesitating the boy dived into the water and swam to the man. The man turned on his back and the boy paddled his legs through the water like crazy to help the man to shore. The man was bleeding in three places and grabbed the boy's hand speaking quickly through gulps of air. The boy could not understand a word. The man seemed to realise this and lifting himself up he pointed repeatedly to the old building at the side of the shipyard which before the war had been used for storage and before that they said it had been the shipyard's oldest foundry. The boy nodded and the man smiled briefly and spoke five words into his ear time and time again. Words that the boy realised were not made from letters that he had started to learn at school. Their sounds were imprinted on his brain forever. The man again smiled briefly and the boy could see that life was draining from him. The man reached inside his jacket and pulled out a small package wrapped in an incredibly soft and fine cloth. He pressed it into the boy's hand and with a final smile full of a mixture of pain and of thanks he closed his eyes. As a couple of the militia approached the boy slipped the package into his pocket.

"Leonid Marlenovich, I now see what you mean by timing the departure 'correctly'," whispered Inspector Bushkin down his mobile phone. He was standing up in a police launch which had several small tarpaulins strapped to its side to cover its police markings. The launch was several hundred metres upstream of the Peter the Great shipyard's dock and slipway. "Everyone will have stopped to listen to the gun salute." The launch had a police driver and two officers sat in the back.

"Precisely," replied Leonid Marlenovich who was standing on the edge of the dock at the Peter the Great Shipyard and signalling to the captain of the yacht carrier for him to set the carrier off to sail down river. "The whole city has stopped. There should not be many boats on the river this evening. A perfect time to leave. Keep your distance from our boat."

"We will," replied Inspector Bushkin steadying himself as the police launch increased its speed. He was not a natural sailor and was not enjoying being on the launch even though the River Neva was flowing very quietly.

The sound of a motor starting up nearby made Leonid Marlenovich jump. The loud bangs of the gun salute had just finished and the sound of the motor was eerily loud in the deep silence which had engulfed the river after the loud bangs. He looked around frantically and could see a shadow at the very end of the slipway down river and he could hear a splashing sound. He waved at the captain of the yacht carrier who immediately put the carrier's engine into reverse and brought the carrier back to the dock. As he jumped onto the carrier Leonid Marlenovich dialled a number on his mobile. Inspector Bushkin's number was engaged. Leonid Marlenovich swore and went to the side of the carrier. He could see the disguised police launch now in the middle of the river and it was at least three hundred yards up stream behind them and keeping its distance as requested. He dialled the number again.

Corley and the men had sat down as their dingy took off from the furthest end of the slipway. Corley had thrown the old army overcoat into the river as soon as they had gone a few metres. He held the black metal box tightly. One of the men was steering the dingy out into the river as the other checked several weapons which were hidden under a black bag in the bottom of the small dingy. He handed Corley a handgun.

"How far is our boat?" Corley asked the man who was steering the dingy.

"Just over half a knot up stream on the other side of the river," came back the reply. "It looks just like a fishing boat."

Corley did not reply. He scanned both sides of the riverbank. There were one or two boats moored up and several others moving slowly in the distance. The dingy was speeding up and Corley had to grip the side of the dingy with one hand and use his other hand to shield his eyes from the water spraying up at them.

The driver of the police launch spotted the dingy moving very quickly straight across the river. It was ignoring the normal rights of way on the river. Instead of crossing the river in a wide circle it was cutting straight across. This was very unusual. He pointed the dingy out to Inspector Bushkin as he increased the launch's speed dramatically. Inspector Bushkin stopped his phone call and looked at the dingy. He took a pair of binoculars which the driver handed to him. There were three men on the boat and all dressed in dark clothing. He could see one of them talking and even at the distance he could tell that he was not Russian. He felt a wave of uneasiness and had to steady himself. From the way the man's lips moved and the complexion of his face his hunch was that they were English or similar. Their competition's timing was also looking correct! But why was the dingy not heading for the yacht carrier. Were there more boats about? His uneasiness was increasing. His mobile was ringing again but he ignored it. He shouted at the driver to head the dingy off before it reached the other riverbank and then turned to the two police officers at the back of the launch and began to give them instructions.

The police launch's rapid change of direction was seen straight away by the dingy and by Leonid Marlenovich on the yacht carrier. Leonid Marlenovich dialled Inspector Bushkin's number for the sixth time. It rang but was not answered. He swore again and then dialled another number. The yacht carrier was now moored up again and he was not going to take any chances. He would get their products offloaded as quickly as possible.

"That launch is coming straight for us and I don't think we will reach our boat before it gets to us," said the man driving the dingy to Corley.

"Can we outrun it anywhere?" asked Corley.

"Unlikely," replied the driver.

"Then turn back the way we came. We'll land and head for the car."

As the dingy started to turn round, the police launch followed and increased its speed even more. Within seconds the waves it was now creating in the river lifted the dingy up out of the water and also lashed against the yacht carrier. In time it was no more than one hundred and fifty yards from the dingy. Leonid Marlenovich called Inspector Bushkin once again as four workers carrying large sacks moved onto the yacht carrier each heading to a different one of the light crafts. They were in a great rush.

"Can we slow them down?" asked Corley. The man who was not driving nodded back with a determined look in his face. He picked up a rifle from the bottom of the dingy.

"At last!" screamed Leonid Marlenovich as Inspector Bushkin answered his phone. "What in God's name are you doing?"

Before he could answer Inspector Bushkin , jumped sideways as he felt a sharp pain on his cheek followed by a small bang at the side of him as glass shattered in one of the side windows of the launch and his shoulder hurt painfully. He swore violently. A burst of fire then raked across the main windscreen of the launch. The police driver ducked for cover and cut the launch's power. A second later one of the other policeman stood up and with a large and heavy gun fired a volley of bullets at the dingy. If the flying bullets were not deadly, Leonid Marlenovich would have watched the scene in a fit of laughter. The tit for tat fire was right out of a gangster film. "Bushkin!" he screamed down his phone. "Stop!"

The policeman's fire had ripped holes in one side of the dingy. The driver kept the engine on full throttle. The dingy started to lose ballast from one side and the driver could not steer it. It was heading straight for the yacht carrier.

"Bushkin!" shouted Leonid Marlenovich again.

"Yes?" came back the reply on a crackling line.

"Get your boat away from here now! You'll have the whole world here in a minute! The last thing we need is attention!"

The phone went dead and Leonid Marlenovich stared at the sight in front of him. The dingy was now some thirty meters away but it had slowed down. It was sinking. The police launch was turning round slowly as the police driver smashed out the glass in its shattered windscreen. Inspector Bushkin sat slumped down in the back of the launch. He had taken the large gun off the policeman who had fired it. Leonid Marlenovich shouted quickly at the workers who jumped off the boat their sacks full. He bent down and then kicked out of sight several white bundles which had been dropped in the race to get them out and off the boats. He then watched as two of the men on the dingy dropped into the water and swam away. The third man was using a rifle to guide the dingy which was now virtually submerged to the end of the yard's slipway. Despite the man's efforts it was drifting to the bow of the yacht carrier. He looked around. The river and its banks had returned to silence. The sound of the bursts of gunfire he could only hope would have been assumed to have been part of the celebrations. The one thing he was sure of, though, was that the man who was now climbing up a ladder on the side of the yacht carrier was definitely not a threat to their operation. The man was struggling to keep hold of the rifle and of an old black metal box. Leonid Marlenovich moved over to him and took both things from him.

"Donald," said Leonid Marlenovich in a voice that could not disguise his amusement, "rather a strange time to take a trip on the river."

Corley was now on the yacht carrier and he took a quick look around himself as he adjusted his jacket and straightened the crease in his trousers. His trousers were wet up to his knees and his shoes were soaked.

"Leonid Marlenovich, good evening," he replied, "it seems we had to turn back." He bent down and picked up a white packet which he had spied under one of the boats.

Leonid Marlenovich had put down the rifle and had opened the black metal box. Both men stopped and looked intently at each. Curiosity was swarming through both their minds and as Leonid Marlenovich looked down at the file and the small objects in the metal box Corley opened the corner of the white bundle. As Leonid Marlenovich put his hand into the box, Corley dropped the white bundle and took the handgun out of his jacket pocket. Leonid Marlenovich smiled broadly and took his hand out of the box.

"Well, well," said Leonid Marlenovich slowly, "and why would there be old British military information here in St Petersburg?"

"Better not to ask," replied Corley lifting up the handgun, "and," he continued pointing at the white package on the floor, "better for me not to ask about that."

"Donald," replied Leonid Marlenovich smiling again, "our deal doing seems to be as strong as it always was. Need we say more?"

"I might just have a loose end to take care of," replied Corley with a mixture of annoyance and determination.

"You don't say," said Leonid Marlenovich. "I have one of my own also!"

Eighty Five

HAMPTON timed his call to catch Vera before she left the office. It was her turn to close the office this Friday evening. Vera picked up the phone as soon as it had rung. Hampton spoke calmly and asked how she was doing and whether there were any matters which she needed to talk to him about. There had been a call from the police but as she had been instructed this had been passed on to the Moscow office. Hampton knew of this and that the authorities did want to talk to him about the shooting but were happy to wait till he returned to St Petersburg. They had nothing they could report from their investigation. Hampton then mentioned the faxed drawings from Alex.

"Alex was so excited about his drawings and wanted me to fax them to you," said Vera brightly.

"That was very helpful. Did Ellen ask you?" asked Hampton.

"No, it was Alex himself when your wife came to pick up your personal post. I will send the originals in the office courier," she said brightly again and then paused. She would soon wish with all her might that she never continued on the subject but after a moment she continued, "as soon as they are back from the printers." The copies were already back and she had given some to Adam but she had forgotten to put then in the office courier. A small white lie about the timing of the copying would cover her mistake and would not do anyone any harm. Her white lie, though, was about to backfire spectacularly and it felt at once to her as if the telephone line had been cut off. The tension down the line was electric and it sounded as if someone was shouting crazily but very faintly in the background, someone thousands of miles away. Then Hampton's voice came down the line as clear as normal.

"Why are the originals at the printers?"

"They are being photocopied in colour," replied Vera who now had the distinct impression that something was not right and that her white lie was definitely unravelling out of control.

"Who for?" asked Hampton his voice became quiet and low.

"For Alex and Ellen," replied Vera conscious now that her own voice was beginning to break up.

"And for anyone else?" This time Hampton's voice was hoarser and with the slightest of menacing edges to it. "You know what these drawings are a copy of, don't you Vera?"

"Not for anyone else," was all Vera could answer before coughing and reaching for her handkerchief. White lie number two.

As she buried her face in her handkerchief images swam in front of her eyes: the cash, the list, the canvas, the crates and now the drawings – could this be the removal of, no the theft of..? As if by instinct she had decided to lie and lie again; how could she get back the colour copies which had already been given to Adam? When she had given them to him, Adam had put them straight into his briefcase. He had listened to what she had said about Alex and said that it probably would not do any harm to give a copy to the guide in the Hermitage. Adam had also met the guide with Alex when they saw the window from the Saint Sophia Cathedral in Kiev. It though would probably not be right to give them to the Committee because that could be potentially really embarrassing to Alex's father! The guide seemed to like Alex a lot and would probably appreciate his efforts and she might even recognise what Alex had drawn. And then, of course, Adam's briefcase had been stolen just like

Hampton's! What on earth could she do? Who on earth could she turn to? Never in her wildest nightmares could she have conceived of the damage a simple photocopy might do to so many people. The scandal could be monumental and it would rock art-loving Russians to the core – and to think she had been so unwittingly instrumental in it all! She could think of no option other than going to the Committee – in Soviet days informing was regarded by the vast majority of people as the worst form of human behaviour possible; now she had nowhere else to go, she would have to take her chances.

Eighty Six

THE start of the evening concert in Palace Square was delayed. Instead of starting at six it did not start until almost seven. The celebrations at the Standart shipyard had taken on a life of their own in the buzz that had followed the Mayor's speech and fuelled by the sudden appearance of crates of vodka in old-fashioned bottles. It was assumed that the city's vodka plant had produced the old-fashioned bottles and a vintage vodka as a surprise for the event but since no-one from the plant had been invited this could not be confirmed. Those who drank the vodka were unanimous in their praise for the subtleness and earthiness of its taste. As they drank their way through the bottles several even began to imagine that the vodka was from the time of Peter the Great himself! The Mayor appeared on the stage in front of the Hermitage set up for the concert just before seven. It was a warm and pleasant evening and the soft summer sunlight shimmied off the Hermitage's frontage.

The Mayor apologised for the delay and once again used his oratorical prowess to win the audience and the assembled performers back on side. The backdrop of the Hermitage with the shimmering rays of sunlight gently bouncing off its green and white façade, the historical setting and the musicians and dancers from the Kirov ballet and other troupes were all going to make this evening something unbelievably special. Something the city had not seen in the best part of a century. He, for one, was holding his head high. The city, Peter's city, was back. The audience clapped madly and shouted their approval as the orchestra struck up and the sounds of the instruments rich with emotion became louder and louder and the concert was underway.

The Miller Lombard office had secured some of the best seats for the concert and the staff and their families had made various pre- and post-concert arrangements to meet for food and drink. Adam had announced that the firm's credit card would be behind the bar in the Senate Bar for an hour before the concert. He had also left a message for Olga saying that he would be in the Senate Bar again after the concert which was expected to finish around nine. Sadly Olga had not proved as cooperative as Adam had hoped. He had not been able to get her on her own after his attack and when he had managed to catch her on the phone in the showroom and he had asked her how her friend 'Lena' was, the reply that came back had floored him. 'Which Lena? I have lots of friends called Lena.' Adam had not probed any further. He felt a clear message to him in her voice not to delve any further. It sounded protective. Maybe she did have lots of friends with the same name. Maybe she had one less now! His visions and flashbacks had faded but were being replaced by an increasing feeling of unease at the back of his mind, perhaps even a touch of paranoia. He decided to wait, to wait until he would see Olga again face to face. He hoped that he might learn something this evening but was prepared to be disappointed.

Anna had not taken up her seat with her colleagues. She had an even better vantage point. She was with the performers at the side of the stage. She was with Sasha. The concert had begun with scenes from the Nutcracker and Giselle ballets and then Rimsky-Korsakov's Flight of the Bumblebee had completed the first part of the concert. Sasha was to perform in the second part which had been described as 'traditional folk dancing and singing'. The third and final part was to be more contemporary music with rumours of disco music to finish. Such bizarre mixes of the classical and modern styles were a new feature of Russian entertainment as artists and audiences sort to break free from the cultural straightjackets of the Soviet era and unpaid musicians resorted to moonlighting in all manner of venues. A top classical violinist could earn a month's wages in one night's performing at a new trendy restaurant as long as he did not mind performing in between a contortionist and a striptease act!

The second part of the concert began with a number of traditional Russian folk dances. The performers seemed to be from several different troops as they went on and off the stage from different places. The music was provided by the orchestra from the Kirov ballet and the final dance in this section was given a warm applause. It was now Sasha's turn. He was directed to the centre of the stage as the orchestra packed up their instruments and quietly moved off to one side. They were replaced by a small group with drums and guitar like instruments. As a spotlight was shone on Sasha and the audience fell silent a huge bang on a drum startled everyone as hands were placed on hearts and nervous laughter drifted across the square. The bang was followed by two more and then silence, a deep silence. Sasha then started. His voice was low and the song delicate with a gently growing chant but his voice swept across the square and resonated off the ground and bounced back from the façade of the Hermitage. Some people quietly started to hum the tune and as Sasha increased his pace one or two other chants rang out. And then another bang, a tremendous bang which echoed off the Hermitage like a bomb going off. The other drums and guitars joined in and the volume of music became deafening but through it all the clear and powerful sound of Sasha's voice ruled. After several more minutes Sasha stopped and the drumming increased to a mind-boggling crescendo. As the drumming reached its climax a violin rang out from the side of the stage and one of the violinists from the Kirov ballet was on his feet and striding across the stage. He was met in the middle by a dancer all in black who it seemed had jumped from out of the audience. The dancer had long black hair and a thick beard. The dancing in the next five minutes, it was later claimed, was not humanly possible such was the speed and the height of the jumps. The dancer finished by whirling around so fast that his whole body was a blur and he disappeared from the stage in a flash and was gone. Once more rumours of the miraculous return of the city's demonic spirit were writ large across Palace Square.

The second interval came as a relief to the audience. Pulses could slow down and heartbeats return to normal. Anna hugged Sasha for as long as she could before handing him over to Valentina Alexandrovna. Sasha was visibly very tired after his evening performance. Anna also hugged Valentina Alexandrovna who whispered to her that she was pressing on with the paperwork now with all the speed that she could muster and that she might have soon good news very, very soon. She did not want to say anything further except that the Mayor himself had been amazed by Sasha and had asked her how best she thought he could be rewarded for such a magnificent performance!

Anna thanked her and said that she would come to the Home to hear more as soon as she was free. She left the performers' area and made her way to the seats that the firm had reserved. She so wanted to tell everyone about Sasha but had to bide her time and to bite her lip. She was so close and the thought of how she could help the Home was constantly in her mind. The powers of attorney were still in her briefcase. She had not even thought of returning them.

The third part of the concert could not compete with the first two parts. Several rock bands did their best and a rising pop star received a warm reception but it would have taken a world famous act to match the skill of the Kirov or the power of the dancing. The firework display from the roof of the Hermitage rounded off the concert, though, in great style. The fireworks only lasted for five minutes but they made a fitting end to what had been a famous evening and the audience dispersed with cheers ringing out across the square and smiles lighting up many faces. The sunlight now had a milky moonlight feel to it and a gentle breeze made people shiver occasionally. Being outdoors so late though was such a contrast to the bleakness of winter which would soon enough descend on the city and keep people indoors in the evenings for months on end.

Anna was talking to Vera about the different arrangements for meeting in bars later than evening when she caught sight of a figure moving towards her. It was Leonid Marlenovich. She excused herself from Vera and walked towards him. He was frowning.

"Good evening, Anna," he said brusquely.

"Good evening, Leonid Marlenovich," she replied. "Did you enjoy the concert? Was Victor Nikolayevich with the Mayor?"

"He was," answered Leonid Marlenovich, "but we may have a problem."

"Really?" said Anna surprised. She could tell Leonid Marlenovich was not his normal confident self.

"Did you arrange for Corley to visit the legal department this afternoon?" he asked sternly.

The look of surprise on Anna's face answered his question. "I did not," she replied, "but I will check with Adam in case he did. I am meeting him soon. How was the visit?"

Leonid Marlenovich paused for a moment. He had thought that Anna was unlikely to be involved unless Corley had asked her to arrange a meeting. But how involved was Adam with Corley? Was the young Englishman also becoming another loose end? "The visit was very short," he replied, "but I should be informed of any visits and meetings beforehand, Anna, you should know that."

"Of course, Leonid Marlenovich, I'll make sure that you are," replied Anna making a mental note to check with Adam as soon as possible.

"Very good," said Leonid Marlenovich.

There had been a noticeable empty seat near the Mayor during the concert. Roman Felixovich's assistant had telephoned the Mayor's office to apologise in advance and to explain that his boss was suffering from a severe migraine and was really disappointed to miss the opportunity to introduce himself properly to the Mayor. The invitation had been in recognition of a significant donation Roman

Felixovich had made to the new Art Committee at the Hermitage to expunge the marine paint fiasco. Made very reluctantly. This had cost Roman Felixovich hard cash. His failure to win the privatisation auction was not the reason for his absence – he genuinely had a problem. There was a faint buzzing sound in his left ear which would not go away. If Roman Felixovich kept his head still for more than a couple of seconds the buzz would start and if he concentrated on the buzz he could hear the voice again. The voice of the dammed child! The song that had infected his mobile phone and had not stopped! He could not have sat through one song, let alone a concert.

He had also made a number of decisions immediately after the auction disaster. Firstly, he would now dedicate all his time and resources to arrange his future success in the privatisations which mattered – the oil companies – he would 'work' even the Mayor himself if he had to. He would amass his own fortune, come what may. He would also take over the Peter the Great Shipyard fully as soon as the next opportunity arose – that had become a matter of pride. Secondly, he would stop payments to Yelena Matrovna and make her life a misery one way of another. He would enjoy the process. And finally, he would solve the damned boy problem himself. He closed his private office early and let his drivers have the evening off. The drivers left the office like a shot, lest Roman Felixovich changed his mind – such largesse from their boss was unheard of. Roman Felixovich took the keys to one of the black Mercedes and put on a baseball hat pulling the cap down over his left ear. Even though the buzz was constant and inside his ear, the act of doing something about it made him feel better. He walked to the Mercedes parked at the back of the Oil & Gas Institute and opened the car boot. He took out a large bag which he put on the passenger seat – as he did so a roll of tape fell out onto the floor of the seat. He swore as he picked it up and put it back on the seat. He was swearing a lot.

The drive to Children Home No. 8. was short and quick as the roads were quiet due to the celebrations. He parked up on the road at the side of the building. He had the keys to the basement where he stored lots of his trading goods and he was going to enter the Home that way. He had time and he would wait. He opened the driver's door and got out of the car. He then opened a door at the back where he normally sat and got in. The side windows and rear windscreen of the car all had blacked out glass. He sat down and checked that he could still see the pavement at the entrance to the Home.

After almost an hour his patience was rewarded. A battered old car pulled up outside the entrance to the Home and a couple of minutes later a woman and a boy got out. A taxi fare had obviously finally been agreed and the woman waved at the driver as the car set off. The boy looked tired as he walked to the entrance but then a sound of singing filled Roman Felixovich's Mercedes. The car's radio was off but the singing got louder. Roman Felixovich wound down a side window slightly and then the sound started to trail off. The boy had gone into the building and the sound stopped abruptly as the door to the Home was shut. Roman Felixovich's shook his head vigorously. And then again. He took off his baseball hat and rubbed his left ear. He shook his head again. The buzzing had gone! It had stopped! It had felt as though it had been sucked through the entrance door and into the Home with the singing. Roman Felixovich was overjoyed. He held his head still for five, six, seven seconds. Nothing. It had really stopped. He banged his car seat with his fist. It had stopped at last. The thought of changing his plan, however, flew out of his brain as soon as it had entered. He sat back to wait.

Sasha got into his bed without changing his clothes and without making a sound. He was very tired. As he lay on his side he felt a lump in his stomache. He adjusted himself and gently pulled his treasured icon from his pocket and held it in both hands. It felt warm. When he was going to be out for the evening he did not dare leave it in the room even in his secret hiding place. He was sure that the other boys would have taken his absence as an invitation to search his bed and all around it. He had deliberately left some chocolate Anna had given him for the other boys to find in the hope that it would curtail their searching. He rubbed the top of the icon gently with his finger. It had a small cross on the top. It was wooden but the end was pointed and very sharp. He knew that if he pressed a finger on the top then it would easily bleed. He pulled the icon to his chest and closed his eyes. Sasha's sleep was disturbed. The exhaustion from his performance at the concert meant that he fell into a deep sleep with his body motionless but his brain racing. He was in a dark place. He tried to open his mouth but he could not. He had to sleep. He had to wait.

The sailors from the Russian, Dutch and British navies were having a ball of an evening. The drinking and the loud singing could be heard in the beer tents and in the streets along the embankments. Very few of the sailors managed to stay in the bars and clubs for very long as burly local bouncers would politely eject them one by one. Only the occasional sailor who had fallen into an inebriated sleep inside was left alone. They would be thrown out when the bars closed and the sailors would then be carried back to their ships before their shore leave finished at six am. The atmosphere was tremendously friendly as sailor after sailor succumbed to the strong beer. Not a punch was thrown.

Adam had been the Miller Lombard 'host' at the concert. Several clients and potential clients had joined him and most of the office staff had turned out. It was judged a great success and Adam quickly managed to say his goodbyes and invite everyone to join him at the Senate Bar. Most politely declined preferring to enjoy a stroll through the streets and canals to soak up the atmosphere. Adam made his way briskly to the bar. Olga was sitting on a stool at the bar. There were two empty shot glasses in front of her and the stool next to her looked as though it had had someone sitting on it. Adam hesitated before going over. He rubbed his shoulder which had just started to ache. As a young woman came out of the toilets and joined Olga at the bar his heart was in his mouth. She had blonde hair styled to frame her face and flow down onto her shoulders. She was sitting there chatting with Olga! He had been so stupid! Why had he worried himself so much for weeks over this girl? She must be a sound sleeper. He had had little experience of sleeping with someone else in the same room since boarding school. Why had he not at least checked? He had panicked. He had been badly hung-over or worse. Of course, he had panicked like mad and that was what had caused him to be haunted by the flashbacks for so long. He felt the blood racing through his veins. His shoulder felt a warm stiffness. He had his mind back. He could restart his life. He walked over to the bar. The two girls turned towards him. He looked straight at Lena and with the most confidence he had shown for years lent over and kissed her on both cheeks.

"Lena! How nice to see you again," he said grinning as he turned and kissed Olga on the cheeks as well.

A few minutes later Anna entered the bar. The bar was quite lively now. A couple of British sailors were slumped over a table near the bar but everyone ignored them. She looked around and quickly located Adam at the bar. She took a step back. Adam was in full flow and laughing and joking like she had never seen him before. He was normally tense and unsure of himself which Anna had put down to his lack of experience with girls. She for one had readily accepted the office gossip about 'boys from British public schools'. Maybe she had gotten it wrong.

"Adam, can I have a quick word?" asked Anna smiling briefly at the two young women. She recognised Olga.

Adam looked at Anna with a brief look of surprise. She had ignored the girls which he thought a little rude but he was in his best mood for a long time. "Of course, Anna," he said and he turned away from Olga and Lena. Anna stood by the bar stool at the other side of Adam.

"I've just seen Leonid Marlenovich," said Anna quietly, "he was a little annoyed."

Adam raised his eyebrow. Adam had enjoyed the celebratory lunch with Leonid Marlenovich and Corley and thought that Leonid Marlenovich was extremely happy with everything.

"Did you set up a meeting at the company for Mr Corley and not tell anyone?" asked Anna who was becoming irritated by the look on Adam's face.

Adam furrowed his brow. "No, I didn't," he replied. "And I would not go near the place myself any time soon!" he joked rubbing his shoulder, "so why would I arrange for Dominic to go there!" His joke fell flat.

Anna looked at him sternly.

"To be honest, Anna, now that the auction is over I'm hoping not to be involved much with the company in the future," said Adam finishing his drink. Anna was about to speak but Olga tapped Adam on the shoulder and he turned round.

"Anna Petrovna," said Olga leaning across Adam, "Adam does not know this yet but he is more closely involved in the Peter the Great Shipyard than you or he could ever imagine!" Olga had spoken the words with some emotion.

Anna looked nonplussed. She knew that Olga had helped Adam but she had thought that that had just been a coincidence. Adam had done research on the company's properties but why would he be more involved in the company? She herself had far greater knowledge of the company.

"Lena," said Olga before anyone else could speak, "can explain her relationship to Victor Nikolayevich." Anna's mouth dropped open. She sat down. "Go on," she said.

"He is...family," said Lena in a soft voice and lowering her head.

"Your uncle or your father?" Asked Anna who seemed to have understood something. Uncles and fathers were a subject close to her heart!

"My father," answered Lena lifting her eyes and looking at Anna.

Adam downed another drink. "Well, what on earth next?" he said shaking his head. He had worried for months that something untoward had happened to her and now she had turned out to be their client's daughter! What kind of parallel universe had he been in! "I am getting another drink." He stood up and moved passed one of the sailors who was slumped on the nearby table. "Want another one, mate?" he said jolting the sailor's arm. "Why not!" Adam answered for him. Another joke which fell flat.

"Wait, Adam," said Anna who had composed herself, "we have to think straight. Your father, Lena, he is an amazing man," Anna's tone was now gentle. This was something which she could never have anticipated. Multiple implications were running through her mind. "Does everyone in the company know this?"

"Some. Leonid Marlenovich and my mother, naturally."

"Who is?"

"Larissa Arkadovna," replied Lena with a brief smile.

Anna nodded. "So that is why you are involved in all of this?"

"Sort of," said Lena with a bigger smile, "I always seem to be helping to keep my father out of trouble. Trouble which most of the time is caused for him by Leonid Marlenovich."

"What kind of trouble?" Anna felt the hairs on the back of her neck tingle.

"All kinds of strange business," said Lena wistfully.

"I see." Anna took a breath.

Lena looked at her and her opinion of Anna was rapidly growing. She had heard a lot about Anna from her father who was constantly singing her praises. "Listen, there is something I need to tell somebody especially if anything should happen to Victor Nikolayevich."

"But he is not in any danger," said Anna before checking herself – there seemed to be a lot which had begun to unravel and she had not yet had time to think through the possibilities. Maybe it was more than just the foreigners around her who were at risk.

"I am not so sure," continued Lena. "Nobody knows what is going to happen. This privatisation is making a lot of people very angry and upsetting a lot of plans."

"Tell me about it," said Adam, rubbing his shoulder.

"What is it, Lena, about your father?" asked Anna.

Lena thought for a moment and then took out a packet from her pocket. It was a small bundle of cloth. She unwrapped the outer layer and inside was a beautiful crimson silk handkerchief.

"This is lovely," said Anna feeling the softness of the silk.

"My father gave these to me three days ago. He had spoken about them for many years and he had them locked in the cupboard in his office. He wants me to put them somewhere really safe." She unfolded the silk handkerchief to show that it contained an old looking necklace, six small balls and a scrap of paper.

"Where did these come from?" said Anna picking up one of the small balls and holding it to the light.

"They are pearls."

"They look very old."

"Over a hundred years, Victor Nikolayevich says. He used to have a full necklace but was forced to sell them pearl by pearl on the black market during the hard years. I saw the full necklace was I was very, very small. It was beautiful."

"Where did it come from?" asked Anna.

"Victor Nikolayevich wants it to remain a secret but I do know that he found it in the Old Foundry building during the Siege. The building was slightly damaged and he found it in some rubble."

Adam had taken the old looking necklace, examined it carefully and frowned. "Is this some form of sick war trophy?" he said slowly with an edge of genuine revulsion rising in his voice.

"I do not know what kind of necklace it is," said Lena visibly upset by Adam's tone.

Anna frowned at him.

"I will show you," he said as he stood up, went over to the nearby table and lifted the drunken sailor's head up.

"Adam, what on earth are you doing?" asked Anna.

"Up you get, mate," said Adam as he held the sailor by the throat and plunged his hand down his neck. He tugged and pulled out a small chain. The sailor flopped back down holding his neck. Adam tossed the chain and the old looking necklace at Anna.

"Identification tags of the British armed forces," he said barley concealing his disgust.

"Wait, wait," said Lena, "there must be some mistake. These were given to my father by a man he saved and the man who gave him a message."

"I don't care," Adam said making a lunge to get them back but Anna stood up and stopped him.

"Let's listen to her, Adam," she said firmly.

Adam sat down.

"I don't know if my father told you the story," continued Lena.

"He has told us lots in recent days," said Anna calmly.

"Going senile some people think," said Adam who himself now seemed visibly upset.

"Adam, please just listen," said Anna.

"During the early part of the Siege my father tried to save a man from drowning in the River Neva," began Lena.

"Yes, he told us that men had fired a lot of bullets at him when he had jumped into the other side of the river. He said that he then dived in to help him to the riverbank."

"Well the man gave him this package and kept repeating words in a foreign language which my father could not understand," said Lena.

"Obviously some German who had killed some British soldier to judge by the tag," said Adam.

"Well that's what could explain it, but.."

"But what?" said Adam. He was genuinely shocked to think that Victor Nikolayevich could have been harbouring such a sick war memento for all these years. "Our firm will resign from advising your father and the Peter the Great Shipyard with immediate effect," he announced standing up.

"Adam," said Anna, "this has nothing to do with being lawyers, this is much more important! Please let's listen!"

Adam thought for a moment and then sighed and nodded.

"But," Lena was repeating, "my father wrote down the sounds that the man had been repeating and the words are not German." She handed the scrap of paper to Anna. It had yellowed and Anna opened it tentatively. She looked at the words.

"Adam you had better help me work this out." She placed the scrap of paper on the bar and they all peered over it.

"'Hot Germans'. The first two words look like. 'HM blue train'. Train? Why would he mention train?"

"The blowing up of the train stations were what effectively sealed the city off for the Siege. It was the speed of this which was such a disaster for us."

"I remember our dinner with Corley," Adam said. "He explained it all in great detail to us. But why would the Germans be 'hot' and why would a train be 'blue'?"

"The man was dying, Adam," said Lena, "these were his last words and my father says he said them to him ten times. What do they sound like to you?"

Adam closed his eyes and repeated the works to himself in his mind several times over. "Hold on a minute," he said quickly, "blue is not the colour it means blew as in blew up and HM," he looked at the sailor's hat with a look of horror spreading across his face, "HM is. I don't believe this. HM means Her Majesty as in Her Majesty's Armed Forces. The British Army!!"

"And," said Anna excitedly, "it is not 'Hot' Germans - it is Not Germans, Lena. Your father has meant 'Not' but has used the Russian letter for N which in Russian looks like a H in English."

"What?" said Lena, "you are saying that the dying soldier said Not Germans Her Majesty, that is the British Army, blew up the trains. But why? You British were on our side against the Germans. Why would you do that?"

"We only joined your side when Hitler invaded you," said Adam sitting back as the implications started to sink in.

Anna's mind was racing. "Lena, you must put the pearls and the silk scarf somewhere safe. I will take these," she said tucking the old tag and the small piece of paper into her bag, "but all of us must not say a word of this to anyone." Olga and Lena both nodded.

Adam could hardly believe Anna's coolness and organisation. They had just unearthed something which could have unspeakable consequences and she had not batted an eyelid. What Adam did not know was that Anna had spotted her own opportunity and she was not going to let it slip.

"Now, Lena, I need to meet with your father somewhere safe tomorrow morning." She took out her mobile. "Can you call him?"

"I will straight away."

Eighty Seven

ANNA and Adam were let into the company's dacha complex by a housekeeper without a word. They walked round to the veranda at the back and Anna smiled as she heard the loud voice of Victor Nikolayevich. He was fussing over a man sitting up in a lounger with a bandage around the top of his chest and a large plaster on the side of his cheek.

"I can't believe it," Victor Nikolayevich was saying, "even the Inspector of Police cannot go about his work now without being attacked. Larissa will take good care of you. I think a trip to the bathhouse and the sauna will do you the world of good until the doctor gets here. Take him over there."

Two young men who doubled as the ineffectual security guards helped him to his feet and over to the bathhouse.

"Anna, my dearest!" shouted Victor Nikolayevich spying Anna approaching, "I am so happy to see you." He threw his arms around her and squeezed her. "I'm glad Lena gave me a call last night. I hope Adam here has been taking good care of you?" he asking winking at Adam.

"It is the other way round, I would say, Victor Nikolayevich," said Adam looking down at the floor as they shook hands.

"But you can always rely on the British in a tight corner," said a voice behind them. They span round to see Corley leaning against the side of the dacha. He was dressed casually. Seeing the look of surprise on Victor Nikolayevich's face he said quietly, "I also had a telephone call suggesting I join you here this morning."

Adam looked at Anna whose return look gave nothing away.

"What ever happened to your Police Inspector, Victor Nikolayevich?" said Corley rapidly changing the subject.

Victor Nikolayevich lowered his voice. "He got caught up in a shoot-out between two mafia gangs. There are rumours that they were fighting over who was going to set up some drug running operation! Here in St Petersburg! And it was on the river not far from our shipyard. I am sure that it will get sorted. Ah! Wonderful! Drinks!"

A young girl approached with a tray full of drinks. "Are you familiar with our kvass, Mr Corley?" asked Victor Nikolayevich.

"Absolutely," replied Corley.

"Well, drink it up quickly. We have a game to play."

"A game?" asked Corley.

"Yes. I think we will be able to talk as well. It is much quieter over there," said Victor Nikolayevich pointing towards the volleyball court. "Do you play?"

"Occasionally," replied Corley.

"That's it settled then. Russia against England. No need for anyone to change. Just take jackets off and shoes too, if you want to."

As they walked over to the court, Victor Nikolayevich put his arm over Anna's shoulder. "Lena said you have some unfinished business with Mr Corley," he said, "good luck, my dear! Let me shake him up a bit for you first!"

"This is for first service," Victor Nikolayevich roared as he hit the ball high in the air and over to the other side. Adam scrambled and managed to get to it knocking it up. Corley launched himself at it smashing it down between Victor Nikolayevich and Anna who hardly moved.

"I think it is our serve," Corley said modestly.

"Um," grunted Victor Nikolayevich, "your serve, yes."

The first three points went to the English until Adam overhit his smash and the serve was passed to the Russians. As Anna launched her serve towards Corley Victor Nikolayevich shouted, "was John Hampton the first to find out?" Corley stopped and looked up as the ball hit the ground in front of him.

"One: three," beamed Victor Nikolayevich, "excellent serve, Anna."

Corley approached the net. "Hampton suspected many things," he said, "but found out nothing and almost got himself killed in the process. I think we will find in the course of time that Hampton has his own agenda."

Anna served again and again Victor Nikolayevich shouted. This time he shouted at Adam, "and as for you, my young friend, do you know that you only survived because of a sweet angel who decided to become your guardian angel!" Adam jerked up and his return shot flew out of play.

"Two: three," added Victor Nikolayevich quickly. The next points were played in silence and the scores were soon tied at thirteen all. Corley and Adam were showing the greater athleticism, Anna the defter touch and Victor Nikolayevich trying all the ruses he could think of whilst throwing his heavy frame at every shot. He and Anna consulted on almost every shot whereas Corley and Adam barley passed pleasantries to each other.

Corley threw the ball up to serve. "Do you have the new instructions for me from you Fund?" quipped Anna and the ball flew into the net. Corley stared over the net. He was about to complain but picking the ball up he looked at Victor Nikolayevich. It was time to get to the point.

"Victor Nikolayevich, you are the one who found the dying soldier. What do you think happened?" he asked.

The air was suddenly tense. Victor Nikolayevich put his hands on his hips and drew his breath in heavily. "I think it was the British and not the Germans who blew up the train station at Mga to cut off the city." Anna and Adam looked at each other, proud they had worked it out but terrified at how Victor Nikolayevich would react next.

"And how does that make you feel?" said Corley aggressively passing the ball chest high to Victor Nikolayevich.

"Very sad," he said slowly, "but so did the whole war. Serve, Anna." The point was played in silence and went to the English as Victor Nikolayevich rather tamely hit his smash in to the net; he was clearly struggling to keep his composure.

As Corley threw the ball up to serve he himself asked out loud. "So does it make sense to tell the world about it now?"

"There's more to it than that," said Victor Nikolayevich angrily smashing the ball back with such power that it hit Adam smack on his shoulder and he tumbled to the side. Anna was about to run over but Victor Nikolayevich put out his arm to block her. "Russian serve," he said calmly.

"What else is there?" said Corley preparing to receive Victor Nikolayevich's serve. Adam was back on his feet.

"He was shot by other British soldiers," came back the reply. Corley managed to knock the serve up but Adam as he heard Victor Nikolayevich's comments completely missed the ball.

"Adam," shouted Corley, "watch the ball for God's sake!"

"But what did he mean?" stuttered Adam.

"What did you mean, Victor Nikolayevich?" said Corley holding on to the ball.

"I mean that you British once you had betrayed us, your ally, by helping the Germans, continued your treachery by killing your own men so that no-one would ever know." Victor Nikolayevich and Corley had both approached the net. Corley did not deny the accusation.

"This is impossible," said Adam more as a question than a statement.

"No, Adam, there is some truth in it," said Corley quietly and not taking his eyes off Victor Nikolayevich, "but it can never be proven."

"But you have admitted it," Adam protested, "you have admitted that we killed our own men and on a day, today, when the Prince of Wales is here to commemorate the bravery of British soldiers on Russian soil."

"And that is why no-one will ever know," said Corley. His words resounded around the court with authority.

"Really?" said Victor Nikolayevich provocatively tossing the ball to Anna. "Match point. Let's serve."

"Wait," said Adam, "we cannot leave it like this."

"Adam," Corley voice was threatening, "the circumstances are complicated."

"Well explain them," said Adam with a firmness in his voice which Anna had not heard before.

Anna had stepped towards the net with the ball tucked under her arm.

"It is true that our original plans for attacking St Petersburg were put to use by the Germans?" asked Adam.

"And by your own soldiers," Victor Nikolayevich continued, "with the full approval of the Chief of Staff and indeed of Mr Churchill himself."

"It was a very confusing time when Hitler suddenly invaded Russia. It would be fairer to say that there were some breakdowns in communications," said Corey flatly.

"In command," Victor Nikolayevich corrected him.

"And yes, I suppose, the breakdown may have been in command. It was decided," he said quietly but firmly, "that the elite group of British soldiers who had infiltrated St Petersburg and blown up the station at Mga to give the Germans the Siege in a way they have never thought possible even in their wildest Blitzkrieg planning," Corley paused for a second and then continued, "should be eliminated and their action buried with them for ever."

"And so they were shot by our own soldiers?" asked Adam slowly as he started to grasp the full implications. "It might be one thing for Britain to cause more deaths and to behave treacherously in dealings with a so-called ally," he said, "but killing our own men to cover it up!" he paused and looked at Anna who dropped her head to avoid his stare. "That destroys," he continued his voice shaking, "that destroys the moral foundation of our whole war effort. This makes a mockery of the deaths of so many, many people in the defence of Europe. In the defence of our moral code!" He sat down.

"War calls for tough choices, Adam," said Corley helping him back on his feet "and you will forget you ever heard this. It is top, top classified and there is no proof anywhere. Anna, please serve."

Anna strolled back. "Before I serve," she said, "you should know, Mr Corley, that I have one of the British soldiers' identification tags," and with that she served the ball at him. He deflected it up and Adam dived to reach it but only managed to send it spinning out of play.

"Match to us!" Victor Nikolayevich clapped his hands gleefully and Anna punched the air like a school girl. Corley walked up to the net. "You are a remarkable young woman, Anna, but you should think carefully about what you have just said. How do you know the tag belonged to one of the men?"

"He was the man rescued from the river and before he died he handed it over," replied Anna. "He also explained what he had done."

Corley did not respond. He looked at Anna, at Victor Nikolayevich and then at Adam. It was the tag which had been missing from the metal box which the soldiers had hidden in the Old Foundry before they had crossed to the boat house from here they had expected to have been picked up by their fellow countrymen and not attacked by them. After they had blown up the station they had been ordered to hide everything that could identify them in case they were caught. One of the soldiers had clearly not obeyed his instructions and even though Corley had retrieved the metal box all it would take would be one tag to prove that British soldiers had been in the city before the Siege. It would be a small step from there to someone discovering what had happened to the soldiers and what the dying soldier, who had been reburied in England, had said. CNN would be on it like a flash! Briefed no doubt by those forces who were out to cause the trouble which Green was so, so desperate to prevent.

Fittingly it was Victor Nikolayevich who spoke next. "Perhaps you did not find everything you wanted in the Old Foundry, Mr Corley?"

"That old building is part of the original shipyard," replied Corley, "and, as you know, Victor Nikolayevich, it holds many, many secrets."

Victor Nikolayevich smiled at Corley. "It does, Mr Corley. And many which should best remain secret, perhaps? Anna, what do you think?"

"I think," Anna replied, "that the ball is right back in Mr Corley's court." Victor Nikolayevich beamed as visions of checkmate spread through his mind. Anna went to the side of the court and bent down in her bag and brought out her mobile phone. "Maybe you can call your office to see if they have made any more progress on the instructions for me." She looked at her watch. "Your Prince will be making his speech in a couple of hours." She threw her mobile phone over the net and Corley caught it nonchalantly and walked to the side of the court.

"I can't believe it. I won't believe it!" Adam was crouched down rubbing his forehead with his fingers. "We British would never do such a thing." He had started to cry.

Victor Nikolayevich put his arm over his shoulder, "it was such a long time ago. Let sleeping dogs sleep, eh?"

"This is abominable," continued Adam.

"There were many abominable things in those days, believe me," replied Victor Nikolayevich heavily.

"But it is a matter of honour. What is there to defend if we ourselves do not believe in honour and justice?"

"I think you need a drink. Calm your nerves. Anna, how are you feeling?"

"We'll soon see." A loud whirling noise made her look up. "Can you hear that?"

"Sounds like a helicopter." They looked towards the dacha and saw Leonid Marlenovich making his way from the sauna.

"I did not know he was here," said Anna slightly concerned.

"Must have just arrived," said Victor Nikolayevich, "now let's get that drink."

Alex had pestered and pestered his mum to take him to the Catherine Palace again. He had been dreaming more and more each night over the last week and most of his dreams seemed to centre on treasures and crashes. It was if his sleeping brain was stuck in the loop of the same film. As it was a Saturday Ellen had finally relented and one of the firm's drivers had driven to the dacha. He had been offered two days off during the next week if he drove on the Saturday and he had been only too happy to accept. Two weekdays off to drive around St Petersburg as an unofficial taxi in a comfortable Volvo would be a very nice little earner. The drive to the Catherine Palace was very short but Ellen had not yet started to drive herself. After the bullet incident and her husband's shooting the decision had easily been taken that she and Alex should always be driven. No exceptions. The investigation into the shooting had still nothing to report but the Mayor himself had assured the Miller Lombard partner in Moscow that the city's police had not uncovered any reason to think that either Ellen or Alex were under any threat whatsoever. If there was the slightest sign then the Mayor's office would provide security directly and immediately. Ellen and Alex climbed into the Volvo.

Roman Felixovich did not know why but for the first time in his life he had started to sing to himself. He was driving his Mercedes out of the city and he was singing. Not current pop songs but songs from his childhood – Russian ballads. He kept looking into the rear view mirror and smiling at himself. He sang a verse or a few lines from one ballad after another. His mind seemed to be full to the brim of ballad after ballad. And with each minor performance he pressed his foot down that little bit more on the accelerator and the car's speedometer slowly moved round and up like mercury rising in a thermometer. He was now on the M10 road and heading out into the country for a ride. He would go through Pushkin and just drive until he found the right spot. He looked at himself in the rear view every few minutes and varied his smile. He deliberately did not use the mirror to look through the car's rear window or onto the back seat.

Sasha had now woken up on the back seat and found himself back in the horrible vision he had fallen asleep into. Everything was pitch black and he could not open his mouth. He tried also to move his hands but they were behind his back and he realised that they were tied with a rope. He could hear a humming noise and strange sounds as if someone was practicing singing in the distance. It sounded like a singing lesson taking place in a room at the other end of the Home. As he could also feel a forward motion under his body he guessed though that he was no longer in the Home but in some kind of vehicle. His nose was not covered and he breathed in deeply. The smell - he recognised it straight away. It was the car that the rich man's driver drove. The car which had taken him to practice his singing in the cathedral. Then why was he in the dark and why could he not open his mouth?

Roman Felixovich could sense that the boy had now woken up. He had moved through the Home in the dead of night without making a sound. He had found out where Sasha slept by telling his driver to take Sasha a music book a few days before as a present and then asking his driver where he had gone. His driver had not suspected anything about the questions because he knew full well that his boss always wanted to know all the details about everything. Sasha had not even moved a muscle as Roman Felixovich had put the cloth with chloroform over his mouth and nose and then lifted him out of his bed, over his shoulder and then out of the room. Had any tiny eyes followed them then they had not made a sound or raised an alarm. Roman Felixovich was pretty sure he had taken the boy without any one seeing and without the slightest trace being left behind. That was how he wanted it. The boy's disappearance into thin air in the middle of the night would be a mystery for the next three hundred years. A mystery really appropriate for this haunted city. The boy would join the devil and that abominable peasant, the peasant who they had had to kill three times over and yet who somehow still seemed to be causing him trouble. Not anymore. They could all finally rot in hell together. The Mercedes was now speeding at a high rate and Roman Felixovich gripped the steering wheel tighter and tighter as he swerved around one pothole after another as the quality of the road started to deteriorate the further he drove from the city.

Sasha could also feel the speed increasing. He tried to move his hands. He was face down on the back seat and covered under layers of cloth. His hands were tied tightly behind his back with a rope. He shuffled his body slowly from side to side and soon he felt the object in his pocket. He started to move his hip and he quickly then managed to push one of his wrists into the object which was making its own way of out his pocket. It was as if his icon was working with him. That it was alive. The threads in the rope around his wrist began to snap as the sharp end of the wooden icon sliced through the fibres.

Roman Felixovich's singing stopped. There was a hooting sound at the side of him. For the tiniest fraction of a second he risked taking his eyes off the road in front of him to peep to his left hand side. He also took his foot off the accelerator slightly. Another hoot. This time it was a double hoot. He risked another sideways glance. His brain was not computing the image he had seen. He gripped the steering wheel even tighter, stared straight ahead and banged his foot down hard on the accelerator pedal. The next hoot was a treble hoot and at the next sound he had to turn his head to the left and look. It was that laugh! The sight at the side of him made him freeze but he kept his foot hard down on the accelerator. He pressed harder and harder and now kept his head turned to the left. He was trying to outrun an old-fashioned steam train which seemed to flying at the side of him. Its driver was waving at him and smiling widely. The train was lifted above the track. The driver had a cap on. He had a long black beard and Roman Felixovich tried with all his might to take his eyes off the driver's face. He forced his head and eyes to look forward. He was now also standing in his seat without noticing. He could now see the railway track on the ground in front of him.

In the back Sasha had now freed his hands, scrambled himself up in the seat and thrown off the blankets. He felt his face and his fingers touched the tape stuck across his mouth. The car was going at a tremendous speed. Before trying to pull off the tape he had the presence of mind to sit up in the seat and put on a seat belt. As he sat upright he looked in the rear-view mirror attached to the windscreen. Its reflection did not show the face of the driver of the car whom he could tell instantly from behind was the rich man who came to the Home. No, it was the old man with the beard and deep, deep blue eyes. He was smiling at Sasha who smiled back instantly.

Sweat was now pouring down Roman Felixovich's face. He gripped the steering wheel so tight that his fingers hurt. His body had started to ache. The hooting and laughing were now all intertwined, each sound competing to be louder than the last and then louder and louder again. The train had a sudden burst of speed and flew in front of the Mercedes. Roman Felixovich flew the steering wheel to the left and the Mercedes lurched across the carriage way into the oncoming lane of traffic on the other side of the carriageway. The Mercedes was now on the wrong side of the road and hurtling along at a fantastic speed.

"Watch out of ahead of us!" yelled Alex who was in the front passenger seat of the Hampton's Volvo. The office driver had already seen ahead and was braking sharply. They were two cars behind a large truck carrying lumber. There were long and wide tree trunks piled up on the truck's trailer and held on by rusty steel ropes. "Wow!" shouted Alex as the lumber truck veered right off the carriage way with a tremendous screech of brakes. It demolished a wooden vegetable stall at the side of the road which was selling large green watermelons. "A car on wrong side!" shouted the office driver followed by a string of Russian expletives aimed at a black Mercedes which was now back on the right side of the road but driving at a crazy speed. It seemed to fly past them. "Driver out of mind," he said quickly to Ellen who had looked sternly at the driver when he had shouted the Russian words which it would have been obvious to anyone were not appropriate. "Where's the truck gone?" shouted Alex. "Mom, we must help! There's a fire extinguisher and a first aid kit in our trunk."

Roman Felixovich now knew that the Mercedes was flying. The train in front of him was flying. It had raced on ahead of him and was getting smaller and smaller. Roman Felixovich could also now see where they were headed. He had to smile and as he did so he relaxed back in his seat. He lifted his foot off the accelerator and took both hands off the steering wheel. He smiled at himself in the rear-view mirror and then looked into the back seat. The boy had put on a seat belt! He had his eyes shut. He was holding a little stick and saying something. Roman Felixovich listened hard for a second. It was a prayer. A prayer! Not that it would do him much good now. But how appropriate. Roman Felixovich folded his arms and smiled at the sight in front of him. It looked as though the building was flying straight at them. It was getting bigger and bigger. It had three bright domes with funny crosses on top. It was a chapel. He had to admire its beauty and peacefulness. As the Mercedes smashed into the building Roman Felixovich went straight through the windscreen. The front and back of the car were then filled with straw. Roman Felixovich had driven the car into a large barn at the side of the road stacked to the roof with bales of hay. There was no chapel anywhere to be seen.

Ellen tried her best but she could not stop Alex jumping out of the Volvo and running round to the trunk. He was back round at the driver's door with a red first aid box in one hand and a small fire extinguisher in the other before the driver could close his door. He took them off Alex with a frown. Ordinarily he would have driven straight off and certainly not become involved in the aftermath of a crash and the slow and lengthy police questioning which would follow. But Alex was his boss's son. Alex rubbed his hands together and complained briefly that his fingers were stinging. He then ran in the direction of the smashed vegetable stall with the driver following him. Ellen too got out of the Volvo as a second black Mercedes drove past her on the other side of the carriage way.

This second Mercedes soon braked to a stop, its tyres screeching. It then turned off the main road and headed for the barn. Yelena Matrovna was in the passenger seat with Roman Felixovich's driver. She had woken in the middle of the night not from a nightmare but from hearing Sasha singing. She lived in a small apartment with an elderly relative which was a short walk from the Home. She had not dressed but had walked to the Home. As she arrived she had seen Roman Felixovich's Mercedes drive off and recognised that it was Roman Felixovich himself driving. Such a sight was completely out of the ordinary. She had immediately called Roman Felixovich's driver and woken him. He had arrived at the Home ten minutes later driving one of Roman Felixovich's other cars. Two police stops and twenty dollars later they had almost caught up with Roman Felixovich. They had watched open-mouthed as he had driven the car right off the road at such speed.

"Wow! Wow! Mom!" shouted Alex. The driver and Ellen were now standing next to Alex and looking down into a dip about one hundred yards in from the road. The truck was on its side and the huge logs had rolled down the hill of the dip and smashed through another small building. A crater about ten yards wide had then been opened up and two logs had fallen into it. The two logs were now standing up like giant telegraph poles.

"Is that a railway line?" asked Alex pointing to the end of a small metal track which could be seen in the crater.

The driver shook his head in response and then said, "no, old mine." He then jogged down towards the truck. Its driver had pulled himself half out of the cab and was shouting at them. Alex's hands were still stinging and then he realised – it was the tingling. But tingling so strongly that it hurt!

"Sasha! Sasha! Sasha!" shouted Yelena Matrovna as they reached the barn.

"Yelena!" replied Sasha his voice very low and hoarse. He too had managed to climb out of a car window. He had ripped the tape off his mouth. It had hurt him and he was crying. Yelena Matrovna swooped him up and covered him in kisses. She put her hand gently over Sasha's mouth and then took it away. His lips had burst and there was some blood. She saw his icon in his hand and she knelt down. She kissed the icon softly and then stood up and hugged Sasha. Roman Felixovich's driver pointed to a body stuck in bales of hay in front to the car. "I'll call an ambulance," he said. As he did they heard the sound of a siren and all three turned round. An ambulance had already arrived. Very oddly it seemed to them all - its driver had a huge smile on his face. He also had a long black beard.

Again there was no stopping Alex. He raced down the dip and as Ellen's heart jumped into her mouth Alex shimmied down one of the logs into the crater. Ellen took off her shoes and bolted down to the crater. She knelt down to look into the crater and thanked God. Alex was only about six feet underground. He was stripping away paper from what looked like a large window. "I told you, mom!" he shouted. "I told you I saw the panels fall off the train in a crash. They must have fallen into the mine and been hidden. They never left Russia!"

Back at the dacha a voice from a loudspeaker out of the helicopter boomed, "stand where you are!" Victor Nikolayevich, Anna and Adam stopped and looked up. The helicopter was now directly above them and the voice repeated its command. A group of camouflaged soldiers were coming over the fence. The company's erstwhile security guards already had their faces ground into the floor. "Drop any weapons, I repeat drop any weapons." Leonid Marlenovich had stopped several metres from them and lifted up his jacket to show a holster. The group of soldiers had surrounded them and the helicopter landed at the side of the volleyball court.

"Might I know whom I have the pleasure of addressing?" asked Victor Nikolayevich. His voice for once had a commanding tone to it.

"Major Checkov from the Federal Security Bureau. You are Pulgarkov, Victor Nikolayevich?"

"Correct," replied Victor Nikolayevich coolly.

"Good." He turned to his men. "Search everywhere."

"Might I enquire what you are looking for?"

"For your sake let's hope we don't find anything. Please line up against the wall."

"We have guests," Victor Nikolayevich said firmly.

"What type of guests?" asked the Major.

"We are entertaining our British investors," said Victor Nikolayevich indicating Corley and Adam, "both citizens of Britain."

The major spoke briefly into his headset.

"They are on Russian soil and will be treated like the rest of you," he said. "Search them."

As Corley and Adam were about to be searched a shout came from the sauna and the group moved over with speed. Victor Nikolayevich indicated to everyone to sit on the seats on the veranda. The FSB Major came jogging back over to the veranda.

"Victor Nikolayevich, did you realise that you have a dead man in your bathhouse?"

"I knew he had been shot, Major, but it did not look serious. We are waiting for the doctor."

"It appears that it won't be necessary. Will you come and identify the body." For some reason it appeared to Anna that the FSB seemed highly satisfied and their attention had been lifted from the rest of them.

A few minutes later a body was wheeled past with its face covered over. There was a commotion at the entrance and in struggled the Chief of Police cursing loudly at the attention of two of the FSB Major's men. They had managed to half take off his gun belt but he was waving his gun in the air wildly and berating them for daring to manhandle a chief of police. On the sight of Major Checkov he quietened down and redressed himself.

"Chief Inspector, I believe one of your senior officers is missing. Are you out to look for him?"

"Who? No. Why? Who?" The Chief of Police was clearly not out looking for anyone. "What makes you say that?" He continued to straighten his jacket and do up his gun belt.

"Very well. Please proceed with what you came for."

"I have been sent on a very important mission and I would request, sir, that your men let me and my men go about their business unhindered."

"Very well. Please what is your business?"

"Victor Nikolayevich, I am to take your to the City Hall immediately."

Victor Nikolayevich looked highly surprised.

"What on earth for?"

"The Mayor himself, sir, requests on behalf of the city and of the country, yes on behalf of the country, that you accept the invitation to join the Prince of Wales today at the ceremony to celebrate the bravery shown by all men, women and children during the Great Patriotic War and the Siege of our city. You must come straight away."

Victor Nikolayevich looked at Anna who smiled. "I will just collect some things."

As he went into the dacha he passed Leonid Marlenovich and Corley chatting quietly. Victor Nikolayevich took Leonid Marlenovich's arm in a tight grip.

"How did Inspector Bushkin's throat get cut?"

Leonid Marlenovich unfastened Victor Nikolayevich's grip and stared at him coolly. He spoke quietly so that only they and Corley could hear. "One should be grateful for British know-how, Victor Nikolayevich, one just never knows when it will come in handy." With that he laughed at Corley and wiped his hands.

Anna and Adam were making their way to the gate. Victor Nikolayevich caught them up. "Would you like a ride with the Chief of Police?"

"That would be great," replied Anna, "I need to go to our office. I have just had a call from Valentina Alexandrovna. A special package is on its way to our office for me."

Victor Nikolayevich and the Chief of Police sat in the back of the car with Anna. Adam took the front passenger seat. He smiled at the police officer driving the car and then did a double take. The driver smiled back.

"I think that with Inspector Bushkin now out of the way," said the Chief of Police with a prolonged wink at Victor Nikolayevich, "I think there will not be any more interference in your night life, Mr Carter." The Chief of Police then nudged Victor Nikolayevich in his ribs with his elbow. Victor Nikolayevich burst out laughing. Adam looked again at the driver who had taken his police hat off. He had a distinct scar above his eye.

"Chief, there seems to have been a big smash up ahead. Shall we stop?" said the driver who then turned to wink at Adam.

"No, we don't want to keep the Mayor waiting," replied the Chief of Police, "put your siren on and drive past."

The police car stopped outside the Miller Lombard office and Anna and Adam got out. They thanked the Chief of Police and Victor Nikolayevich who would not let Anna go without a big hug.

"Try and watch the television," said the Chief of Police as the car drove off, "Victor Nikolayevich will be on it shortly."

Anna opened the door to their office. There was a small but thick brown envelope in the letter box. It had the logo of the Mayor's office on it. Anna tore the envelope open. Inside was a residency permit with Sasha's name on it, a Certificate of Adoption and a hand written letter from Valentina Alexandrovna. Anna burst into tears. She now officially had a young brother. Adam sensing that Anna would not like him to see her tears went into the meeting room and switched on the TV.

St Petersburg it seemed had become the centre of the world for news, if only for one day. CNN had split its screen into four sections in an attempt to disseminate the different 'breaking news' stories from the city. The first section showed a police launch full of bullet holes tied up at a dock. A reporter was reporting from the dock on a momentous day for the Russian security forces, the FSB, which had scored a major success in stopping a suspected start-up operation in the drugs trade in the city. "We understand," announced the reporter, "that the operation was masterminded by an Inspector in the local police force with ties to local mafia bosses who was killed in a shoot-out on the quayside between rival gangs. No drugs were found but the FSB is sure it has thwarted the operation before it could start. We hope to have a full analysis and further comments later in the day."

The second section was running footage of the Mayor of St Petersburg and His Royal Highness the Prince of Wales awarding the Order of the Cross of St Peter to Victor Nikolayevich Pulgarkov, the General Director of the Peter the Great Shipyard, for lifetime services to the city. The screen then cut to the Prince of Wales giving a speech. He proclaimed that Peter the Great himself would have been proud of the bravery shown by Victor Nikolayevich both as a young boy, during the terrible Siege of the city, and now as a leader of one of Russia's most promising companies battling its way through the dramatic changes caused by Russia joining the world economy. It was a fluent and kind speech and Adam guessed that it must have been written by the Prince himself for once. Adam then listened as the channel went on to explain that the day held more honours for Victor Nikolayevich as he was named as one of the founding trustees of a Russian British Charitable Fund to be based in St Petersburg to modernise all the city's children's homes and to invest in extra staff and new medical and recreation facilities at the homes. The British Government has agreed to match dollar for dollar some five million dollars already raised by the Russian founders of the new fund who were the beneficiaries of an anonymous donation. The section of screen then cut to the Children Home No. 8. in St Petersburg where a group of young children were jumping up and down and shouting wildly and at the tops of their voices. A young boy with light blue eyes stood closest to the camera. He was grinning widely despite what looked like a burst lip.

"Anna, I know you said that the deal you wanted was for the British Government to match your donation, but how did you get hold of so much yourself?" shouted Adam. "Five million dollars!" Adam genuinely could not believe it.

"You remember those powers of attorney from the Fund which are in my name?" said Anna coming into the room and grinning. "Let's just say that Mr Corley has gone a lot further than simply just fulfilling his investment obligations to the company!"

The third section returned to more visual news. It showed an overturned truck and a large crater in the ground. The crater had been cordoned off. The report said that a potentially large haul of lost works of arts may have been unearthed by the spilling of a truck's load of logs into an old mine shaft. Part of the findings were believed to be panels similar to those in the Amber Room which used to be considered by many as the Eighth Wonder of the World. The Hermitage Art Committee had called for a forensic analysis of the panels as soon as funds and experts could be mobilised. An 'off the record' comment hinted that this may well disprove the widely held belief that the Amber Room was destroyed in a fire in Germany. A young American boy was being lauded as possibly the world's youngest treasure hunter for his role in being the first to uncover the panels in the crater. Adam took a double take as a photograph of Alex holding a panel flashed on to the screen. He then listened intently as he heard the name of his own firm being mentioned. At the same time the Hermitage Art Committee was delighted to announce its first major success continued the report. Five major Impressionists paintings which had been discovered in one of the basement rooms in the Hermitage had been safely and confidentially transported to

Chicago where they were being restored by American experts. This was being financed by a law firm called Miller Lombard and special mention was given by the Committee to Vera Bogomolov, one of the firm's legal secretaries, who had played a key role in arranging the restoration of the paintings after the shooting of her boss. The paintings were expected back in the Hermitage in two to three months. Adam looked at Anna and then back at the television.

The fourth section was running a report about a driver who had had a miraculous escape when his Mercedes had a mechanical fault at high speed and left the road and hit a barn. The camera showed an ambulance leaving the site of the barn. Its bearded driver smiled into the camera. His deep blue eyes were laughing. The driver of the Mercedes was rumoured to be one of the city's fastest rising businessmen - a man by the name of Roman Felixovich Yusupov who in recent days was said to have become obsessed with recovering his family's vast Tsarist wealth which had been taken from them in the Revolution. His family was also notorious for the lead role it played in the infamous murder of the mad monk Rasputin who once again had become the source of many, many rumours in the city in recent months.

"Sasha!" shouted Anna as she looked back at the second section. "The boy in the Home, Adam, that is Sasha, he is my uncle's grandson and we have just adopted him! He is my new brother. The Mayor himself signed the papers today. He is Russian but he was born in Romania." Anna hugged the papers she had just received to her chest.

"And that is Alex, there, Anna, holding that panel," shouted Adam. "He is so obsessed about art and treasure and he is always hunting for things!"

"And they look so alike!" replied Anna. "Let me get my photo of Sasha from my desk."

"And I'll get my photo of Alex. I took it at the Hermitage on our last visit," replied Adam feeling a sudden sense of dread. It was spooky, frightening even, that they both had recent photographs.

A minute later they returned and put their photos on the table. They both looked at them and stood in silence. The boys were almost identical and the most striking similarity was their blue eyes. Adam was the first to speak. "How old is Sasha?" he asked softly.

"No-one knows," started Anna, "I mean no-on knew," she continued, "until now!" She sat down her heart racing. She opened the brown envelope and scanned the letter in it from Valentina Alexandrovna. "His date of birth is 17th December, 1985, which makes him nine years old."

"Alex's birthday," said Adam sitting down with his hand shaking, "is 17th December as well and he is nine, too." He paused and then grabbed Anna's hand. "No-one else in our law firm knows this, Anna," he said with a gulp, "but Ellen told me after the shooting. They adopted Alex as a baby from an orphanage – in Bucharest!"

As soon as Adam had said this, the door to the meeting room flew open with a tremendous bang. They both stared into the doorway but all they could hear was the sound of gentle contented laughter and the shattering of a glass as it slowly and quietly hit the floor.